The moment their lips met, the kiss turned so hot that it could have started a wildfire.

The morning's adventure had driven both of them to the edge of desperation.

What she needed was to close her eyes and focus on the man who held her in his arms instead of everything else that was happening to her.

He deepened the kiss. She loved the taste of him, the feel of his body, the way he clasped her tightly. She'd been craving this since last night, and the terror of the past few hours had only intensified her emotions.

She forgot where they were, forgot everything except the need to get close to him—as close as two people could get.

CARRIE'S PROTECTOR

BY
REBECCA YORK

First published in Great Britain 2013
by Mills & Boon, an imprint of Harlequin (UK) Limited,
Eton House, 18-24 Paradise Road, Richmond, Surrey TW9 1SR

© Ruth Glick 2013

ISBN: 978 0 263 90364 5
ebook ISBN: 978 1 472 00727 8

46-0713

Harlequin (UK) policy is to use papers that are natural, renewable and recyclable products and made from wood grown in sustainable forests. The logging and manufacturing processes conform to the legal environmental regulations of the country of origin.

Printed and bound in Spain
by Blackprint CPI, Barcelona

Award-winning, *USA TODAY* bestselling novelist Ruth Glick, who writes as **Rebecca York,** is the author of more than one hundred books, including her popular 43 LIGHT STREET series for Mills & Boon® Intrigue. Ruth says she has the best job in the world. Not only does she get paid for telling stories, she's also an author of twelve cookbooks. Ruth and her husband, Norman, travel frequently, researching locales for her novels and searching out new dishes for her cookbooks.

For two little eagles, E12 and E14,
who met untimely deaths in Decorah, Iowa.

Chapter One

Carrie Mitchell had made the biggest mistake of her life. And if she had it to do all over again, her actions would be exactly the same.

"Ready?" the dark-haired man waiting ramrod straight at the bottom of the stairs asked.

She dragged in a breath and let it out before speaking. "As ready as I'm going to be."

"Then let's get it over with."

He stepped outside and motioned for her to wait as he looked around the exterior of the safe house where she'd been staying for the past week.

Really, the visual inspection was unnecessary, she thought. Nobody could get past the electric fence and the motion detectors, or through the main gate without the proper security codes.

Still, he made her linger inside before motioning her out the door, then led the way toward the black town car they were taking into D.C. The car was bulletproof, a precaution Carrie wished they could have done without. But her father, Douglas Mitchell, was rich enough to make his own rules when it came to his daughter's safety—or anything else. An ordinary man would have relied on the FBI to protect his only child. Dad wanted an armored car and an elite private security team to keep her safe. The driver was already behind the wheel, a guy named Joe Collins, who was one of the guards who had been with her for the past week.

The man who held the car door open was Wyatt Hawk, the one in charge. Carrie didn't like him much. Maybe that wasn't fair, because she couldn't really say she knew him. He kept himself so closed up that she'd had little chance for an in-depth conversation with him.

He was tall and muscular and good-looking in a kind of tough-guy way that she might have admired from a distance—if she'd had the choice. You could imagine him as the bodyguard for a mob boss, although that wasn't his background. He was supposed to have retired early from the CIA, but he never talked about his former life.

The other security men at the safe house were much more open about their backgrounds. They were all ex-cops, and they'd been friendly, perhaps to counteract Wyatt's aloof demeanor. Gary Blain was a black man in his fifties, with a shaved head and broad shoulders. Hank Swinton was around the same age, with a bit of gray invading his sandy hair. And Rodrigo Garcia was a little younger, with classic Hispanic features.

They'd made her feel protected as they'd tried to lighten her isolation. In contrast, Wyatt always had an open book in front of him at the dining table, probably to discourage conversation. One of the few things she knew about him was that he liked World War II spy novels.

She'd joined him a time or two in the basement gym. He'd stuck to his routine of weight machines and hard-driving pumping on the elliptical trainer to the sounds of classic rock.

She never pushed herself as far. For her, exercise wasn't a religion. It was just a way to keep in reasonable shape so she could crawl around in the woods taking pictures of wildlife.

Which was how she'd gotten into the worst trouble of her life.

Last Thursday she'd been practicing her profession, happily eavesdropping on an eagles' nest in D.C.'s Rock Creek Park, the sprawling wooded area that ran through the north-west section of the city. She'd been using her telephoto lens to capture the family life of the parents and their two babies, photographing them off and on since before they'd hatched.

The photos were to illustrate a piece she was doing for *Wildlife Magazine* on raptors in urban areas.

She was creeping through the underbrush out of sight of the eagles' eighty-foot-high, thousand-pound nest when she spotted three young Midwestern-looking men in jeans and T-shirts in a nearby picnic area.

She could see they hadn't come for a meal. They were sitting at one of the tree-shaded wooden tables, speaking in low voices. Two of them were chain-smoking and littering the ground with the spent butts. Every so often, one of them would look around nervously.

At first she'd paid them only minimal attention. Then, as she moved to get a different angle on the nest, she started to get the gist of their conversation, and the back of her neck began to tingle.

She heard the words *bomb, Capitol Police* and *best place to inflict maximum damage.* Her heart was pounding as she swiveled cautiously in her hidden position, switching her camera's focus from the eagles' nest to the men. After taking their pictures, she wanted to flee, yet she knew that just their faces might not be enough to identify them. Her every move stealthy, she made her way back toward the road, intent on getting their license plates, as well. Her own car was parked on the other side of the picnic area, because it was a better approach to the eagles' nest.

Finally she was on the verge of pressing her luck too far. The men were still talking as she circled back the way she'd come, knowing she'd better get out of the woods before they spotted her.

But she realized it was already too late when she heard a shout of alarm.

"Hey, somebody's spying on us."

Her heart in her throat, she started running flat out for her car, hearing the crack of twigs and the rustle of underbrush behind her. She fumbled in her bag for the car remote, clicking the lock as she pelted through the woods.

She was only seconds ahead of them as she jumped into the driver's seat and started the engine. As she pulled away, she heard the sound of gunfire.

The back window and a taillight shattered as she sped away. But she made it onto Military Road and out of the park, and they didn't pick up her trail because they'd had to double back and circle around to get to the other parking area. She'd made it to the nearest police station, and the rest was history.

Her attention snapped back to the present when Wyatt spoke.

"You okay?" he asked.

"Yes."

"The Federal prosecutor has the pictures you took of the men. All you have to do is tell him exactly what you heard and exactly what happened."

"Then I suppose I'll have to show up in court for Bobby Thompson's trial." He was the only one of the men who had been identified and arrested. He was locked up in a maximum-security facility while the others were still at large.

"Not for months."

"Does that mean we're going to be together for months?" she asked, sorry she couldn't keep the snappish tone out of her voice.

"Not necessarily," Wyatt answered. Not if he could help it. He wanted out of this situation, but not until he got a suitable replacement.

He slid Carrie a sidewise glance, noting the way she was

twisting her fingers together in her lap. He wanted to reach over and press his hand over hers, but he kept his arms at his sides because he knew that touching her was a bad idea.

His gaze traveled to her short-cropped dark hair. When they'd first met, it had been long and blond, but he'd made her cut and dye it—to change her appearance. She hadn't liked it, but she'd done it—then refused contact lenses that would change her blue eyes to brown. And there was no way to disguise her high cheekbones, cute little nose or appealing lips. She was still a very attractive woman, even with the change in her hair and the nondescript clothing he'd purchased for her. As they rode into town, she looked like a Federal employee who'd come in on a Saturday to catch up on her work.

They made the rest of the trip into the District in silence, a silence he'd tried to maintain since he'd first met her. She probably thought he didn't like her. The problem was just the opposite. He liked her a lot. She had courage and determination, and she wasn't like a lot of rich women who thought that the world owed them special consideration. She was hardworking, smart and good at her job. She had all the qualities he admired in a woman, which was why he couldn't allow himself to get close to her.

To his relief, the long ride was almost over. At least they wouldn't be confined to the backseat of a car for much longer. While she talked with the prosecutor, he could wait in the reception area.

"The building's just ahead," he said in a low voice, breaking the silence inside the sedan.

Beside him Carrie sighed. "I guess the sooner I get this over with, the sooner I get my life back."

"Makes sense," he answered, wondering if she ever would get her life back. Would she ever feel safe again tramping around in the woods by herself, photographing the subjects she loved to capture in their natural environment? For just a moment he pictured himself going on those expeditions with her, carrying her equipment, making sure that nobody got out of line with her and no wild animals attacked her. Then he ruthlessly cut off that avenue of thought before it could go any further. He and Carrie Mitchell were from two different worlds. She had had every advantage growing up. She could have lived off her dad for the rest of her life, but she was trying to make a name for herself in a difficult profession. He was an ex-spook who came from a family in Alexandria, Virginia, that was barely making it. His dad drove a cab. His mom was a waitress, and he'd known he wanted a different life, which was why he'd joined the army and then the CIA. He'd seen a lot of the world, but he was home now and working private security. And even if their backgrounds matched better, he was too damaged to even think about a relationship with someone like her—or anyone else, for that matter.

They were meeting Skip Gunderson, the Federal prosecutor, in a yellow-brick government building as nondescript as Carrie's clothing. Five stories tall, with a security barrier at the entrance. As a precaution, it wasn't the building where Gunderson normally worked. The meeting was at another facility that was off the radar of the D.C. press corps.

That was one of the unfortunate aspects of this whole situation. Although Carrie's identity was supposed to be confidential, somehow a cable news reporter had gotten wind of her name. Now everyone and his brother knew that she was the woman who had foiled a major terrorist plot. At least they hadn't been able to ferret out the location of the safe house where she was staying. Or photograph her disguise—he hoped.

"Showtime," Carrie murmured, as the big car made a right turn and pulled up at the metal stanchions that blocked the entrance to an underground garage. Next to the barrier was a guardhouse, where a man in a blue uniform and police-type cap stood as if he had an iron pipe rammed up his butt.

Wyatt watched him. Usually these guys were relaxed, but the guard's posture pegged him as being on edge.

As their car stopped, he stepped out.

Wyatt hadn't seen him before, but then, he hadn't seen a lot of the men assigned to security duty at this place.

"Identification, please," the guard said to Joe Collins, the driver, who rolled down his window and reached into his pocket for the papers.

Wyatt had heard the request every time they'd arrived here, yet today something was just a bit off—perhaps the hint of edginess in the man's voice or the way he had his cap pulled down low. That thought had barely crossed Wyatt's mind when the man raised his arm, aiming an automatic pistol toward the open window of the car.

Acting on instinct and experience, Wyatt pushed Carrie down, blocking her body with his as he pulled out his own weapon and wrenched himself around to face the guard.

He was a split second too late to prevent disaster.

Joe went down in a spray of blood. Wyatt fired at the bogus guard, striking him in the chest and knocking him backward into the glass booth. But undoubtedly, he wasn't the only threat. Before the man hit the ground, Wyatt lunged across the car and opened the opposite door, pushing Carrie out ahead of him.

She gasped as she came down on the hard cement of the driveway.

"Sorry. We've got to get the hell out of here, but not onto the street."

Looking up, he confirmed that assessment as he saw eight armed men racing down the driveway toward them—men who didn't look like cops or security guards.

Carrie followed his gaze, gasping as she took in the situation.

Grabbing her hand, he helped her up, leading her toward the right and behind a row of cars in the garage, giving them some cover. But he was badly outnumbered and outgunned. He wasn't going to shoot it out with these guys in the garage if he could help it.

"This way."

He'd studied the layout of the building, and he hurried her along the wall and around a corner to a service door and was relieved to find it unlocked.

"We have to call the police," she whispered when the door closed behind them.

"No. We can't trust the police or anyone else. *Somebody* gave up the meeting."

As he spoke, he considered their options. Going down would trap them in the lower floors of the garage. Which left only one alternative.

"We're going up."

They had just reached the third level when Wyatt heard gunfire blasting below.

He led Carrie through a door into the building, then pulled out his cell phone and speed-dialed the safe house.

Gary Blain answered. "Wyatt? Is something wrong?"

"Yeah. We're in the building where Carrie was supposed to meet the prosecutor. Somehow the terrorists knew we were coming."

"Is she all right?"

"Yes. But there are shooters in here."

"Where are you?"

"Near the south stairwell. Armed men were blocking the garage entrance. Can you pick us up on the roof?"

"Negative. Unless we get clearance for a helo flight into D.C."

Wyatt answered with a curse.

A burst of gunfire from below interrupted the conversation.

"Gotta go."

He led Carrie down the hall to another stairwell then up

two more levels. He was pretty sure the attackers had thought they'd get him and Carrie in the garage, which meant they probably hadn't stationed anyone up here. Yet.

Cautiously he opened the door and looked out into the hallway. Nothing was moving—particularly the dead body lying in a pool of blood in the center of the tile floor.

When he hesitated, Carrie pressed against his back and looked over his shoulder.

"Oh, God," she breathed as she gazed at Skip Gunderson, the Federal prosecutor she'd been coming to meet.

"We can't stay here," Wyatt said.

But when he glanced back at Carrie, he saw the blood had drained from her face and she had gone stock-still.

"Carrie!"

Her gaze stayed on Gunderson. "We have to…" she whispered.

He gripped her arm, squeezing hard. "I'm sorry, but there's nothing you can do for him now."

When she still didn't move, he tugged on her arm. "Come on. Before we end up the same way."

He watched her expression harden as she shook herself into action and let him lead her down the hall, although she kept looking back.

"This is my fault," she said, as he tried to determine the best place to hide.

"You're not responsible."

She made a snorting sound. "Of course I am. He was here to meet me."

"Because he was doing his job. Maybe you should blame the building security for letting terrorists in here. Or whoever leaked the meeting information."

He hurried Carrie down the hall, opening doors as they went. Most led to small offices, but one was larger, which had the potential for more hiding places. He stepped inside, looking around. The blinds were partially closed, which would give them more cover. Crouching behind the broad wooden desk was too obvious, but a bank of storage cabinets blocked the view from the door.

"Get back there."

"What about you?"

"I'm coming."

Carrie hesitated, then crossed the room and wedged herself into the corner. Crossing to the desk, he opened drawers, looking for anything useful. When he found a box of pushpins, he threw them onto the polished tile floor, watching them scatter. Then he crossed to the cabinets and stepped in front of Carrie, gun drawn.

Of course, if he had to shoot, he'd alert every terrorist in the building.

As he pressed his back to her front, he could feel the tension humming through her.

"Wyatt?"

"I'm here to make sure you get out of this." He wanted to turn around and take her in his arms. He wanted to stroke her back and hair to comfort her, but he knew that facing the enemy was more important than giving her reassurances.

Down the hall, Wyatt could hear rapid footsteps and doors opening and slamming shut again. When the door to the office where they were hiding opened, every muscle in his body tensed. He saw a shadow flicker on the wall—the shadow of a man holding a machine gun. The guy stood still for a moment, then started across the tile floor toward their hiding place.

Chapter Two

Wyatt waited, his body coiled for action.

In a couple of seconds, if the trap he'd set didn't work, the invader was going to spot them—and shoot. But before he reached their hiding place, the man stepped on the pushpins and lost his footing.

Wyatt sprang around the corner, reaching for the guy's gun arm and pulling him forward across the slippery surface. Off balance from the pins and the man yanking on his arm, the gunman scrambled to stay upright while he tried to get his weapon into firing position. Before he could do either, Wyatt kicked him square in the back, sending him sprawling on the tile floor, yelping as the sharp points of the pins dug into his hands and face.

He was a blond guy, young and muscular, and totally unprepared to be attacked by the quarry he was hunting.

Wyatt was on him as he went down. As the guy struggled to respond to the changed circumstances, Wyatt raised his own weapon and bashed the terrorist over the head with the gun butt. The man went still.

"Cover him," he told Carrie, handing her his Sig while he looked for something to tie the guy up.

She held the weapon in a two-handed grip. He noted that she was savvy enough to stand a couple of yards away so that the man couldn't grab her leg if he came to and went into attack mode.

Wyatt's glance raked the desk. Grabbing the phone, he yanked the cord from the wall, then disconnected the cord from the phone to the receiver.

While Carrie kept the gun trained on the guy, Wyatt tied him up using both cords. When he was finished, he took a closer look at the terrorist's appearance. Definitely not from the Middle East. In fact, he looked like a typical Midwestern farmer with sunburned skin, blond hair and pleasant-enough features.

"You know him?" Wyatt asked. "Was he one of the men in the park?"

"No," Carrie answered.

"Well, that's a clue to the scope of the organization. Looks like the initial three you spotted in the park weren't the only ones involved in the plot."

She nodded.

As Blondie started to stir, Wyatt took back the gun while he debated what to do.

The man's eyes blinked open. When he tried to move and found that his hands and feet were secured, he swung his murderous gaze from Wyatt to Carrie and back again. Carrie recoiled, but Wyatt ignored the threatening scowl. "How many men are in the building?"

"Enough to kill you and the bitch."

"I don't think so." He wanted to ask how the terrorists had discovered the time and location of Carrie's meeting with the Federal prosecutor, but he knew that would only be a waste of time.

The guy smirked at him. "You won't get out of here alive. And once you're dead, there won't be anyone to testify against Bobby."

"They have the pictures she took of your meeting."

"So what? In this day and age, they could be faked. And—"

To stave off another smart remark, Wyatt bashed him on the head again, and he went still.

Carrie made a low, distressed sound. "Why did you do that?"

"Don't tell me you wanted to keep listening to his line of crap?"

"No."

Wyatt found packing tape in one of the desk drawers, and wound it around the guy's head and over his mouth so he couldn't call for help. Then he pulled him behind the desk.

"It looked like you handled my gun all right," he remarked.

"Yes. My father made sure I was able to protect myself."

"Good."

He handed her his automatic and took the terrorist's weapon for himself before crossing to the door and looking out. The hall was clear. But they'd come back when they realized their buddy was missing.

Wyatt led the way, and they sprinted to the end of the hall and into another office.

He locked the door, even knowing it would be a dead giveaway to their position. At least it would buy them a few seconds if somebody tried to get in.

"Up here the windows open. We can get out," he told Carrie.

"Five stories up?"

"There are step-back roofs." He hurried to the window and slid the glass open.

Carrie looked out, seeing the roof below them. "It's pretty far."

"Not if you lower yourself by your hands. I'll go first."

She kept her gaze on him. "You're all business. All the time. I should be thankful for that."

He bit back a retort. There was no time for anything but escape from a building that had turned into a death trap.

He slung the weapon over his shoulder, then climbed out

the window and lowered himself, thankful that he was in good shape.

Controlling his descent, he eased down the wall, then let himself drop the four feet to the gravel surface of the roof below. Turning, he held up his arms to Carrie.

She shook her head. "I can't do that."

"You don't have to. I'll catch you. Hurry, before they find us."

She stuffed the gun into her shoulder bag, which she wrapped across her chest, then maneuvered herself out the window. Turning around, she lowered herself until her body was dangling from the frame. But her grip wasn't strong enough, and she fell. Wyatt was there to catch her, taking her weight as she came hurtling down.

They both wavered on their feet, then he steadied them.

"Thanks," she said.

"We've got to do that again."

She made a strangled sound but followed him to the edge of the roof. Again he went first, lowering himself to his full length, then dropping six feet to the roof below.

When he turned and glanced up, he saw Carrie watching him. She looked as if she wanted to protest; instead, she grimly climbed over the edge and lowered herself by her arms. This time she must have made a concerted effort to control her descent. She didn't let go until her full length was dangling from the edge. Again he caught her and staggered back, almost losing his balance. But he stayed on his feet, then went to check the next drop-off point.

A scuffling sound made him whirl around. He saw that Carrie had turned and was holding the pistol he'd given her in two hands—pointed at a man who was looking over the edge of the roof above, his weapon aimed downward.

Carrie fired, hitting the would-be assassin in the arm. Before he could recover, Wyatt delivered a chest shot, and the man went down, toppling over the edge and landing on the gravel surface a few yards from where they stood.

Carrie gasped as she stared at the body.

Wyatt hurried back to her, catching her look of horror as she realized what she'd done.

"I...I think he couldn't believe a woman had the guts to fire at him."

"His mistake," Wyatt said in a gritty voice. "Thank God you did."

She stood rigidly, and he reached for her hand.

"Gotta go."

At his touch, she shook herself into action, and he hustled her to the edge of the roof. This time there was a bonus feature: a ladder leading down to ground level.

Wyatt sent Carrie down first, alternately covering her descent and checking for more pursuers on the roof above. When he joined her, she was shaking, and he knew she was still reacting to what had happened.

"I shot a man," she whispered as though she were just now taking it in.

He pulled her toward him, at the same time easing her against the side of the building where it would be harder for anyone looking down from above to see them. Wrapping his arms around her, he held her close. "You shot in self-defense. He was going to kill you."

"It's not like shooting at a target."

He didn't point out that he'd fired the kill shot. Or that he'd killed a lot more men. This was no time for a philosophical discussion on the morality of protecting oneself.

She let her head drop to his shoulder, clinging to him, and he cradled her against himself, breathing in her scent, absorbing the curves of her slender body before easing away.

"We can't stay here. Another one of them could come across the roof at any minute. And there's a big clue up there about which way we went."

She shuddered, then looked around. "Why didn't we see any cops?"

"They may not know about it yet."

While he'd been holding her, he'd been thinking about escape routes. Before coming down to the government building with her today, he'd scouted out the area around the building as well as the interior, and he was mentally plotting a route that would get them onto the city streets.

He looked up one more time, scanning the roofline for terrorists before leading Carrie away from the building, toward a chain-link fence topped with barbed wire. He was wondering how they were going to get over it when he saw that the lock on the gate was broken and the barrier was open a crack.

"This must be how they were going to get away," he muttered as he pushed the gate farther open.

She nodded, following him through and into an alley.

He looked at the assault rifle in his hand. "I guess I can't take this out onto the street." First he used his shirt to wipe off his fingerprints. Then he set the weapon on the ground before hustling Carrie along the alley.

When they had turned a corner, putting another building between them and the scene of carnage, he called the safe house.

Gary Blain answered again. "Wyatt?"

"Yes. We got out of there. We're coming back. We won't have the town car."

"Thank God you're okay." He paused. "What about Collins?"

"He didn't make it."

Gary absorbed that bit of bad news, then asked, "What are you going to do for transportation?"

"There's a Zipcar agency a couple of blocks away. We can rent one of those."

"Be careful down there, man."

"I always am."

When he hung up, Carrie looked at him. "What's a Zipcar?"

"Cars you can rent by the hour. Like bicycles in Europe."

"I didn't know about that, either."

Probably a function of her living in a million-dollar condo in Columbia Heights with a spectacular view of the city. He was tempted to say something about her dad's money making it unnecessary for her to rent anything, but he decided there was no point in needling her. Not after they'd narrowly escaped getting killed—and after he'd seen what she was made of. He'd known she had the guts to turn in men plotting against the U.S. government. He hadn't known the rest.

"Are you going to call the police now?" she asked, breaking into his thoughts.

"We still can't trust them. We still don't have a handle on how those guys found out about your meeting. For all we know, the terrorists have a spy in the D.C. police department."

She winced. "How would that be possible?"

"It just takes one bad cop who wants to supplement his income."

"But he'd know he'd be setting us up to get killed."

"Some people will do just about anything for money. Do you know how many people got killed because Aldrich Ames, that turncoat in the CIA, blew their cover?"

"I don't know the exact number, but I get your point."

"Which means I'm not taking any chances," he answered as he led her down Tenth Street to the storefront with the Zipcar office.

The blond young man behind the counter, wearing a dress shirt and tie, looked up as they stepped in.

"We'd like a vehicle with four-wheel drive," Wyatt said.

Carrie looked surprised but said nothing.

"How long will you be needing it?"

"At least a day."

"There will be extra charges if you turn it in later."

"Understood."

"Driver's license?"

Beside him Carrie tensed. He touched her arm reassuringly, then dug into his wallet and pulled out an alternate ID.

He handed over a license that said he was Will Hanks.

The clerk filled out the paperwork, and they were out of the office and on the road in less than fifteen minutes.

Carrie sank into the passenger seat of the Chevy Equinox, leaned back against the headrest and closed her eyes. He watched her take a few moments to catch her breath before she turned to him. "You always carry fake ID?"

"Yeah." His gaze alternated between her and the road. "You did good back there."

"What choice did I have?"

"A lot of people would have gone to pieces or frozen up when the crap hit the fan. You didn't."

She huffed out a breath. "I guess I didn't go to pieces when I spotted those guys in the park, either."

"True."

She made a snorting sound. "One minute I was taking pictures of a happy little eagle family. Then I was in the middle of an action-adventure movie."

"More real than 3-D."

"Yeah. When they shoot at you in a 3-D movie, you can't get killed."

He turned onto Connecticut Avenue and took that route toward the suburbs.

"Why did you get a four-wheel-drive car?" she asked.

"We might not be going in the front entrance to the safe house," he answered, then switched the subject. "I want to find out who ratted you out. Who knew about your meeting downtown?"

She sighed. "I did discuss it with my dad because he wanted to stay informed."

"He asked me questions about the meeting, too."

She turned her head toward him. "But he wouldn't tell anyone. He doesn't even trust the government. He hired you and your team because he wanted to keep me safe."

Wyatt nodded. "Other people are at his house. Someone might have heard."

"No one there would set me up like that."

Although Wyatt heard the note of conviction in her voice, he wasn't so sure. He'd be the judge of who might have betrayed Carrie. Right now, though, his primary goal was to get her back to safety, and he needed to make sure nobody was on their tail.

He wanted to speed back to the safe house, but he allowed himself to go no faster than five miles above the speed limit as he watched the rearview mirror for any signs that they were being followed. He saw none.

Pulling out his phone again, he dialed the secure number. This time he waited eight rings, but nobody picked up. A very bad sign.

Instead of leaving a message, he clicked off.

"What?" she asked.

"Nobody answered."

"What does that mean?"

"I don't know, and I don't like it."

They were on a secondary road that led through the rolling Maryland countryside. As he'd suggested he might do, he turned off onto a dirt track that circled the safe-house property, staying on the alert for signs of trouble.

"What are you doing?"

He gave her a quick look. "I'm not taking you in there until I know everything's all right."

"It's supposed to be secure. That's why it's called a safe house."

"And right now the vibes are all wrong."

"Then why are we going back at all?"

"A couple of reasons. There's equipment in there that I need. And the rest of the team could be in trouble."

THE NEWS OF the ambush at the Federal Building had hit the cable channels. Tuned in to the CNN broadcast, the watcher felt anger flare up. A lot of money had crossed hands—for results—and now it looked as though everything was going to hell in a handbasket.

After clicking off the TV, the individual walked down the hall, stepped into a darkened bedroom and dialed a cell phone number, hand tightening on the phone while waiting for someone on the other end of the line to pick up.

"Yes?"

The caller spoke in a low, steady voice, working hard to hold back screams. "What the hell is going on?"

"A glitch."

"You call that a glitch? The attack on the Federal Building has hit all the major news stations. The only bodies they found were that Federal prosecutor—what's his name—Skip Gunderson? And two of your guys. I assume that means the agent and the girl got away."

"Yeah. A real screwup."

"There better not be any blowback."

"The dead guys won't talk. And we got the rest of our men out before anyone else showed up."

"How did you make such a mess of a simple assignment?"

"You neglected to tell us how good Wyatt Hawk is."

"I'm as surprised as you are." The caller made a throat-clearing noise. "Where are Hawk and the girl?" Maybe that news would be better.

"We don't know for certain. We figure they'll come back to the safe house. We can get them there."

"You're sure?"

"It's a good bet."

"What if that doesn't work out?"

"We go to plan B."

"That's just perfect."

Before the caller could ask another question, the man on the other end of the line hung up, leaving nothing but dead air.

The caller had thought of a foolproof scheme. Apparently, that held true only if you weren't working with morons. More proof that if you wanted something done right, you'd better do it yourself. Too bad it took special training to handle this job.

FIFTY MINUTES AFTER leaving the Zipcar office, Wyatt pulled the Chevy Equinox into the woods, torn between bad and worse alternatives. He could leave Carrie in the car or hiding in the underbrush while he went in to find out what was going on at the hideout. Unfortunately, that would mean she was vulnerable if someone was lurking nearby. Or he could take her with him, which would expose her to whatever danger might be waiting ahead.

He made a decision and turned toward Carrie. "I don't want to leave you here unprotected. We're going to approach the house from the right side. I want you to stay behind me, and do exactly what I say. If I tell you to hit the deck, you do it." His gaze burned into hers. "Got that?"

"Yes."

"Wait in the car until I signal you to get out."

She answered with a tight nod.

Hoping he could count on her not to freeze up, he climbed out of the vehicle and checked the area before motioning for her to follow.

As they approached the property line, they came in low, making themselves as small a target as possible. The first real evidence that something was wrong hit Wyatt when they reached the electric fence. He threw a stone at it and was only half surprised to find that it was no longer working. Somehow the current to the wires had been disrupted.

He threw another stone, then took a chance and crept

forward to touch the fence. Nothing happened. Dead as a drowned rat.

Again he considered leaving Carrie but decided against the tactic.

He was able to lift the wire fence and scoot under, then hold it for her.

She came up beside him, her gaze focused on the house.

"It's quiet," she whispered.

"Too quiet. You might think we'd hear the TV. Or guys talking."

Too bad he didn't have a pair of binoculars. But he hadn't anticipated the need to spy on a facility that had been perfectly safe when they'd left.

His instincts warned him to turn around and get the hell out of there, but he couldn't do it. Not when he felt an obligation to the men who'd taken this assignment with him. What if they were injured? Or being held under threat of death?

"Stay low," he whispered.

Carrie did as he'd asked.

Taking his time, he moved forward until they came to the flat stretch, where the fields for a hundred yards around the structure had been cleared to make it difficult for anyone to sneak up on the safe house. Great planning when you were on the inside, but not so advantageous if you were trying to get close to the house.

Unfortunately, he found he didn't have to get close to understand what had happened. The evidence was big as life and twice as plain—a body lying sprawled across the back steps.

Chapter Three

Carrie heard Wyatt mutter a curse.

Alarmed, she followed the direction of his gaze.

From her hiding place, she saw a dark-skinned man with a shaved head lying at the bottom of the back steps, his arms spread and a gun still clutched in his hand. As she realized who it was, her chest constricted painfully. The man was Gary Blain, one of the bodyguards who'd gone out of his way to be nice to her during guard duty. It looked as though he'd been trying to get away when he'd been gunned down.

She choked back a sob. Another casualty. On her account. "No."

Wyatt put his arm around her shoulder, pulling her against his side, and she turned toward him, closing her eyes and pressing her forehead against his chest.

"Well, we know why he didn't answer the phone," he said in a raspy voice.

"What about the rest of them?"

"We've got to assume they're dead, too. Probably in the house. And Gary almost got away."

"My fault—again," she whispered.

"No. The bastards are determined to get you. When we escaped from the Federal Building, they probably came here. Or maybe they sent a team here as a precaution in case we got out of the trap they'd set."

"How did they know about this place?"

"Obviously, somebody gave away this location."

"Could they have followed you? I mean, sometime earlier?"

"I don't think so," he answered, but she heard the tiny note of doubt in his voice. Still, he continued, "We have to assume it's the same person who told them about your meeting this morning."

Carrie fought the sick feeling rising in her throat. Death and destruction were following close on her heels. It was hard to imagine everything that had happened today and harder still to believe that someone was deliberately trying to kill her. But apparently, that was what happened when you ratted on terrorists.

"What are we going to do?" she murmured.

"For starters, thank God that we didn't go charging in there."

"You mean thank your instincts."

"Whatever," he answered dismissively. "We'd better get the hell back to the car before somebody spots us."

Even as he spoke, it was already too late. Lookouts must have been stationed in all directions, because in the next second, gunfire erupted from inside the house, and men charged outside, sprinting in their direction.

Wyatt grabbed Carrie's hand, leading her back the way they'd come, heading for the screen of trees. Behind them she heard running feet closing the gap.

Lord, no.

"On my own turf, I've got a little surprise to slow them down," he said. He reached into his pocket, pulling out something that looked like a cell phone. As they ran, he pressed a series of buttons. In back of them, small explosions began to erupt from the grass, sending sprays of dirt and stones into the air.

She heard a loud curse, as someone behind them took a hit.

The explosions continued, but Wyatt didn't slow his pace, so she kept running beside him, her lungs burning as she struggled to keep up with him.

She was beginning to think they were in the clear when the gunfire stopped. But after the last explosion, she heard a sound that made the hair on her arms prickle. Someone must have escaped Wyatt's trap and he was pounding along behind them.

At first the thuds were faint. Whoever was back there had lost ground because of the charges, but he was catching up, and now he began shooting as he went.

Wyatt whirled and returned fire, but his weapon was no match for his opponent's. Unfortunately, they were still a long way from the electric fence and the car, and she could hear the pursuer steadily gaining on them.

She glanced at Wyatt, seeing the grim set of his jaw. Apparently, he didn't think they were going to make it to the fence.

When they came to a place where the land had been contoured into several small hills and valleys, Wyatt stopped.

"Get down. And stay down, no matter what happens."

She remembered when she hadn't liked Wyatt. Now she obeyed his orders without question, because she knew that was the only way she was getting out of this trap alive.

Dropping behind a hillock, she dragged in great gasps of air and pressed her hand against her side, her gaze fixed on the man who was charging toward them, firing his weapon as he ran.

She ducked and slung her arms over her head, as if that would stop a bullet. Her heart was pounding as she waited for Wyatt to drop the guy. But in the next moment, Wyatt made a strangled sound and fell back against the ground.

Carrie felt her heart stop. He'd been hit!

With a whoop of victory, the gunman closed the last few

yards between them and swung his weapon toward her, taking a long moment to meet her terrified gaze.

"Don't," she whispered.

But Wyatt obviously had no intention of letting her get murdered. He leaped from behind the mound and shot the guy in the back at point-blank range. The attacker went down with a gasp of surprise.

Wyatt charged toward her, snatching the assault rifle from the man's grasp.

"Why didn't you shoot him before he got so close?" she gasped as she stared at the terrorist. He was another perfectly normal-looking young man. If you saw him on the street, you never would have known what was in his mind.

"Because I only had one bullet left, and it had to count," Wyatt answered.

He turned to look back the way they'd come, and she followed his gaze toward the bodies of two men sprawled in the field. Neither was moving.

"Are they dead?"

"We can't go back to find out. Come on. Before another one comes after us," he said.

Reaching down a hand, he helped her up. She swayed on her feet for a moment. Then they ran back toward where they'd left the car. She was out of breath when they reached the fence, and he held it up for her. She dived beneath the wires, and he followed.

They made it to the vehicle, and she allowed relief to flood through her as she climbed in and locked the door. Wyatt shoved the weapon he'd appropriated onto the floor between his seat and the console, then turned the ignition and slammed the shift into Drive, speeding away before any other terrorists could figure out what had gone wrong with their foolproof plan.

She sat for a few moments gripping the edges of her seat, willing her heart to stop pounding and her breath to slow.

Against all odds, they had gotten away again. Thanks to the man beside her.

"Are you okay?" he asked.

"Yes."

Then she remembered the sound he had made as the terrorist was charging toward them. When she opened her eyes and swung her gaze to the left, she saw the blood oozing through the fabric of his shirt.

"You really are hit," she gasped out. "You weren't just pretending to get his attention."

"It's not bad."

"How do you know?"

"I can move my arm all right. I can drive. The bone's not broken."

"You have to—"

"—get us the hell out of here before they figure out which way we went."

She saw the set of his jaw as he kept driving along the narrow country road, watched him grimace when he had to turn the wheel, putting distance between them and the safe house that was no longer a refuge.

She wanted to ask what they were going to do now, but she was sure he'd tell her when he figured it out. It was amazing how much her thinking had changed in the past few hours. She'd thought Wyatt was a grim lone wolf, and she had wondered why her father had hired him. Now she understood that he was the best man for the job. Maybe the only man. Could anyone else have saved her life so many times today?

She heard him curse under his breath, and alarm shot through her.

Jerking upright, she looked in all directions but saw no suspicious cars.

"What?"

"I shouldn't have gone back there," he muttered, and she knew he was blaming himself for the latest shoot-out.

"You had your reasons."

"They were a mistake."

He clenched his teeth, and she could tell he was fighting the pain in his arm. If she'd known where they were going, she would have ordered him to let her drive, but the safe house was in an isolated part of the county, accessible only from a series of narrow, winding roads, an area she barely knew.

All she could do was divide her attention between their surroundings and Wyatt, watching the sinister red patch on his sleeve grow bigger as he drove.

He saw her watching him. "It's not an artery."

"Glad to hear it."

"I'd already be dead if it were."

She made a snorting sound.

He kept driving, clenching his teeth every time he made a turn and checking the rearview mirror frequently to make sure they weren't being followed. When signs of civilization began appearing, he slowed his speed. Finally they approached a strip mall, and he pulled into the parking lot of a drugstore, finding a spot near the door. "I'm going to stay here. Can you go in and get a few things?"

"Of course."

"I need gauze pads, antiseptic, adhesive tape, and if they have men's shirts, get me something I can wear that's not bloodstained."

She nodded and climbed out, looking around to make sure nobody was paying any attention.

Inside, she grabbed a shopping cart and took a moment to orient herself, then headed for the first-aid section. She found the required items and added a bottle of painkillers, a bottle of water and a roll of paper towels. Then she went to the clothing department. It wasn't large, but she did find a long-sleeved, button-down-the-front sports shirt that looked as if it would fit Wyatt.

At the cash register, she started to reach for her credit card, then remembered a credit transaction could be traced. Instead, she paid in cash and hurried back to the car. Wyatt was sitting with his head thrown back and his eyes closed. They snapped open, and his hand went to the gun when she opened the passenger door. When he realized it was her, he relaxed.

He'd gotten them to the shopping center, but now his skin was gray and covered with perspiration. He was in shock.

"You're not in any shape to drive," she said.

She expected an argument, but he got out of the car and walked unsteadily to her side. She switched places with him, then drove around the back of the shopping center.

He stared around in surprise. "What are you doing?"

"Having a look at your arm."

The strip mall backed up onto a wooded area, and she drove to the side of the blacktop, parking under some low-hanging maple trees.

"Let me get my shirt off."

He heaved himself up and climbed out, where he stood studying the area. When he established that they were alone, he started unbuttoning his shirt. She could see that moving his arm was hurting him.

Joining him, she said, "Let me."

Standing in front of him, she began working the buttons, exposing his broad chest, which was covered with a dark mat of hair and what looked like an old scar.

"What happened to you?" she asked as she gently touched the scar.

"I was in a war zone," he clipped out, telling her by his tone that he wanted her to drop the subject.

Pressing her lips together, she tried not to focus on his buff physique as she helped him take his good arm out of his sleeve, then gathered up the fabric so that she could ease the other sleeve down his arm. The blood had already stuck the fabric to his skin, and he made a small sound as she peeled the shirt away. There was a trash can nearby. Balling up the shirt, she started toward it.

He stopped her with a firm command. "No. I don't want any evidence left around here."

"Oh, right."

He walked back to the passenger seat and sat down heavily, giving her access to the arm. Gingerly, she examined the wound. It looked as if the bullet had torn a path across his skin, leaving a deep canyon in his flesh.

He turned his head and inspected the track. "It's not bad. Which is good, because spending time in an emergency room could be dangerous."

"Why?"

"That's a logical place to look for me."

"How would they know you were hurt?"

"I left some blood on the ground."

She made a low sound. She had been so wound up with getting away that she hadn't even noticed.

After opening the paper towels, she pulled a couple off, wadded them up and wet them with the water, then gingerly wiped at the dried blood on his arm, being careful not to start the wound bleeding again.

She'd barely spoken to the man in the week she'd been with him. In the space of a few hours, she'd gotten to know him a lot better. Now she felt the intimacy of this encounter. He was half-naked, and she was tending to him with hands-on closeness. She might have tried to speed through the first aid. Instead, the situation made her want to linger. Too bad they were parked in the back of a shopping center, a location that wasn't exactly private.

"How did my father happen to hire you?" she asked.

"He was looking for someone to guard you, and he got a recommendation from one of my former bosses at the CIA. I guess he liked what he heard."

"You quit the Agency?"

"I got into a situation in Greece."

"What kind of situation?"

"I got my partner killed," he snapped.

"It probably was as much his fault as yours."

"Her."

"Oh."

"I should have known better than to get involved with her." The way he said it told her this was another subject he didn't want to talk about. She wouldn't press him. Not now when he was injured, although she couldn't help wondering what had happened.

She opened the bottle of antiseptic. "This may sting."

He answered with a tight nod.

She poured the clear liquid onto his arm, hearing him wince as it pooled in the wound.

When she was satisfied that she'd cleaned it well, she taped on the gauze pads.

Next came the shirt, which she pulled out of the bag and unbuttoned. Reversing the process, she helped him get his arms through the sleeves, which turned out to be about an inch too short, so she left the cuffs unbuttoned.

Before she finished, a blast from a car horn startled her, making her lose her balance and fall forward, pressing her breasts against Wyatt's face. Quickly she pushed herself away. Turning, she saw a white Jeep with an orange dome light on top. A middle-aged man in a security guard's uniform was leaning out the driver's window, staring at them with narrowed eyes.

"This side of the lot is for store owners and employees only. You can't come back here and make out," he said in a stern voice.

When she started to object that they'd been doing no such thing, Wyatt put a hand on her arm.

"Sorry, Officer," he said.

"Button up your shirt and move along."

"Yes, sir," Wyatt answered.

She'd never expected to hear him cave in the face of authority, and she knew he probably hated doing it, but she also knew he was avoiding any kind of confrontation, avoiding having the guy come over and see the bloodied shirt or the gun in the car. While Wyatt and the guard had exchanged pleasantries, she'd bundled the supplies back into the drugstore bag and thrown them in the backseat. Now she hurried around to the driver's door. The security guy stayed where he was while she pulled away, then followed her to the parking lot entrance. She waited for the light to change and pulled out, heading down the road in the opposite direction from where they'd come.

Wyatt had leaned back in his seat but now he sat up suddenly and cursed.

Carrie's gaze shot to him in alarm. "What?"

"We have to get rid of that gun."

"Like throw it in the bushes?"

"No. Like put it in the trunk."

He craned his neck to look at a road sign. "Turn off on a side road and look for a place where there aren't any houses."

She followed directions, and they both got out. She blocked the view from the road while he stowed the weapon out of sight.

Back in the car, he directed her to the Intercounty Connector. When they'd gotten onto the high-speed road that cut across the D.C. area, he said, "Get off at Route 29 and head for Columbia. There are a lot of motels over there. Find something that's part of a midpriced chain."

When they reached Route 29, she slowed, and he looked at her inquiringly. "What are you doing?"

"I have to call my father and tell him I'm okay."

"When we know we're safe."

"He'll be worried."

"We'll be in Columbia in less than thirty-five minutes. If

you were dead, he'd know it. The news stations would have already broadcasted it."

She winced.

He leaned back and closed his eyes, and she took the highway he'd suggested, which turned out to be a toll road that cut across Montgomery County to Howard County.

ALTHOUGH THE SAFE house had been deemed an easy target, four men had been given the job of taking it down and waiting for Carrie and Wyatt to return. Now two of the men were dead and one was wounded. The guy who was still functional walked down the access road and into the woods, where he and his partners had parked a white van out of sight. The standard anonymous utility vehicle. In this case, perfectly suitable for getting rid of the bodies of three large men who'd been at the wrong place at the wrong time. And two terrorists who'd gotten themselves killed by taking off after the fleeing man and woman.

The four-man team had caught the hired guards by surprise because the bitch they'd been minding had been out of the house, which was reason enough for them to relax. The unwanted visitors had disabled the security system at the safe house—as a further means of gaining access unawares. Nobody had been looking out the windows when they'd crept up through the fields and made the dash across the cleared land around the house. Only one of the guards inside had been on his toes enough to make it outside, and he hadn't gotten any farther than the back steps. Too bad his body had alerted the guy with Carrie Mitchell that something was wrong at the house. And too bad he'd come sneaking up from the side yard. Apparently, he was an efficient and cautious fellow.

The men who'd taken the house were named Harry, Sidney, Jordan and Bruce. Sid was the only one not wounded or killed.

He wished he'd turned down the job. He hadn't signed up for this gig because of any ideological convictions. He was in it strictly for the cash. Now he was cursing himself for getting lured in by easy money. It flitted through his mind to climb in the van and drive away. Then keep driving. He already had the first payment from the patron who'd hired him and the others.

But he didn't think escape was a practical solution. You didn't just quit a job like this. Once you were in, you were in for the duration. And from where he was sitting now, it looked as though it was going to be a longer haul than he'd been led to believe. The only way they were getting out of this was to finish the mission—or die trying. Harry and Jordan were already dead. And Bruce had a mangled leg. Two of the guys in the downtown end of the operation had also bought the farm.

Although Carrie Mitchell and her bodyguard had made it out of the area, Sid didn't call in for instructions right away. Instead, he spread tarps in the back of the van and started the annoying process of loading the five bodies into the vehicle before cleaning up the blood on the floor inside the house and moving dirt around to cover the blood outside, as per the instructions he'd been given to leave as little evidence as possible.

Bruce watched him work with dull eyes. Usually he was the one in charge. Now he was in too bad a shape to do more than nurse his wounded leg. "I'm hurt bad, man," he moaned.

"We'll get you back to headquarters."

"Shouldn't I be in the hospital?"

Sid gave him a considering look. "Hang on. That's what you'd say to me if our situations were reversed."

"It's a long way back to the hideout."

"Not that far, and it's real private."

Bruce cringed, probably thinking that his partner was considering leaving him in the same condition as the bodies. He closed his mouth and let Sid finish the quick and dirty cleanup. The rushed job wouldn't hide the evidence if the cops came in with luminol. But it was probably going to be a long time—if ever—before the authorities got to the safe house.

Who was going to call them? Not Wyatt Hawk. He was too conscious of maintaining the secrecy of his assignment. Which was going to make it difficult to find him and the woman. Hopefully, plan B would flush them out. And hopefully Sid could go back to his normal life of petty crime.

Chapter Four

As Carrie drove toward Columbia, she glanced at Wyatt. He was sitting with his head back and his eyes closed. She wanted to reach out and press the back of her hand to his cheek, but she had the feeling that if she did, he'd come instantly alert, and she'd find a gun pointed at her side. Which meant it was prudent to keep her hands on the wheel.

She knew Wyatt was being cautious when he'd asked her to drive so far away from the safe house. Would the terrorists really start checking every motel within a twenty-mile radius of their last known location? She doubted it, with so many motels in this area. But maybe they'd do it if they were desperate enough. And they'd certainly seemed determined to stop her from testifying.

Beside her Wyatt made a strangled sound, and her eyes snapped to him, seeing him looking around and getting his bearings.

"How are you feeling?" she asked.

"Okay."

Probably it was a lie—designed to reassure her. How could he feel okay after getting shot?

He shook his head and started to stretch, then stopped abruptly, undoubtedly because the pain in his arm had hit him. He dragged in a breath and let it out.

"How long was I sleeping?"

"A half hour."

"How close are we to Columbia?"

"We're here, but I don't know where to find a motel. They built the place so you can't find anything."

He laughed. "It was the original plan not to spoil the view with big signs. Then they realized that they needed to make the commercial areas more obvious." He looked around. "Head down Route 108, then turn at the Palace Nine shopping center. You'll find the right kind of motels along 100 Parkway."

She took his advice, stopping at a chain that advertised breakfast along with a room for less than a hundred bucks a night.

"You stay here. I'll check in," he said.

"Why?"

"Because I don't want the clerk to see a man and a woman together and remember the two of us if anyone comes asking questions. And a lone male is less suspicious than a lone female."

She nodded and pulled into a parking space near the door. When he got out, she watched him steady himself against the car door, then square his shoulders.

She gave him a critical inspection as he headed for the lobby. He looked like a guy who wasn't feeling 100 percent, but there was no way to know that he'd been shot a little more than an hour ago.

She glanced around, glad to see that nobody was paying her any particular attention.

PATRICK HARRISON STRUGGLED not to let his taut nerves overwhelm him. He spared a quick glance at his watch. It had been two hours since he and Carrie's father had heard the news of the attack in Washington, D.C., and he felt the tension humming around the comfortable, wood-paneled home office.

He sat in one of the leather guest chairs. Douglas Mitchell sat behind his broad rosewood desk. They were both staring at a flat-screen television tuned to CNN. There had been nothing new to report for the past hour and a half, but the commentators were attempting to fill the air. At the moment the network was running a background piece on the Mitchell family, discussing the way Douglas Mitchell had taken the twenty million dollars he'd inherited from his father and turned it into over a billion—by buying up companies in distress and gutting them. The tactic had made him popular with the investment group he'd formed but not so much with the men and women who'd lost their jobs under his tender loving care.

Next came candid shots of Carrie as a teenager riding in horse shows and more shots of her all grown up and out on dates in D.C. with various eligible bachelors. She was also shown with her father on a trip to Europe they'd taken two years ago. There were no shots of Patrick, of course. He was invisible as far as the family history was concerned.

Next were some of the nature pictures Carrie had taken close to home and across the U.S. Patrick realized that if she survived this ordeal, her career was going to get a big boost. Or if she died, perhaps her pictures would sell for hundreds of dollars more than they had the day before.

Patrick shot a glance at Douglas's rigid profile. The man had one hand pressed to his forehead as though trying to ward off a headache.

Patrick tried to make his voice reassuring. "Carrie's in good hands. I'm sure she got away."

Douglas whirled around in his swivel chair, his eyes fierce. "I'm not interested in your half-assed opinion. You don't have any more information than I do." He was as wired as a cat caught in a clothes dryer. Of course, he had a right to be. Since the moment his daughter had come home to the Mitchell estate to tell him about overhearing a terrorist plot, he'd been sick with worry about her.

Not that you could tell what he was feeling, unless you

knew him well enough to see below the surface of his bluff exterior.

His attitude came across as annoyance and anger, but Patrick had been with him long enough to understand the old man's anxiety. His daughter had come forward to testify against a gang of domestic terrorists, putting herself in immediate danger. She'd been hiding out for a week, and she'd gone downtown to meet with the Federal prosecutor. Unfortunately, the terrorists had been waiting for her and her bodyguard, Wyatt Hawk.

From the news accounts, it seemed that Hawk had gotten her out of the building. But where were they now?

Patrick took a calming breath. He'd known Carrie all his life, and he hated feeling as though there was nothing he could do, but he didn't see any effective course of action open to him.

The old man picked up his phone and punched in Hawk's cell number once again. The results were the same as every other time Douglas had tried to make the call. There was no answer.

"Damn him!" the elder Mitchell growled. For a moment, it looked as if he would throw the phone across the room.

"Remember your blood pressure," Patrick murmured.

"I don't need your damn advice," Mitchell shot back, slapping his hand against the desk. After a moment, he took a breath and said, "Sorry. I'm on edge. I shouldn't take it out on you."

"I understand."

"But I need to know what's going on." This time he dialed the safe house where Carrie had been staying for the past week. The results were the same.

"What can I do to help?" Patrick asked.

"Bring me a scotch and soda."

"Is that wise?"

"Don't question me."

Patrick sighed and got up. Again he sneaked a glance at his watch. How long was this ordeal going to last?

Maybe he could have a drink, too. And maybe he'd have another discussion with Douglas about hiring security for himself, although the man was firm in his conviction that he didn't need it.

He had just crossed the thick carpet to the bar when a noise alerted him that something was wrong. He whipped around to see two men standing in the office doorway. They wore ski masks over their faces and carried automatic weapons.

Patrick leaped toward the desk, putting himself between Douglas and the two men.

"What the hell?" Douglas turned.

"Out of the way." One of the men charged toward Patrick and hit him on the side of the head with the butt of a gun. He cried out in pain and went down, struggling to cling to consciousness.

While he was on the floor, the other intruder crossed to Douglas Mitchell. "Come on."

"Where?"

"You'll find out." The man grabbed Douglas by the arms and hustled him toward the door. When Douglas struggled, the man shoved a gun into the older man's back. "Cooperate, or you're going to get killed."

The man turned to address Patrick. "Tell Carrie Mitchell that if she doesn't turn herself in, her father's dead."

"We…we haven't heard from her," he managed to say.

"Well, you'd better hope she calls. And oh, yeah, if you contact the cops, you can kiss Mitchell's ass goodbye."

THE LONGER CARRIE waited for Wyatt to come out of the motel office, the more her tension grew. So many bad things had happened in the past few hours that she couldn't stop herself from waiting for the next one.

To her relief, Wyatt returned with the key in under five

minutes and directed her to a room around back. One room. She didn't love that arrangement, but she understood why he'd done it.

Inside, the accommodations were pretty standard, with two queen-size beds and enough room so that they could keep out of each other's way.

Wyatt pulled back the spread on one of the beds, kicked off his shoes and lay down heavily.

"I'm going to call my father," she said.

"Go ahead."

She dug her phone out of her purse and clicked it on. It beeped immediately.

"There are messages for me."

"Call your father first," he said as he leaned back against the pillow and closed his eyes.

"Right." She clicked the automatic-dial button for her father's house. The call was answered on the first ring, not by Douglas Mitchell. It was Patrick Harrison, her father's chief of staff. His mother had been a maid in their house, and she'd died in an automobile accident twenty-five years earlier. Since there had been no relatives willing to take the three-year-old boy, her father had unofficially adopted Patrick, and he'd been a member of the household ever since. He'd gone to college at Ohio State, then come back home to work for the senior Mitchell.

"Carrie, thank God," he said. "I've been trying to call you, but there was no answer." He sounded near hysterical.

She kept her own voice calm as she answered, "Wyatt told me to turn off my phone so they couldn't use it to pinpoint our location."

"Are you all right?"

"Yes. But the men at the safe house are dead." She gulped. "All except Wyatt. We were going back there, but it was an ambush. Like at the Federal Building."

"Thank God you're all right," he said again.

Something in the tone of his voice told her he wasn't just worried about her.

"What happened?" she asked, praying that her father hadn't had a heart attack or a stroke.

"There's no easy way to say this."

"Then spit it out!"

"Your father's been kidnapped."

"Lord, no!"

At the sound of her raised voice, Wyatt surged off the bed. Crossing to her, he took the phone out of her hand.

"What did you just tell Carrie?" he demanded, clicking on the speaker so that they could both hear.

"Her father's been kidnapped."

"How? Where?"

"Two men came to the house."

"Are you all right?" Carrie interjected.

"One of them hit me with the butt of his gun, but I'm okay. They're demanding that Carrie turn herself in, or they'll kill Douglas. And they said they'll kill him if I call the police."

Carrie gasped, hardly able to believe what she'd just heard.

"Are you sure it's the terrorists?" Wyatt demanded.

"I...guess. I don't know for sure. Who else would they be?"

"What did they look like?"

"They were wearing ski masks."

"Is there anything else you can tell me?"

"I was on the floor, hanging on to consciousness by my fingernails."

Carrie made a low sound. "I'm so sorry."

"It's okay. I mean, I'm still here. Maybe so I could give you the message about your father."

"Yeah," Wyatt agreed.

Patrick switched subjects. "Where are you?"

"Somewhere safe," Wyatt answered.

"We have to go home," Carrie said.

"No." Wyatt fixed his gaze on her. "Patrick just said that

men broke in and took your father, but they want you. They'll keep him alive as long as they don't have you. If you turn yourself in, you're dead, and so is he."

Carrie stared at Wyatt. A few minutes ago he had seemed as if he needed a good night's rest before he would be fully functional. Now he looked like the agent in charge again. "I want to know what happened, but I'm not going to take that information now, in case this call is being traced."

"By whom?" Patrick asked.

"The terrorists. I'll call you back soon."

"But—"

Wyatt clicked off.

ON THE OTHER end of the line, Patrick Harrison cursed. Slamming down the phone, he stood for a moment, struggling to control his temper as he reminded himself to breathe in and out slowly. Hawk had said he would call back. When, exactly?

Patrick had just been through a terrible ordeal, and now he didn't like the way Wyatt Hawk was handling the situation. No, for starters, he didn't like it that Hawk was on the case at all.

Patrick had come up with the initial list of bodyguards. Then he'd found something questionable in the guy's background. He'd told Douglas not to hire Hawk, but the man had always had a mind of his own. He might listen to advice, then do the exact opposite because he was sure he knew better. In this case, he'd decided to go ahead with the former CIA operative, even though the man had messed up on his last job.

Patrick had lived with Douglas Mitchell's arbitrary decisions for years. Since he'd come back from college to work for the old man, he'd thought more than once that he should have struck out on his own. But he'd been comfortable here, and when Douglas had made him a good offer, he'd known that the man wanted him to stay—and valued his work ethic.

But he'd found out soon enough that working for Douglas

could be an exercise in frustration. Never more than at this moment. He'd have liked to have Carrie home at the family compound so he'd know exactly where she was. But Hawk had her stashed Lord knew where. It could be somewhere close. Or they could be in the next state by now.

He banged his fist against the rosewood desk, then struggled for calm again. Hawk had said he'd call back. Then Patrick would get more information. Or not, depending on Hawk's mood.

He cursed again, more softly this time. Wyatt Hawk was turning out to be the biggest mistake he could imagine making.

CARRIE'S STOMACH ROILED as she stood in the middle of the room, clutching her cell phone. "My father—"

"—is a hostage."

"Which is my fault. And the men who snatched him hurt Patrick."

"Carrie, none of this is your fault. You were just doing your duty as a citizen. What were you going to do, let them blow up the U.S. Capitol and pretend you hadn't heard anything?"

When she started to protest, Wyatt reached for her and pulled her close, pressing her face to his shoulder. "We have two jobs here. The first one is to keep you safe. The second is to get your dad back."

"What if I think that's the wrong order?" she asked in a strained voice.

"It's not. And we *will* get him back."

"How?"

His tone was soothing as he rubbed her back. "We don't do it by running off without a plan. We've got to consider all the angles and proceed carefully."

He kept his arms around her, rubbing her neck and shoulders, and she leaned into his strength as she thought back over the awful conversation with Patrick. Thank goodness she hadn't been alone. If Wyatt hadn't stopped her, she would probably have told Patrick where she was, and the terrorists could be on their way to the motel already if they'd been listening.

"They can't find us through the phone?" she murmured.

"We didn't speak long enough for them to trace the call. But I want to get rid of both our phones so they can't use the GPS."

She nodded against his shoulder.

"Are you feeling better?" he asked.

"Shouldn't that be my line?"

He managed a low laugh. "I'm fine."

"You were shot a little while ago. You were resting when I got ahold of Patrick."

"I've been hurt before, a lot worse than this."

"That scar on your chest."

"Yes."

"And you were in the hospital, right?"

"I said it was worse than this." He eased away from her. "We need to get a couple of prepaid phones so we can use them and throw them away."

"Okay."

He gave Carrie a direct look. "You trust Patrick?"

"Of course!"

"Who else is at your house?"

She thought for a moment. "There's Inez, our maid."

"How long has she been with you?"

"Fifteen years."

"Does she need money?"

"Everybody needs money."

He nodded. "Who else could have heard you talking to your father about your plans to hide out?"

She felt as if she was being interrogated, but she knew he needed to know the answers. "There's a gardening crew that comes by a couple of times a week. They could have been eavesdropping."

"Anyone else?"

"Not on a regular basis."

His eyes narrowed, and she could see he was considering contingencies. "I don't want to leave you here, and I don't want to take you to the store, but I think that sticking together is better at the moment."

She nodded, assuming he was probably afraid she'd call Patrick if he left her.

He carried the cell phones to the bathroom and crushed them under his heel, then stuffed the pieces into his pocket.

She winced, thinking about the contacts and the pictures he'd just destroyed.

He glanced at her, apparently reading her expression. "You can get a new one later."

"Right."

"I'm going out first." He opened the door and looked out, then crossed to the car and motioned for her to follow.

As she got in the car, she asked, "They couldn't have found us here already, could they?"

"Probably not, but I didn't think they would show up at the safe house before we got back there. It appears that this operation is bigger and better organized than we assumed initially."

"Oh, great."

Minutes after they'd entered the motel room, they were back on the road.

This time, Wyatt took the driver's side. She wanted to protest that he should be resting, but she was pretty sure he wouldn't pay any attention to the suggestion. Obviously he was the kind of man who wasn't going to let a woman drive him unless he was incapacitated.

As he drove, he tossed away the pieces of the phones, then turned to her. "I have Patrick's bio. He's been with you for twenty-five years, right?"

"Yes."

"And does he have any reasons to dislike your family?"

"Why would he? My father did everything for him. He treated him like a son, actually. He had a bedroom down the hall from me. He ate all his meals with us. My father sent him to the same private school I went to. He paid his tuition at Ohio State."

"So he was a good student?"

"Yes."

"Did he ever give your father any trouble?"

"You mean like rebelling?"

"Yes."

"He and I did a couple of stupid things—like borrow my dad's car when we were both fifteen."

"What happened when your dad found out?"

"He didn't. We covered for each other."

"You like him?"

"He was as close to me as a brother." Memories flooded her. "We hung out together, because Dad was usually busy. You could say he was the kind of father who didn't have a lot of time for his kids, but I knew he loved me."

"We were talking about Patrick, not your dad."

"I was trying to explain why Patrick and I were so close."

"And he loved Patrick?"

She hesitated. "That might be too strong a word. I know he's fond of him. And he's certainly come to rely on him." Again she paused before continuing. "Patrick didn't have to come back and work for Dad, but he did that on his own."

"Okay." Wyatt checked the rearview mirror. "What about your mother?"

"Dad never talks about her."

"When's the last time you saw her?"

She thought for a moment. "When I was maybe six. I went into her room, and she was packing." The pain and confusion of that long-ago moment came zinging back to her again. "She said she loved me, but she needed to leave. She said she'd be back to see me, but she never came back."

"Why?"

"At the time I thought she'd abandoned me. Now I think my dad kept her away. I heard him and his lawyer talking once. Dad said that he'd given her a lot of money, and he wasn't springing for any more."

"Why do you think she left?"

"I think Dad was more wound up with his work than he was with her."

"Like with you and Patrick?"

"Yes."

"Could she be holding a grudge? Could she be angry enough to...try to hurt him?"

Carrie turned her head toward Wyatt. "Wait a minute. What are you trying to say? That my father wasn't kidnapped because of a terrorist plot?"

"I'm trying to look at every angle. Were you ever romantically involved with Patrick?" he asked.

The question startled her. "What business is that of yours?"

"I'm trying to understand the family dynamics."

"Patrick and I were never close that way," she clipped out, hoping he'd drop the subject, but apparently, he wasn't ready to do that.

"Did he ever try anything—and you rebuffed him?"

She sat perfectly still, remembering.

"From the look on your face, I take it the answer is yes."

"Once, at the pool, he came up behind me and put his arms around me."

"What did you do?"

"I swam away."

"How did he take that?"

"He never...tried again."

"How old were you?"

"We were teenagers. Would you drop it now?"

"Okay," he said, although she gathered from the tone of his voice that he wanted to keep interrogating her.

THIRTY MILES AWAY, things were unraveling for a key player in the unfolding drama.

The phone rang. And the caller ID said the number was unpublished.

Just let it ring, an interior voice advised. But that could turn out to be worse than picking it up.

Still, the hand that lifted the receiver wasn't quite steady.

"Hello?"

"You know who this is?"

"Yes."

"You're late on your payment."

"I'll have it in a few days."

"That's what you said last time."

"I swear I'll have it."

"You can't keep relying on our goodwill."

The line went dead, and the hand that replaced the receiver was shaking so hard that the instrument rattled.

Was there any way out of this? There had to be.

Chapter Five

"Tell me why someone else besides the terrorists could have kidnapped my father," Carrie said.

She watched Wyatt heave in a sigh and let it out before answering.

"It's all over the news. Someone could have taken advantage of the plot to go after him when he's vulnerable."

"Why?"

"That's what I'm trying to figure out. What do you know about his enemies?"

She didn't like the way he'd put that. He'd flat-out assumed that there were people who wanted to hurt her father.

"He didn't talk to me a lot about his business."

"But you do know something."

"He and a guy named Quincy Sumner had a pretty public fight over a piece of land they both wanted."

"And your father won."

"Yes."

"We'll put Sumner on our list. Where does he live?"

"Fairfax, Virginia."

They had arrived at the drugstore. This time they went in together. After buying four cell phones, Wyatt took Carrie on a quick run through the cosmetics and toiletries departments, where they bought some of the basics that they'd been forced to abandon at the safe house. He also bought her a sun hat.

When he'd removed the tag, he put it on her head, pulling it down firmly to cover part of her face.

As they returned to the parking lot, he turned to her. "I'm going to call Patrick back, but I want to do the talking."

"What if I want to talk to him?"

"Let me deal with him. I'll put on the speaker so you can hear."

She gave a little nod. She didn't like it, but it was probably the best course, given the state of her emotions.

On the prepaid phone Wyatt dialed the Mitchell house.

Patrick picked up immediately.

"Where the hell have you been?" he demanded.

"Getting phones. Tell us what happened."

"Is Carrie there?"

"Yes," she answered, then forgot all about letting Wyatt handle the call. "When did you find out I was in trouble?"

"Your dad got a computer alert about a shoot-out in the Federal Building. He turned on the television, and we were both watching, so we didn't hear anything until armed men appeared in his office and threatened to kill him."

Carrie moaned. "Was he all right?"

He repeated what he'd said earlier. "I told you I was on the floor at the time. I couldn't see much, but he walked out under his own power. They said they'd exchange him for you."

"Surrendering to them would be foolish," Wyatt snapped.

"Then what are you going to do?" Patrick asked.

"I'll get back to you on that."

"If you come home, we can work together on this."

"You're kidding, right?" Wyatt said. "You just told me that they strolled into the house. It's not safe for Carrie there."

Patrick made a frustrated sound. "I guess you're right." Then he asked again, "Where are you?"

"It's safer if you don't know. What if they came back and tortured you for information?"

"I wouldn't talk."

Wyatt answered with a mirthless laugh. "Everybody talks when they're in enough pain."

"I have to know Carrie's going to be okay."

"I am," she answered, the response automatic. She wasn't okay, but she was still alive, thanks to Wyatt Hawk.

Patrick's voice was an unwelcome counterpoint to her thoughts.

"You need more protection," he said.

Before she could answer, Wyatt jumped back into the conversation. "Like I said, that didn't work out so well last time."

"We need to discuss this," Patrick countered.

"There's nothing to discuss. You're not in charge of keeping Carrie safe."

"I could fire you."

Wyatt laughed. "I work for Douglas Mitchell, not you, and we're getting off now."

"Wait. When will I hear from you again?"

"I don't know."

"What if the kidnappers call?"

"Tell them to email me." Wyatt gave an email address.

"I may need to get in touch with you."

"You can use the same method."

"I may need to have quicker access."

"I'll keep checking my mail."

He clicked off before Patrick could ask another question.

Carrie closed her eyes and leaned back in her seat. "If you're guessing wrong, they could kill my dad."

"I don't think they will."

"But you're not sure."

"I'm sorry. We can't be absolutely sure of anything—except that they want you dead, and they'll try any method to get to you."

"My dad's health isn't that great. I was already worried that the stress of my being in danger would give him a heart attack or a stroke."

"Sorry," he said again. "My job is protecting you, and taking you home isn't the way to do it."

She gave him a direct look—and the only answer that made any sense. "I understand." After a moment, she added, "You said Patrick could email you, but you left your laptop back at the safe house, and you can't get mail on a cheap disposable phone, can you?"

"No, but I'm going to get another computer now. Then we'll pick up some clothes."

She could see he was thinking several steps ahead, while she was just trying to keep her nose above water.

Their next stop was one of the big computer and appliances chains, where Wyatt bought a midpriced laptop, using the credit card with the fake identity. Nearby was a discount department store where they each bought underwear and a couple of changes of clothing. He also bought Carrie a pair of sunglasses.

"This is costing you a lot," Carrie observed.

"Your dad can add it to the bill when we get him back."

She didn't bother saying she wasn't positive of that outcome.

By the time they were finished with the shopping expedition, Carrie was feeling worn-out. And she couldn't imagine how Wyatt was holding up. His wound might not be life-threatening, but it should have been more than enough to slow him down.

"We should eat something," he said.

She wasn't hungry, and she'd been feeling tense the whole time they were in the department store.

"We should call Patrick again," she said.

"I'd rather communicate by email."

"You said these phones can't be traced."

"Someone could have tapped into the phone system at your father's house. I'd rather not give them any information."

She sighed. "You have to set up that computer before you can get mail."

He nodded. "We can pick up dinner and eat in the room. That will save time. What do you want?"

She shrugged. "It's hard to think about food."

"But we both need to fuel up, with something simple and basic."

He drove to a fast-food burger chain and ordered loaded burgers, French fries and milk shakes for both of them. After getting the food at the drive-through window, they headed back to the motel, where he made a survey of the parking lot before pulling into the space in front of their unit.

She was still feeling wired, but she knew she needed to eat. After unpacking the food, she sat at the table, nibbling on the burger.

"Drink the milk shake," Wyatt advised. "You can use the calories."

She took a dutiful sip and found that she wanted more. Wyatt sat down across from her, interspersing eating and sipping with setting up his computer.

The room had a flat-screen television, and she picked up the remote and turned on CNN. The content of the broadcast gave her a shock. It was all about Carrie Mitchell.

She watched in fascination as they showed the Federal Building where the ambush had taken place, then old pictures of her and even some of her friends talking about her.

One was Pam Simmons, who had ridden in horse shows with her. Another was an editor who'd bought some of her nature photos.

She studied the pictures of herself. Most of them were old. And in all of them her hair was different from the way it looked now, which was good. A shot of her standing with her father made her heart squeeze. She must have made some kind of sound, because she looked up to find Wyatt watching her.

"I'm a celebrity."

"Unfortunately."

"I had no idea I would attract so much attention."

"The shooting's big news. Bigger than the original terrorist plot."

"Why?"

"You foiled the plot, making it a nonevent. The shooting's the real deal."

She sighed.

"You really want to keep watching that?" he asked when a shot they'd seen before flashed on the screen again.

"I guess not." She flicked off the television, then switched her attention to Wyatt, studying his face for signs that he was in pain and seeing what he probably wanted to hide. "How's your arm?"

"It's been better." He went back to work, and she watched him from under lowered lashes. He was competent and efficient. She'd seen that from the beginning. She hadn't understood his level of commitment to her. Or was that just part of the job? She hoped it was more than that.

"I can get my mail now," he finally said.

She waited, feeling her heart rate accelerate, while he accessed the mail system.

"There's a message from Patrick. Marked *urgent*."

"What does it say?"

"'The terrorists contacted me. They said—'"

Before he could finish, she grabbed the laptop and turned it toward her. "'—ask Carrie Mitchell if she wants to be responsible for her father's death.'"

THE WORDS BURNED into Carrie's mind and soul. She leaped up and charged around the table, heading for the bag with the phones.

Wyatt was on his feet seconds behind her, stopping her as she grabbed for one of them. He took it out of her hand before she could switch it on. "Don't."

"I have to call him."

"That's what they want. That's why they set this up. It sounds like the phone at your father's place is almost certainly tapped."

"I can't stand by and let them kill him."

"They won't."

She gave him a fierce look. "You keep saying that, but he's not *your* father. He's mine, and I'm not going to be responsible for killing him."

"You won't be."

The stress of the day was suddenly too much for her. She'd held herself together until this moment. Now she felt hot tears well in her eyes.

Wyatt saw them. Lifting her into his arms, he carried her to one of the beds, leaning over to lay her gently down. When she saw him looking at her, she rolled away from him, curling into a ball, embarrassed that he was seeing her go to pieces.

He muttered something she couldn't hear. She felt him ease onto the bed and reach for her. Turning her toward him, he took her in his arms.

She hated crying in front of him, hated this whole situation, but she was too stressed out to contain the sobs that wracked her body.

Carrie had learned not to show her emotions. When she'd cried in front of her father, he'd gotten angry or annoyed and told her to "grow up." His attitude had pushed her away. She'd tried to act like she didn't need him, which was perhaps why she felt so devastated by his getting kidnapped. Maybe she was feeling guilty because their relationship had never been filled with the warm, fuzzy father-daughter moments that she saw in sitcoms. Or maybe nobody had that, and it was simply a Hollywood illusion.

And speaking of illusions, what about the way she felt in Wyatt's arms now? Warm and safe. Perhaps even cherished.

Or was she making that part up because of the way he held her and stroked her?

She didn't move away when her sobs subsided. Neither did he. He kept her close, stroking his hands over her back, brushing his lips against her hairline.

The light kiss stunned her. This man who had held himself aloof was trailing his lips against her face.

For most of their short acquaintance, she had told herself that she didn't like Wyatt Hawk, that she didn't need him. But everything had changed with the first blast from the man pretending to be a security guard at the Federal office building.

Wyatt had shot him dead. He'd gotten her out of the car and into the building, under fire. And that had only been the first time he'd saved her.

Now she felt emotions rushing through her.

They flip-flopped as he eased away from her, then stood, running a hand through his hair.

"I'm sorry. That was inappropriate," he said.

She didn't know what to say. Was it? Or had she invited intimacy without realizing it?

She took her lower lip between her teeth. Maybe he was right. Maybe he was doing her a favor by getting off the bed, although it certainly didn't feel like it at the moment.

"We should try to figure out who blew the whistle on your meeting," he said.

"Who do you think it is?"

"I've got an idea where to start."

DOUGLAS MITCHELL'S EYES blinked open. He couldn't see much because he was in a darkened room. But he knew he was lying on a narrow bed, like something in a child's room, only not as comfortable.

He felt disoriented, but that was nothing new. He'd been feeling this way for the past six months, hiding his fuzzy thinking because he didn't want to admit anything was wrong with him.

He moved his left hand, tugging at the cold metal around his wrist. When he tried to move his arm off the bed, something stopped him. A rope, he thought, but he couldn't be sure in the dark.

He closed his eyes again, trying to breathe evenly, trying to calm himself. If he got too upset, his blood pressure would go up, and he might have a stroke. That wouldn't do him any good—or Carrie, either.

He took blood-pressure medication and a whole bunch of other pills. He didn't think the men who were holding him captive had brought his pills.

But why would they? They were going to kill him anyway.

That thought sent a frisson of fear rippling through his mind.

He fought to calm himself.

Think!

Could he get away? Trick them somehow?

He didn't know, but he had to try. For Carrie.

His heart constricted when he thought about his daughter. She was so brave. So together. He'd never told her how much he loved her or how much he admired the way she'd taken charge of her life. Now he might never have the chance.

He pushed that thought away and tried to focus on what he needed to do.

But thoughts swam in and out of his head the way they often did these days.

He could almost remember when the fuzzy feeling had started. Almost, but not quite.

But he wouldn't give in to the brain fog. He had to keep going, projecting the iron will that had always stood him so well.

Thank the Lord he'd had Patrick to help him keep his finances straight—and make decisions about Carrie.

Patrick had combed through a list of security experts and picked Wyatt Hawk to keep Carrie safe. No, wait. Patrick hadn't picked Hawk. He'd recommended someone else. But Douglas had thought Hawk was better. Had that been a mistake?

He cursed under his breath. Had he made a foolish decision that had jeopardized his daughter's life?

He went from cursing to praying. He hadn't prayed in years, not for himself. But he could pray for Carrie, couldn't he?

She must still be safe. Or why would these men be holding him captive?

He wasn't sure about that. He wasn't sure about anything beyond his hostage status.

When the doorknob turned, he closed his eyes and pretended to sleep.

A shaft of light fell across his face, and he heard men talking.

"How long do we have to keep the old guy?"

"Until we know the daughter's taken care of. Then we can wash our hands of him."

"She won't know the difference if we off him now."

"That's against the boss's orders."

The door closed again, but the men must have been standing right on the other side because Douglas could still hear their voices. He strained to hear the rest of the conversation.

"The boss is a pain in the ass."

"Yeah. But we're getting paid enough to put up with it. We already got a payment."

"Not enough. I want more of it now. As a gesture of good faith, you know."

The voices faded away, and Douglas sat up in the bed. Had he really heard that conversation, or had he made it up to fit the situation? In his current state, he honestly didn't know.

CARRIE LAY WHERE Wyatt had left her on the bed. She'd thought about curling her body away from him. Instead, she'd kept her gaze on him as he walked into the bathroom and splashed cold water on his face, then walked to the table and pulled his computer toward him.

She'd almost gotten in over her head with him a few moments ago. But he'd done her a favor by pulling away.

Or *was* it a favor?

She felt too confused to make up her mind about that. Maybe because she'd had so few intimate relationships with men.

Wyatt had asked her about Patrick. She'd never thought of *him* that way. He'd always been too much like a brother to her.

In college, she'd had some relationships, but they'd been with guys who'd turned out to be looking for more of a bed partner than a life partner.

Or maybe that was her fault. Maybe she'd given off vibrations that had kept them from getting too close to her.

If you didn't feel good about your relationship with your father, could you feel good about your relationships with other men?

She'd never gotten that analytical about it. She'd just always known that it was hard for her to trust anyone with the intimate emotions she'd always kept to herself.

That didn't seem to be true with Wyatt Hawk. She wanted to feel close to him. But was she deliberately picking a guy she knew wouldn't let it happen?

She hated second-guessing herself. And him.

Was the danger swirling around them making her reach out toward him? Or was there something real developing between them—if both of them were willing to take the chance and let their guard down?

Chapter Six

Wyatt kept his gaze away from Carrie and forced his mind back to what he was supposed to be doing—figuring out who could be responsible for both the ambush and the kidnapping.

He walked to the table and picked up his computer, opening a web browser.

"You mentioned a Quincy Sumner?" he said.

"Yes."

"He lives in Fairfax?"

"Yes."

He put in the name and the Virginia city and came up with several hits right away. After scanning them quickly, he raised his head.

"It's not him."

"How do you know?"

"He's dead."

"He is?" she asked, surprise in her voice.

"Yeah. He had retired—then had a heart attack on the golf course a few months ago."

"Dad didn't mention it."

"Maybe he doesn't even know." Wyatt studied the obituary, looking for names of next of kin. "I suppose it's possible that someone in his family could still hold a grudge against your father, but it seems unlikely that they'd be executing such an elaborate plan."

From the bed, Carrie murmured in agreement.

Wyatt bent his head to the computer screen again. "I've got some other ideas," he said as he scrolled through some of the files he'd stored in his mail system.

"Like what?"

"Let me check an address." He found the house he was searching for, then looked up. "I think the next step is to have a talk with Aaron Madison."

"Who is he?" Carrie asked.

"Another Federal prosecutor. He was working with Skip Gunderson."

"And you think he might know something?"

"He was in a position to know. This time you stay here, and keep the door locked." He closed the computer and stood up, thinking that going to Madison's house would get him away from Carrie for a while. And right now, he needed that distance. He'd done something stupid, and he didn't want to remain in the way of temptation.

But she apparently didn't understand his point of view—on any level.

"Uh, I don't think so."

He turned and faced her. "You don't think what?"

"I don't think you're leaving me here."

"It's the safest alternative."

Carrie stood and crossed the room, putting a firm hand on his arm.

He turned and looked at her. "Your father hired me to make judgment calls. It's safer if you stay here."

"Nothing's safe."

"But there's less risk keeping out of sight."

"That's not what you said before."

"The situation's changed."

"If you're going to talk to Madison, I'm going with you," she repeated. "I'm the one they're trying to kill, and I have the right to know what's going on."

He wanted to say they were trying to kill him, too. He wanted to add that she would be the next person to get any information he picked up, but he knew she wasn't going to accept that.

He sighed. "Okay." Walking over to the bag of clothing they'd bought, he pulled out black jeans and a black, long-sleeved polo shirt, which he took into the bathroom and put on.

When he came out, she gave him a curious look. "Are we going to talk to the man or break into his house?"

"You never know."

"Give me a minute."

She grabbed similar dark clothing and stepped into the bathroom. When she closed the door, he thought about leaving her in the motel but decided not to take the underhanded approach.

She came out a few moments later, and he handed her the hat and sunglasses he'd bought. "Put these on."

When she had complied, he studied her, trying to assess how much she looked like the woman he'd just seen on television. She'd lost weight since he'd met her, which made her face more angular.

"I can't wear the sunglasses after dark," she muttered.

"You'll wear them to the car now." He stopped and gave her a direct look. "And the same rules apply as when we were in the field outside the safe house. If I tell you to do something, you have to obey me."

"You mean like an S-and-M master?" she shot back.

He snorted. "You know what I mean."

"Yes."

"Then let me go out first."

"You wouldn't have tried to make me stay here if you thought it wasn't safe," she pointed out.

"Yeah, but I'm not taking any chances. When I give you

the all clear, don't run to the car. Walk like we're here on a fun vacation."

"In Columbia?"

"Maybe you're planning a shopping trip to the Columbia Mall."

When she laughed, he said, "The point is, we don't want to attract any attention."

There were no problems on the way to the car. When Carrie had settled into her seat, he pulled out of the parking space. Twisting the wheel made his arm hurt, but he figured the pain would keep him focused. Beside him, Carrie took off the sunglasses, tucked them into her purse and folded her hands in her lap. She sat very still, and he wondered if she was thinking she shouldn't have come along.

Finally, she cleared her throat. "Tell me about Aaron Madison. Why do you think he could be a problem?"

"He certainly had access to the information about your trip downtown."

"Didn't a lot of government people?"

"Not really. They were trying to keep it under wraps so nothing bad would happen."

She made a dismissive sound. "Well, that certainly worked out well." After a few moments of silence, she asked, "What else about him made you wonder?"

"It's hard to say. There's something about him that I can't put into words. I guess you'd call it a hunch that he could be a problem. Maybe because he always seemed on edge when I talked with him."

"Meeting with me was a big responsibility. That could be why."

"Maybe," he said, but he was still wondering if it was something more sinister.

They rode in silence for a while before she asked, "Where does he live?"

"Bethesda," he answered, naming a close-in, expensive D.C. suburb.

"Won't his family wonder why we're dropping in after hours—or at all?"

"He doesn't have any children, and he and his wife, Rita, recently separated," he answered, glad to put the focus on Madison again.

"Do you know why?"

"No. I only know that she moved out a few months ago and got an apartment in one of the luxury buildings near the D.C. line."

"Isn't it unusual for the wife to be the one to leave?"

"Yes. That's one of the things I noticed."

"You had him investigated?"

"Not with any depth." He tightened his hands on the wheel. "Which may have been a mistake."

He waited for a comment on that, but she said nothing about his investigative skills. Instead, she said, "I met him briefly."

"How did he seem?"

She thought for a moment. "Anxious not to spend too much time with me. Now that I think back on it, I felt like he didn't want to get to know me very well."

Not a good sign, Wyatt thought as he drove down Route 29 to the Beltway, where he got off at the Connecticut Avenue exit, then took Bradley Boulevard, which was a shortcut to the section of the posh suburb where the Madison house was located.

Wyatt turned onto Wisconsin Avenue, then onto a side street where the houses were mostly brick two-stories that looked as though they had been built in the forties or fifties. Large trees marched up the green parkway between the curb and the sidewalk, and all the lawns and shrubbery were well maintained. It was obviously an upscale environment.

"A solid old neighborhood," Carrie remarked as she peered into the gathering darkness. "Which house is it?"

"157." He pointed to a redbrick colonial where most of the lights were turned off. When he got to the end of the block, he turned the corner, then did it again, putting them on the street in back of the Madison house.

"What are you doing?" Carrie asked.

"Taking precautions. I don't want anyone to know we're here."

"It would make for a quicker getaway if we parked closer."

"You think we'll need to get away fast?"

She shrugged. "I hope not. I guess I was thinking of what they do in action movies."

As they walked up the sidewalk and around the corner, Wyatt kept their pace moderate, as if they were out for an evening stroll. As far as he could see, there was no one else doing the same, and he hoped no one was looking out their windows trying to figure out who the man and woman were.

As they walked past parked cars, he looked inside but found them empty.

They reached 157 and turned into the driveway, which was about twenty-five yards long and sheltered by a tall hedge between Madison and the neighbors. At least that gave them a bit of privacy.

Carrie stared at the large two-story looming before them. "How can the guy afford all this on a government salary?"

Wyatt's thoughts were running along the same lines. "Maybe he inherited money. Or maybe he's got another source."

Wyatt walked softly up the blacktop driveway, trying to make as little noise as possible, listening for sounds from the house or the surroundings. There were none.

He got to a place where someone who pulled up in a car could turn off and take a path of wide stepping stones to the front door. Instead, he kept walking along the driveway. Carrie followed, and he was glad she wasn't asking questions.

They arrived at a six-foot-tall wooden fence to the backyard. The gate was standing open. Wyatt stepped through and looked around, then motioned for Carrie to follow. Inside the yard he led her toward the back door, which featured glass panes in the top half. Like the gate, it was standing ajar.

Beside him, she drew in a quick breath. "What's going on?" she whispered.

He shook his head, drawing his sidearm as he peered through the glass into the empty kitchen, where cabinets stood open and boxes of cereal and pasta had been thrown from the shelves onto the counters and the floor.

He cursed under his breath, wishing he'd insisted that Carrie stay at the motel. But she was here now, and he had to deal with it.

"Stay by the door," he whispered.

Entering the kitchen, he held his gun in a two-handed grip, swinging it in all directions, looking for whoever had made this mess. There appeared to be no one in this part of the house, but he took a quick run through the first-floor laundry room, then the living room and dining room before motioning Carrie to follow. Both rooms were in disarray, as though someone had conducted a search without caring how much mess they made.

"It's spooky." Carrie wrapped her arms around her shoulders. "What do you think happened?"

"Someone was searching—in a hurry."

"Are they gone?"

"It looks that way, unless they did the same thing we did and parked around the corner."

They walked quietly down a short hall toward the front of the house. On one side were double doors that led to a home office. Wyatt could see books pulled from the bookcase, the rug turned up, credenza drawers open. There was also a glass and a bottle of Jack Daniel's spilled on the rug.

It was a worse mess than in the kitchen, but there was something even more disturbing—a pair of men's shoes and trouser-clad legs sticking out from one side of the desk.

Carrie gasped.

"Stay back."

Wyatt rushed forward and found the man he'd been looking for lying on the floor behind the desk.

Aaron Madison was in his early forties with a receding hairline. Once, his features had been handsome. Now his face was battered, and his glasses lay on the floor near the wall, shattered. His eyes were closed, but one was badly swollen. His nose was smashed, and his lips were split and bloody. His shirt was open, and Wyatt saw that a knife had been used to carve up his chest, but not so deeply that he was going to die right away.

He'd hoped to spare Carrie the gruesome sight, but he knew she was right behind him.

"Oh, Lord," she gasped as she stared at the man. "Who did this to him?"

"I hope it's not someone trying to get information about you."

When she sucked in a sharp breath, he wished he'd kept that thought to himself. As he knelt beside Madison, he pressed two fingers to the man's neck, where he felt a faint pulse.

"He's alive." Barely, he thought. "Someone worked him over. The same someone who trashed the house. I'm going to call an ambulance."

The man's good eye fluttered open and focused on Wyatt. "Too late," he whispered. "Internal injuries…bad."

"Who did this?"

Instead of answering, Madison asked, "Wyatt Hawk? What…are you doing…here?"

"A hunch. Who did this?"

Again Madison ignored the question as though it were dangerous to tell what had happened to him. Even now.

"They didn't get into the safe," Madison whispered. He dragged in a rattling breath.

"You need—"

"To tell you the combo…twenty-six right." He paused. "Fifteen left." Again he stopped to catch his breath. "Double right turn to seventy-two."

After delivering the message, he closed his eyes again. Wyatt gripped his shoulder. "Where is the safe?"

"Behind…medicine cabinet in bathroom down the hall."

"Stay with him," Wyatt said to Carrie. "See if he can tell you anything else."

Carrie knelt beside the man. "You need medical attention," she murmured.

Wyatt left the gun with Carrie and hurried down the hall to the bathroom. The medicine cabinet stood open, and the contents were scattered around the small room, but the cabinet itself was undisturbed. It was not a standard model but an ornately carved wooden box that was fixed to the wall with hooks above the top pediment. The bottom rested on a bracket.

Wyatt lifted the cabinet up, detaching it and setting it on the floor, revealing a safe embedded in the wall. Quickly he began spinning the dial, working the combination that Madison had given him.

Twenty-six right, fifteen left. Double right turn to seventy-two. With the last turn, the lock clicked, and he pulled the door open. There was a wad of folded bills inside—ranging from twenties to hundreds. Beside them was a small notebook. Wyatt left the money and took out the book, thumbing through the pages. There were number notations, but he couldn't tell what they meant, exactly. He'd have to ask Madison.

A noise behind him made him whirl. It was Carrie, her face stark.

"I guess he didn't make it?"

"No," she choked out.

"Did he say anything?"

"He looked at me and said he'd been stupid."

"That's all?"

"Yes."

"Did he know who you were?"

"I think so." She swallowed hard. "He must have betrayed me, and—"

"Don't jump to conclusions."

"It has to do with me!"

"But maybe not the way you think." Wyatt held up the book. "We don't know how he's connected to the ambush, if he is at all, but I think this is what the people who searched the house were looking for."

"Lucky we didn't run into them."

He nodded and handed the book to her, watching as she flipped through the pages. "What is it?"

She shook her head. "No idea."

As they stood in the bathroom, he became aware of a background noise that grew and swelled—a siren coming closer. "The cops are coming," he muttered. "We'd better split."

"What about Madison?"

"We can't do anything for him."

He reached for a tissue from the box on top of the toilet tank and wiped his fingerprints off the safe dial. Had he touched anything in the office where the cops could get prints? He hoped not.

The siren was getting louder. "Come on."

He sprinted back down the hall and grabbed the gun she'd left on the floor.

"Sorry," she muttered.

"Not your job."

He led her into the kitchen and out the door. On the street, he could see flashing red and blue lights. They couldn't get out that way, but could they get out at all?

Silently cursing the bad timing, he led her into the backyard, around a swimming pool and over to the back fence, which was about six feet tall. Too bad Madison had been so conscientious about enclosing the pool.

When he saw Carrie eyeing the fence, he said, "Let me go first."

He hoisted himself up and scrambled over. On the other side there were rails where he could rest his feet. Reaching down, he grabbed Carrie's hand, helping her up and over. They both dropped to the ground in the yard behind Madison's.

From the other side of the fence, they heard running feet in the driveway, but now they were screened from view.

"Come on."

Thankful that he'd followed his instincts and parked on the opposite street, Wyatt started across the yard in back of the Madison house, another suburban oasis, also featuring a pool.

Before he and Carrie had made it halfway, a dog began to bark, and he cursed again. It sounded medium-size, and maybe the cops would think the animal was barking at *them*.

Apparently, the canine was in the house. Hoping the owner wasn't going to let it out, he kept moving through the yard.

Lights were already flicking on in the house, and he ducked low as he reached the neighbor's gate and swung it open.

They hurried through, and he thought they were going to make it to the street without further incident when floodlights clicked on, illuminating the yard.

Grabbing Carrie, Wyatt threw them both into the shrubbery moments before a door opened.

He waited with his heart pounding, peering out and seeing a man dressed in jeans and a button-down shirt standing in the light coming from the front hall. Wyatt had a gun and the homeowner probably didn't, but he wasn't going to shoot anybody.

Beside him he could feel Carrie waiting tensely and put a reassuring hand on her arm.

Seconds ticked by. Praying that the guy wasn't stupid enough to put himself in danger, Wyatt forced himself to wait. Finally he heard the front door shut again. He stayed where he was for another minute, but he knew that the cops could come this way any moment.

"Got to move," he whispered. "Stay in the bushes."

They crawled through the shrubbery to the next house and waited again.

When he heard more footsteps, he tensed. This time it was a patrol officer, coming along the sidewalk, shining his light into the greenery.

Chapter Seven

Wyatt pressed Carrie down, flattening himself on top of her, hiding his face and hoping that their dark clothing would keep them from being discovered.

With his mouth near her ear, he whispered, "Don't look up."

Tension zinged through him as the cop made his slow way up the sidewalk.

When Wyatt heard the footsteps stop, every muscle in his body tightened as he ran scenarios through his mind.

They were on the run from terrorists, and maybe he could explain why they'd decided to question Aaron Madison, but he knew that if the cops found them, they'd be in for a long interrogation—which would put Carrie in danger because there was no way of knowing who was feeding information to the bad guys.

Hoping he wasn't going to have to assault the officer, he waited with his muscles coiled. Below him he could almost feel Carrie vibrating with nerves.

When the footsteps moved on, he and Carrie both stayed where they were. Finally he lifted his head, slid off of Carrie's body and crawled far enough forward so that he could see out. The street and sidewalk were clear.

"I'm going to get the car," he said. "You stay here."

He braced for her objection, but she must have remembered his caution about following his directions.

"I have to keep low, so it might take some time," he whispered.

"Okay."

"Watch out for me. I'll drive up the block with my lights off."

Again she murmured her assent.

He stayed low to the ground, wishing he could move faster. It was hard going, especially with his wounded arm throbbing. After passing three houses, he decided to take a chance on standing.

Fighting the impulse to run, he walked the rest of the way to the car, then climbed in and shut the door quickly to kill the light. He threw the switch, so the light wouldn't turn on when he opened the door again, and started the engine, then drove at a normal pace toward the house where he'd left Carrie.

When he eased to the curb, she emerged from the bushes and raced toward the car.

Once she was inside, he turned on his headlights so he wouldn't look suspicious and pulled away before she'd buckled her seat belt.

As they rounded the corner on the perpendicular street, he could see several pairs of flashing lights in front of the dead man's house.

He turned the other way, still driving like a responsible citizen as he made his way back toward Wisconsin Avenue.

"Will they know we were there?" Carrie asked.

"I don't know. Depends on if we left prints. Or if someone spotted us and reported they saw a man and a woman go into the house."

"That doesn't prove it was us."

"No. But they might make assumptions."

She picked up Madison's book from where Wyatt had stuffed it between the seats, switched on the reading light and thumbed through the pages. "I'd like to know what this signifies. Some numbers have a plus in front of them and some have a minus."

"And there are dates?"

"Yes. I guess that meant something to him."

She turned to the last few pages. "In this part, it seems to be all minuses. Wait, here's a plus."

"What's the number?"

"Twenty thousand."

"Interesting. What are the minus numbers?"

"Smaller. Five thousand. Three thousand. Two thousand." Carrie sighed.

"Do the dates start before you saw the terrorists in the park?"

"Yes."

"So it might not be related. Let's put the book on hold and see if the murder made the news yet."

She switched off the reading light, turned on the radio and found the all-news station. They sat through some sports scores, political news and ads before an announcer said, "Police are investigating the murder of a U.S. Attorney at his home in Bethesda, Maryland, this evening. Aaron Madison had been severely beaten before his death. Two people—Carrie Mitchell and Wyatt Hawk—are wanted for questioning in conjunction with the murder."

Carrie gasped. "What?"

Wyatt put a hand on her arm. "Quiet. I want to hear the rest of it."

The newsreader was saying, "Earlier today, Mitchell was supposed to meet with a U.S. Attorney in connection with a terrorist plot she allegedly overheard. That official, Skip Gunderson, was also found dead in the offices where he was scheduled to meet Mitchell. She and Wyatt Hawk have been missing since the morning incident."

Carrie turned to him, her face suffused with panic. "It's too quick for fingerprints."

He worked to keep his voice steady. "Like I said, somebody could have seen us sneaking around. It could be the person who called the cops." Wyatt clenched his hands on the wheel. "But how did they know my name? That was never made public." He turned toward her. "We're back to the set of people who knew your father hired me."

"If the cops catch us…"

He swallowed, then told her what he'd been thinking but hadn't wanted to say before. "They can hold us on national-security grounds."

"Why?"

"Because this all started with a terrorist plot."

"You're talking about them holding us forever without a lawyer?"

"Right."

"But I'm the one who turned the terrorists in."

"And now a lot of people are dead, and nobody can be sure of your motives."

They rode in silence for a while. Up the road Wyatt saw flashing red and blue lights.

"Oh, Lord. A cop car," Carrie breathed. "Is he after us?"

"If he were, he wouldn't just be sitting there," Wyatt answered, hoping he had assessed the situation correctly. Still, he started looking for a place to turn off and saw none.

Beside him, Carrie had clenched her fingers together in her lap. He reached out and laid a hand on her arm.

"It's probably a traffic stop."

She didn't answer, but when they got close enough he saw that he was right, and they drove by without the cop leaping into the road and pointing a gun at them.

Beside him, Carrie whispered, "I hate to clench up every time we see a motorist pulled over."

"The police don't know about this car. Nobody saw it near Madison's house, and I rented it under a different name."

She nodded.

"And we're going to stay under the radar. But first…"

When he pulled into the parking lot of a small grocery store, she looked up. "What?"

"We can get a few things to eat. What do you want?"

"Surprise me," she said without much enthusiasm.

"Slide down in the seat while I'm gone."

She did as he'd asked, and he made a quick trip through the store, getting some premade deli sandwiches, drinks and snacks.

When he returned to the car, he found her watching for him but didn't bother to remind her that she'd been supposed to stay down.

They made it back to the motel, where Wyatt drove around the parking lot a couple of times before finding a spot near their door. He had Carrie wait while he checked the room, then motioned for her to follow. She came inside and leaned against the closed door.

"I hate this," she murmured as she picked up the remote and pointed it at the television. She caught an account of the information they'd already heard—along with something new. This time there was a picture of Wyatt, taken when he was still with the CIA.

He muttered a curse.

Carrie stared at the picture. "I guess it's not recent."

"Thank God for small favors."

He put the milk and juice he'd bought into the small refrigerator.

"Want a drink?"

"Are you offering me liquor?"

"No. Maybe orange juice or soda water."

"Juice."

He poured them both a drink and watched her trying to relax as she took small sips.

He wanted to put his arms around her, but he knew it was a lot more prudent to keep his hands off of her. Too bad they couldn't get some distance from each other. But he couldn't let her stay in a separate room now—not even a suite. He wanted her where he could see her—except when she was in the bathroom.

"Watch a movie," he said.

"I won't be able to concentrate."

"It's a better choice than worrying."

She kicked off her shoes, pulled down the spread, then got up and opened one of the bags from the discount department store, which she took into the bathroom. He heard the toilet flush, then water running in the shower, and he remembered that they'd spent part of the evening lying in the dirt. She was in the shower for a long time. When she emerged from the bathroom, she'd changed into a clean shirt and pair of jeans. Probably the way to go, he decided.

"Feel better?" he asked.

"Yes. A shower always helps."

She brought over one of the sandwiches and unwrapped it, then started flipping channels. He didn't want to watch the television, and he didn't want to watch her.

Instead, he took a quick shower, keeping his wounded arm out of the water, and changed, then took the other sandwich to the table, where he ate and studied the book he had taken from Madison's house.

Suppose the notations were for money either received or owed on a given date? What would that mean? Was he involved in some business—possibly an illegal enterprise, which he conducted on a cash-only basis? Suppose he'd been keeping the information from his wife, and she'd found out and left him?

Perhaps Rita Madison could solve the mystery of the notations. The next logical step would be to visit her, if they could do it without attracting attention.

He glanced over at Carrie and saw that she had slumped down on the bed, and was now asleep.

He called her name softly, but she didn't answer. He found the remote where she'd laid it and clicked off the television, killing the background noise in the room. Then he took the remains of the sandwich off the bed and threw it away.

Carrie was lying on top of the covers. He figured he should wake her so she could get properly into the bed. Then he decided that it would be better to simply let her sleep because she had had a hell of a day, and he knew she needed to rest.

Which created a problem. He could try to stay awake to keep guard, but he'd had the same horrible day—worse, if you factored in getting shot. If he didn't get some sleep, he was going to be in bad shape tomorrow, when he'd need his wits about him to figure out what the hell was going on.

He walked to her bed, looking down at her for a few minutes and listening to her even breathing.

At the safe house, he'd tried to avoid direct contact with her, but he'd studied her covertly. Now he allowed himself the pleasure of taking in her delicate features, the long lashes fanning her cheeks, the short, dark hair that certainly wasn't her natural look but worked, because she'd be beautiful with any hairstyle or color.

He drank his fill of her face, then let his eyes travel downward, pausing at the creamy hollow at the base of her throat, the swell of her breasts, the curve of her hips. He imagined himself climbing into bed with her, taking her in his arms, caressing all the sweet places he longed to touch. When he found himself getting hard, he turned away and grabbed the bag of supplies she'd bought at the drugstore as well as one of the bags from the department store.

After quietly closing the bathroom door, he took off his shirt and then the bandage. His arm hurt when he flexed it, but there was only a little blood on the gauze pads he'd removed. Turning so that he could study the wound in the mirror, he saw that it looked as if it was healing okay. He poked at the margins, finding them tender but not swollen. After applying more antiseptic, he redressed the wound.

When he exited the bathroom, he left the light on and the door ajar. Looking at the clock on the table between the beds, he saw that it was after eleven. He wasn't expecting trouble, but sleeping in his clothes wasn't a bad idea.

He kicked off his shoes and turned down the spread on his bed. He kept himself awake for an hour researching Aaron Madison on the web. Finally, when his eyes became heavy-lidded, he eased down on the bed and reviewed everything that had happened in the past fifteen hours. It seemed like too much for one day. But he knew that it had all been real.

He closed his eyes, knowing that any hint of danger would bring him awake.

CARRIE WAS TOTALLY unaware of her surroundings. At first she slept soundly, the events of the day acting like a drug to wipe out her consciousness. The blissful peace lasted for a few hours. Then from one moment to the next, she was plunged into a dream. A dream that made her gasp. She struggled to pull away, but it held her fast, its grip like a choke hold around her neck.

A silent scream rose in her throat, but it never reached her lips as she fought against the terror of the dream.

She knew at once what was coming, a repeat of her day, only this time the colors were somber, and ominous music was playing in the background, as though she was watching another television program. But this time she wasn't a spectator. She was in the middle of it, and she knew from the music that something bad was going to happen.

Suddenly she was in the backseat of the big black car on the way to meet Skip Gunderson, the Federal prosecutor. It was her duty. She'd known that all along, but as she sat next to Wyatt, tension vibrated through her. She was waiting for the worst, because this time she knew what was going to happen. She was back where she had been with Wyatt at the beginning. He'd been cold and distant. Now he sat like a statue, his gaze fixed in the distance.

"Wyatt?"

He didn't answer, didn't even turn his head toward her. She wanted to reach out and grab him, but she knew it wouldn't do her any good.

Her nerves pulled taut as a rubber band about to snap when the car stopped at the barrier outside the garage. Even knowing what was coming, she couldn't make herself leap away. The fake guard thrust his arm into the car and shot at them, just as he had that morning, and Wyatt finally moved, shooting the man before pulling her out of the car.

She relived her flight with Wyatt into the building. Only this time it was different. This time she was sure they would never get away. Wyatt was running through endless brightly lit corridors, with terrorists leaping out of doorways and shooting, the bullets smashing into the hallway floors just behind them. It was all so real and vivid that she knew she and Wyatt were going to die.

She moaned, struggling to fight her way out of the awful nightmare, her head thrashing back and forth. When she felt arms restraining her, she cried out and tried to wrench away, sure that one of the terrorists had grabbed her and was holding fast.

She struggled against him, kicking out with her feet and slamming hands into him, hearing him grunt in pain.

He was speaking, and she tried to focus on the words.

"Carrie. It's okay. Carrie, it's Wyatt."

"Wyatt?"

Her eyes blinked open, staring up into his face.

"Wyatt?" she said again.

"Yes."

She dragged in a breath and let it out as she realized she'd been kicking and hitting him.

"I hurt you. Oh, Lord, I'm so sorry."

"I'm okay."

She knew it was Wyatt above her. She wasn't sure of much else. She wasn't in her condo in D.C. Or at her father's estate. She wasn't at the safe house. But she was lying in bed with her clothes on.

Then reality slammed back into her. The nightmare was a replay of reality. Her new reality.

"You were having a bad dream," he murmured.

"Yes. And you were so distant…like you were at first, and I hated that."

The moment the words were out of her mouth, she wished she could take them back.

"I'm sorry."

"It wasn't your fault. It was my subconscious." She winced, wondering if that sounded any better.

A shaft of illumination came from the bathroom. Because she needed to look away from him, she swung her head toward the clock, but she was lying at the wrong angle to see it.

"What time is it?"

"Four in the morning."

"I woke you up." And she'd given away the fear she'd tried to suppress, but it had invaded her sleep. She wasn't sure which was worse.

"It's okay. Do you want to talk about it?"

Not really, she thought. But she owed him an explanation.

"It was what happened this morning. You took me down to the Federal office building. You shot that fake security guard. Then the terrorists were chasing us through the building. We were running down corridors, and they were always behind us—shooting."

He had been looming over her. Now he eased down beside her, stroking her arm, then her hair. "That must have been terrifying."

"I was sure we wouldn't get away."

She rolled toward him, seeking the warmth of his body. She didn't want to think about the dream, and she didn't want to talk about it anymore.

"It's all right, sweetheart," he murmured, his mouth close to her ear.

Sweetheart. Had the endearment somehow slipped out because he was trying to reassure her? Or had he meant it? And was there a way to find out?

Overcome with emotions, she turned her head, so that her lips brushed his mouth.

When she sensed that he might draw away, she cupped her hand around the back of his head to hold him where he was. This morning the idea of kissing Wyatt would never have entered her mind. He'd been too distant and unapproachable. Now she knew that he'd wanted her to see him that way because he'd been trying to keep their relationship strictly professional.

Since this morning she'd learned to see him differently. And she'd learned something about herself, too. In her life she'd made sure she needed nobody besides herself. Now she needed this man in ways she couldn't even understand.

Their lips held, and she clung to him, because her world—the world where she had lived all her life—had come crashing down around her head, and Wyatt Hawk was the only point of stability in a universe that had turned itself upside down.

If he drew back now, reality would crumble. When his lips pressed more firmly to hers, she returned the kiss. She knew she wanted comfort from him, but she wanted—needed—so much more. And she knew in that moment that he needed the same things she did, knew it from the way he began to feast on her, with hunger and passion and perhaps the edge of desperation.

They'd been through hell today. And they had only each other.

Her heart started to beat faster, and faster still when he gathered her closer and his hands moved restlessly across her back. His touch had begun as comforting; now it spoke of a sensuality she hadn't dared to hope he possessed.

Or perhaps she had known and sensed that he had buried it deep inside himself. And she had brought it to the surface.

That knowledge made her heart leap.

It was a potent combination. The man who had signed on to protect her and had proved his worth a thousand times over. And the man who had proved he cared more about her than himself.

For long moments he stroked her, caressing her breasts, her hips, her bottom, sending ripples of sensation over her skin, sensations that sank into her body, heating her from the inside out. How could she ever have thought him cold? His mere touch took her breath away.

As she felt the heat build between them, she closed her eyes, clinging to him, rocking with him on the bed. When she felt his erection pressing against her middle, she knew without a doubt where they were headed, and she rejoiced in the knowledge—until the moment when she felt him pull away.

Her eyes blinked open and stared into the dark depths of his. "Wyatt?"

His voice had turned gritty. "You know we can't do this."

"Why not?" she asked, somehow managing to keep her voice even. "We both want—"

He pressed his fingers against her lips, preventing her from finishing the sentence. "Wanting isn't the issue. We've both been through an emotional roller coaster today. You're reacting to the dream and to almost getting killed. I'm..."

This time he was the one who stopped.

"You're what?"

"Taking advantage of you."

"No."

He might be putting it that way, but she knew it wasn't the truth. He wasn't taking any more than he was giving.

"You're in a fragile emotional state," he added.

She swallowed. He could be speaking the truth as he knew it, but she didn't want to hear his assessment of the heat that had flared between them.

He sat up and ran a hand through his dark hair. Then he moved to the side of the bed and got up, putting several feet of space between them as he stood there breathing hard.

She was also struggling to control her breathing, and listening to the wild pounding of her heart.

She wondered what would happen if she got off the bed and reached for him. Would he come back and take up where they'd left off?

It was tempting to try it, but she didn't want a second rejection.

Instead, she got up and pulled the covers aside so that she could climb in.

"Are you going to be okay?" he asked.

She might have told him she wanted to be held. Instead, she said, "Yes," and fixed the pillow more comfortably under her neck as she closed her eyes.

She could feel him watching her for a few more moments. She thought he'd get back into bed. Instead, as she watched through slitted lids, he walked to the table where he'd left his computer and sat down, leaning toward the screen as he accessed material she couldn't see.

She kept covertly watching him, sure she wouldn't get back to sleep. But finally she surrendered to fatigue. The next time she opened her eyes, she smelled coffee.

Blinking, she looked at Wyatt, then at the clock. It was after nine.

"Why didn't you wake me up?"

"You needed the sleep. They have breakfast here. I got us

both something. Better than last night's stale sandwiches." He kept his voice matter-of-fact, as though nothing personal had happened between them in the night.

If he could do it, so could she. "Thanks."

He set down a cardboard tray with coffee, juice, cinnamon buns and hard-boiled eggs. She joined him at the table, and they both drank coffee and ate.

"What were you working on when I fell asleep?" she asked as she glanced toward his computer.

"A couple of things. I got the address of Madison's wife, but I'm afraid that if we go over there, we're going to run into a bunch of people."

"If we get some dressier clothing, we can go in as friends of her husband, then ask to speak to her privately."

"That might work. But it could be dangerous."

Setting down her coffee cup, she picked up the remote control and turned to CNN. She and Wyatt were still of interest, starting with a rehash of the attack at the Federal Building and progressing to speculation about whether they had been at Aaron Madison's house.

"His poor wife," Carrie murmured. "Even if they were having problems, his death has to be a shock."

DOUGLAS MITCHELL MOVED restlessly on the narrow bed. His captors had let him get up to go to the bathroom. Then they had secured his hand to the bed again. And they'd given him a bottle of water and a sandwich. Something from a deli, he judged.

He sat in the dark, eating the food slowly and drinking the water.

He wasn't sure how long the men had been holding him. He shook his head. Sometimes it felt as if he'd been here for hours, sometimes days, and the sense of time distortion was maddening.

One thing he did know: Carrie must still be on the loose.

These men hadn't captured or killed her because he was still alive.

He clenched his teeth together, hating that he was at the mercy of these men.

He'd seen three of them when they'd let him out for his bathroom break. They were all young. In their late twenties and early thirties, he judged.

And they all looked like American men from the Midwest. Not what he'd consider typical terrorists.

Well, maybe they were, if you thought about Timothy McVeigh. But McVeigh had been a fanatic. These guys had talked about getting money for what they were doing. Did that mean they didn't care about their terrorist plot?

He took another swallow of the water. Should he drink it all or save some for later?

Maybe saving it was best. But maybe he should eat more of the sandwich. It wouldn't keep, would it?

It was still hard to think about what to do, but it felt as though his mind wasn't quite as fuzzy as it had been.

Did he recognize this house? He wasn't sure, but he thought it looked familiar.

He remembered a friend talking about his own mind being fuzzy. The guy had been on a gazillion medications, and he was having problems with his memory. Then his doctor had cut back some of his meds, and he'd started thinking better.

Could that be his problem?

Chapter Eight

Wyatt gave Carrie a direct look. "I have to think Madison's involved."

"It could be a coincidence," she argued.

"You mean his house getting searched and his getting killed the same day you're supposed to meet Gunderson and someone tries to kill you? Highly unlikely."

"Then we should go with the paying-our-respects-to-the-widow plan."

"And if there's a TV truck outside, we drive past."

"And then what?"

"Go on to the next best lead."

"Which is?"

"I'm thinking."

When Carrie finished her breakfast, she took the toiletries she'd bought into the bathroom and got dressed.

"We're going to have to stop at a more upscale department store," he said as he eyed her jeans and T-shirt.

She nodded.

"I wish we didn't have to go out in public."

"I'll be quick," she answered, starting to mentally plan what she could buy. If she got a dress, she'd also have to buy stockings and good shoes. Probably it was better to stick to dress slacks and a dark jacket.

"Are we checking out?" she asked, as he gathered up his belongings.

"Probably better not to stay in the same place for two nights."

"Then we should get suitcases, too."

She gathered up the things she'd bought and put them back into the bags.

"Put on your hat," Wyatt said.

"I actually hate hats."

"When this is over, you'll never have to wear one again."

And would he be around to see her with the dye out of her hair and the length back? Did she want him to be?

The answer was yes, but she couldn't focus on that. Right now she had to make sure there was life after hiding out.

He repeated the security procedures from the night before, then motioned her to the car.

They drove to the Columbia Mall.

"Macy's is probably the best bet," she said.

"Okay. I'll get slacks, a dress shirt, a sports jacket and loafers, then meet you in the luggage department. And one more thing. The store probably has security cameras, and there will be cameras outside the building where Mrs. Madison lives. Keep your gaze down, like you need to watch your feet to walk straight."

"You think the police will be looking at cameras here?"

"Like I said, it's always better to be prepared. If somebody thinks they've spotted us, the cops might go back over the security tapes."

Inside they split up.

Carrie had never liked clothes shopping. And she liked it even less this morning because she kept wondering if anyone was watching her. To minimize her exposure, she tried to streamline the process. First she picked up slacks she thought would fit. Then she found a black blazer with narrow white stripes and paired it with a simple white knit top. Her selections fit and didn't look too bad with the low shoes she'd worn to the meeting with Gunderson that never happened. She took the tags off the new clothing and brought them to the checkout counter, then asked the clerk to put what she'd been wearing in the store bag.

At the luggage department, she didn't spot Wyatt at first. Then a tall man in a navy sports jacket and gray pants turned around, and she realized she'd been totally faked out. She'd seen him in only casual clothing, looking like a rough-around-the-edges secret agent. But he was very polished in the dressier outfit, as if he could fit right into a boardroom.

"You clean up pretty well," she murmured.

"You do, too," he answered, eyeing her conservative yet flattering outfit.

He paid for the luggage, and they went back to the car. After stowing the department-store bags in the one of the suitcases, they headed back the way they'd come the day before, taking the same route to the Beltway and then to Wisconsin Avenue.

"We should plan how we're going to represent ourselves to various people," Wyatt said.

"Okay. How do you want to play it?"

"I think that if anyone else is with Rita—or asks how we know Aaron—we say we're friends from the country club."

"Which club?"

He named a well-known club off of Connecticut Avenue in Chevy Chase.

"What if people who really knew him there are around?"

"Unlikely. They kicked him out six months ago when he couldn't pay the membership fees."

"And you know all that how?"

"I researched him on the web after you went to sleep. Then I did some more poking around in the morning."

"What else did you find out?"

"That his credit cards were maxed out. I also know that

his wife has a trust fund from her family. She used it to buy her apartment."

"So she wasn't dependent on her husband."

"Right. Which is lucky for her."

"Describe her to me, so I don't start talking to another guest like she's the widow."

"She's a good-looking blonde woman in her late thirties. Her hair is in a short pageboy. Her makeup is always impeccable. She's the kind who takes good care of herself and wouldn't allow an ounce of extra fat to spoil the look of her size-four figure."

"It sounds like you don't approve of slender women."

He gave her a quick look, then glanced back at the road. "I don't like this obsession in our society with trying to look model thin."

"There are a lot of people who are overweight."

"Yeah. A weird contrast."

They drove in silence for another few minutes before Wyatt cleared his throat.

"Yes?" she asked.

"About our cover story... Maybe we should pretend to be a married couple."

After he dropped the comment, silence hung between them for a few seconds. Carrie could imagine he hadn't liked making the suggestion, and she couldn't stop herself from needling him.

"Why, exactly?"

"Because that's the easiest explanation of why we're showing up together. Do you have a better idea?"

"We both worked downtown with him."

"Rita probably met the office staff," he shot back.

"Right. I guess we have to use the country-club story—and false names, too."

"Since I'm already Will Hanks," he said, using the alias

he'd used at the rental-car place and the motel, "you can be Carolyn Hanks."

"You came up with that fast. Were you already thinking about my name?"

He nodded.

"Carolyn Hanks and Will Hanks," she said, trying out the names. "If we get a chance to talk to Rita, maybe I should be the one who starts the conversation."

"Why?"

"Because it will be woman to woman, and she may say things to me that she wouldn't say to you."

He thought for a moment. "Okay, that makes sense, but maybe we need to have a legend planned so we don't get caught in any traps."

"What's a legend?"

"A spy's cover story. What if you lost your first husband a few years ago, and you have some idea of how she feels."

"We're getting into an elaborate scenario, don't you think?"

"We need to be prepared."

"Then what did you do with Aaron at the country club? Golf? Tennis? Do we know what he did there?"

He made a dismissive sound. "I can't fake my way through golf or tennis. Let's say we met in the weight room."

"Okay," she answered, remembering that Wyatt had been a faithful user of the weights at the safe house. The memory stopped her for a moment. Living with him and using the weight room had been part of her routine for a week. Now that seemed like another life. In fact, her whole world had been turned upside down and righted again—with yet a different view of reality each time.

They arrived at Rita Madison's apartment building, which was one of the expensive high-rises near the upscale shopping complex at Wisconsin and Western. They drove by, checking out the environment.

"No TV trucks," Carrie said.

"Let's hope reporters aren't hiding in the bushes."

She gave him a sharp look. "Do you think they would?"

"You never know what they're going to do. Like I said, I'm wondering how they got my photo."

The comment set Carrie's teeth on edge, and she kept her guard up as they walked back toward the building and stepped into the lobby. Apparently, it was the kind of place where you didn't get past the first floor unless you lived there—or were announced.

"May I help you?" asked an older woman in a dark suit who was standing behind a counter resembling a hotel check-in desk.

Wyatt approached her, and Carrie followed.

"We're here to pay our respects to Rita Madison, apartment three fifteen."

The woman pulled a long face. "Yes, it's so sad. We heard it on the news last night. Mrs. Madison only moved in a few months ago."

"After she separated from Aaron?" Wyatt asked.

"Yes."

"We were hoping they'd get back together," Wyatt said, as though he was an old friend of both of theirs.

Still, he broke off the conversation before it went any further.

When the elevator door had closed behind them, he said, "We don't want to call too much attention to ourselves."

She nodded, thinking that he should have been an actor. He was good at slipping into a persona. Like he'd done with her. At first at the safe house, she'd thought he was cold and distant because that was what he'd wanted her to think. Then she'd known it was a pose. And what about his relationship with her now? Was there any way to know what he was really thinking?

She stopped trying to puzzle it out as they reached the third floor and the elevator doors opened.

As they walked down the hall, she saw that the door to

number 315 was ajar, probably so that Mrs. Madison didn't have to keep getting up to let visitors in.

They walked into a marble-floored vestibule that could have been the front entryway to a good-size house. Beyond was a living room with very formal furniture—reproductions of seventeenth-century English pieces, Carrie judged.

She spotted Rita Madison right away. She saw the blond hair and the slender form, although the woman had not taken the care with her makeup that Wyatt had described. She was speaking to a man in a black suit wearing a black shirt with a white collar. Her minister. Other people stood around the room. Some were talking quietly while others were drinking coffee or eating from small plates of food.

Carrie looked toward the dining table and saw that various buffet items had been set out. A young, dark-haired woman in a black uniform stepped into the room and began collecting dirty plates and glasses. It was a pretty good spread for having been organized at short notice.

Rita Madison must have been keeping one eye on the door. She glanced up, spotted them and stiffened. For a moment, Carrie thought she had recognized them from the news reports of the murder. Or could the police have shown her pictures of them?

Then she told herself that the woman was probably only wondering who these people were that she didn't know. Was Rita worried about her husband's associates? Did she think some of them might show up and cause trouble?

Carrie hated having to speculate on every small thing that happened. It would be great to have her nice, normal life back. Or would it? That life hadn't included Wyatt Hawk. When this was over, she could imagine that he'd walk away from her—because he thought it was the right thing to do. Never mind what she thought.

She struggled to put those particular speculations aside as she crossed the room with Wyatt at her side.

"Mrs. Madison?" Carrie said. "I'm sorry to be meeting you under such sad circumstances, but we wanted to stop by and pay our respects."

The minister touched her shoulder. "I'll just go and get some coffee and leave you to greet your guests."

It looked as if Rita wasn't sure she wanted the man to leave her side. But she didn't stop him from heading into the dining room, where he started filling a plate at the buffet table.

The widow turned to Carrie. Her voice was cool as she asked, "Who are you?"

Wyatt answered. "We know…or rather I knew Aaron from the club. He and I used to get into conversations in the weight room. We had a little competition going about how much we could bench-press."

"Yes, Aaron was very competitive," Rita murmured.

"I'm Will Hanks. And this is my wife, Carolyn," Wyatt said.

"Nice to meet you." She stopped and sighed. "I guess that's not the right way to put it. I'm not sure what the right way is."

"I know," Carrie said sympathetically. "I lost my first husband a few years ago, so I know what you're going through."

Rita nodded.

"I'm wondering if we could speak in private," Wyatt said.

"About what?"

"Something Aaron wouldn't want us discussing in front of a bunch of people."

The words must have raised alarm bells, because she gave Wyatt and Carrie a penetrating look.

"Could we please talk privately?" Carrie said again. "It's important."

The woman hesitated, glancing around the room. Lowering her voice, she said, "I guess you're not going to murder me if we step into the bedroom."

"Hardly," Wyatt answered.

She turned and walked quickly down the hall, and they followed.

Carrie gave Wyatt a look that said, *Easier than I expected.* He gave her a cautious look in return.

They reached a large bedroom, decorated in similar style to the rest of the apartment.

Once inside, Rita closed the door, then crossed to the bedside table and bent down to open a drawer. When she turned to face them again, she was holding a small revolver in a hand that wasn't quite steady.

Carrie choked back a gasp. Beside her she could feel the tension radiating through Wyatt's body.

"You're lying about how you knew Aaron. I think you'd better tell me what's going on," the widow said in a hard voice. "Or maybe tell me why I shouldn't call 911."

Carrie's heart leaped into her throat as she looked from the gun to the angry eyes confronting her. As she struggled to speak, Wyatt said, "We came to you because we're in trouble, and we hope you can help us."

"You're the couple the police are looking for, aren't you?"

"Yes."

"Did you kill my husband?"

"No."

"But you were at his house last night. And everything you've said about your background is a lie. You didn't know Aaron."

"I met him because he was involved in Carrie's case," Wyatt said. "I'm sorry we made up a story, but we needed a reason to walk into your home, because we need to ask you some questions."

"What do you know about my husband's death?"

"When we arrived at the house he was lying on the floor, bleeding," Wyatt answered. "There was nothing we could do for him."

Rita made a moaning sound. "If I'd been there…"

"They probably would have killed you, too," Wyatt said.

Carrie watched a shudder go through the woman.

To Carrie's relief, she lowered the gun. But she didn't put it down. "Tell me what you found."

"The house had been searched by someone who didn't care about making a mess. Aaron was in his office. He was struggling to give us information—before it was too late. He gave me the combination to his safe."

Mrs. Madison's eyes widened. "His safe."

"Did you know what was in it?"

"Aaron never gave me the combination. What did you find?"

"For one thing—money. Which is still there."

"And a book with notations that we can't decipher." Wyatt kept his gaze on the woman's face. "I want to show you what we found. I'm going to reach slowly into my pocket so you can see exactly what I'm doing. I'm not armed. Don't shoot me."

Moving very slowly as promised, he slid his hand into the pocket of his sports coat and pulled out the little book he'd taken from the safe. Carrie hadn't even known that he'd brought it along.

"Can you tell us what it is?" he asked.

Chapter Nine

Rita reached out and took the book from Wyatt, looking as if she was testing its weight in her hand.

"Have you ever seen this before?" Wyatt asked.

"I don't think so." She riffled through the pages, looking at the sets of numbers.

She shook her head. "This appears to be something Aaron hid from me."

"Why?"

"Maybe he was ashamed of what it represented."

"Because?" Wyatt pressed.

Carrie's breathing stilled as she waited to hear more.

"I think these are notations of his gambling wins and losses," Rita said.

"Gambling?" Wyatt asked, clearly surprised by the unexpected answer.

As Rita put the gun back into the drawer, her expression turned sad. "I didn't know it when we married, but he was heavily addicted. At first he won, and I wondered where he got the extra cash, since he couldn't be making that much money as a junior prosecutor. We had a confrontation, and he bragged about how good he was at picking horses and playing blackjack. Then his luck changed. He never talked about it, but I knew from the way he was acting.

"I suspected he owed a lot of money. I was so frightened

about what would happen if he couldn't pay. I begged him to get help, but he wouldn't do it. That's why I left him."

Carrie thought about the woman's family background. "Couldn't your parents cover his debts?"

"I'd asked them to bail him out a few years ago. They'd made it clear that they wouldn't do it again."

Carrie nodded.

"So he might have done something for money—something that he wouldn't have considered under other circumstances?" Wyatt pressed.

She gave him a pleading look. "I don't know. I didn't want to know." She clenched and unclenched her fists. "Once he sold a piece of jewelry that had been in my family for generations. After that, I put my valuable pieces in a safe-deposit box—one where he didn't have the key."

Carrie nodded sympathetically.

"It was like he was on drugs," Rita went on, speaking more to herself than to them. "A sickness he couldn't free himself from. I tried to help, but I couldn't reach him. Not on that."

Carrie put a hand on her arm. "We're both sorry to be pressing you, and I'm sorry that we made up a story about Wyatt's knowing your husband, but we're in a terrible situation. In the last few days, there have been two attempts on our lives. We're trying to figure out who's behind the attacks. I mean, besides the obvious answer of the terrorists."

"I can't imagine what you're going through, and I'm sorry I pulled a gun on you."

"It's understandable," Wyatt answered, "given that the cops are making it look like we're suspects. Did they tell you anything they haven't said in public?"

"No. Just that they wanted to talk to you about…what happened last night."

Wyatt's expression turned grim. "I think we'd better leave," he said. He gave the widow a direct look. "They may be looking at security tapes from the building, and they may

ask what we said to each other. I'd appreciate your not telling
them we were here. But if you're forced to, you can say we
came here looking for information." He fixed his gaze on her.
"Did you talk to the police about Aaron's gambling problem?"

She flushed. "No."

"You might want to tell them."

"Why?"

"It gives them another motive for his murder—one that
doesn't lead back to us."

She nodded. "You said there was money in the safe? Could
you give me the combination?"

"Yes." Wyatt gave her the numbers and the directions,
which she wrote down on a piece of paper and put in the
drawer with the gun.

"Thank you."

Carrie stepped forward and hugged her. "I'm so sorry for
your loss, and I'm sorry that we had to approach you this
way."

"I understand."

"We'd better go," Wyatt said. "And again, we're sorry for
the intrusion."

"Let me go back to the living room and make sure the
coast is clear," Rita said.

When she'd left the room, Carrie looked at Wyatt. "You
think Aaron Madison could have told the terrorists where
and when I was meeting—for money?"

"It could be. He'd do anything he had to—if the mob was
going to come after him for money."

"The mob?"

"He wasn't placing bets with the Easter Bunny."

Before Carrie could reply, Rita hurried back into the room.
"There's a police detective Langley in the living room."

"What's he doing here?"

"He wants information about Aaron. I hate to tell him
about the gambling."

Carrie clamped her hand on Wyatt's arm. "What about us? If they find us here, they'll take us down to the station house."

"I'm thinking." He turned to Rita. "Is there another way out of the apartment?"

"There's a service door in the kitchen, but you have to get back to the living room before you can use it."

Wyatt looked at Carrie. "You can change clothes with the maid."

Carrie stared at him. "What?"

"That will get you out of here."

"What about you?" Carrie asked.

"I'm going to have to use another method." He turned to Rita. "Ask the maid to step in here." When she'd gone, he turned to Carrie. "We've got to make it look like Rita and the maid weren't cooperating with us, which will be better for both of them when the cops start asking questions."

"How?"

"We're going to force them."

Mrs. Madison was back with the maid in a few moments. When she stepped into the room, Wyatt pulled out the gun he'd concealed under his jacket.

Rita and the maid, whose name tag said Pamela, gasped.

"My partner needs to wear your uniform. Take it off," he said to the maid in a harsh voice. "You can wear my partner's clothing."

When she stared at him in dumb shock, he growled, "Hurry. We don't have a lot of time. Or do you want me to take it off of you?"

Pamela began hastily unbuttoning her uniform, while Carrie took off her slacks and jacket. The uniform was a little large on Carrie, but it would have to do.

When the clothing exchange was finished, Wyatt turned to the maid. "Get in the bathroom and stay there. You, too," he said to Rita. "And keep your mouths shut for the next twenty minutes."

She looked shocked but did as he'd asked.

When he'd closed the door behind the women, he turned to Carrie.

"Walk down the hall to the kitchen, and leave the apartment through that door. Exit the building through the service entrance," he said to her. "Meet me at the car."

She answered with a tight nod.

Wyatt grabbed a chair and tipped it up so that the back held the bathroom door closed. Then he turned back to Carrie.

"You'd better get going."

Her heart was pounding as she asked, "How long should I wait at the car?"

"No more than ten minutes. If you hear sirens, get the hell out of here."

"I—"

"Go."

She gave him a fierce hug, then made herself step away. Everything they did was crumbling into a mess, but she wasn't going to just turn herself in to that detective in the living room.

Trying to look normal, she walked down the hall. When the police detective's gaze flicked her way, she forced herself to keep walking, then breathed out a sigh as she stepped into the kitchen. Every moment she expected him to come charging after her, but nobody followed. With a sigh of relief, she stepped into the corridor and closed the door behind her. She should have asked where the service entrance was, but she'd been too shocked to think of that detail.

When the elevator arrived, Carrie stepped inside and studied the buttons. There was one for the lower lobby, and she thought that might be the right place. Or maybe she could go out through the garage.

At the lower level, she exited and looked around, remembering that Wyatt had cautioned her to keep her head down. She could see she was definitely in a service area. Upstairs, there had been marble, polished chrome and the smell of air freshener. Down here, there were cinder-block walls, cement floors and the smell of laundry detergent. A sign had various directions on it—pointing to the laundry room, the trash room, the storage room, the garage, and deliveries.

She could get out through the garage or the trash room. Which was better? she wondered as she headed down the hall. Probably she'd encounter fewer people in the trash room.

The sound of voices stopped her, and she stepped around a corner as two women in maid's uniforms passed. They paid her no attention, and she walked right on past.

Praying the cops hadn't stationed someone to guard the exit, she stepped inside the trash room. Nothing assaulted her but the smell of ripe garbage.

At the other end of the room was a door that led outside. As she entered a rectangular area at the end of a wide driveway, she let out the breath she'd been holding. She'd feared she wouldn't get out of the building, but here she was in the open air. Still, she couldn't let down her guard. Surely there was a camera out here. Forcing herself not to run, she walked up a ramp and found herself in an alley between two apartment buildings.

After hurrying down the narrow cement lane to the street, she paused to get her bearings, then decided that the car must be on the street to the right.

She'd been terrified that she'd be caught before she could get away. Now that she was outside, she found herself praying that Wyatt would show up quickly. If she reached the ten-minute limit, she'd have to decide what to do.

That was the least of her problems, she realized, as she spotted two uniformed officers walking down the street checking the license plates on the cars.

UPSTAIRS, WYATT walked to the sliding glass doors that made up most of the bedroom wall.

When he opened the curtains, he found a wide balcony with a couple of expensive patio chairs and a table between them.

He opened the doors and stepped out, looking down at the three-story drop.

Wishing he'd come prepared, he scanned the bedroom and saw nothing immediately useful. With a grimace, he glanced at the bathroom door, then he stripped the spread off the queen-size bed and pulled the top sheet free.

But now what? He had one sheet and three balconies before ground level.

Using his teeth, he started a tear in the fabric, then ripped it in half. He took the two halves outside and tied one to the railing, testing the knot. If he fell, it was going to be a long drop to the ground.

But he had no other options at the moment. The women in the bathroom could start yelling. Or the cop in the living room could come back to find out what was keeping Rita.

When the knot on the sheet held, Wyatt pulled it into a narrow rope. With the second sheet tied around his waist, he stepped off the side of the balcony, using his legs to take some of the pressure off his arms. Still, the bullet wound stung as he descended to the next level down. Glancing at the curtains on the bedroom window, he saw that they were closed and thanked God for small favors.

There was no way to get the first half of the sheet free, so he had to leave it where it was like a signpost announcing his escape route. With a grimace, he tied the second sheet to the current railing and repeated the procedure, climbing over the side and lowering himself down as fast as he could.

A muffled scream made him almost let go of the sheet as he reached the balcony below. Looking toward the window, he saw an elderly woman dressed in a bra and panties standing inside the bedroom staring at him in horror.

"Sorry," he called out and turned quickly away. He didn't

have another rope, but he was close to the ground. Probably the woman was calling 911, he thought as he climbed over the railing and lowered himself as far as he could before letting go. He landed on the lawn at the side of the building and wavered on his feet.

Thankful that he hadn't twisted an ankle, he took a moment to straighten his clothes, then headed for the street where he'd left the car, praying he was going to find Carrie waiting.

Chapter Ten

Carrie was nowhere in sight.

Wyatt's heart started to pound again as he saw instead two cops standing near the car. The car that had an assault rifle hidden in the trunk.

Taking a deep breath, he reminded himself that the officers didn't have X-ray vision.

Were they responding to the woman who had seen him come down the building? Had the detective upstairs come into the bedroom, found the women in the bathroom and called for backup? Or did these guys just happen to be checking the area? If he turned around and headed the other way, he'd seem suspicious. If he kept walking toward them, they might recognize him, but he figured his best option was to keep going.

Trying not to look as though his heart was racing, he passed the car. Once he'd gotten by the cops, he started trying to figure out where Carrie might be. Probably she'd seen the uniforms, too, and walked past. That was, if she hadn't already been arrested.

He couldn't stop doubts from chasing themselves around in his mind. He was supposed to be protecting her, and he'd gotten them both in a mess of trouble by going to Rita's apartment. The way he had two years ago in Greece by sleeping late when he should have been on his toes. That slipup had cost his partner her life.

He shuddered. This wasn't like that at all. He hadn't made a mistake because he was too involved with Carrie. He'd wanted information from Rita Madison, he'd taken a calculated risk and he'd learned something they didn't know before.

And now he had to find Carrie.

Trying to think the way she would, he headed for the shopping center, cursing himself for not giving her one of the untraceable cell phones. But when they'd left on this fact-gathering expedition this morning, he'd assumed they were going to stay together.

He reached the shopping area and started looking in stores.

As he walked past a coffee shop, Carrie came out, still wearing the maid's uniform, as he'd assumed she would be.

He felt a flood of relief as he saw her and noted his own profound relief mirrored on her face. Their eyes met, and he fought the need to stop and take her in his arms. Instead, he kept on walking, hoping the moment hadn't called attention to them.

She fell into step behind him as he kept moving down the street toward the main shopping area, hoping he looked as if he was a guy out killing some time—or maybe picking up something for his wife. When he turned into one of the upscale department stores, she followed him.

He paused inside the doorway, looking around as though he was trying to locate a particular department.

Several shoppers passed, and Wyatt pretended that he and Carrie had simply come in at the same time.

When they were alone for a few moments, she spoke. "What are we going to do?"

"Better not to be seen together. You spend about five minutes in the ladies' room. I'm going back to the car and hope that the cops have moved on. I'll drive over and pick you up at this exit."

She looked down at her clothing. "I'm wearing a maid's uniform."

"Maybe you're out shopping on your lunch hour. You can change into something else later."

A woman with a shopping bag was approaching the exit where they stood, and he stopped talking abruptly.

As though they'd simply bumped into each other casually, Carrie nodded at him and started walking toward one of the clerks at the jewelry counter, where he presumed she was asking for directions to the ladies' room. He walked toward the shoe department, stopped to look at a couple of oxfords, then exited the store. Turning back the way he'd come, he headed for the car. As he approached, he saw that no one was paying any attention to the vehicle. Was it a trap?

If he'd had an alternate means of transportation, he would have left the car where it was. But he hadn't even thought he'd need one false identity—let alone more. The alternate driver's license and credit card had simply been a precaution. Renting another vehicle under the same name wasn't going to help. And stealing a car was too risky.

After unlocking the car, he climbed in and sat for a moment gripping the wheel before pulling out of the parking space and heading back the way he'd come. When he slowed near the store exit, Carrie came out and looked right and left before walking rapidly toward the vehicle and climbing in. Before she'd had a chance to buckle her seat belt, he drove off, turning down Western Avenue and then into a residential area.

Carrie sat with her head back and her eyes closed, and he couldn't stop himself from reaching over and laying his palm over her clenched hands. She knitted her fingers with his, holding on tight.

"I was scared," she finally said.

"So was I. When I came back to the car and found you weren't there."

"And I was frightened for you. What happened upstairs? How did you get away?"

"I tore up a sheet and used it to climb down from the balcony."

She sucked in a sharp breath.

"I made it." He laughed. "After I scared the bejesus out of an old lady in her underwear two levels down."

Despite the gravity of their situation, Carrie laughed, too, and he liked the sound.

Wyatt kept driving, making several turns past upscale houses with well-kept landscaping. As far as he could see, no one was following them, but there was one more thing he had to check. He found a driveway with tall hedges on either side and pulled in.

"What are you doing?"

"Making sure nobody put a tracker on the car."

"Could they do that?"

"It's not likely, but I need to be certain," he said, thinking that a lot of things that weren't likely had happened since he'd taken the job of protecting Carrie Mitchell.

CARRIE WATCHED WYATT get out of the car. Bending over, he ran his hand under the front bumper and along the sides, moving slowly and repeating the process in back and on the other side.

When he got back in, he looked relieved. "I think we're okay."

"Are we?" she asked, not just thinking about the transmitter.

They were sitting in a car screened by tall bushes on each side, making a private little enclave on a residential street. Before he could start the engine again, she shifted out of her seat and reached for him across the console.

Would he resist the embrace? She held her breath, waiting to find out what he would do. To her relief, he leaned into her, sighing as he gathered her closer.

"Lord, Carrie," he murmured as he ran his hands up and down her back and into her hair.

"I was so worried about you," she whispered.

"Yeah. Likewise."

She was so relived he was all right. That she was all right. That they were back together again. And all she could think about was getting close to him, feeling the reassurance of his arms around her again. Craving as much of him as she could have, she hoisted herself over the console, into his lap. Because his legs were long, his seat was far enough from the wheel to make room for her.

She had never been wild and reckless, but she felt that way now. Without giving herself time to change her mind, she straddled his lap so that the hot, needy place between her legs was pressed to the front of his jeans.

He made a strangled sound. Before he could change their positions, she tipped her face up and found his mouth. The moment their lips met, the kiss turned so hot that it could have started a wildfire. The morning's adventure had driven both of them to the edge of desperation.

What she needed was to close her eyes and focus on the man who held her in his arms instead of everything else that was happening to her.

He sipped from her mouth, then deepened the kiss. She loved the taste of him, the feel of his body, the way he clasped her tightly. She'd been craving this since last night, and the terror of the past few hours had only intensified her emotions.

She forgot where they were, forgot everything except the need to get close to him—as close as two people could get.

His tongue dipped into her mouth, exploring the line of her teeth, then stroking the sensitive tissue on the inside of her lips, sending hot currents curling through her body.

She knew he had tried to keep his distance from her because he thought it was the right thing to do. And she knew now that he had given in to the heat building between them.

His hands stroked up and down her ribs, gliding upward to find the sides of her breasts, then inward, across her nipples. At the same time, she felt the erection that had risen behind the fly of his jeans pressing against the part of her that needed him most.

Earlier she'd been wearing slacks, but the maid's uniform was more convenient. If she took off her panties and unzipped his fly, they could do what they both craved.

Her breath shuddered in and out as he undid the buttons at the front of the dress and slipped two fingers inside, dipping under her bra to stroke her nipple, sending heat shooting downward through her body.

She could do the same thing, she thought, as she unbuttoned the front of his dress shirt enough to ease her hand inside, playing with his crinkled chest hair. She found a flat nipple, feeling it stiffen at her touch. Sliding back a little, she reached for his belt buckle.

Before she could undo it, the sound of a car horn went through her like a shock wave.

Chapter Eleven

Jerking away from Wyatt and back into the passenger seat, Carrie looked wildly around for the source of the intrusion into the private world they'd wrapped around themselves and saw a Cadillac in the street behind them. As she turned to stare, the woman driver honked again.

Wyatt swore under his breath, turned the key in the ignition and backed out of the driveway, easing around the luxury car.

An older woman with dyed blond hair was staring daggers at them. Rolling down her window, she stuck her head out and called, "How dare you use my driveway for a dalliance with the maid!"

"The maid?"

Oh, right. She was still wearing the borrowed uniform.

Carrie felt her cheeks flame and ducked her head, trying to hide her face.

Wyatt slammed the gearshift into Drive and pulled around the circular driveway, his mouth set in a grim line.

"I'm sorry," she whispered.

"Not your fault," he answered as he sped away. "That wasn't going much further anyway. The first time I make love with you, it's not going to be in the front seat of a car in someone's driveway."

She digested that comment. "Did I hear you right?"

He gave her a sheepish look. "I didn't mean to say that."

"But it's what you were thinking."

"Forget it."

"I don't think so."

She wasn't going to forget something like that, because it was too good a window into his state of mind.

Wyatt wanted to make love to her. And he would. It was just a question of when.

She could continue the very interesting conversation, but she didn't think that would get her anywhere. Instead, she filed it away for future reference. Very near future.

Changing the subject, she asked, "What did I miss upstairs after I left?"

"Just my daring escape."

She felt a shiver go through her. He might joke about it, but it had been a very risky way to get out of the apartment.

"I made it," he said, as if reading her thoughts.

"Thank God. But now what are we going to do?" she asked.

"Try another approach." He turned his head toward her for a moment. "Would you have called Patrick Harrison if I hadn't gotten back to the car?"

"I don't know."

"But you were thinking about it."

"What should I have done if you hadn't come back?"

She saw him tighten his hands on the wheel, then deliberately relax them. "Withdraw a bunch of money from your bank account. Disappear."

"I don't know how to do that."

"You're smart. You'd learn," he said, but she wondered if he really believed it.

"You can't disappear forever."

"Some people do. Like that woman who was in the Weather Underground who made a new life for herself. Or that mob boss who vanished for a decade."

"Then you read years later that they were captured."

"Or not. There are plenty you *don't* read about."

"Maybe you'd better give me some tips. You know, in case I actually need to do it."

"Go to a rural graveyard, find a child born the same year you were and died when she was a few years old. Take her identity. Then move to another location where nobody would know about her. After that, say you lost your Social Security card and need a new one."

She shuddered. "That's awful."

"It works." He cleared his throat. "Back to Patrick. I don't trust him."

"Why not?"

"Because I don't trust anybody. And because he's close to this situation."

"That doesn't make him guilty. And I know he wouldn't do anything to harm me."

"Are you sure?"

She gave him a sharp look. "As sure as I can be of anyone. I told you—we grew up together."

"And you always got along?"

"Didn't we already talk about this?"

"I'm trying to get as much information as I can. I want to go back and question your father's maid—and see what I can get off his computer. And I'm not sure I want Patrick around when we do it." He checked the rearview mirror. "Give me some more background on him."

She thought back over the years that they'd been together. "There was a period when he was a teenager when he…resented my father, and he did some things that you could consider rebellious. But I did, too."

"Like what?"

"Him or me?"

"Both of you."

"There was a boy in school that I liked. I sneaked off to see him and had a girlfriend cover for me."

"That's it?"

"Do I have to tell you everything?"

"No." He glanced over at her. "What about Patrick?"

"Maybe the worst thing he did was borrow one of my dad's cars—and drive it up on a curb. He whacked up the axle, and then he asked me to help him get it fixed without my dad finding out."

"Did you?"

"Yes."

"Nice of you."

"He'd done things for me."

"Like what?"

She sighed. "Once when I was in sixth grade, I didn't want to go to school. I got him to help me put a thermometer on a lightbulb, then cool it down again so it looked like I had a temperature of a hundred and one."

He laughed. "You needed Patrick to help you do that?"

"Well, he caught me in the act, and then he said he wouldn't tell my dad." She swung her head toward him. "Your turn. What did you do bad?"

"So you can hold it over my head?"

"I don't want to be the only one confessing."

He thought for a moment. "There was a kid in my neighborhood who organized a bunch of us to steal car radar detectors and GPSes."

"Did you get caught?"

"I felt bad about it and quit."

She knew they were both using the conversation to keep their minds off their current problems.

"And what else? Did you seduce lots of girls when you were a teenager?"

"Actually, an older girl seduced me. Since you opened up the subject, who was your first? Not Patrick, I hope."

"I told you, I didn't think of Patrick that way. It was a guy in college," she said in a clipped tone.

"A one-night stand?"

"No. We had a relationship. Then he decided it wasn't working out."

She hoped from the way she'd said it that he'd take the hint and stop the interrogation. "How did we get into this?" she muttered.

"We were trying to decide if we could trust Patrick. You think that if we went back to your house, he wouldn't tell the terrorists you were there?"

"He wouldn't."

"*You* may be certain of that. *I'm* not taking a chance with your life. I want to talk to the maid, and I don't trust him to know where you're going to be."

"Then what are you going to do?"

"Get him out of the house. I want you to call him and set up a meeting."

"Where?"

He looked around. "We're near the Macomb Street playground. That's probably as good a place as any. We can scope it out first to make sure it sounds like a legitimate location for a meeting."

They drove down Connecticut Avenue, then turned onto Macomb Street. The tree-shaded playground was empty, and Wyatt found a nearby parking spot.

"Be right back," he said, getting out to look around the area.

When he returned, he said, "Tell him that you're alone and that you'll meet him in an hour at the closest picnic table to the gate." He gave her a direct look. "Can you say that without making him think that you have no intention of showing up?"

"Yes," she snapped.

"And see if you can make sure Inez is there."

"I know what I'm doing."

When he handed her the cell phone, she dialed her home number.

Patrick answered immediately.

"Carrie?"

"Yes."

"Where are you?" He sounded on edge.

"I'm in D.C."

"At your apartment in Columbia Heights?"

"No."

"You should come home."

"You know I can't. It's not safe for me to go there. The terrorists could be watching the place, but you can meet me."

"Where?"

"I'm at the Macomb Street playground."

"A playground?"

"It seemed like a place nobody would look for me."

"Is Hawk with you?"

She glanced at Wyatt. "I'm alone."

"Why?"

She kept her voice even. "We decided that it would be better to separate for a while."

"I thought he was sticking to you like glue."

"I'll tell you about it when we meet."

"When?"

"I can't stay around the park—or anywhere else—too long. I'll leave and come back in about an hour. Can you get here then?"

"Where is it?"

She gave him the directions, then stumbled a bit before she asked, "Uh…who will be in charge at home, in case the kidnappers call?" As she said the last part, she felt her chest tighten. She'd been keeping her mind off of what might be happening to her father, but she'd just brought it front and center.

"Inez will be here," Patrick answered.

Carrie glanced at Wyatt and knew he'd heard.

"There's been no word about Dad?" she asked, fighting to keep her voice even.

"No. I'm sorry. Carrie…"

Wyatt squeezed her arm. When she turned to him with a questioning gaze, he pointed to his watch.

"Get here in an hour," she said to Patrick.

She hung up before he could say anything else, then glanced at Wyatt. "Was that okay?"

"Yeah, but I didn't want him to get a fix on this phone."

She nodded.

He started the engine. "The sooner we get to your house, the better. When he realizes you're not at the park, he'll come tearing home. We don't want to be there when he does."

PATRICK HARRISON PUT down the receiver, fighting to control the trembling of his body.

Carrie had vanished from the face of the earth, and he'd been terrified that she wouldn't get in touch with him. He'd told himself he knew her very well. He'd come to realize that she wasn't as reliable as he'd like.

But she had finally called, and his spirits lifted. Things were definitely looking up.

He paced back and forth, debating what to do. It looked as though his best bet was to simply meet—and take it from there. He'd have liked to get her away from the park before Wyatt Hawk came back, but he realized that the chances of keeping her out of the clutches of her bodyguard were slim.

He turned around to find the housekeeper, Inez, watching him.

"Is there any news?" she asked.

"No. I'm going out."

"Where?"

"It's better if I don't tell you," he said carefully.

"All right," she answered in the same tone, her gaze fixed on him.

He'd never been entirely comfortable with the woman, because he'd never been sure of her loyalties or her motives. Now he wanted to tell her to clear out, but somebody had to be at the house. He could feel her gaze on him as he exited the room and headed for the garage, where he'd parked the Lexus sedan Douglas Mitchell had bought him. It wasn't the car he would have chosen for himself. But that was the way the old man operated. He thought he knew best, and he didn't care what anyone else thought. Which might have been the reason he'd gotten himself kidnapped.

CARRIE TRIED TO calm the beating of her heart as Wyatt headed up Connecticut Avenue toward Chevy Chase Circle.

When he pulled into a gas station she looked at him questioningly.

"What are we doing?"

"Do you want to go out there in a maid's uniform?"

She'd forgotten what she was wearing and glanced down at herself. "Right."

"You can change in the ladies' room."

He popped the trunk, and she opened her suitcase, taking out jeans and a T-shirt. When she came back out, she stuffed the uniform into the suitcase and climbed into the car again.

As they headed for Potomac, Maryland, she felt her nerves jangling. She hadn't been home since she'd made a quick trip to the family estate after the terrorist incident. Wyatt hadn't wanted her to go back to her condo, so she'd gathered up some clothing from her old room and stuffed it into a suitcase, under Wyatt's watchful eyes. Back then he'd made her uncomfortable. Now she thought she understood him better. He was opening up in ways she never expected. More than opening up. That unguarded comment about making love to her had floored her. She was going to have to make sure he didn't forget about it. Actually, thinking about how to get him into bed was a lot more pleasant than thinking about the coming meeting with Inez. Carrie had always thought she and the housekeeper got along, but had she been wrong about the relationship all along? She didn't know whom to trust anymore.

"What do you know about Inez?" he asked as they drove.

"She's from Nicaragua. She came here on a work visa fifteen years ago, and my father got it extended so that she's a permanent resident."

"She's been with you fifteen years?"

"Yes."

"Is she married?"

"I never heard that she was."

"She left a husband and a son back in Nicaragua."

Carrie's head whipped toward him. "You know that how?"

"I had her checked out."

"Then why were you asking me what I knew about her?"

"To see if she'd told you the whole story. Do you think your father knows about the husband and child?"

"I...don't know. He never talked to me about it," she added, wondering if he'd kept the information to himself. Or if maybe he'd used it to keep Inez in line.

She knew he was ruthless, and using private information wouldn't bother him.

"Maybe she didn't abandon them," she said, defending Inez. "Maybe she sent money home to them."

"I found no record of that."

Carrie glared at him. "You were thorough."

"That's my job. Would she take drastic measures if she thought your father had dug into her past and was going to send her home?"

"You mean like cook up a terrorist plot? Then have him kidnapped? That sounds far-fetched. Where would she get the contacts?"

"It sounded far-fetched that a Federal prosecutor would take money to tell someone when you had a secret meeting downtown. But it looks like that's what happened. What if someone forced Inez to work with them?"

"Let's not assume the worst."

"You know I always assume the worst."

"What else do you know about Inez that's bad?" she challenged.

"Nothing," he said curtly, looking annoyed as he kept driving, but she wasn't going to apologize for asking her questions. He was the one who had started the conversation.

They rode in silence the rest of the way to her father's house.

Long ago, Potomac had been the home of big estates, horse riding and fox hunting. Gradually, most of the exclusive acreage had been subdivided into developments, but there were still some big properties left, including the Mitchell estate.

Her anticipation mounted as they turned onto Trotter Hill Road.

"Why are you driving past?" she asked, as Wyatt failed to turn in at the entrance.

"I don't want anyone to know we're going to your house, and I don't want to get trapped."

"You think someone is watching the property?"

"Again, we need to make the assumption."

He went an eighth of a mile down the road and turned in at their nearest neighbor's house, where there was a big for-sale sign at the end of the driveway.

"It belongs to the Butlers," she said.

"I know. I checked it out. The husband died, and the wife moved to Florida."

"What, did you check the whole neighborhood?"

"Just the properties on either side of your dad's. Mrs. Butler is holding out for her asking price. But she was too cheap to hire a security company to keep an eye on the place."

They parked around the back of the house.

"And I suppose you also figured out the best route to get there from here?" Carrie asked.

"Yeah. Around the bramble patch, not through it."

They walked past the swimming pool, across the manicured lawn and onto the rougher, unkempt fields beyond, skirting the bramble patch Wyatt had mentioned.

"I used to pick raspberries and blackberries here," Carrie murmured.

"Enough for a pie?"

"Sometimes. And they were good on my cereal in the morning."

"Patrick doesn't exactly seem like nature boy. Did he go berry picking with you?"

"Sometimes."

"So he's been out here?"

She nodded, wishing that everything didn't have a sinister implication.

They walked through a stand of white pines that had been planted long ago to shield the Mitchell property from the neighbors' view, then paused at the edge while Wyatt pulled a pair of binoculars from a knapsack he'd brought along.

"Where did you get those?"

"The same place we bought the clothes. They're not the best model around, but they'll do."

He scanned the house. "It looks quiet. I haven't been inside, except that time you stopped to get your clothes on the way to the safe house. The bedrooms are in the wing on the left, correct?"

"Yes."

"And the breakfast room is in the middle."

"Overlooking the pool."

"I don't suppose the back door is going to be unlocked."

"It shouldn't be."

He scanned the property again. "The garage door is open, and it shouldn't be, either."

"I guess Patrick was in a hurry to get to the meeting."

"We'll go in that way, but I want you to keep low as we

approach. And run as fast as you can to the back wall of the house."

He went first, bending over so that running looked awkward, but she followed his example, darting around the pool area to the side of the house and then the garage.

There was no sign that anyone had spotted them. Was Inez even here?

Inside the garage, Wyatt asked, "Where is the housekeeper likely to be?"

"Anywhere. She's either working or resting."

Wyatt walked quietly to the door that led to the house. It was locked, but he took a credit card from his wallet and inserted it between the door and the jamb. After a few moments, the door opened.

"Not very secure," Wyatt muttered.

"There's a dead bolt. Patrick must have left it open."

As they stepped into the mudroom, Carrie fought a strange sensation of detachment. She'd lived here most of her life, yet now she felt totally divorced from the house. When she got out of this mess, would she even want to come back here?

And why not? she asked herself, knowing that it had something to do with Wyatt. He hadn't said so, but she sensed that he didn't approve of her father's lifestyle.

They were moving quietly down the hall when a door opened and they came face-to-face with Inez, a small, plump woman with graying hair pulled back in a bun. She was wearing a black uniform not unlike the one that Carrie had put on at the Madison house. The housekeeper screamed when she saw intruders in the house and tried to slam the door, but Wyatt caught it with his hand and held it open.

"Stay here," he ordered.

"*Madre de Dios,*" she said when she realized that Carrie was one of the intruders. "What are you doing here?"

"We need to look around here."

"But Mr. Patrick was going to meet you."

"How do you know?"

Inez's face flushed. When she spoke, her Spanish accent thickened. "I was listening to the conversation. I was worried about you, and I wanted to talk to you, but I knew I couldn't do it."

Carrie answered with a tight nod.

"Do you often listen in on private conversations?" Wyatt asked.

"When I'm concerned about Señor Mitchell and Señorita Carrie."

He kept his gaze fixed on her. "So you know what's been going on?"

"You mean that Señorita Carrie was attacked when she went downtown. And, of course, I know about Señor Mitchell being kidnapped."

"Were you here when it happened?"

She shook her head. "No. I was out getting groceries."

"Convenient," he answered.

Inez raised her chin. "What is that supposed to mean?"

"That you might have wanted to be out of the house during the abduction."

"How would I know there was going to be an abduction?"

"You tell me."

"I didn't." Her voice quavered, and she sounded on the verge of tears.

"It's okay," Carrie murmured. "He's just being cautious."

"*Sí.*"

"Did Mr. Mitchell know that you left your husband and child to come here?" Wyatt suddenly asked.

Inez rounded on him. "I did not leave my husband and child. In my country, women have few choices. *Mi esposo* was a man who always got what he wanted. He wanted to marry another woman. He kicked me out of the house, and when I tried to get my son, he told me I'd better stay away from the house or he'd kill me."

the look on the housekeeper's face that she noted the relationship that had developed between Carrie and her bodyguard. Apparently, Inez was right. She didn't miss much.

PATRICK HARRISON GOT up from the wooden picnic table where he'd been sitting and paced back to the street.

He'd been at the playground for twenty minutes, and he didn't like the way this was shaping up. Carrie had said she'd be here, but so far, she was nowhere in sight. Neither was her damn bodyguard.

He made his hand into a fist and punched the chain-link fence that surrounded the play area. It looked as though he'd driven all the way into town for nothing.

There couldn't be any mistake about where they were supposed to meet, could there?

He walked outside the fence and looked up and down the street. Still no Carrie. He pulled his phone out of its holster and held it in his hand. He'd tried to call back and found that Carrie had contacted him from a phone that could only make outgoing calls, so there was no use trying to find out where she was. He wanted to tell her how worried he was about her. He wanted to beg her to show up, but he simply couldn't do it—not even in this age of instant communications.

How long should he wait before giving up and going home? Or maybe she'd gotten in touch with Inez? Maybe he should call her and find out if she'd heard anything.

THE PHONE RANG and all three people in the Mitchell house went stock-still.

Hope and pain laced through Carrie as she looked at Wyatt. "It could be the kidnappers."

"I'll get it," Inez said.

Wyatt didn't have time to give her instructions before she picked up the receiver.

"Hello?"

Wyatt and Carrie both moved close to her so they could hear who was on the other end of the line.

"Have you heard from Carrie?" a voice asked. It was Patrick, and he sounded upset.

Inez clenched the receiver more tightly and glanced from Carrie to Wyatt. "No. Should I have?"

"She was supposed to meet me," Patrick said. "But she hasn't shown up, and I'm worried about her."

"I don't know anything about it."

"You sound strange."

"I'm just, you know, on edge. I'm worried about Señorita Carrie, too. And her father."

"There's no use waiting here. I'm coming home."

"Maybe she'll show up where you are. What if she comes and you're not there?"

"I'm coming home."

The line clicked off, leaving the three of them staring at each other.

"We don't have much time," Wyatt said. "He could be right around the corner."

"It sounded as if he's still down there," Carrie said.

"Unless he was calling to test Inez." Wyatt turned to the housekeeper. "You keep watch. If you see him coming up the drive, let me know. I'm going to search his room." He turned to Carrie. "You get your cameras. Well, maybe not all of them. Anything we take might have to be abandoned."

She winced. "Okay."

"While I search Patrick's room, you see if you can get into your father's computer."

"It's password protected."

"Do your best." Wyatt charged off down the hall to Patrick's room, then stopped at the door. Would the guy have some warning system or a camera in there?

He examined the closed door and the floor around it to

make sure Patrick hadn't used any device to indicate an unwanted visitor.

Wyatt opened the door and stepped into the room. The shades were drawn, and he flicked the light switch so that he could look around. His first thought was that Patrick was a neat freak. Nothing was out of place. Nothing was sitting around. It could almost have been a room in a luxury hotel where people came and went without leaving their personal belongings. Scanning the bookshelves, he saw some volumes of popular fiction, separated from books on business. He ran his hands along the volumes, intent on finding out if one of them was really a hidden camera.

There were no cameras in the bookshelves, and he couldn't identify anything on the walls that was taking his picture, either. He went into the bathroom and checked the medicine cabinet, finding only the usual toiletries. Patrick didn't seem to be on any kind of medication, or nothing that he kept where a visitor could find it.

Visitor? That stopped him short. Patrick probably wasn't expecting anyone to come in here. Which might have made him careless.

Wyatt returned to the bedroom and opened the closet, riffling through the neatly hung shirts, jackets and pants, all arranged by color. He didn't know a lot of men who enjoyed shopping for clothes, but Patrick had a lot of them, and the labels were good ones. Apparently, he liked his sartorial comforts.

He should have asked Carrie what the guy did for fun. There was no indication here of what that might be.

He opened drawers, finding carefully folded underwear and T-shirts. All of them looked as though he'd gotten Inez to iron them.

In the sock drawer, Wyatt hit pay dirt. There was a slight irregularity in the shelf-lining paper, and when Wyatt lifted it up, he found a manila folder.

When he pulled it out, he found something interesting. It was a carefully compiled and annotated employment history on a security man—named Wyatt Hawk.

INEZ STOOD IN the hallway feeling sick inside. She didn't like what she was about to do, but what choice did she have?

First she peeked into Patrick's room, where she saw Señor Wyatt searching through dresser drawers. Satisfied that he was busy, she walked down the hall to the office and saw Señorita Carrie sitting at the desk trying to get into the computer.

She could have told her the password, but then she'd have to admit how much snooping she'd done around here.

She'd watched Señor Mitchell type in the letters and numbers, and when he'd been out of the office, she'd done it herself to make sure they worked.

Before Señorita Carrie could turn around and find her standing there, she went down the hall to the front of the house, where she looked out the window as she'd been instructed. She saw no cars coming up the driveway, but she didn't expect to see anyone. Not yet.

Her heart was pounding as she moved to the kitchen and checked to make sure that neither of the other people in the house was watching. When she was satisfied she was alone, she took the receiver off the hook and dialed a number.

"Hello?" a voice said.

"Is this Home Depot?" she asked.

"You have the wrong number."

"Okay. Sorry."

She hung up quickly, knowing that she had delivered the required message. It had to do with the place she'd asked for. *Home Depot* meant Carrie was in the house.

She pressed her fist against her lips, then pulled herself together and went back to the window.

Chapter Twelve

Wyatt riffled through the folder he'd found in Patrick's drawer, noting that the information wasn't totally about him. There were also several other guys who specialized in security work, but it seemed he was the star attraction.

He thumbed through the pages and found he knew some of the men. Cal Winston was a good choice for a protection detail. So was Drake Inmann. They would both have been excellent for the assignment, but from the amount of material on each, it looked as if they'd been taken out of the running early on.

He went on to his own work history, reading about his early army training at Fort Bragg. His CIA experience in a number of countries around the world. The spy operation that had gone bad in Greece was highlighted in yellow.

So they knew about his biggest failure, but Patrick had made a notation next to it, saying that Douglas had accepted Patrick's recommendation of Hawk.

Wyatt stared at the page with narrowed eyes. If this was to be believed, Patrick had been the one who'd recommended him. Because he thought Wyatt was the most qualified, or what?

A sound behind Wyatt alerted him that he was not alone. He whirled around to find Carrie standing in the doorway.

"Sorry I startled you."

"I guess I'm jumpy."

"We both are. What did you find?"

"Work experience of several security men—me included. Did you know Patrick recommended me for your bodyguard?"

"No."

"Did you have any input into the selection or talk to him about it?"

"No."

Wyatt held up the folder. "There are several other candidates in here. Good men. Why do you think he picked me?"

"I have no idea."

He wanted to ask if she thought it was because he'd made a bad mistake in Greece, but he didn't want to open the subject to discussion.

"Where did you find the file?" she asked.

"In his sock drawer."

"He was hiding it?"

"Looks like it." He switched subjects abruptly. "Were you able to get into your father's computer?"

"Yes. The password is my birthday."

"Not too original. What did you find?"

"The usual things. His list of contacts. A list of his medications. Angry letters he's written to various companies complaining about their products and services. There's also a file of family pictures. He must have had them scanned and put into the computer."

"Anything useful?"

"The bills he paid and his bank records. It looks like some money has been moved around."

"Let me see." Wyatt put the folder back where he'd found it and glanced around the room, trying to ensure he left no trace of his search.

"Was he always such a neat freak?" he asked Carrie.

"Not at first." She stopped and thought. "My dad used to

criticize him for the way he kept his room. That made him much neater."

"Kids respond to their parents in one of two ways. Either they do what's asked of them, or they do just the opposite."

She laughed. "I guess."

"Were you as neat?"

"No. One of my acts of rebellion."

They headed down the hall again. In the office Wyatt got a listing of the files and started scanning the contents. He rummaged in a drawer for a thumb drive and stuck it in the machine. He had just started copying files when Inez came running down the hall, her face a mask of panic.

"Mr. Patrick is coming up the driveway. He'll fire me if he finds out you've been here. What should I do?"

"Just act naturally, as if you've been ironing his T-shirts," Wyatt said. He hadn't copied all the files he wanted from Douglas's computer, and it looked as though he wasn't going to get to do it.

"Come on."

He shoved the thumb drive into his jacket pocket and headed for the back of the house, but it was already too late. The front door slammed open and Patrick charged into the house.

Wyatt looked at Carrie. *Where can we hide?* he mouthed.

She looked wildly around, then pointed to the back door.

"He'll see us."

"I have an idea."

Out in the front hall, they could hear Patrick interrogating Inez.

"Were they here?" he demanded.

"Who?"

"Carrie and Hawk."

"Why would they have come here?"

"You tell me."

"I…I…don't know."

"You were alone here the whole time?"

"Of course."

The voices faded as Carrie led Wyatt to a shed a few yards from the edge of the pool deck. It filled a gap in the wall of tall shrubbery that enclosed three sides of the pool. When she opened the door and stepped inside, he followed her into a small enclosure that housed the pool's pump and large plastic cans of chemicals. They closed the door behind them, shutting out most of the light.

"Doesn't he know about this place?" Wyatt whispered.

"I don't know, but you can bar the door, and he won't be able to get in."

It seemed crazy for Carrie to be hiding in her own house—from her father's chief of staff, a man she had known almost all her life. But Wyatt couldn't shake the conviction that it would be dangerous for Patrick to find them here.

Carrie rummaged through the equipment and found a metal bar, which she slipped through two slots in the door.

"This door locks from the inside?" he asked, his voice low.

"I had one of my father's workmen put it on for me years ago," she answered.

"Why?"

"You see how the pool's enclosed. When I was a kid, a friend of my dad used to visit with a big dog that scared me. I'd be in the water or on a chaise, and he'd come charging outside. If I thought I couldn't make it to the house, I'd come in here."

The sound of footsteps made Carrie stop speaking abruptly.

Wyatt listened as the steps crossed the pool deck. He reached for Carrie, thrusting her behind him and turning to face the door.

He tensed, preparing for a confrontation as the door rattled, but it didn't open.

Outside, he could hear Patrick drag in a breath and let it

out. "Carrie, you're in the pool shed, aren't you? I remember you used to hide in there."

She made a muffled choking sound but didn't answer.

"Listen to me," he continued. "I made a big mistake. I helped your father pick a bodyguard, and I recommended Wyatt Hawk."

At the sound of his name, Wyatt tensed.

"I thought he was the right man, but now I think I was wrong. I'm so worried about you. Let me protect you. Or I can call one of the other guys your father was considering."

In the dark, Wyatt could feel Carrie stiffen behind him. What if she believed Patrick? What if she took him up on the offer? Was he going to have to kidnap her to keep her safe?

He waited with tension bubbling inside him.

Patrick was also waiting for an answer. To Wyatt's relief, Carrie said nothing, and Wyatt certainly wasn't going to give away their hiding place. After long, tense moments, they heard the man kick the door.

"Get the hell out of there," he bellowed.

When they didn't answer he said, "Have it your way."

He gave the door one more kick and hurried away.

"What's he going to do?" Carrie whispered.

"I think he's going to get something he can use to break in."

"He's angry."

"Yeah." Wyatt grabbed the bar from the door, turned and shoved it through the slats in back of the shed. With a mighty heave, he pulled one free and then another.

"Go out that way," he said.

She moved around him and wiggled through.

Wyatt replaced the bar in the door, then turned back to the escape hatch. He was bigger than Carrie, and he had to twist to get his body through the narrow opening, gritting his teeth as the boards scraped the arm where he'd been shot. Behind him, he heard rapid footsteps coming back, then Patrick was rattling the door, but it held.

"Come out!" he shouted.

When they didn't respond, he started bashing the door with something heavy.

Wyatt pressed the boards he'd removed back into place. They wouldn't hold if Patrick shoved on them, but for the moment they looked okay.

"Come on," Wyatt whispered. Taking Carrie's hand, he started running across the field, hearing Patrick whacking at the shed door and cursing.

They were almost across the field when the sound of a vehicle in the Mitchell driveway made him turn. He saw a green van speeding toward the house.

"Who's that?" he whispered.

She turned and followed his gaze.

"The gardeners."

"This is their regular day?"

"I don't know."

Pointing toward the woods, Wyatt motioned for Carrie to duck low and run for the shelter of the trees. He followed, staying between her and the truck.

They had just made it to the little woods when the sound of gunfire echoed behind them.

Douglas Mitchell's eyes blinked open. He was still in the darkened room, still lying with his left hand fastened to the bed. But something was different this time.

He stayed very still, thinking about everything that had happened. Carrie had overheard terrorists plotting when she'd been taking nature photographs in the woods. She'd talked to the police, and then everything had gone to hell in a hand-basket.

She'd been hiding out with Wyatt Hawk and some other

men he'd hired to protect her. She'd been safe, until she'd gone down to D.C. to talk to the Federal prosecutor.

Those details had been insubstantial in his memory. He hadn't known if they were real or if he'd made them up. Now he *knew*.

His mind had been very dim, as if all his thoughts were filtering through a glass of motor oil. Now the oil had been washed away, and his mind was functioning again.

Again?

He stopped to think about that. How long had he been feeling as though everything was all balled up in his mind?

Six months. That sounded right. For the past six months he hadn't felt like himself. Then men had captured him and locked him away from the world, and he was somehow thinking straight again.

He ground his teeth together, unable to believe that his mental state was just a coincidence.

In his mind he went back over the past few months—and the past few days, and a terrible conclusion began to dawn on him.

He wanted to howl with rage, but that wouldn't do him any good. Instead, he looked around, and made a startling discovery. He knew where he was. He'd been out of this room to go to the bathroom, and the place had looked vaguely familiar. Now he knew.

This was a guest bedroom in the vacation house he owned down on the Severn River.

Good God. He was being held captive on his own property—a location that he knew well. Was there some way he could escape? Or some way he could get a message to Carrie?

There was so much he wanted to say to her. Not just about where he was being held. Things that he should have said to her years ago.

First he had to get free of this place so he could warn her what was going on. But how was he going to do it?

Chapter Thirteen

At the blast of gunfire, Carrie stopped in her tracks.

Wyatt grabbed her arm and pulled her forward, into the shadows of the trees.

Someone had arrived in a truck that looked as if it belonged to the gardeners. Whoever it was had started shooting, and Wyatt didn't know if the fire was directed at them or at Inez and Patrick. But he wasn't going to stay around to find out.

They made it into the woods, where they stood panting. Wyatt looked back toward the house and saw several men in green uniforms standing outside. The hedges around the pool prevented him from seeing Patrick or Inez.

"What if they're hurt? We have to go back," Carrie said between breaths.

"We can't."

"But—"

He shook his head, silencing her. "We have to get the hell out of here."

He led her back the way they'd come, across the fields and into the manicured yard of the house that was for sale.

"Wait," he ordered, leaving her beside the back wall while he cautiously looked into the car.

It appeared to be untouched. As far as he could tell, whoever was shooting hadn't figured out that they'd left their vehicle here.

He came back and motioned for Carrie to follow him. They both climbed into the car, and he drove away. But he hadn't made a clean escape. As he headed away from the Mitchell estate, he looked in the rearview mirror and saw a car exit the property and come speeding in their direction. Not the green van. A different vehicle.

His curse had Carrie's head jerking toward him.

"What?"

"Somebody figured out where we were," he answered as he pressed his foot to the accelerator.

Carrie swung around in her seat, her gaze zeroing in on the pursuer.

"Hang on," he advised. He took a curve at a dangerous speed and kept going. A truck was ahead of them. Wyatt blasted his horn and swung out into the oncoming lane. He made it back onto the right side of the road just in time to miss crashing into a sedan coming the other way.

Beside him, Carrie gasped, but she didn't ask him to slow down. They had come to the more populous part of Potomac, and he chose a development at random, slowing down as he turned into a street lined with large two-story houses. He followed the entrance road for several hundred yards, then chose one of the side streets at random. From there, he wound his way through the development.

"Keep looking in back of us," he told Carrie. "Let me know if you see anyone following."

She did as he'd asked.

"Nothing?"

"I don't see anyone."

He breathed out a sigh, then left the development through a back entrance and made his way toward Route 29.

Beside him, Carrie relaxed a little.

"I have to call Inez," she whispered.

"You can't."

"But—"

"It could be dangerous for her if the terrorists are there. They'd know you were in contact with her."

"They know we were there, don't they?"

"Yeah. But they don't know your relationship with her."

"You think it's the terrorists?"

"That's my best guess."

"But there was shooting. Maybe two different groups. What does that mean?"

"The cops and the terrorists? The Feds and the terrorists? Or maybe Patrick opened fire on them," he said as he kept driving. "He was pretty angry. Out of control, I'd say."

"Yes," she whispered.

"Have you ever seen him that way?" Wyatt asked.

"No."

"So maybe the pressure is making him unstable."

"Because he's worried about me and my father."

"Maybe."

She sighed. "I understand the need to let off steam. If I start screaming in frustration, you may have to gag me."

"You won't."

"How do you know?"

"You've got your act together."

"Yes, but I feel like I'm getting people killed or putting them in danger every time I turn around. I feel like I shouldn't have gone home."

She gave Wyatt a defiant look, pulled out her phone and called the Mitchell home number.

Inez answered.

"Are you all right?" Carrie asked.

"Yes. We—"

Wyatt grabbed the phone and clicked it off. "That's all you need to know," he growled.

She glared at him and he could see her struggling for calm.

"They're okay, and we got some important information."

"Like what?" she demanded.

"We have some files from your father's computer, and we know he's got—" He stopped and wondered how to phrase the end of the sentence.

"Dementia," she said.

"Not necessarily."

"That's what Inez said. She said that Patrick's been taking over more and more of his business dealings."

"We know the business part, but she might not be interpreting the rest of it correctly."

Carrie dragged in a breath and let it out. "I'm trying to remember what he's been like. I didn't notice any difference—except that he wasn't saying much. And he got angry more easily."

"That can be a symptom. But we don't really know what was going on with him. There's simply too much happening for everything to get cleared up in a few hours. We'll find out the true story when we find your father."

"And you think we will?" she asked, her voice cracking.

"Yes." He reached for her hand, lacing his fingers with hers. "I'm sorry," he whispered.

"Not your fault."

"So you don't go along with Patrick's theory that I'm the wrong man for the job?" he asked in a gritty voice.

"No! I'd be dead a dozen times over without you."

"Maybe I've been making wrong decisions that got us into trouble."

"Do you really believe that?"

"No. I think that we're up against a...conspiracy that's bigger and more organized than anyone suspected."

"A conspiracy?"

"That's the best way I can describe it."

When he pulled to the shoulder of the road and then into a clearing, she looked at him questioningly. "What are you doing?"

"Checking for a tracker again. Making sure nobody put one on our car while it was parked at that other house."

WYATT CLIMBED OUT and went through the same procedure that he'd gone through earlier. He felt along the undersides of the bumpers, then along the undersides of the chassis. He stopped abruptly when his fingers encountered a small piece of plastic that shouldn't have been there.

His pulse pounding, he pulled it out and held it up. He hadn't expected to find anything, but here it was.

Opening the door, he eased back into the car and held the thing up.

Carrie's eyes widened when she saw it. "What is it?"

"A GPS locator."

"How long has it been there?"

"You know I checked after we left Rita's apartment."

"Yes."

"It must have been put there while we were parked at your neighbor's house."

She kept staring at the thing. "Who would do that?"

"For all I know, it could have been Inez."

"When?"

"While we were busy."

"But she warned us that Patrick was coming."

He shrugged. "This is just more proof that we don't know what the hell is going on." He turned the thing in his hand. "It could have been Patrick. He could have done it before he came up your driveway."

She looked as if she didn't want to believe either alternative, but she nodded slowly.

"And he'd have good reason. You lied to him about where you were going to be, and he wanted to make sure he had his own means of finding you."

"I don't like thinking that."

"I don't like thinking any of this. I mean, as long as we're speculating...it could be the cops."

"Why would *they* do that?"

"They might want to find out what we're up to."

"Wouldn't they just arrest us?"

"Maybe not, if they thought we were involved in your father's kidnapping."

She made a strangled sound. "That's awful."

"This whole thing is awful." Something in his expression must have alerted her that another thought had struck him.

"What?"

He laughed. "I was wondering... Maybe the bad guys and the cops both showed up back there and they were shooting at each other."

She shook her head. "Yeah, maybe they can eliminate each other."

"I wouldn't count on it. Remember, a car drove away."

The conversation brought his thoughts back to Rita Madison. Like what had she said to the cop who'd been in her apartment after she told him about Wyatt Hawk locking her and the maid in the bathroom? She'd seemed to want to help him and Carrie, but he could have totally changed her mind by locking her up. He kept his gaze on the tracker, not wanting to open that line of speculation with Carrie.

One thing he knew: they had to get moving.

He got out of the car again and put the tracker on the ground. He was going to crush it under his heel, then thought better of it. Let the bastards think they'd simply stopped moving. That would give him and Carrie a head start to somewhere. After walking into the woods and setting the tracker down inside the circle of an old automobile tire, he got back into the car.

Carrie looked at him expectantly. "You want them to think it's still working?"

"Yes."

"If they had the tracker, why didn't they follow us?"

"I guess to make us think that we'd lost them. Or if there were two sets of guys at your house, one could have the tracker and the other could have followed us."

"Oh, great." She kept her gaze on him. "Where are we going now?"

"When we drove away from your neighbor's, I was thinking about the Baltimore suburbs. Now I have the feeling that's too obvious. When they realize they don't know where we are, they're going to start beating the bushes." He flapped his hand. "I guess we need to go somewhere I can look at the information on the thumb drive."

"A motel?"

"Probably."

He heard her draw in a breath and let it out before speaking. "Somewhere nice. I want to feel like I'm not a fugitive."

"What do you have in mind?"

"What about Frederick? It's not that long a drive, and it's a tourist area with a lot of bed-and-breakfast places."

He thought about it, then punched the small city into his GPS. He wasn't concerned with luxury accommodation, but he knew Carrie could use some kind of respite. If he'd had the option, would he have kept the information about the tracker to himself? Although he would have liked to spare her the worry, at the same time he couldn't in good conscience withhold information from her. But perhaps he could make her hiding place pleasant. After he took care of one more problem.

When he neared Frederick, he stopped at a shopping center on the outskirts of town.

"What are we doing?" she asked when he pulled up in front of a hardware store.

"Getting some electrical tape and scissors."

"Because?"

"If they found the car, they probably also took down the license number."

She winced.

"I believe I can make it look different."

After purchasing the supplies, he drove the car to a secluded section of the parking lot, got out and examined the front license plate. The first digit was the number one, and he used the tape to turn it into an *E*. He did the same with the plate on the back. If you stood ten feet away from it, he thought, the ruse should work.

Then he headed for the old-town area of Frederick, which had been in existence since Colonial times and was at the center of Civil War activity in the state.

Like many other older communities, it had gone through a period of decline, then began to prosper again, partly due to people moving out from Baltimore and Washington, where housing was more expensive, and partly due to the Colonial charm of the downtown area, where many restored buildings housed antiques shops and restaurants.

When they drove past a Victorian house with a B-and-B sign out front and extensive gardens all around, Carrie pointed. "Try that place."

"Spur-of-the-moment decision?"

"Yes."

He slowed and pulled to a stop down the block. "We'd better get our story straight before we go in."

"Okay, what's our story?"

"We're on a road trip traveling around Maryland and Virginia. We stop when a place strikes our fancy."

"And where are we from?"

"The D.C. suburbs. I work for the government—in a hush-hush job that I don't talk about—and you…teach…what?"

"Photography. So I can answer questions if I have to." She kept her gaze on him.

"Do you remember the names we were using?"

"Carolyn and Will Hanks."

"Right."

"And we're married?" she asked.

"Do you want to be?" he countered, wondering why he had put it that way.

"Yes."

He swallowed. "Okay."

Wyatt turned around and pulled into a gravel drive, and they got out of the car together. Carrie reached for his hand as they walked toward the front porch.

A few moments after Wyatt had rung the bell, a pleasant-looking middle-aged woman came to the door.

"Can I help you?"

"We're hoping we don't need a reservation to get a room."

"Not at all. Come in."

"We're the Hankses," Wyatt said, as they stepped into a spacious front hall. He looked to the left and saw a living room furnished with comfortable couches and chairs and what looked like antique chests and tables. On the right was a dining room with several tables.

"I'm Barbara Williamson."

"Nice to meet you," Carrie answered. She then said, "We want your best room."

"Are you celebrating something?"

"Not really, but we're having a very nice road trip, and I want to continue with the top-of-the-line experience."

"Our best room is in a private building out back. Would you like me to show it to you?"

"Yes."

They followed Mrs. Williamson through a large modern kitchen to a building that might have once been a carriage house. Unlocking the door, she showed them into a two-room suite. The sitting room was comfortable and cozy. The bedroom had a wide canopy bed. And through a doorway was a large luxury bathroom with a soaking tub, a shower and a double sink.

"Perfect," Carrie said.

"We can pay in advance," Wyatt said.

"If you like. Breakfast is between eight and nine-thirty."

"Would it be possible to have a tray brought over?" Carrie asked.

"That can be arranged. What time do you want it?"

Carrie looked at Wyatt.

"Eight," he answered.

He paid in cash before they carried their luggage into the guest cottage.

"I'm sure she didn't recognize us or anything," Carrie said.

"That seems to be the case. Wait here for a minute."

She stood in the middle of the sitting room while he set one of their suitcases on a stand. Then he began walking around the little cottage. If need be, they could get out one of the back windows, he decided.

When he turned from the window, he found Carrie standing in back of him. She turned and the expression on her face told him that she was preparing to push him—and push herself.

"Is this the kind of place where you'd like to make love to me for the first time?" she asked in a breathy voice.

He swallowed hard. "I shouldn't have said that. Do you usually ask that kind of question?"

"Never. But in this case I think I have to. Please answer the question."

"Yes," he said, his throat so tight that he could barely speak. Still, his bodyguard's mind was working, and he was thinking they were at a location where it was unlikely the terrorists would be looking for them.

"You could be making a terrible mistake," he managed to say.

"I don't think so."

CARRIE HAD BEEN warned. But she stood her ground, swallowing hard as she met his gaze.

She knew he wanted her, but she wasn't quite prepared for the masculine potency of his look. Yet he made no move to close the distance between them. As she watched a muscle in his jaw clench, she knew that he would not reach for her unless she made the first move.

Was reaching for him enough? Perhaps not.

Quickly, before she could tell herself she was doing the wrong thing, she pulled off the T-shirt she was wearing and tossed it onto the floor. Then she reached around to unhook the clasp of her bra, which she sent to join the shirt.

She saw his eyes burn as they took in the sight of her breasts. If she hadn't been sure of what she wanted, the scorching look on Wyatt's face might have sent her running. Instead, in one smooth motion she slid her jeans and panties down her legs and kicked them away so that she was standing in front of him, naked.

He stayed where he was, and for a terrible moment she thought that she had made a mistake.

Chapter Fourteen

Then Carrie saw the fire in his eyes flare. He began to do what she had done, unbuttoning the dress shirt he wore and tossing it away. Next he unbuckled his belt, then slid his slacks and briefs down his legs until he was as naked as she was—and fully aroused.

"I knew you would be beautiful," he said, ending with a low sound of need as he closed the distance between them and pulled her into his arms.

It had all happened so fast that her head was spinning. The shock of his naked body against hers was like a flare of electricity between them.

She was unable to hold back a gasp as his hands caressed her back and shoulders, then slid down her spine to stroke the curve of her bottom.

She did the same, touching him in all the places she could reach.

As the two of them rocked together, they found each other's mouths in a savage kiss that had been building since the first time they had met. Only neither one of them had understood the implications of that meeting.

She kissed him with a driving need that she hoped said all the things she wanted to say to him. And he returned the passion, making the blood pound through her veins.

When his mouth lifted, his breath was ragged, and the skin

of his face was stretched taut. "Tell me to stop," he said. "I can still stop if I hear you say no."

"I thought I'd already made that impossible," she answered. "What else do I need to do?"

Reaching between them, she found his erection and clasped him in her hand, feeling the hot, solid weight of him.

He made a strangled sound that ended with a laugh. "I give up. But you'd better stop if you don't want this to be over before it's barely begun."

As she dropped her arm to her side, he moved her far enough away so that he could lift and shape her breasts in his hands, then stroked the hardened tips as he slid hot kisses onto her neck and shoulders. There were no coherent words to express what she was feeling, only the low, breathy sounds of two people caught in a spiral of hunger for each other.

She forgot where they were or where they had been. Forgot everything but the taste of him, the feel of his hands and mouth on her hot flesh, the overwhelming satisfaction of being with him like this.

He took her hand and led her to the bed, where he turned back the covers. When she lay down, he followed her onto the yielding surface.

Reaching up, she stroked his face, ran her fingers over his lips, heard him draw in a shaky breath.

Slowly, almost reverently, he reached for her, holding her close and dropping tiny kisses over her cheeks, her hairline, her ears, before coming back to her mouth for a long, lingering kiss as his hands molded her breasts.

"I dreamed of all the ways I wanted to touch you and kiss you," he said in a thick voice, then lowered his head to one distended nipple.

She cupped the back of his head, caressing his thick hair as he began to draw on her. His hand sought the other peak, pulling and tugging, sending heat rocketing downward through her body.

Lost in a world of sensation, she could only lie against the pillows, her hands dallying over his back and spine.

When his mouth returned to hers, it was infinitely gentle and tender as his hands moved down her body, stroking and caressing their way to the swollen folds of her sex, sending a surge of sensation through her, making her arch her hips toward him.

He knew how to please a woman, how to feed her arousal almost beyond endurance. Her need built until she was clinging to him, calling his name, begging him to fill the empty ache inside her.

"Wyatt, I need you. Don't make me wait."

He levered his body over hers, and she guided him into her. He made a sound of gratification deep in his throat, telling her how much he needed her.

It was the same for her. She had no words to say how good this was. She could only continue to touch him and kiss him.

When he began to move, she was lost to anything but the power of this man—in her, over her, surrounding her.

He set the rhythm, and she knew this joining was too intense to last for long. The tempo quickened, lifting her to a high plane where the air was almost too thin to breathe. She clung to him, feeling her body quicken, then burst with sensations so intense that she cried out with the pleasure of it.

She felt him go rigid, heard his shout of satisfaction as he followed her into the whirlwind. They clung together as they drifted back to earth.

He rolled to his side, and she moved with him, hugging him to her as they lay together on the bed.

He gathered her close, his lips skimming her hair, her damp face, her lips.

When the cool air on her damp skin made her shiver, he reached to pull the covers over them and settled beside her.

As the silence stretched, she understood that neither of them was sure about what to say. Everything had changed.

Yet at the same time, nothing had changed. For the past half hour she had thought only of him. Now reality intruded again. They were on the run from men who had vowed to kill her. And the only thing that stood between her and them was Wyatt Hawk.

He held her for long moments, and she allowed herself the luxury of drifting off to sleep in his arms. She wasn't sure how long she slept, but when the light began to fade, she woke when he started to ease away.

She reached out and grabbed his wrist.

"I'm sorry. I didn't mean to wake you."

The tone of his voice made her turn her head and look at him. "Don't say we shouldn't have made love," she murmured as he sat up.

"Are you a mind reader?"

"No, I've learned to read Wyatt Hawk."

"I was hired to keep you safe."

"You are."

"Do you call this keeping watch?"

"We're in a bed-and-breakfast where nobody knows us."

"I'm hoping that's true."

"I think we should test out the theory of whether this was a good idea or not."

"What do you mean?"

"This." She sat up and reached for him, pulling him into her arms and lifting her mouth to his.

She was shocked at how aggressive she'd become, but apparently, she was going to have to make her wishes clear, at least until they were out of danger and Wyatt stopped telling himself he was neglecting his duties.

At first, she knew he was thinking he should drag himself out of bed. But as she kissed him and touched him, she knew she was having an effect on him. And she was gratified when he let her drag him down to a horizontal position again.

She kept him busy for another hour, finding out what he

liked and loving the way he returned the favor as they explored each other's bodies.

She was smiling when she finally lay back against the pillow, totally satisfied.

Wyatt stayed beside her for a few minutes, then cleared his throat. "I'd like to take you out for a good dinner, but I think it's better if I bring something back."

"Agreed."

He climbed out of bed, and she admired his body as he found his clothes and pulled them on.

"What do you want?" he asked.

"Surprise me."

He left the cottage and was gone for half an hour, during which she showered and got dressed. When he came back, she caught the tempting aroma of Italian food.

"I got veal and chicken," he said. "You can have your pick."

"Good choices. We can share."

He'd even bought a bottle of wine, which they also shared. The meal gave her a glimpse of what life could be like with Wyatt Hawk under normal circumstances.

In the next moment, she brought herself up short. She shouldn't be thinking about life with Wyatt. At least not until they'd rescued her father—and figured out what to do about the men who were after them.

But they'd made love, and she wasn't into one-night stands. She'd been thinking about the future all along. The problem was getting her dinner companion to think along the same lines.

Toward the end of the meal, he seemed preoccupied.

"Earth to Wyatt Hawk," she said.

He looked up. "Sorry. I was thinking about what I'm supposed to be doing. You know, my job."

He pushed away from the table and brought over his laptop. As he waited for Douglas Mitchell's files to load, he said,

"Keep everything in the suitcase, in case we need to make a quick getaway."

"You think we will?"

"Like I said, be prepared."

She cleaned up after the meal, then sat beside him, watching him scrolling through information, before stopping to read something more carefully.

"What?"

"I'm seeing notations of money transfers."

She leaned over and looked at the screen, which showed a spreadsheet. "From where to where?"

"I'm not sure. The institution names are coded." He looked up at her. "Would he be trying to hide money to avoid paying taxes on it?"

She sighed, thinking about his business practices over the years. "He might. He didn't like giving the government more taxes than he absolutely had to."

"And most of his income was from investments?"

"Yes." She stared at the numbers on the screen. "I guess there's no way to figure out where the accounts are?"

"Not all the files are here. I need more information."

She stood up and paced to the window, looking out into the darkness. Had her father been doing something shady with his money? Or what if the problems Inez had mentioned were making him act erratically?

She wished they had the rest of the files, but they weren't going back to her father's house for them.

"You should get some sleep," Wyatt said.

"What about you?"

"I want to see if I can get anything more out of this stuff."

She climbed into bed, and after the day she'd had, she was asleep almost instantly.

The next thing she knew, Wyatt was putting a hand on her arm.

Her eyes blinked open, and she saw him standing beside her, wearing a T-shirt and jeans.

"Hi," she murmured.

"Sorry to wake you up, but I want to get out of here early."

"What time is it?"

"Six-thirty. Get dressed, and I'll ask Mrs. Williamson if we can eat early."

When he started to pull away, she sat up and gave him a quick kiss.

He kissed her back, but she wondered if he was regretting getting so close to her yesterday.

As he left the cottage, she climbed out of bed and stretched, then padded into the bathroom.

WYATT LEFT CARRIE in the cabin and walked through the back garden toward the main house.

He could hear classical music playing as he stepped through the back. Other guests must be up, he thought as he heard Mrs. Williamson talking to a man with a deep voice.

Then the man's words reached him, and he went very still as he heard the name Carrie Mitchell.

He couldn't hear Mrs. Williamson's response, but just the mention of Carrie's name was enough for him to know that he had to get her the hell out of here.

Either this guy was from the police or the Feds, or he was pretending to be a cop.

For several seconds he debated what to do while cursing himself for leaving his gun back at the cottage. And for what he and Carrie had been doing yesterday. He'd known it was a bad idea, but he'd let her—

He stopped that thought cold. *Don't blame that on her,* he told himself.

Quickly he backed out the way he'd come and ran through the garden to the cottage. When he burst in, Carrie was just pulling on a T-shirt.

"What?" she asked when she saw the expression on his face.

"Someone's found us."

"The terrorists?"

"I don't know."

"What are we going to do?" she asked, her voice filled with panic.

"Ambush him. He doesn't know we know he's here." He pulled the curtains aside and peered out the window, then cursed.

"What?"

"I only heard one guy talking to Mrs. Williamson, but two of them are heading this way. We're going to try to take them without shooting."

"How?"

"They think they've got surprise on their side."

He was still silently cursing as he tried to revise his plans. He wanted to send Carrie out the back window, but he had no idea if the two guys were coming in the front or if one of them was going around back. Presumably, they were both armed, and he had only one weapon. Looking wildly around, he spotted the twin brass lamps on the bedside tables. After pulling them out by the cords and popping off the shades, he kept one for himself and shoved the makeshift club into Carrie's hands.

The lamps had a longer reach than using the butt of his gun to whack the guys. Or would it be better to shoot the bastards and run? That made sense unless it really was the authorities coming to apprehend them.

His thinking time was cut off abruptly by a knock at the door.

Ask who's there, he mouthed to Carrie.

"Who is it?" she called out.

"Breakfast from Mrs. Williamson."

Carrie glanced at him for instructions.

Stall, he mouthed.

"We're not dressed," she said. "Give us a minute."

He bent to Carrie's ear. "Open the door and step back against the wall, beside me."

Her face was pale as she approached the door. "Just a minute." Reaching out, she turned the knob and stepped beside Wyatt, who was already in position against the wall.

Two men barreled into the sitting room, guns drawn.

Wyatt took the first intruder down with a sharp blow to the back of the head, using the lamp. The man dropped with a satisfying groan of surprise.

The other stopped short, figured out the trap and tried to whirl toward Wyatt, but he tripped over his buddy, who was lying on the floor by the door. Carrie slammed him with her lamp. Wyatt gave him another blow just to make sure he was sufficiently immobilized.

He handed Carrie his gun as he stepped around the two men. "Cover them."

"Who are they?"

"We'll try to find out."

He closed the door, then bent to the unconscious men, rifling through their pockets.

Each of them had a wallet with what looked like a Federal identification card.

Carrie saw the cards and drew in a quick breath.

"They could be fake. I want to tie these guys up and ask some questions."

He was looking around for something to use when he heard the sound of police sirens in the distance.

Carrie's eyes widened. "How did they find us?"

"I didn't hear the whole conversation this guy had with Mrs. Williamson. Maybe she saw a news report about us and figured it out. Maybe she was suspicious of these guys and called the cops. Whatever's going on, we can't stay here."

He grabbed the suitcases, stuffed his laptop inside and headed for the door, ushering Carrie ahead of him. As soon as they'd gotten into the car, he started off, taking a loop road around the property. As they reached the exit, he saw a police car driving toward their cottage. It stopped, and two uniformed officers got out.

He didn't stay to find out what was going to happen next. Exiting the property, he headed toward the center of Frederick.

"How did those men find us?" Carrie asked in a thick voice.

"Like I said, if it's the cops, Mrs. Williamson could have called them. Or if it's the terrorists, when they realized the tracker was gone, they started beating the bushes."

"Like how?"

"They must have drawn a radius around where I left the tracker, then began searching places where we might have driven to."

"That would take a lot of manpower."

"Which makes it sound like they're desperate to find us."

"If we can't go to a motel or a bed-and-breakfast, what are we going to do?"

"Either find a place to sleep in the car or do some breaking and entering."

She sucked in a sharp breath. "I don't like that."

"Neither do I, but we may not have much choice."

CARRIE TURNED HER head to look at Wyatt's grim profile. "You're thinking that we could have gotten caught while we were making love," she said.

"You're damn right."

"You had no way of knowing that was going to happen."

"I told you, my job is guarding you, not setting you up to get captured or killed."

"You didn't. I was the one who started it."

"And I should never have gotten so close to you."

The words stung, but she understood where they were

coming from. He'd made a mistake. Or she'd put him in a position where it was almost impossible for him to turn away from her. That hadn't been a smart move on her part. To put it mildly. But she'd wanted him, and she'd gotten what she'd wanted. At least for that moment. She hoped she hadn't won the battle and lost the war.

She cut him another glance and saw that his grim expression hadn't changed. It made her feel like she had that first week at the safe house, when he'd deliberately kept his distance from her. He was doing it again. This time she understood why.

She wanted to reach out and lay her hand over his, but she didn't do it because she knew what reception she would get. Better to try to play by his rules until this was all over. Then she could go back to where they had been. Or could she?

Beside her, Wyatt cleared his throat, and she tensed.

"I was thinking we should look for a place to hide out," he said slowly. "But now I think that won't work."

Chapter Fifteen

"What do you mean?" Carrie asked. "Where else could we go?"

"What if we went back to Rock Creek Park, to the place where you first saw those guys plotting?"

A shiver went through her when she remembered her last visit to that location. Catching her reaction, he pressed his hand over hers.

"Sorry. I guess it's not the place you'd choose to visit."

She swallowed. "Why do you want to go there?"

"Because we may find something there that we can use."

"I'm pretty sure the D.C. cops and the Park Police scoured the woods."

"But maybe they weren't looking for the right thing. Maybe if you'd been along to point them in the right direction, they would have come up with something useful."

She nodded, remembering that all she'd wanted to do when she'd heard the terrorist plot was get out of there.

"The police wouldn't let me come back."

"Because they were being supercautious."

"And we're not?"

"In this case, it's the last thing anyone would expect."

He had been heading toward Baltimore. When he came to the place where the road split, he took the Route 270 option—toward D.C.

"LETTING YOU GET up to use the bathroom is a pain in the butt," one of Douglas Mitchell's captors muttered.

"Sorry."

"Yeah, this prisoner thing is getting old," the other guy added. "Next time maybe we'll leave you to pee in your pants."

"Why are you doing this to me?" Douglas asked. "It's for money, right? I can pay you more than whoever hired you to do this."

"Shut up if you don't want to get whacked," the first one said.

Douglas clamped his lips together as he sat down on the hard iron bed while the young man fastened his arm to the side rail again. There was a metal cuff around his wrist and a metal bolt attached to the bed. But the middle part of the bond was some kind of nylon rope. The young man standing over him set down a paper plate beside Douglas on the bed. The plate had a peanut butter and jelly sandwich. Beside it was a bottle of water. The men left the food and drink, then marched out of the room. It was obvious that they'd expected this hostage situation to be over a lot sooner, and now they were taking out their annoyance on their captive.

After they closed the door, Douglas listened intently. He could hear angry voices raised, men arguing with each other.

"We were supposed to be outta here by now."

"When are we going to get our money?"

"And what about Bobby? We just leave him hanging out to dry?"

"He shouldn't have got his ass caught."

Douglas strained his ears, but he didn't hear anything else for a few moments. Then another of the men spoke up.

"I say we see how much we can get out of the old guy."

"That wasn't the deal."

"The deal is what we can make it."

There was more arguing, but they'd apparently moved too far away for him to hear clearly.

How many of them were out there? Altogether, he'd seen four, but he suspected there were more men involved.

Douglas took a couple bites of the sandwich and washed it down with some water. He hadn't eaten peanut butter and jelly since he'd been a kid. It tasted comforting, and he wondered why he hadn't asked for it more recently.

He finished the sandwich, then reached into his pocket and pulled out something he'd found in the bathroom. A broken piece of glass that had fallen behind the toilet. If he'd been paying to have the house cleaned, he would have been angry that there was something sharp in the bathroom.

Instead, he was elated. It was a weapon, and maybe he could use it to saw through the nylon rope that held him to the bed. It would take a long time, but he had nothing but time—until these men got the word that his daughter was dead. Then they wouldn't need him anymore. He cursed under his breath, thinking of Carrie and himself. Then he firmed his lips.

He turned the rope over so that the bottom side was up. Then he laid the raw edge of the glass against the fibers and began to pull it back and forth with a sawing motion. Of course, trying to get free was risky, which was why he was working on the bottom of the rope. If his captors figured out what he'd been trying to do, they would surely punish him. Maybe even kill him. But he had to take the chance.

He glanced up, looking around the room. Could he get out the window if he freed himself? And how would he get away? He knew there was a boat down at the dock. Maybe he could escape by water. He'd have to figure out that part when he got free.

NEITHER CARRIE NOR Wyatt spoke much on the trip into D.C., except when Wyatt cursed as he hit the usual morning Beltway traffic.

She knew he was tense. She was, too, but she tried to tell herself they were doing something positive—so far as they could do anything that would help them.

They took Connecticut Avenue into the District, then turned off onto Military Road, heading for the part of the park where she'd been taking pictures when she'd heard the men talking—and disrupted her whole life.

"You were photographing an eagles' nest?" he asked, as they drew near to the picnic area.

"Yes."

"And you remember where it was?"

"Yes. I've been there a lot of times. I've got pictures of the parents getting the nest ready for laying eggs, pictures of the just-hatched babies, pictures of them growing up. I was going to do an article on the eagle family."

He nodded, and she wondered what he thought about her fascination with the eagles. Sometimes she wondered the same thing. She loved the domestic details of raptor life. But not the domestic details of human life?

Had she used her nature photography work as an excuse to stay out of relationships? She hadn't thought of that until this moment, and she mulled over the concept as she directed him to the right part of the park.

It was still early, and no one was at the picnic site. Still, as she'd expected he would, Wyatt didn't stop immediately but drove slowly past, scouting out the location.

"I parked around the other side, and came in through the woods," she said, pointing out a side road that wound through the park. It wasn't like Central Park in New York or any park that had been tamed into a human notion of what would make a good outdoor play area. Instead, most of the acreage was woodland that had been left pretty much as it had been before the city had grown up around it. There were deer, squirrels, raccoons and all sorts of wildlife in the area. Probably even coyotes that had made it that far east, although she hadn't seen any. And, of course, lots of birds.

They pulled up in a shaded area, and she led Wyatt through the woods to the huge oak tree where the eagles had made their nest about eighty feet from the ground.

"I wonder how much the babies have grown since I was here last," she whispered.

"Are they afraid of people?" he asked.

"Not really. I mean, anybody who tried to climb up and bother them would probably get their eyes pecked out. Plus the eagles are at the top of their food chain, so they're not worried about predators. There are some threats to the eggs and the young birds. Like raccoons. But the parents guard the nest. The mother's on there with them at night, and the father is on a nearby branch." She kept talking, relating more eagle facts to keep her mind off her last visit here.

But she finally asked, "The terrorists wouldn't be watching this place, would they?"

"More likely they'd avoid it," Wyatt answered.

They moved quietly through the trees, and she pointed toward the oak, then upward where the parents had built their giant nest in a triangle formed by three large branches.

Wyatt stared at the structure. "Impressive."

"It's about the size of a Volkswagen Beetle and weighs a thousand pounds."

"Hard to believe that two birds can build something like that."

"The male picks the location and does most of the nest building. And the female helps keep it in good shape. It's amazing what size branches they can bring in."

"You've obviously spent a lot of time watching them."

"Yes. And there are websites where you can read about eagle behavior. One of my favorites is in Decorah, Iowa."

"Did you name these birds?"

"I thought about it, but they're wild creatures. I called the parents Mom and Dad and the two babies RC One and RC Two."

"For Rock Creek?"

"Yes."

He nodded, looking up at the nest, but she saw he was dividing his time between it and the surrounding woods.

As she focused on the nest, one of the young eagles moved to the very edge of the nest and looked down at them from its high perch.

Wyatt stared at the large black bird. "You're telling me that's a bald eagle?"

"Yes."

"But he's all black."

"They don't get white feathers on their heads and tails until they're four or five years old. These are only a few months old. The last time I was here, they hadn't branched yet," Carrie murmured.

"What does that mean?"

"It means fly to a nearby branch that's within easy reach of the nest."

"I guess that gives new meaning to the phrase 'branching out.'"

"Yes. That must be where it came from. After that, they fledge. Which means fly away from the home tree before coming back."

As they watched, the young bird flapped its wings and took off in a graceful glide to another tree about fifty yards away.

She and Wyatt watched it land about forty feet up on the trunk of another oak. Not on a branch that could hold its weight. Something else.

"What's he standing on?" Wyatt asked.

"No idea. There are leaves in the way."

"He wasn't over there before?"

"Like I said, the last time I was here, the juvies were too

young to fly. I'd never seen any of them out of the nest until just now."

She followed Wyatt as he walked closer to the spot where the eagle perched, staring up at him. "He's not standing on anything natural," he muttered.

He moved to a different angle, and trained his binoculars on the bird.

"I can't see exactly what it is. Too many leaves."

He looked up and down, judging the distance from the ground to the first branch.

"I think I can get up there—if you give me a lift."

"Why do you want to?"

"There's just something about the location…" His voice trailed off, and he shrugged. "Can you make a stirrup out of your hands?"

"Yes."

He put down the binoculars then emptied his pockets, setting his wallet and everything else on the ground. "Ready."

She did as he'd asked, gritting her teeth as she took his weight.

"Sorry," he muttered. She struggled to hold steady while he reached for the lowest branch. He got his hands around it and began to pull himself up. When he winced, she remembered that he'd gotten shot in the arm a few days ago.

"Should you be doing that?" she asked.

"Have to."

He clenched his teeth and pulled himself up to the branch, then climbed onto the horizontal surface. After a moment, he hoisted himself up another level.

The young eagle, who had been looking down at the man invading his space, took off, flying to another tree a little farther away.

Carrie stood back where she could get a better view of what Wyatt was doing. Her stomach knotted as she watched him pull himself to a higher level.

Finally, he was even with the spot where the eagle had been standing.

When she heard him curse, she caught her breath.

"What?"

"Tell you when I get down."

He stayed where he was for several more minutes, and she wondered what he was doing.

Finally he came down, moving rapidly. When he got to the lowest branch, he used both hands to lower himself and jumped the final few feet, flexing his legs as he hit the ground. When he straightened, she saw that he had tucked something inside his shirt.

"What?"

"Come on. We're getting the hell out of here."

Wyatt put everything back in his pockets, then took Carrie's hand, leading her back toward the spot where they'd parked.

As soon as they were in the car, he drew out the thing he'd carried in his shirt.

"A video camera?" she asked.

"Yeah."

He put the camera on the console and drove away, alternating between looking ahead and checking the rearview mirror. It wasn't until they'd turned onto Connecticut Avenue that he breathed out a little sigh.

"I guess we got away." He turned toward her. "Someone was working surveillance on the area."

"But it's not unusual to have cameras trained on eagles' nests."

"That camera wasn't focused on the nest. It was pointed toward the ground."

"But why?"

"Because whoever put it there was hoping to see something, and I don't think there are cameras stationed to catch people making out at every picnic area in Rock Creek Park."

She absorbed that information. "You mean someone else knew that the terrorists were meeting at that particular location?"

"That's one explanation."

"But if they did, why didn't they move on them? Were they waiting for evidence?"

"And you stumbled into the middle of the plot? But if they were already tracking the terrorists, that means they knew about the plot weeks or months ago," Wyatt answered.

"They'd have what the terrorists said recorded, so they wouldn't need my testimony."

"Right."

"So what's going on?"

"You could say that the terrorists didn't know about the camera. They only knew that you had stumbled into their plot, and they were desperate to stop you. Remember, one of them is in custody. If you don't testify against him, they think there's no case." He dragged in a breath and let it out. "There's another way to look at it."

"Which is?"

"That someone knew you would be there and wanted to get pictures of you."

"That doesn't make sense. Why would they do that?"

Instead of answering, he asked, "Who knew where you were going to be doing nature photography?"

"I didn't tell anyone where I was taking photographs that day. But I did talk to my father about the eagles' nest. I told him I'd been watching them, and I told him some of the same things about eagle nesting behavior that I told you."

"Interesting. Which means Inez or Patrick could have overheard the conversation."

"Yes," she whispered.

"You talked to him over the phone?"

"Yes. Also, I was out there for dinner about a month ago.

Then later I came out to get some clothes I wanted. I also picked up one of my lenses."

"And you said why?"

"Maybe. I can't remember."

They were both silent as they considered the implications. Carrie watched Wyatt's grim expression as he headed toward Bethesda.

"So what if there's a conspiracy against *you?*"

She shuddered. "That would mean someone went to an awful lot of trouble."

"You have a better explanation?"

"Can we see what's on the camera?"

"Maybe." They had reached the Bethesda business district, and he slowed down, then pulled into a parking space in front of an electronics store.

"Wait here. Duck down so you're not so visible."

He got out, and she followed directions, scrunching down so that only the top of her head showed at window level. As she sat there, she could feel her heart pounding. She'd known all along that she was in trouble. It seemed that more and more stuff kept piling on.

Instead of thinking about that, she tried to focus on something constructive. They needed a place to hide out, and they had limited options. An idea struck her, but she didn't know how Wyatt would react.

When he came back, he had the camera inside a bag with something he'd purchased.

"What did you get?"

"A cable that will let me download the camera's contents to the computer—if there's anything to see."

Chapter Sixteen

"What's the chance of that?" Carrie asked.

"It depends on how much storage is in the camera. It could be like store surveillance that erases the footage every week or so."

She nodded.

"Now we have to find a place where we can look at it."

"I was thinking about that," she said.

"Where?"

"Dad owns some property on the Severn River, in Arnold, Maryland. We have a house there, where we used to spend time in the summer."

"You don't use it now?"

"I think he still likes to stay there occasionally, but I haven't been with him."

"It's a possibility, but there's a chance the terrorists could know about it. And I'd like to stay closer to the D.C. area if possible."

She nodded. "What are you thinking?"

He looked at her for a moment. "Sometimes the army clears an area of insurgents and then there's no reason to go back. We can use that technique in reverse."

"What do you mean?"

"We can go back to the Butlers' house. The one next to

your dad's." He paused. "I wasn't thinking about breaking in when I did my research."

"Maybe we don't have to use the main house. There's a guest cottage on the other side of the pool."

"Do you remember if it's got a direct line of sight to your dad's property?"

"I don't think so."

"Well, it's the last place they're likely to think we'd be, so we'll take a look at it."

She sighed. "I guess breaking into the guesthouse of someone you know is better than breaking into the house of a stranger."

He stopped at a commercial area, and he pointed to the array of fast-food restaurants. "Italian last night. What's your pleasure for brunch?"

She studied the options. "Let's go with Mexican."

"I wouldn't have figured you for that kind of food."

"Why not? I spent a summer in Costa Rica. Dad sent me to learn Spanish. I know Mexican isn't exactly the same, but it's similar. Well, the rice-and-beans part."

"Why did he want you to learn Spanish?"

"It was my idea. I was in high school, but I already knew I wanted to be a photographer, and I thought I'd probably travel in Latin America."

"That's very goal oriented."

"Yeah."

They pulled into the drive-through line, ordering burritos and tacos along with large cups of iced tea.

After paying for the purchases, they headed toward her father's house, giving her the feeling that they were traveling in circles.

When Wyatt drew near the Butler property, he kept alert for surveillance, then he drove slowly up the access road. He parked in the woods out of sight of the road and turned to Carrie.

"Wait until I give you the all clear. We might have to make a quick getaway."

He left the engine running as he took a quick circuit around the house, then checked for line of sight from the guesthouse to her father's place.

Still, he didn't motion for her to get out.

She saw him inspecting the door and windows of the guesthouse, and she figured he was checking for an alarm system.

Next he stood in front of the door, and she couldn't see what he was doing.

When he stepped back, she expected him to tell her to join him. Instead, he held up his hand, and she waited while he disappeared into the house. He was back in less than a minute and motioned her to get out of the car.

She turned off the engine, pulled the keys from the ignition and joined him at the open door. They both stepped inside, and she looked around at the cozy room.

Mrs. Butler hadn't bothered to clean out the cottage. She'd left the room furnished, and Carrie saw a couch, a couple of comfortable chairs, a dining set and a kitchen area along one wall.

She set the bags of food down on the table and flopped into one of the chairs.

"Long day," Wyatt said. "And it's only noon."

She nodded.

Wyatt set the camera and his laptop on the table beside the food.

As they ate, he booted up the computer and attached a USB cable from the camera to the computer.

She moved her chair around so that she could see the screen.

"I'm going to rewind to the beginning."

For a moment, the image on the screen was only black dots, and she thought maybe there was nothing to see. Then it cleared up and she got an image of men on the ground. "The terrorists," she murmured.

"Setting things up," Wyatt agreed.

They disappeared, and there was a long stretch of nothing but birds, squirrels and deer—and sometimes Carrie taking pictures of the eagles' nest.

"They were checking up on me."

"Right."

"There was probably more than one camera, and this was the only one left," Wyatt said.

He fast-forwarded through the normal forest footage. Finally the men came back.

"Is that the day I showed up and heard them?"

"We'll find out."

Before moving out of the shot, the men glanced up at the camera and at other trees where there must have been more spy cams.

"What are they looking at?" she asked.

"Checking to make sure everything's in place."

Then she saw herself, moving through the woods, her own camera in hand as she approached the eagles' nest.

Her breath caught as she stopped short. "That must be when I heard them."

"Yeah. Which makes it a pretty good guess that they were waiting for you."

"Could they send those images to a remote location?"

"Probably."

He stood up and paced the living room. "Your overhearing them was all a setup, I think."

"But why?"

"I don't know yet."

Carrie moved restlessly in her seat. She didn't want to think about what this hidden footage meant, and she found herself searching for another subject to focus on.

She knew Wyatt wasn't going to like her next question.

Chapter Seventeen

Carrie finished a bite of burrito and looked up at the man who'd spent almost every waking minute with her since they'd gotten in that town car to go downtown.

"You told me you blame yourself for your partner's getting killed in Greece. Why was it your fault?"

It wasn't until the words were out of her mouth that she realized they probably sounded like an accusation to him.

He reared back as though she'd come at him with a baseball bat.

"That's not relevant."

"I think it is."

"Because you don't trust me?" he asked in a gritty voice.

"Because I want to hear what's making you so sure that you did the wrong thing."

He slapped his drink back onto the table and glared at her, but she didn't back down.

"What kind of assignment were you on?"

"We were posing as a tourist couple traveling around the country looking at ancient sites, but we were really tracking down a terrorist cell."

"In Greece?"

"Yeah, they thought it was a good place to hide out."

When he didn't elaborate, she prompted him. "Did you find them?"

"We traced them to a fishing village, and then we lost their trail."

"And then what?"

"We spent the night at a little pension." He kept his voice hard. "And we made love that night. Which we shouldn't have done, of course."

"Whose idea was that?"

He shook his head. "It was a mutual decision."

Getting the information was like pulling teeth because he kept stopping. And every time he did, she felt her own tension mount. But she'd started this, and she wasn't going to let him off the hook, even if she was going to hate what she heard. "And then?" she asked again.

"And then in the morning when I woke up, Gina wasn't in the room."

"You'd told her to go out and do something?"

His voice jolted up a notch. "I'd told her not to go off on her own. I'd told her to stay with me, and she didn't obey orders."

The look on his face made her insides twist, but she stayed where she was and let him tell the rest of the story in his own way.

"We'd been talking to some of the locals, and it looked like they might have some information, if we could gain their trust. I think she had some kind of idea that she could locate the terrorists and get credit for her big discovery. Instead, she was struck by a car along the road as she was walking toward the center of town. It was set up to look like a hit-and-run accident. Two years have passed and they've never found out who plowed into her."

"It could have really been an accident."

"I don't think so. I think the terrorists knew we were getting close, and they wanted to send me a message."

"How can you blame yourself for that?"

"I blame myself for not having better control of the situation."

"It sounds to me like she had made her own decision, and you couldn't do anything about it."

"I was the senior agent. The one in charge!" he shouted.

"And you felt guilty about sleeping with her. Maybe that was unprofessional. But the rest of it wasn't your fault. She didn't have to go out in the morning. You weren't even there when she was killed."

He glared at her. "You're making assumptions."

"So are you."

When she started to speak again, he stood up and marched out of the guest cottage. She could see him standing by the pool, his back to her and his shoulders rigid.

She knew he was angry at her, questioning assumptions that he'd carried around for the past two years, but he meant too much to her to just keep her mouth shut.

He was clenching and unclenching his fists, and she was pretty sure he wanted to drive away and leave her at the guest-house. But he couldn't do it because he had an obligation to her and her father.

She picked up her burrito and took a bite, but the food felt like cement in her mouth. After washing it down with a sip of iced tea, she got up and went into the bathroom, where she splashed water on her face. Then she walked into the bedroom of the guest cottage, kicked off her shoes and lay down on the bed. Maybe if she wasn't in the living room Wyatt would come back inside.

When she heard him in the living room, she tensed. His footsteps stopped, and she thought he might be wondering where she'd gone. Then he charged across to the bedroom.

"Come on."

"Where?"

"I spotted Patrick's Lexus leaving the property, and I want to follow him."

She jumped up, put her shoes back on and followed Wyatt to the car.

As he took off down the drive, she buckled her seat belt. "I thought you wanted to go back to Dad's house and get into his computer again."

"Yeah. It was a tough decision, but I decided that following Patrick is more important."

Neither of them mentioned the previous discussion, and she wasn't going back to it now.

She was glad they had something to focus on besides the two of them as Wyatt drove back toward the D.C. area, staying back so that Patrick wouldn't know he was being followed. The technique was nerve-racking, because a couple of times Wyatt lost sight of their quarry, but he reappeared again each time.

"I don't believe he's thinking about being followed," Carrie murmured.

"Why not?"

"Because he's not doing anything evasive."

"Yeah, unless he knows we're here, and he's leading us into a trap."

She sucked in a sharp breath. "Why would he do that?"

"I don't have a handle on his motivation. I only know that I don't trust him."

She nodded, trying to rearrange her picture of Patrick Harrison. She'd known him all her life, and she'd considered him a friend. But now she couldn't be sure of him. Or of Inez, for that matter.

Wyatt let a couple of cars get between him and Patrick as they merged onto the Capital Beltway, and he stayed a few cars back.

With the volume of traffic, it was easier to follow him without danger of being spotted as he headed toward the city, but Patrick got off on the exit leading to Wisconsin Avenue.

When Patrick reached the Bethesda business district, he turned off onto a side street, then slowed as he came to a

Starbucks, peering in the window. He pulled into a parking garage, and Wyatt and Carrie drove past.

"I think he's meeting someone there," Wyatt said. "I'm going to find a parking place. You follow him, but don't let him see you."

"Right."

She got out and pretended to be inspecting the handbags in the window of a specialty shop.

Patrick came out of the parking garage and walked rapidly back to the Starbucks, not paying attention to anyone around him.

He went inside, and she wondered what she should do.

A few minutes later, a woman came up the block, heading for the same coffee shop. Carrie blinked, wondering if her eyes were giving her the correct image. She kept staring, unable to believe what she was seeing.

Patrick was meeting Rita Madison.

The idea blew her mind.

Once Rita was inside, Carrie edged closer, moving to the window where she could peek inside. Rita and Patrick had their heads together, speaking to each other.

When Rita started to look up, Carrie pulled back so that she was no longer visible through the window.

At that moment, she sensed someone behind her and froze.

"It's me," Wyatt whispered. As she relaxed, he asked, "Who's he meeting?"

"You won't believe it. Rita Madison. And she looks more like her old self than last time we saw her—at least the way you described her."

"What do you mean?

"She's got on makeup. And she must have had her hair done."

"Interesting. Like she's out of mourning real fast." He waited a beat and put his hand on Carrie's arm, drawing her away from the window. "If I leave you alone here for a few minutes, will you be okay?"

"Of course."

"Stay out of sight. I'll be back as quickly as I can. If they come out, go into the shop next door."

She nodded.

WYATT FELT HIS stomach knot. He was leaving her in a vulnerable position, but there were two urgent pieces of business, and he couldn't take care of both of them at the same time. Praying that nothing would happen to her while he was gone, he sprinted down the block, hoping he could accomplish his mission in time. Lucky for him that they were near the same electronics shop where he'd picked up the USB cable earlier.

He rushed through the door and stopped short when he saw several customers waiting in line.

Pushing his way to the counter, he said, "I need a GPS tracker."

"You have to wait your turn, buddy," the guy to his right said in a loud voice.

"This is an emergency," he said.

"What? Your wife is hanging out with another guy?"

"Something like that."

The clerk pointed to a section of electronics devices hanging on the wall.

Wyatt strode to them, grabbed a package and looked at the price. He also scanned the directions and found the batteries he needed. He came back to the counter and threw down two fifty-dollar bills.

"Hey, wait," the clerk called out.

"In a hurry," he shouted over his shoulder.

He was out of there two minutes after he'd entered, and he didn't know if he'd taken too much time.

His next stop was the garage where he'd seen Patrick pull in. He started jogging up the ramp, looking at the cars, opening the package as he ran. He found Patrick's Lexus on the third level and stood panting while he opened the GPS and shoved in the batteries. When a green light went on, he knelt down and stuck the thing under the front bumper, hoping that this ploy was going to work.

Again he sprinted back the way he'd come, heading for the Starbucks and wondering if he was going to bump into Patrick or Rita on the way.

He got back to find Carrie where he'd left her.

"They're still in there?"

"Yes."

She stepped back, and he took her position, watching the man and woman talking inside. It looked as though they knew each other pretty well. What the hell was going on with them?

Patrick broke off to get in the coffee-order line, and Rita sat down at a table, her back to the window, presumably so that she could keep an eye on Patrick.

There were several people in line in front of him, and he moved slowly to the front.

Behind Wyatt, Carrie asked, "Where were you?"

"Tell you later."

"Let me see what's happening in there."

He and Carrie exchanged places again. After a few minutes, Carrie backed away.

"They're pushing their chairs back. I think their meeting is over."

He took her hand and hurried her to the next shop, which turned out to sell handbags.

"Can I help you?" the clerk asked.

"I want to find something special for my wife," Wyatt said.

When Carrie gave him a questioning look, he wondered why he'd used that word. But it had just come out of his mouth unbidden.

Carrie picked up a leopard-print purse and pretended to be interested while Wyatt kept his gaze on the street.

"Isn't it pretty?" the clerk said. "It's on sale for twenty percent off."

Carrie nodded, dividing her gaze between the purse and the entrance to the coffee shop. First Patrick came out and walked back toward the parking garage.

A few minutes later, Rita emerged and hesitated. For a moment, Wyatt was afraid that the woman was going to come into the purse shop, but she kept walking down the street.

"Come on," Wyatt said to Carrie.

As he started to leave the shop, the clerk called out, "That purse is a closeout. I can give you a better deal."

"Thanks so much," Carrie answered, "but we're still thinking about what to get."

Once on the street they headed in the direction that Rita had taken, putting other shoppers between themselves and their quarry. She turned down the cross street and walked to a nearby bank, where she disappeared inside.

Wyatt motioned Carrie to a passageway between two shops, where they waited in the shadows.

"What do you think they were doing?" Carrie asked.

"I'm not sure, but I assume it's nothing on the up-and-up. I mean, how do they even know each other?"

Carrie shook her head.

Rita was inside the bank for twenty minutes. When she emerged, she wore an annoyed expression.

"I guess that didn't go well."

"Are we going to follow her?" Carrie asked.

"If we can do it without her spotting us." They trailed half a block behind as Rita walked in and out of a couple of shops, then headed for the garage where Patrick had parked.

They waited until she'd disappeared inside, then got into his rental. By the time they'd paid, Rita's car was already down the block, but Wyatt caught up and kept pace with her. The surveillance did not turn out to be particularly productive, since she was only heading back to her condo.

When she turned into the garage, Wyatt continued on past.

"Now what?" Carrie asked.

"We go back to Patrick."

"You mean follow him home?"

"I hope that's not where he's going. The reason I left you alone outside Starbucks was to buy a tracker, like the one someone put on my car. And I slapped it under Patrick's bumper."

"Good thinking."

"But I'm betting he wasn't even looking. We can follow him and find out where he's going." As he drove, Wyatt got out the other part of the device, a GPS that kept them apprised of Patrick's location. Douglas Mitchell's chief of staff was heading along the Capital Beltway again.

"He could be going home."

"We'll see." Wyatt switched the subject back to Rita. "What if Rita was feeding us a bunch of bull when we talked to her?"

"About what?"

"Everything. What if that book has nothing to do with gambling debts?"

"Then what?"

"We have to find out."

Instead of heading for the Mitchell estate, Patrick took I-95 toward Baltimore.

He skirted around Baltimore and turned in the general direction of Annapolis. Wyatt stayed well back because there was no need to keep the vehicle in sight. They could follow perfectly well using the GPS.

Carrie caught her breath as he swung onto East Oak Road.

"I think I know where he's going."

Wyatt turned his head toward her, then back to the road. "Yeah?"

"Remember I told you about the house my father owns on the river in Arnold? This is the route you take to get there."

"Patrick's going to your father's house? That's an interesting development. Okay, tell me everything you remember about the property."

She organized her thoughts.

"It was an old bungalow that my dad bought maybe thirty years ago and fixed up. The property's worth a lot because it's right on a bluff overlooking the river. The access road is about a hundred yards long. The house is one story. There are three bedrooms and a great room. Nothing fancy. In back there's a gravel walkway and stairs that lead down to a dock. Dad keeps a motorboat there."

"Is there a garage?"

"Yes, a big detached one on one side."

"So cars could be hidden inside."

"Yes."

"Is there a lot of cover on the grounds?"

"Yes. Lots of trees and shrubs. And probably underbrush that's grown up, since I don't think Dad has a gardener down here."

They stayed well back as Patrick headed down the road, then disappeared onto a long drive winding through a wooded lot that completely hid the dwelling from view.

"What's he doing here?" Carrie murmured.

"I guess we'll find out."

Wyatt continued for another hundred yards until he found a place where he could turn off. When he climbed out, he checked his Sig.

Carrie eyed the weapon. "You're expecting trouble?"

"I don't know what to expect. I mean, why is Patrick here at all? Did Rita send him here? Or did something he told her give him the idea?"

Carrie shrugged, trying not to think the worst of a man she'd considered a friend for all of her life.

She hadn't been to this house by the river in years, but memories came flooding back as they stepped off the road and into the underbrush. She'd loved this place when she'd been a kid. Playing in the woods. Swimming in the river. Fishing from the pier. She and Patrick had made forts in the woods. Later, when they'd gotten older, they'd been allowed to take the motorboat out on the river. In the early days, there had been no air-conditioning in the house, and they'd slept out on the screened porch.

"There's a path through the woods," she whispered.

Or there had been. When she tried to find it, she found that nobody had kept it up, and the forest had closed in around the almost imperceptible trail.

"You'd better show me the way," Wyatt said, although it was obvious he didn't like the idea of her going first.

She took the lead position and started moving as quietly as possible toward the house, avoiding brambles and patches of poison ivy.

From the road, it was an uphill slog, and Carrie tried to keep the house in sight so that she wouldn't get lost as they navigated the wilderness area.

They passed a dilapidated structure.

"What's that?" Wyatt asked.

"That was one of the forts Patrick and I built. We used to play pioneer out here."

When they reached the edge of the woods, Wyatt stopped short. The house looked deserted, and Patrick's car was the only one in sight, parked beside a large heap of brush and sticks that had been piled up in the front yard and left there. He had turned his vehicle around, making it look as if he was poised for a quick getaway.

Carrie focused on the car and breathed out a little sigh when she saw Patrick through the window. He must have stayed in there for a few minutes. Now he was stepping out.

"What has he been doing all this time?" Carrie whispered.

"Don't know. Stay here."

As he got out of the vehicle, Patrick was focused on the house, not what might be in the woods behind him.

Wyatt sprinted forward and caught up with the man while he was still twenty yards from the building.

Pressing a gun into Patrick's back, he said, "Raise your voice or make a sudden move, and you're dead."

The other man went stock-still.

"What…what are you doing here?" he sputtered.

"I'll ask the questions," Wyatt answered. "Turn around and walk back toward the woods." He emphasized the order with a jab from the gun.

Patrick's gaze fixed on Carrie, and his eyes widened.

"You."

She raised one shoulder in a little shrug.

"Move."

Patrick finally unfroze from his position. Wyatt stayed behind him, marching him into the woods, where he couldn't be seen from the house—if there was anyone inside. Wyatt still didn't even know that.

He moved around to face Patrick. "What are you doing here?"

Patrick responded with a look of panic.

"Is someone here?" Wyatt prompted.

Carrie jumped into the conversation. "Did it have something to do with Rita?" she blurted, and Wyatt gave her a quick glance, sorry that she'd mentioned the other woman's name. He'd wanted to save that information as a surprise after he'd gotten the initial version of Patrick's story.

"What about Rita?" Patrick asked cautiously.

"You met with her," Carrie answered.

The look of panic on Patrick's face changed to one of cunning.

"Don't say anything else," Wyatt advised Carrie. "I want to find out what he's got to say."

Her face contorted, and he knew she realized that speaking impulsively might not be such a good idea.

"She asked to meet with me," Patrick said.

"About what? How do the two of you even know each other?"

"After her husband died, she contacted me because she knew about your being on the run."

Patrick turned to Carrie. "She gave me some information about your father. It's right here."

"About Dad?"

Patrick put his hands up. "I'm reaching into my pocket. I won't make any sudden moves." As he put his hand in his jacket pocket, Wyatt saw Carrie step closer to the man, no doubt eager to see what he had to show her.

"Stay back!" he shouted.

But it was already too late. Carrie darted forward, getting between Patrick and Wyatt's gun.

In the next second, Patrick grabbed Carrie, holding her in front of himself as he pulled out a gun and pressed it to her neck.

Chapter Eighteen

Wyatt froze.

"Drop your gun or I'll shoot her," Patrick ordered. "And don't think I won't do it."

"Patrick?" Carrie whispered.

"Shut up," he growled, and she clamped her lips shut.

Wyatt's only option was to obey.

Still holding Carrie, Patrick bent down and scooped up the weapon. But the man wasn't very good at hiding his intentions. As he held one gun on Carrie, he raised the hand with Wyatt's gun and fired.

Wyatt was already ducking behind a tree. More bullets followed him into the woods, but he could tell that Patrick wasn't much of a shot with his left hand. Ducking down, Wyatt waited in the shadows of the trees.

Behind Patrick, the door to the house opened. Peeking from behind a tree, Wyatt saw two young men emerge, both carrying guns. They looked like the terrorists he'd seen at the Federal Building and at the safe house.

"What's going on?" one of them shouted to Patrick.

"Carrie Mitchell and Wyatt Hawk showed up. I've got her. Hawk's in the woods. I've got his gun. You can blow him away."

The idea of leaving Carrie in Patrick's clutches made Wyatt's stomach knot, but he wasn't going to do her any good if he was dead.

As he turned and ran back the way he'd come, a bullet whizzed past him, and he heard the pounding feet of the pursuers.

He ducked low, making for a tangle of brambles and diving in, scratching himself as he hunkered down.

The two men were coming through the woods, mowing down underbrush as they searched for him.

Wyatt cursed under his breath. He hadn't been sure of Patrick's role in this plot. He still wasn't sure, but he knew that the man was willing to kill Carrie to get what he wanted.

Which was?

Wyatt felt his throat constrict. In the past few minutes, it had become clear that this whole plot had been about killing Carrie, and every second that passed put her in more danger.

Desperately, he tried to figure his best course of action.

The sounds in the woods told Wyatt that the men pursuing him had separated. From Wyatt's hiding place, he saw one of them approaching his location, but his attention was focused on something farther on—the fort that Carrie had pointed out on their way up from the road.

PATRICK MARCHED CARRIE into the house. As soon as they were inside, he said, "Take off that purse and toss it over here."

She removed the strap from across her chest, and he upended the purse onto the floor, then pushed her into a chair in the great room. "Stay there if you don't want to get hurt—yet."

She watched him sort through the contents of the pocketbook. When he found the cell phone, he slammed it against the floor, spewing out its guts.

"Is that what you used to call me and get me to drive into D.C. so you could search the house?"

"No."

"Liar. You were hiding in the pool shed, weren't you?"

She didn't answer.

There were three other men in the house watching her and Patrick. One was blond. His leg was bandaged, and he was leaning on a crutch. The two others had dark hair. Ordinary-looking young men, all of them. She recognized them as the terrorists from the park.

Patrick looked at them with an expression she recognized. He was pleased with himself and going to rub it in.

"You couldn't get her, but here she is," Patrick said.

"You're going to tell us you planned to have her show up?" the blond asked.

"No, but I know how to take advantage of a situation."

Carrie's stomach roiled. She was coping with her altered view of Patrick—and the stupidity of what she'd done. She'd trusted Patrick, and she'd been so desperate to get information about her father that she'd let him trick her into getting close, and now she was trapped.

"Where is my father?" she asked.

"Shut up," he snapped.

The blond young man leaned on his crutch and kept his gaze on Patrick. "This isn't working out the way it was supposed to. I'm shot in the leg. Bobby's still in custody, and he's not going free, is he?"

"It's not my fault that he got caught."

"This whole deal was your idea."

"Rita Madison's idea," Patrick corrected.

"How?" Carrie gasped out.

Patrick spared her a glance. "I said shut up."

"I trusted you."

"Oh, really? Is that why you sent me on that wild-goose chase into D.C. and hid in the pool shed?"

She could tell that really bothered him, and she knew she'd better answer carefully. "I didn't want to do it, but Wyatt insisted."

"Blame him," Patrick snarled.

"Patrick, I thought you and I were friends."

"Oh, sure. On a limited basis. You and your father always thought you were better than me."

"No. Of course not."

All along she'd thought Patrick was on her side, but now she understood that their friendship was only an illusion. She saw the hatred on his face. Hatred that she wouldn't have believed if she hadn't seen it for herself.

Still, she couldn't stop herself from trying to reach him. "Don't you understand that Dad gave you every advantage?"

Patrick snorted. "Not like he gave you."

"I'm his daughter."

"And I was always just an afterthought. Or later, someone convenient he could use for jobs that needed getting done."

Seeing she wasn't going to get him to change his mind, she asked, "You hatched this whole plot?"

"No. It was Rita's idea. But I liked the way she thinks. Big."

"But why?"

"After the way her husband was pissing away money with his compulsive gambling, she needed some cash, and I knew where I could get it. She had the connections to pull off what looked like a terrorist attack—and to set you up."

Carrie gripped the arms of the chair where she sat, trying to anchor herself to reality when the whole world felt as if it was sliding out from under her. Everything she'd thought about the past few days was all wrong. "Are you saying it wasn't really a terrorist attack at all?"

"In a way, it was. An attack on you and your father, actually." He laughed. "Rita knew exactly how it would go once you ratted out the 'terrorists.' She knew you'd end up down at the Federal Building."

"But why set up an elaborate scheme?"

"Don't you know the insurance policy your father bought you pays triple if you're killed in a terrorist attack?"

"He bought me an insurance policy?"

He grinned. "Well, I did it for him. He was so out of it that he didn't even know."

She felt sick as she stared at him in disbelief, trying to re-arrange years of thinking. Her father had done everything for this man, and it turned out that all he felt was resentment for not getting more. He'd hidden it well. She hadn't suspected a thing, but Wyatt had obviously had a very different view of her father's chief of staff. He hadn't trusted him from the beginning, and she should have listened to him.

Although bitterness had festered in Patrick for years, she wondered if he would have acted against her and her father without Rita.

But it was clear that he was enjoying crowing about his exploits, and she wanted to keep him talking, because the longer she stalled, the better chance Wyatt had to rescue her, and she had no doubt that he could do it.

"How did you meet Rita?" she managed to say.

"I was driving your father to a reception at her country club, and the old man let me come in and mingle with the guests. Rita and I hit it off right away."

"It was her idea to kidnap my father?"

"Yeah."

"Do you know where he is?"

"As a matter of fact, I do."

As they had gone back and forth in their revealing con-versation, Patrick had taken his gaze off the blond man with the crutch. Now the blond pulled out a gun and pointed it at Patrick.

"Enough of this blathering."

Patrick stared at him in disbelief. "I'm in charge here."

"Not anymore." He punctuated the announcement by rais-ing the gun and firing.

Carrie stared in disbelief as Patrick staggered back against the wall, blood spreading across his left shirtsleeve.

FROM HIS HIDING place, Wyatt heard a gunshot. Then everything was quiet again.

Lord, had Patrick or someone else in the house shot Carrie? What was going on in there?

Rage boiled up inside Wyatt—rage and disregard for his own safety. As one of the pursuers came close to the bramble thicket, Wyatt sprang out and grabbed the man, taking him totally by surprise and throwing him to the ground.

The gunman tried to twist around, tried to get his weapon into firing position, but Wyatt slammed his gun hand against a rock, and the man screamed.

"Eric?" the other guy shouted from what sounded like twenty-five yards away.

When Eric tried to answer, Wyatt slammed a fist into the man's face.

Blood leaked from his mouth, but he kept struggling. Wyatt pulled him up and slammed him against the ground, knocking the wind out of him.

He felt as though he had superhuman strength as he grappled with the guy, slamming him against the ground again and again until he went limp.

Wyatt picked up Eric's weapon, just as the other man came charging through the underbrush.

He saw Wyatt and fired.

A MUFFLED BLAST came from outside, then another. Two gunshots. Carrie's heart began to pound. When she started to spring out of the chair, one of the dark-haired men put a hand on her shoulder and pushed her down again.

"Stay put," he ordered.

"That's Eric or Cory taking care of your friend. What's his name? Wyatt?" the blond-haired man said.

"No," Carrie breathed. She *would not* believe that Wyatt was dead. Not the Wyatt Hawk who had saved her and himself so many times since the attack at the Federal Building.

These men had to be wrong. They couldn't see what was happening out there. They were just guessing, and if *she* had to guess, she'd say that it was the other way around. Wyatt had eliminated the threat from the other two men.

IN THE WOODS, the bullet missed Wyatt and hit Eric. Wyatt shot at the man charging forward, felling him with a slug to the chest. As he toppled over, Wyatt sprang up with Eric's gun in hand. When neither of the attackers moved, he knelt by each of them in turn, feeling for a pulse in the neck. There was none in either man.

He turned away from the two attackers he'd downed.

How many more were in the house, and was he in time to save Carrie?

With a gun in each hand, he ran toward the house through the woods. But when he reached the open area at the edge of the trees, he stopped.

At the moment he didn't give a damn what happened to himself, but he had to stay alive—to rescue Carrie. For so many reasons. But the one that came zinging into his mind was—he loved her.

The thought was so powerful, it nearly felled him.

He loved her? That conviction had slipped out without his conscious knowledge.

But as soon as he admitted it, he knew it was true. He'd fought against it with all the emotional resolve he could muster. In spite of that, he'd fallen in love with her, and if he couldn't save her life, there was no point in saving his.

Stopping behind a tree trunk, he scanned the facade of the house. All the shades were drawn, and as far as he could tell, nobody was looking out. Still, instead of rushing right to the dwelling, he moved cautiously through the woods, circling around so that he could come at the house from another angle.

He had to succeed. He was Carrie's only hope.

Chapter Nineteen

Carrie looked in horror from the gunman to Patrick and back again.

Patrick's mouth began to work, and words slowly came out of his mouth. "Bruce, why did you do that?"

"This deal was supposed to be easy. She was supposed to die in the woods. Then it was going to be at the Federal Building. But the whole thing is turning to crap. Nothing's gone the way it should. I rounded up a whole crew of guys for you. And look what's happened. We lost George and Perry downtown. We lost Billy to the Feds. We lost Harry and Jordan at the safe house. I got shot there. And we haven't gotten more than a couple of thousand dollars out of this."

"You will," Patrick wheezed.

"The hell with your insurance-policy bull. I want you to grab that money you got out of the old man's account when he was drugged up and transfer it to us."

"That's *my* money," Patrick objected.

"Not anymore. I want it in a bank account where I can get my hands on it. And if you don't do that right now, you're dead. Or maybe I'll shoot you in the kneecap next time, then carry you to the computer so you can get that cash."

Patrick's face was ashen. "I need medical attention."

"You mean like I got after the safe house?"

"That's not my fault."

"Well, you just have a flesh wound. You'll live." The blond man looked at Carrie. "We may need you for a while."

"Want me to put her in with the old man?" one of the other terrorists asked.

"Come on, Sid—do you think it's smart to put them together where they can plot something sneaky?"

"I guess not."

"My father's *here*?" Carrie gasped.

Nobody bothered to answer her. The man who had pushed her down into the chair pulled her up and kept a tight hold on her arm as he escorted her out of the room. As she walked, she was processing information. Inez had said her father was acting demented. But it wasn't because his mind was deteriorating. It was because Patrick had been drugging him so he could get access to his financial resources.

The other man yanked Patrick up and led him to a computer on a table along the wall across from the front door.

The last she saw of him, he was wincing as he sat down in the chair. No doubt he'd be transferring the money he'd stolen from her father's account, as the gunman had ordered.

As Sid led her down the hall, she looked at the closed doors. There were three bedrooms in the house, and her father must be in one of them—if these men were telling the truth.

She swallowed hard, then called out, "Dad?"

"Carrie?" her father shouted from behind the nearest door.

At the sound of his voice, she felt her heart stop then start to beat in double time. Her father really was here.

"No talking," Sid warned.

Unwilling to give up this opportunity, she ignored her captor and kept talking to her father. "Are you all right?"

The dark-haired man slapped her across the face so hard that her ears rang. "If you try that again, I'll shoot you," he growled as he dragged her farther down the hall.

In the far bedroom, he pulled out handcuffs and fastened her to the brass headboard.

"This mess is all your fault," he said bitingly.

"My fault? That's crazy. I was just minding my own business when I heard your plot."

"And now look what's happened."

The murderous look in his eyes told her he couldn't see the situation rationally. Better to shut up and try to figure out how to escape.

To her relief, he stomped out of the room, and she breathed out a little sigh. She was safe for the moment, but what about Wyatt?

Her throat clenched. "Wyatt," she whispered. "Oh, Lord, Wyatt, please be okay. What would I do without you now?"

The life she'd made for herself had been fine until she'd heard the terrorist plot in the park. Then it had turned upside down, and Wyatt Hawk had stepped in to right it again. At first she'd hated being forced into living with him. Then she'd come to realize that he gave her something she'd never had before. He wasn't just her bodyguard. He was a man who could be her partner—if he'd allow himself to think in those terms. But could he? And what had those shots outside meant?

She yanked on the cuff that held her to the bed. She had to find a way to free herself and her father. And then she had to find Wyatt.

A tall order, but she wasn't going to simply sit here and wait for the men out there to come back and kill her.

AT THE BACK of the house, Wyatt heard something that made his heart leap. Carrie called out to her father, and he answered. They were both alive, thank the Lord.

He listened to the sound of a door opening. Someone moved around before the door closed again.

The action was followed by profound silence.

Cautiously he crept toward the window. When he looked inside, he saw Carrie sitting on a bed, pulling at a pair of handcuffs that secured her left wrist to the bed.

After waiting for a moment to make sure that the guy who had cuffed her wasn't coming back, he tapped lightly on the window. She looked around, her eyes widening as she saw him.

Wyatt, she mouthed as she pressed her hand over her heart.

He felt a choking sensation. Putting his hands against the window glass, he pushed at the sash, but it was locked, and breaking the glass would bring the bad guys running.

When she saw what he was doing, she stood and tried to get to the window, but her cuffs kept her from getting close. After looking over her shoulder toward the door, she began to tug at the bed, moving it inch by inch closer to the window.

She would tug, then wait to make sure nobody had heard the legs scrape on the floor, then move it again, but apparently, the men were busy in the living room.

It took her several minutes to get close enough to the window to reach the lock. She unlatched the lock with her free hand, then pushed the window up. As soon as she opened the window a crack, Wyatt reached under and helped her shove it up.

Stepping back, she gave him room to climb through the window, and he made it into the room and took her in his arms, holding tight.

"Thank God you're all right," they both said at once.

"I heard a shot," he said.

"One of the men shot Patrick. He was working with them. But it sounds like the crazy scheme was Rita's idea. If I had to guess, I'd say she had her husband killed by the guys out there."

He nodded, looking at the cuff that held her wrist to the bed.

Taking out a Swiss Army knife, he used one of the implements to manipulate the lock on the cuffs. When he heard the lock click, he pulled the cuff off of her.

She threw her arms around him again and held tight.

"How many men are here?" he asked.

"Three plus Patrick. A blond guy named Bruce who has a wounded leg—from the safe-house assault—and a couple of dark-haired men. One of them is Sid. I don't know the other one's name, but I saw him at the picnic area. I assume some of them were at the Federal Building."

"And I assume each of them is armed."

"Yes. But Patrick is out of commission. The one named Bruce shot him in the leg."

"Why?"

"I guess to make him understand that bad things were going to happen if he didn't get my father's money out of the bank account where he'd stashed it."

Wyatt muttered a curse. "I guess this isn't going the way Patrick expected."

"Yes, and there's more. Apparently, Patrick was drugging my father—giving him something so he couldn't think straight. And so Patrick could have the run of his computer."

She gave him a pleading look. "My father did everything for Patrick. Why did he turn on him?"

"You said your father was…difficult. If *you* felt that way, how did a guy who wasn't a real member of the family feel?"

She nodded.

"We can talk later."

"Yes, my father's here. We have to free him."

"I heard you call to him. Where is he?"

"In the next bedroom."

"I guess we're going through the window again."

He helped her outside onto the ground, wishing he could make her get the hell out of there before the men inside discovered what was happening, but he knew from experience that she wasn't going to take orders unless she thought they made sense.

BACK IN THE great room, Bruce pushed himself up using his crutch.

He looked at his partners. "I expected Eric and Cory back here by now."

The other men nodded.

"You don't think that Wyatt guy could have gotten them, do you?" Larry, the third man, asked.

"They're good."

"Maybe he's better. And they should have taken the assault weapons. Get them out." He thought for a moment, then turned to Sid. "And maybe you should go back and get the prisoners. If anything's going to happen, we can use them as human shields."

"Right."

Sid started toward the back of the house.

WYATT AND CARRIE moved silently to the other window. Apparently, Douglas Mitchell had heard them, because he came over to the window and looked out cautiously. He was also wearing a cuff, but there was a length of yellow rope attached to it and the end was frayed.

He unlocked the window and pushed up the sash.

"I sawed through the rope," he said as he started to climb through the window.

He was halfway out when Wyatt and Carrie heard a shout behind him, then a blast from a gun.

Douglas made a startled sound, toppled through the window and landed hard on the ground.

Carrie bent to him.

"Dad? Dad?"

Wyatt leaped to the window and returned fire into the bedroom. Whoever was shooting inside ducked back into the hall. A moment later, footsteps pounded toward the great room.

Douglas pushed himself up, looking dazed. Wyatt saw a streak of red along the side of his head that disappeared into his hair. When he felt the track of the bullet, he found that it had traveled across the man's skull.

"It's a graze," Wyatt said as he helped the older man to his feet. "We can't stay here. Come on."

"Where?" Carrie asked.

"Out of the line of fire."

Carrie and Wyatt each took one of her father's arms, holding him up as they hurried him toward the woods.

They had almost reached the shelter of the trees when they heard shots behind them. This time it was automatic weapons firing.

They pulled her father into the woods. Blood dripped down the side of his face, and his skin was pale, but he was still on his feet.

When they were behind the trees, Wyatt spun around and returned fire. "You have to get your dad out of here," he said to Carrie, reaching into his pocket and handing her the car keys. "I'll hold them off. If I'm not there in ten minutes, take off without me."

When Carrie hesitated, he said it again. "Go. You have to get your father to safety."

He watched panic, fear, determination chase themselves across her face. He could see she didn't want to leave him, but she didn't want her father in danger, either.

"Have the engine running for a quick getaway. I'll follow you."

She reached for him, pulling him close. "I can't let you do this."

"You have to."

She clung to him for another moment, then took her father's arm and moved him farther into the woods.

Wyatt stayed behind the tree. The last time he'd been entrusted with a woman's life, he'd let her get killed. It wasn't going to happen again.

He studied the house. It was quiet. There were still three

of the terrorists in there, all armed. The ones who'd come after him in the woods had been using automatic handguns. The ones in the house had switched to more powerful guns.

They'd use their superior firepower to rush him, and maybe he could stop them. But by then Carrie would be gone—if she followed orders.

CARRIE HELPED HER father through the woods, trying to hurry. When he stumbled, she held him upright.

"We can't leave Wyatt," she murmured as she helped him along.

"Agreed. But what are we going to do?"

"Are you all right?"

He laughed. "I'm a tough old bastard."

"You're not a bastard."

"Of course I am. I was always tough on you and Patrick. I've gotten worse. I can see that now."

"Don't blame yourself for this."

He scoffed, then was silent for several moments.

They made good progress through the woods. It was easier going than when she and Wyatt had approached the house. The downward slope helped, and they had already cleared some of the brush away as they came up.

Her father spoke again. "I made a big mistake."

"Dad…"

"Let me say this. I knew Patrick resented his place in our household. I tried to make him feel more like he belonged, but it was never going to work. I should have encouraged him to go out on his own. Instead, it was easier to let him take over some of my workload."

"You couldn't know what he'd do."

"I do now. He drugged me and started draining money from my accounts."

Did her father know that Patrick had also taken out a massive life-insurance policy on her? If he didn't, she wasn't going to mention that nasty detail.

As she helped her father through the woods, she racked her brain for a plan that would get Wyatt out of there.

He had told her to drive away. It was the right thing to do—for herself and for her father—but she couldn't leave Wyatt up there waiting for the men in the house to rush him.

The terrible image of that gun battle made her heart pound. He thought he was doing the right thing, but she wasn't going to let him sacrifice himself for her—not if she could do something about it. But what?

They made it to the car.

"Lie down in the backseat. I'll get you to the hospital as soon as I can," she said to her father.

"I'm all right. What are you planning?"

"I'm thinking," she answered, picturing the scene at the top of the drive. Wyatt was in the woods. There was a huge brush pile in the front yard next to Patrick's car. And beyond that a circle of blacktop at the end of the driveway.

Opening the glove compartment, she rummaged inside. When she found a box of matches, her hand closed around them.

"I've got an idea," she told her father. When she told him what it was, his breath caught, but he didn't try to talk her out of it.

She turned on the engine and checked the gas gauge. Plenty of fuel.

After cutting the engine, she climbed out and pulled off her slacks, then removed the cap from the gas tank. Using a stick, she stuffed one pant leg down into the tank. When she pulled it free, she saw it had acted like a wick, soaking up gasoline.

Next, she walked along the shoulder of the road for several yards and found a rock about the size of a baseball. Being careful not to touch the soaked part of the pant leg, she tied the rock into the garment. When she'd finished her preparations, she turned the car around and started up the driveway toward the house. The tricky part came next, but it seemed like her only option.

As the car came into view on the access road, the men inside the house started shooting, and she ducked low, clenching her hands on the wheel. But it seemed that Bruce, Sid and the other guy were too far away for accuracy. If they got her, it would be with a lucky shot.

Staying low, she pulled up on the far side of Patrick's car, using it and the brush pile for a shield as she climbed out.

Screened by the car and the heap of sticks and dried foliage, she lit a match and touched it to the end of the gas-soaked pant leg, rearing back as it flamed up with unexpected fury. As the heat leaped toward her, she heaved the garment toward the brush pile. The rock she'd tied inside the pants carried it forward, and it landed in a nest of dried vegetation and weathered wood that caught fire almost instantly.

Carrie crawled back the way she'd come, gravel digging into her hands and knees. As she climbed back into the car, a heavier volley of gunfire erupted from the terrorists, and she heard Wyatt returning fire from the woods, keeping the men in the house.

She waited with her heart pounding, willing the smoke to billow up enough for her to risk driving close enough for Wyatt to jump in.

It seemed to take forever, but finally she thought she had created enough of a smoke screen.

Ducking low, she took off, heading for the patch of woods where Wyatt had made his stand, and she saw him lean out from behind the tree and shoot toward the house, giving her cover.

When she drew close, he dashed through the smoke and leaped into the passenger seat. Even through the fire and smoke, shots followed her as she sped backward down the drive, then turned around and kept going. Some of the bullets hit the vehicle.

"Is everyone okay?" she shouted.

"Yes," her father and Wyatt both answered.

"I told you to get out of here," Wyatt growled.

"I wasn't going to leave you."

The gunfire faded behind Carrie as she sped down the drive. She had done it. They had gotten away.

Then her eyes widened as she reached the end of the access road, which was now blocked by a large black SUV.

Chapter Twenty

Men leaped from the SUV, and Carrie saw that they were wearing vests that said FBI. She also saw that they were aiming weapons at them.

"FBI! Come out with your hands up!" a tall man shouted.

"We'd better do it," Wyatt said between clenched teeth as he set his weapons down.

In the backseat, Douglas sat up.

As Carrie climbed out, she wished she was wearing more than a shirt and panties.

"I'm Wyatt Hawk and these are Carrie and Douglas Mitchell. Three of the armed terrorists are still up the hill in the house," Wyatt said as soon as he was out of the vehicle. "Patrick Harrison is also up there. They shot him."

While he was speaking, other agents circled around him and looked into the car. One of them reached under the dash and opened the trunk, then walked to the back of the vehicle.

"There's an assault weapon in here," he reported.

"Captured from the terrorists," Carrie answered.

She held her breath, then sighed in relief as the Federal agents conferred, then lowered their weapons.

"I'm Agent Fitzgerald," the man who'd been speaking said. "What's on fire up there?"

"I started a fire in a pile of brush in the driveway so I

could get Wyatt out of there," Carrie answered as she lowered her hands.

Wyatt and her father did the same.

"How did you get here?" Wyatt asked.

"The maid, Inez, got your license number when you were at the estate," Fitzgerald answered. "You got away from the Mitchell house just as we arrived in the gardener's van."

"If that was you, who was shooting?"

"The terrorists had gotten there ahead of us. They took some shots at us, then got the hell out of there."

Carrie caught her breath. "And Inez is okay?"

"Yes." The man addressed Wyatt. "We had your make and model, but we didn't pick you up on a traffic camera until a half hour ago. We saw you'd altered the plates."

Carrie sucked in a breath. "Inez was helping you?"

"Yes. She was reluctant to work with us, but we persuaded her to cooperate. She put a tracker on your car." He gave Wyatt a wry look. "But you found it and got rid of it."

"I thought the bad guys had put it there," Wyatt said.

"Yeah, well, we weren't coordinating very well—seeing as we didn't know whether you were part of the plot."

Carrie's voice rose in outrage. "Part of the plot? He's the only reason my father and I are alive."

"You gotta admit, your activities looked suspicious," Fitzgerald answered.

"Because we didn't know who we could trust. You do understand what's been going on?" she prodded. "Patrick Harrison and Rita Madison hatched a very elaborate scheme to kill me and get money from my father."

Fitzgerald nodded. "We're going to need more details from you. Like, for example, this started off looking like a terrorist plot against the government, but it appears to have been directed against the Mitchell family all along."

"Correct," Wyatt said.

"We'll tell you everything we know," Carrie said, then looked at Wyatt for confirmation.

He nodded. "It seems the men at the house were hired help."

Several agents peeled off and started up the driveway on foot. Above them came the sound of a helicopter.

"We'll get the rest of them," Fitzgerald said.

"You have Rita Madison?" Wyatt asked.

"We brought her in for questioning after intercepting a phone call she made to Harrison's cell phone. But that's not enough to arrest her. We have to prove that she's part of the conspiracy."

"Patrick claims it was her idea," Carrie said. "Maybe you can get them to rat out each other."

"Hopefully," Fitzgerald answered.

"And do you happen to have something I can wear?" Carrie asked.

One of the men went back to the SUV and brought her a pair of trousers. They were too long, but she rolled up the legs.

A siren told them another emergency vehicle was approaching. It turned out to be an ambulance.

Wyatt looked at Carrie. "You go with your father to the hospital."

"Where are you going?"

"I have to show them where to find the bodies in the woods."

She sucked in a sharp breath.

"Bodies in the woods?" Fitzgerald inquired.

"Yeah, two armed men came after me, and I defended myself." Wyatt looked at Fitzgerald. "Come on. I'll show you."

Carrie watched Wyatt and one of the agents disappear into the woods, wondering when she was going to see Wyatt again. Or *if* she was going to see him.

He'd saved her life. Now he had the perfect opportunity to disappear.

An FBI AGENT named Gleason followed the ambulance to the hospital. He stayed with Carrie while her father was treated.

"He needs to go home and rest," she told Agent Gleason when her father joined them in the waiting room.

Gleason considered the request and turned to the elder Mitchell. "We can talk to you tomorrow."

"Thank you."

The agent looked at Carrie. "But I want you down at headquarters."

"Is Wyatt Hawk there?"

"Yes, but you can't see him now. We need to get your stories separately."

"To make sure we tell you the same thing?" she asked.

"It's the usual procedure."

She sighed, knowing there was no point in arguing. She ached to see Wyatt, but the sooner she got this over with, the better.

Her father spoke up. "Carrie, I'm sorry you had to go through all this."

"I'm fine. Thanks to Wyatt Hawk."

"We both owe him a lot."

"Yes."

"And there's a lot I want to apologize for. There's nothing like thinking you're going to die to make you realize what's important."

She swallowed hard. "I found that out, too."

They hugged, and she waited with him until a cab picked him up.

She spent the next three hours with the FBI, telling her story, confirming details and asking questions.

"Did Rita have her husband killed?" she asked.

"No, it was the mob. They wanted their money. It added up to more than forty thousand dollars. He'd stolen twenty thousand by forging his wife's name on a check, but it wasn't enough to pay them off. We assume he was planning to disappear."

"That's the twenty thousand dollars he had in his safe and noted in his little book?"

"What book?" Fitzgerald asked.

"Before he died, he gave us the combination to his safe, and Wyatt found the book and the money. We thought he'd gotten a payment for telling the terrorists when I was going to be at the Federal Building."

"Yeah, that would have made sense, only it was Rita who told them. She probably got the information from his computer."

"We followed her and saw her go to her bank. She looked angry when she came out."

"She must have found out that the money was missing."

The phone rang, and the agent picked it up. After listening for a few minutes, he swung back to Carrie. "Patrick is under guard in the hospital, and he's telling us everything he knows, trying to cut a deal."

"Good. Well, good that he's talking. I don't care what happens to him now."

They had more questions for her, but finally the session wound down, and she decided to take a bathroom break. On the way back, she stopped short when she saw Wyatt talking in the hall to one of the agents.

He looked up, spotted her and went very still.

She walked up to the two men and addressed the agent. "Mr. Hawk and I need to talk—privately."

"Of course." He pointed toward a nearby door.

She turned and walked toward the door, hoping she looked confident even though her chest was so tight that she could barely breathe.

For a moment, she thought Wyatt wasn't going to follow her, but he stepped inside a room that was furnished like a lounge with comfortable sofas and chairs and a couple of square table and chair sets.

Turning, she faced him.

"Were you going to leave without seeing me again?"

"That might have been the best thing."

"Why? Because you're a coward?"

Anger flared in his eyes. "Of course not!"

"But you thought it would be easier to just walk away from me."

"It would be better for you."

"Why?"

"Because I'm a former CIA operative who isn't fit for polite society."

Her anger jolted up. "Don't give me that old story. You think because your partner did something stupid in Greece, that you have to keep punishing yourself?"

When he didn't answer, she asked, "Do you love me?"

He went absolutely still.

"Are you afraid to tell me the truth?"

She saw him drag in a breath and let it out. "No. I love you," he said in a barely audible voice, then said it again more strongly.

She closed the distance between them, throwing herself into his arms, and he caught her, clung to her.

They held each other for long moments before she raised her head and he lowered his. Their lips met in a long, passionate kiss.

Carrie reached behind him and locked the door.

"What are you doing?"

"Making sure nobody can come in here," she answered as she reached for his belt buckle.

"This is the J. Edgar Hoover Building. You can't do that here."

"Watch me."

He swore under his breath, but he helped her free himself from his pants and helped her off with hers. They had been through hell together over the past few days, and she couldn't be subtle about the emotions churning through her. She needed him, and she needed him now. And it looked as though he felt the same desperation. He kicked his pants away and kicked a chair aside so that he could set her on one of the tables.

She spread her legs for him, guiding him to her, gasping as he entered her.

He went still immediately, his face strained.

"Carrie, did I hurt you?"

"No."

She sealed the reassurance with a hard kiss, her hands clasping his shoulders then moving down his back to his butt as he began to move inside.

They were both too emotionally charged for the lovemaking to last long. She felt her inner muscles contract, felt her whole body quicken as an all-consuming climax seized her. Moments later, he followed her into the maelstrom. They clung together for long moments before he eased away and picked up her borrowed pants, handing them to her.

"In case they send an assault team to break in, you know," he said as he found his own pants.

When they were both dressed again, he scooped her up in his arms and carried her to the sofa. Sitting down, he cradled her in his lap, and she nestled against him.

"Tell me you're not going away," she murmured.

The long silence made her stomach knot.

"Wyatt?"

"You really want me to stay?"

"Yes. I love you."

His breath caught. "You hardly know me."

"Maybe I don't know a lot about your background, but I know exactly who you are. You showed me over and over when we were on the run." She raised her head and looked at him. "You're the bravest man I've ever met."

"But—"

"No protests."

She pressed her fingers to his lips. "I'd never met a man I wanted to spend my life with. I thought I'd always be alone, so I focused on my work. When I first met you, I thought you were another overbearing male."

"I was trying to keep my distance."

"I figured that out. And I appreciate it. But everything changed when you risked your life to save mine."

"I was doing my job."

"And more. So much more," she murmured, raising her head to kiss him again.

She knew they hadn't settled everything. But he wasn't going to walk away from her, and they had the time to work out the details. Maybe he'd even like the idea of coming with her on some photo shoots—to places she'd feel uncomfortable by herself.

She was going to ask him about that when a loud knock sounded at the door.

"You alive in there?" someone called out.

"Yes," Wyatt answered in a husky voice. "We were having a private debriefing."

She stifled a giggle.

"Oh, yeah. Well, the two of you are free to go—and find a room," the voice added. "But we'd like you to be available."

"We'll be at my apartment in D.C.," Carrie called out.

Footsteps departed.

"I hope they're not waiting outside when we open the door," she said.

"They're FBI agents. They're discreet."

She grinned at him, and he grinned back. She'd never

seen Wyatt Hawk so relaxed, and she liked it. They needed more of that and every other good thing. Together. For the rest of their lives.

* * * * *

She tried to pull away, but his hold was firm. "I'm not your prisoner. You're not responsible for me."

He was close enough that she could see the muscle in his jaw jerk. "I am. Make no mistake about that."

His bare chest loomed close enough that all she had to do was reach out and she would be touching his naked skin. She let her eyes drift down across his chest, following the line of hair as it tapered down into the open V of his unbuttoned jeans.

She flicked her eyes up. His breath was shallow, drawn through just slightly open lips. His eyes seemed even darker.

And then he closed the distance between them and pulled her body up next to his, fitting her curves into his strength.

FOR THE BABY'S SAKE

BY
BEVERLY LONG

All the characters in this book have no existence outside the imagination of the author, and have no relation whatsoever to anyone bearing the same name or names. They are not even distantly inspired by any individual known or unknown to the author, and all the incidents are pure invention.

All Rights Reserved including the right of reproduction in whole or in part in any form. This edition is published by arrangement with Harlequin Enterprises II B.V./S.à.r.l. The text of this publication or any part thereof may not be reproduced or transmitted in any form or by any means, electronic or mechanical, including photocopying, recording, storage in an information retrieval system, or otherwise, without the written permission of the publisher.

This book is sold subject to the condition that it shall not, by way of trade or otherwise, be lent, resold, hired out or otherwise circulated without the prior consent of the publisher in any form of binding or cover other than that in which it is published and without a similar condition including this condition being imposed on the subsequent purchaser.

First published in Great Britain 2013
by Mills & Boon, an imprint of Harlequin (UK) Limited,
Eton House, 18-24 Paradise Road, Richmond, Surrey TW9 1SR

© Beverly R. Long 2013

ISBN: 978 0 263 90364 5
ebook ISBN: 978 1 472 00728 5

46-0713

Harlequin (UK) policy is to use papers that are natural, renewable and recyclable products and made from wood grown in sustainable forests. The logging and manufacturing processes conform to the legal environmental regulations of the country of origin.

Printed and bound in Spain
by Blackprint CPI, Barcelona

As a child, **Beverly Long** used to take a flashlight to bed so that she could hide under the covers and read. Once a teenager, more often than not, the books she chose were romance novels. Now she gets to keep the light on as long as she wants, and there's always a romance novel on her nightstand. With both a bachelor's and a master's degree in business and more than twenty years of experience as a human resources director, she now enjoys the opportunity to write her own stories. She considers her books to be a great success if they compel the reader to stay up way past their bedtime.

Beverly loves to hear from readers. Visit www.beverlylong.com or like her at www.facebook.com/BeverlyLong.Romance.

For Mary, Linda, Karen and David. Family,
and friends, too. We're lucky!

Chapter One

Liz Mayfield had kicked off her shoes long before lunch, and now, with her bare feet tucked under her butt, she simply ignored the sweat that trickled down her spine. It had to be ninety in the shade. At least ninety-five in her small, lower-level office.

It was the kind of day for pool parties and frosty drinks in pretty glasses. Not the kind of day for sorting through mail and dealing with confused teenagers.

But she'd traded one in for the other years ago when she'd left her six-figure income and five weeks of vacation to take the job at Options for Caring Mothers—OCM.

It had been three years, and there were still people scratching their heads over her choice.

She picked the top envelope off the stack on the corner of her desk. Her name was scrawled across the plain white front in blue ink. The sender had spelled her last name wrong, mixing up the order of the *i* and the *e*. She slid her thumb under the flap, pulled out the single sheet of lined notebook paper and read.

And her head started to buzz.

You stupid BITCH. You going to be very sorry if you don't stop messing in stuff thats not your busines.

The egg-salad sandwich she'd had for lunch rumbled in her stomach. Still holding the notebook paper with one hand, she cupped her other hand over her mouth. She swallowed hard twice, and once she thought she might have it under control, she unfolded her legs and stretched them far enough that she could slip both feet into her sandals. And for some crazy reason, she felt better once she had shoes on, as if she was more prepared.

She braced the heels of her hands against the edge of her scratched metal desk and pushed. Her old chair squeaked as it rolled two feet and then came to a jarring stop when a wheel jammed against a big crack in the tile floor.

Who would have sent her something like that? What did they mean that she was going to be *very sorry?* And when the heck was her heart going to stop pounding?

She stood and walked around her desk, making a very deliberate circle. On her third trip around, she worked up enough nerve to look more closely at the envelope. It had a stamp and a postmark from three days earlier but no return address. With just the nail on her pinkie finger, she flipped the envelope over. There was nothing on the back.

Her mail had been gathering dust for days. She'd had a packed schedule, and it probably would have sat another day if her one o'clock hadn't canceled. That made her feel marginally better. If nothing had happened yet to make her *very sorry,* it was probably just some idiot trying to freak her out.

That, however, didn't stop her from dropping to the floor like a sack of potatoes when she heard a noise outside her small window. On her hands and knees, she peered around the edge of her desk and felt like a fool when she looked through the open ground-level window and saw it was only Mary Thorton arriving for her two-o'clock appointment. She could see the girl's thin white legs with the terribly annoying skull tattoo just above her right knee.

Liz got up and brushed her dusty hands off on her denim shorts. The door opened and Mary, her ponytail, freckles and still-thin arms all strangely at odds with her round stomach, walked in. She picked up an OCM brochure that Liz kept on a rack by the door and started fanning herself. "I am never working in a basement when I get older," she said.

"I hope you don't have to," Liz said, grateful that her voice sounded normal. She sat in her chair and pulled it up to the desk. Using her pinkie again, she flipped the notebook paper over so that the blank side faced up.

Mary had already taken a seat on one of the two chairs in front of the desk. Pieces of strawberry blond hair clung to her neck, and her mascara was smudged around her pale blue eyes. She slouched in the chair, with her arms resting on her stomach.

"How do you feel?" Liz asked. The girl looked tired.

"Fat. And I'm sweating like a pig," Mary replied.

Liz, careful not to touch or look at the notebook paper, reached for the open manila folder that she'd pulled from her drawer earlier that morning. She scanned her notes from Mary's last visit. "How's your job at the drugstore?"

"I quit."

Mary had taken the job less than three weeks earlier. It had been the last in a string of jobs since becoming Liz's client four months ago. Most had lasted only a few days or a week at best at the others. The bosses were stupid, the hours were too many or too few, the location too far. The list went on and on—countless reasons not to keep a job.

"Why, Mary?"

She shrugged her narrow shoulders. "I gave a few friends a little discount on their makeup. Stupid boss made a big deal out of it."

"Imagine that. Now what do you plan to do?"

"I've been thinking about killing myself."

It was the one thing Mary could have said that made Liz grasp for words. "How would you do it, Mary?" she asked, sounding calmer than she felt.

"I don't know. Nothing bloody. Maybe pills. Or I might just walk off the end of Navy Pier. They say drowning is pretty peaceful."

No plan. That was good. Was it just shock talk, something destined to get Mary the attention that she seemed to crave?

"Sometimes it seems like the only answer," Mary said. She stared at her round stomach. "You know what I mean?"

Liz did know, better than most. She leaned back in her chair and looked up at the open street-level window. Three years ago, it had been a day not all that different from today. Maybe not as hot but there'd been a similar stillness in the air.

There'd been no breeze to carry the scent of death. Nothing that had prepared her for walking into that house and seeing sweet Jenny, with the deadly razor blade just inches from her limp hand, lying in the red pool of death.

Yeah, Liz knew. She just wished she didn't.

"No one would probably even notice," Mary said, her lower lip trembling.

Liz got up, walked around the desk and sat in the chair next to the teen. The vinyl covering on the seat, cracked in places, scratched her bare legs. She clasped Mary's hand and held it tight. "I would notice."

With her free hand, Mary played with the hem of her maternity shorts. "Some days," she said, "I want this baby so much, and there are other days that I can't stand it. It's like this weird little bug has gotten into my stomach, and it keeps growing and growing until it's going to explode, and there will be bug pieces everywhere."

Liz rubbed her thumb across the top of Mary's hand.

"Mary, it's okay. You're very close to your due date. It's natural to be scared."

"I'm not scared."

Of course not. "Have you thought any more about whether you intend to keep the baby or give it up for adoption?"

"It's not a baby. It's a bug. You got some bug parents lined up?" Mary rolled her eyes.

"I can speak with our attorney," Liz said, determined to stay on topic. "Mr. Fraypish has an excellent record of locating wonderful parents."

Mary stared at Liz, her eyes wide open. She didn't look happy or sad. Interested or bored. Just empty.

Liz stood up and stretched, determined that Mary wouldn't see her frustration. The teen had danced around the adoption issue for months, sometimes embracing it and other times flatly rejecting it. But she needed to make a decision. Soon.

Liz debated whether she should push. Mary continued to stare, her eyes focused somewhere around Liz's chin. Neither of them said a word.

Outside her window, a car stopped with a sudden squeal of brakes. Liz looked up just as the first bullet hit the far wall.

Noise thundered as more bullets spewed through the open window, sending chunks of plaster flying. Liz grabbed for Mary, pulling the pregnant girl to the floor. She covered the teen's body with her own, doing her best to keep her weight off the girl's stomach.

It stopped as suddenly as it had started. She heard the car speed off, the noise fading fast.

Liz jerked away from Mary. "Are you okay?"

The teen stared at her stomach. "I think so," she said.

Liz could see the girl reach for her familiar indifference, but it had been too quick, too frightening, too close. Tears welled up in the teen's eyes, and they rolled down her smooth, freckled cheeks. With both hands, she hugged her middle. "I didn't mean it. I don't want to die. I don't want my baby to die."

Liz had seen Mary angry, defensive, even openly hostile. But she'd never seen her cry. "I know, sweetie. I know." She reached to hug her but stopped when she heard the front door of OCM slam open and the thunder of footsteps on the wooden stairs.

Her heart rate sped up, and she hurriedly got to her feet, moving in front of Mary. The closed office door swung open. She saw the gun, and for a crazy minute, she thought the man holding it had come back to finish what he'd started. She'd been an idiot not to take the threat seriously. Some kind of strange noise squeaked out of her throat.

"It's all right," the man said. "I'm Detective Sawyer Montgomery with Chicago Police, ma'am. Are either of you hurt?"

It took her a second or two to process that this man wasn't going to hurt her. Once it registered, it seemed as if her bones turned to dust, and she could barely keep her body upright. He must have sensed that she was just about to go down for the count because he shoved his gun back into his shoulder holster and grabbed her waist to steady her.

"Take a breath," he said. "Nice and easy."

She closed her eyes and focused on sucking air in through her nose and blowing it out her mouth. All she could think about was that he didn't sound like a Chicago cop. He sounded Southern, like the cool, sweet tea she'd enjoyed on hot summer evenings a lifetime ago. Smooth.

After four or five breaths, she opened her eyes. He looked at her, saw that she was back among the living and let go of her waist. He backed up a step. "Are you hurt?" he repeated.

"We're okay," she said, focusing on him. He wore gray dress pants, a wrinkled white shirt and a red tie that was loose at the collar. He had a police radio clipped to his belt, and though it was turned low, she could hear the background noise of Chicago's finest at work.

He reached into his shirt pocket, pulled out a badge, flipped it open and held it steady, giving her a chance to read.

"Thank you, Detective Montgomery," she said.

He nodded and pivoted to show it to Mary. Once she nodded, he flipped it shut and returned it to his pocket. Then he extended a hand to help Mary up off the floor.

Mary hesitated, then took it. Once up, she moved several feet away. Detective Montgomery didn't react. Instead he pulled his radio from his belt. "Squad, this is 5162. I'm inside at 229 Logan Street. No injuries to report. Backup is still requested to secure the exterior."

Liz stared at the cop. He had the darkest brown eyes—almost, but not quite, black. His hair was brown and thick and looked as if it had recently been trimmed. His skin was tanned, and his lips had a very nice shape.

Best-looking cop she'd seen in some time.

In fact, only cop she'd seen in some time. Logan Street wasn't in a great neighborhood but was quiet in comparison to the streets that ran a couple blocks to the south. As such, it didn't get much attention from the police.

And yet, Detective Montgomery had been inside OCM less than a minute after the shooting. That didn't make sense. She stepped forward, putting herself between the detective and Mary.

"How did you get here so quickly?" she asked.

He hesitated for just a second. "I was parked outside."

"That was coincidental," she said. "I'm not generally big on coincidences."

He shrugged and pulled a notebook out of his pocket. "May I have your name, please?"

His look and his attitude were all business. His voice was pure pleasure. The difference in the two caught her off balance, making her almost forgive that he was being deliberately evasive. There was a reason he'd been parked outside, but he wasn't ready to cough it up. She was going to have to play the game his way.

"Liz Mayfield," she said. "I'm one of three counselors here at OCM. Options for Caring Mothers," she added. "This is Mary Thorton."

The introduction wasn't necessary. The girl had been keeping him up at nights. Sawyer knew her name, her social security number, her address. Hell, he knew her favorite breakfast cereal. Three empty boxes of Fruit Loops in her garbage had been pretty hard to miss. "Miss Thorton," he said, nodding at the teen before turning back to the counselor. "Is there anybody else in the building?"

The woman shook her head. "Carmen was here earlier, but she left to take her brother to the orthodontist. Cynthia, she's the third counselor, just works in the mornings. We have a part-time receptionist, too, but she's not here today. Oh, and Jamison is getting ready for a fund-raiser. He's working off-site."

"Who's Jamison?"

"He's the boss."

"Okay. Why don't the two of you—"

Sawyer stopped when he heard his partner let loose their call numbers. He turned the volume up on his radio.

"Squad, this is 5162, following a gray Lexus, license Adam, John, David, 7, 4, 9. I lost him, somewhere around Halsted and 35th. Repeat, lost him. Keep an eye out, guys."

Sawyer wasn't surprised. He and Robert had been parked a block down the street. Sawyer had jumped out, and Robert had given chase, but the shooter had at least a two-block advantage. In a crowded city, filled with alleys and side streets, that was a lot. Every cop on the street in that general vicinity would be on the watch now, but Sawyer doubted it would do any good. Mirandez's boys would have dumped the car by now. He turned the volume on his radio back down.

"Why don't you two have a seat?" he said, trying hard to maintain a hold on his emotions. They hadn't gotten the shooter, but maybe—just maybe—he had Mary Thorton in a position where she'd want to talk.

The counselor sat. Mary continued to stand until Liz Mayfield patted the chair next to her.

Facing both women, he said, "I'd like to ask you a few questions. Are you feeling up to that?"

"You okay?" Liz Mayfield asked Mary.

The girl shrugged. "I suppose."

The woman nodded at Sawyer. "Shoot," she said.

Mary snorted, and the pretty counselor's cheeks turned pink. "Sorry," she mumbled. "We're ready. Proceed. Begin."

Wow. She was a Beach Boys song—a regular California girl—with her smooth skin and thick, blond hair that hung down to the middle of her back. She wore a sleeveless white cotton shirt and denim shorts, and her toenails were the brightest pink he'd ever seen.

What the hell was she doing in a basement on the south side of Chicago?

He knew what he was doing there. He was two minutes and two hundred yards behind Dantel Mirandez. Like he had been for the past eighteen months.

And the son of a bitch had slipped away again.

Sawyer crossed his legs at the ankles and leaned back against the desk, resting his butt on the corner. He focused his attention on the teenager. She sat slouched in her chair, staring at the floor. "Ms. Thorton, any ideas about who is responsible for this shooting?"

Out of the corner of his eye, he saw Liz Mayfield sit up straighter in her chair. "I—"

He held up his hand, stopping her. "If you don't mind, I'd like to give Ms. Thorton a chance to answer first."

"I don't know anything, Cop," the teen said, her voice hard with irritation.

Damn. "You're sure?"

Mary raised her chin. "Yeah. What kind of cop are you? Haven't you heard about people in cars with guns? They shoot things. Duh. That's why they call them drive-by shooters."

It looked as if she planned to stick to the same old story. He walked over to the window and looked out. Two squad cars had arrived. He knew the officers would systematically work their way through the crowd that had gathered, trying to find out if anybody had seen anything that would be helpful. He didn't hold out much hope. In this neighborhood, even if somebody saw something, they wouldn't be that likely to talk. He heard a noise behind him and turned.

"I'm out of here." Mary pushed on the arms of her chair and started to get up. "I've got things to do."

He wasn't letting her off the hook that easy. "Sit down," he instructed. "We're not done."

"You can't tell me what to do," Mary shouted.

You can't tell me what to do. The words bounced off the walls, sharp, quick blows, taking Sawyer back seventeen years. Just a kid himself, he'd alternated between begging, demanding, bribing, whatever he'd thought would work. But that angry teenage girl hadn't listened to him, either. She'd continued to pump heroin into her veins, and his son, his precious infant son, had paid the ultimate price.

Sawyer bit the inside of his lip. "Sit," he said.

Liz Mayfield stood. "Detective, may I talk to you privately?"

He gave her a quick glance. "In a minute." He turned his

attention back to Mary. "I'm going to ask you one more time. What do you know about this shooting?"

"What I know is that you talk funny."

He heard Liz Mayfield's quick intake of breath, but the woman remained silent.

"Is that right?" Sawyer rubbed his chin, debating how much he should share. "Maybe I do. Where I come from, everybody talks like this. Where I come from, two drive-by shootings in one week is something worthy of note."

Mary lowered her chin. Liz Mayfield, who had remained standing, cocked her head to the side and studied Mary. "Two?" she asked.

Sawyer didn't wait for Mary. "While Ms. Thorton shopped in a convenience store just three days ago, the front windows got shot out," he said.

"Mary?"

Was it surprise or hurt that he heard in the counselor's voice?

The teen didn't answer. The silence stretched for another full minute before Liz tried again. "What's going on here?" she asked.

"There ain't nothing going on here," Mary said. "Besides me getting bored out of my mind, that is."

"Somebody's going to get killed one of these days." Sawyer paced in front of the two women, stopping in front of Mary. "How would you like it if Ms. Mayfield had gotten a bullet in the back of her head?"

"I got rights," Mary yelled.

"Be quiet," he said. "Use some of that energy and tell me about Mirandez."

"Who?" the counselor asked.

Sawyer didn't respond, his attention focused on Mary. He saw her hand grip the wooden arm of the chair.

"Well?" Sawyer prompted. "Are you going to pretend you don't know who I'm talking about?"

"Stupid cops," Mary said, shaking her head.

He'd been called worse. Twice already today. "Come on, Mary," he said. "Before somebody dies."

Mary leaned close to her counselor. "I don't know what he's talking about. Honest, I don't. You've got to believe me." A tear slid down the girl's pale face, dripping onto her round stomach. He looked away. He didn't want to think about her baby.

"If I can go home now," Mary said, looking up at Liz Mayfield, "I'll come back tomorrow. We can talk about the adoption."

The woman stared at the teen for a long minute before turning to him. "Mary says she doesn't know anything about the shooting. I'm not sure what else we can tell you."

Sawyer settled back against the desk and contemplated his next words. "That's it? That's all either of you has to say?"

Liz Mayfield shrugged. "I'd still like a minute of your time," she said, "but if you don't have any other questions for Mary, can she go home?" She brushed her hair back from her face. "It has been a rather unpleasant day."

Maybe he needed to describe in graphic detail exactly what unpleasant looked like.

"Please," she said.

She looked tired and pale, and he remembered that she'd already about passed out once. "Fine," he said. "She can go."

Liz Mayfield extended her hand to Mary, helping the girl out of the chair. She wrapped her arm around Mary's freckled shoulder, and they left the room.

He had his back toward the door, his face turned toward the open window, scanning the street, when she came back. "I'm just curious," he said without turning around. "You saw her when I said his name. She knows something. You know it, and I know it. How come you let her walk away?"

"Who's Mirandez?" she asked.

He turned around. He wanted to see her face. "Dantel Mirandez is scum. The worst kind of scum. He's the guy who makes it possible for third graders to buy a joint at recess. And for their older brothers and sisters to be heroin addicts by the time they're twelve. And for their parents to spend their grocery money on—"

"I think I get it, Detective."

"Yeah, well, get this. Mirandez isn't just your neighborhood dealer. He runs a big operation. Maybe as much as ten percent of all the illegal drug traffic in Chicago. Millions of dollars pass through his organization. He employs hundreds. Not bad for a twenty-six-year-old punk."

"How do you know Mary is involved with him?"

"It's my job to know. She's been his main squeeze for the past six months—at least."

"It doesn't make sense. Why would he try to hurt her?"

"We don't think he's trying to hurt her. It's more like he's trying to get her attention, to make sure she remembers that he's the boss. To make sure that she remembers that he can get to her at any time, at any place."

"I don't understand."

"Three weeks ago, during one of his transactions, he killed a man. Little doubt that it wasn't the first time. But word on the street is that this time, your little Miss Mary was with him. She saw it."

"Oh, my God. I had no idea."

She looked as if she might faint again. He pushed a chair in her direction. She didn't even look at it. He watched her, relaxing when a bit of color returned to her face.

"I'm sure you didn't," he said. "The tip came in about a week ago that Mary saw the hit. And then the convenience store got shot up. She got questioned at the scene, but she didn't offer anything up about Mirandez. I've been following her ever since. It wasn't a coincidence that my partner and I were parked a block away. We saw a car come around the corner, slow down. Before we could do anything, they had a gun stuck out the window, blowing this place up. We called it in, and I jumped out to come inside. My partner went after them. As you may have heard," he said, motioning to his radio, "they got away."

"It sounded like you got a license plate."

"Not that it will do us any good. It's a pretty safe bet that the car was hot. Stolen," he added.

"Do you know for sure that it was Mirandez who shot out my window? Did you actually see him?"

"I'm sure it wasn't him pulling the trigger. He rarely does his own dirty work. It was likely someone further down the food chain."

She swallowed hard. "You may be right, Detective. And I'm willing to try to talk to Mary, to try to convince her to cooperate with the police. You have to understand that my first priority is her. She doesn't have anyone else."

"She has Mirandez."

"She's never said a word about him."

"I assume he's the father of the baby," he said. "That fact is probably the only thing that's keeping her alive right now. Otherwise, I think she'd be expendable. Everybody is to this guy."

Liz shook her head. "He's not the father of her baby."

"How do you know?"

She hesitated. "Because I've met the father. He's a business major at Loyola."

"That doesn't make sense. Why isn't he tending to his own business? What kind of man lets his girlfriend and his unborn child get mixed up with people like Mirandez? He knows about the baby?"

"Yes. But he's not interested."

"He said that?"

"Mary is considering adoption. When the paternity of a baby is known, we require the father's consent as well as the mother's."

"I guess they're not teaching responsibility in college anymore." Sawyer flexed his hand, wishing he had about three minutes with college boy.

"Can't download it," she answered.

Sawyer laughed, his anger dissipating a bit. "And where does Mirandez fit into this?" he asked. "You saw her face when I said his name. She knows him all right. The question is, what else does she know?"

"It's hard to say. She's not an easy person to read."

"How old is she?"

"She turned eighteen last month. Legally an adult but still very young, if you know what I mean."

"Yeah, well, she's gonna be young, foolish and dead if she doesn't get away from Mirandez. It's only a matter of time." He wanted Liz to understand the severity. "Otherwise, if I can prove she was at that murder scene, then she's an accessory and that baby is gonna be born in jail."

"Well, that's clear enough." She turned her head to look at her desk. She took a deep breath. "It may not have anything to do with Mary."

He lowered his chin and studied her. "Why do you say that?"

She walked over to the desk and flipped over a piece of notebook paper. She pointed at it and then the envelope next to it. "They go together. I opened it about a half hour ago."

He looked down and read it quickly. When he jerked his

head up, she stood there, looking calmer than he felt. "Any idea who sent this?"

She shook her head. "So maybe this has nothing to do with Mary. Maybe, just maybe, you were busting her chops for nothing."

For some odd reason, her slightly sarcastic tone made him smile. "I wasn't busting her chops," he said. "That was me making polite conversation. First time you ever get something like this?"

"Yes."

"Anybody really pissed off at you?"

"I work with pregnant teenagers and when possible with the fathers, too. Most of them are irritated with me at one time or another. It's my job to make them deal with things they'd sometimes rather ignore."

He supposed it was possible that the shooting wasn't Mirandez's work, but the similarities between it and the shooting at the convenience store were too strong to be ignored. "I imagine you touched this?"

She nodded.

"Anybody else have access to your mail?"

"Our receptionist. She sorts it."

"Okay. I'll need both your prints so that we can rule them out."

She blew out a breath. "Fine. I've got her home number. By the way, they spelled my name wrong," she said. "That doesn't necessarily mean it's not someone who knows me. Given that *business* is also spelled wrong and the grammar isn't all that great, I'd say we're not dealing with a genius."

"They still got their point across."

She smiled at him, and he noticed not for the first time that Liz Mayfield was one damn fine-looking woman. "That they did," she said. "Loud and clear."

"Why don't you have a seat? I'll get an evidence tech out

here to take your prints. That will take a few minutes. In the meantime, I've got a few questions."

She rolled her eyes. "I'll just bet you do," she said before she dutifully sat down.

Chapter Two

"Hey, Montgomery, you owe me ten bucks. I told you the Cubs would lose to St. Louis. When are you going to learn?"

Sawyer fished two fives out of his pocket. He hadn't expected his boys to win. But he'd been a fan since coming to Chicago two years earlier and going to his first Cubs game at Wrigley Field. He wasn't sentimental enough to believe it was because of the ivy growing on the walls that it somehow reminded him of home. He liked to think it was because the Cubs, no matter if they were winning or losing, were always the underdog. Sort of like cops.

He folded the bills and tossed them at his partner. "Here. Now shut up. Why does the lieutenant want to see us?"

"I don't know. I got the same page you did." Robert Hanson pulled a thick telephone book out of his desk drawer. "It's a damn shame. Veronica spent the night, and she's really at her best in the morning. Very enthusiastic."

"Which one is Veronica?"

"Blonde. Blue eyes. Nice rack."

That described most of the women Robert dated. Sawyer heard the door and looked up. Lieutenant Fischer walked in.

"Gentlemen," their boss greeted them, dropping a thick green file on the wood desk. "We've got a problem."

Robert sat up straighter in his chair. Sawyer stared at his

boss. The man looked every one of his fifty years. "What's up?" Sawyer asked.

"We've got another dead body. Looks like the guy was beat up pretty good before somebody shot him in the head."

"Mirandez?" Sawyer hissed.

"Probably. Our guys ID'd the deceased. Bobbie Morage."

Sawyer looked at Robert. "Morage was tight with Mirandez until recently."

Robert nodded. "Rumor has it that Morage was skimming off the top. Taking product home in his pockets."

Lieutenant Fischer closed his eyes and leaned his head back. "No honor among thieves or killers."

"Any witnesses?" Sawyer asked.

His boss opened his eyes. "None. Got one hysterical maid at the Rotayne Hotel. She found him on her way to the Dumpster. Look, we've got to get this guy. This makes three in the past two months. Eight in the past year."

Sawyer could do the math. He wanted Mirandez more than he'd wanted anybody in fifteen years of wearing a badge.

"Are you sure you can't get Mary Thorton to talk?" The lieutenant stood in front of Sawyer, his arms folded across his chest.

"I don't know. Like I told you yesterday, she's either in it up to her eyeballs, or she's just a dumb young kid with a smart mouth who doesn't know anything. I'm not sure which."

"What about her counselor? What was her name?"

"Liz. Elizabeth, I guess. Last name is Mayfield."

"Can she help us?"

"I don't know." Sawyer shook his head. "If anyone can get to Mary, I think she's the one. She said she'd try."

"We need the girlfriend. Push the counselor if you need to."

Sawyer understood Lieutenant Fischer's anxiety. People

were dying. "She does have her own issues," he said, feeling the need to defend the woman.

Lieutenant Fischer rubbed a hand across his face. "I know. You get any prints off the note she got?"

"Nothing that we couldn't match up to her or the receptionist. We got a couple partials, and we're tracking down the mail carrier to rule him or her out. I don't know. It could be coincidence that she got this and then Mirandez went after Mary Thorton again."

"I don't believe in coincidence," Lieutenant Fischer said, his voice hard.

Sawyer didn't much, either. "I'll go see her now."

"I'll go with you," Robert offered, clearly resigned that Veronica was an opportunity lost.

Blonde. Blue eyes. Nice rack. Liz Mayfield had green eyes, but other than that, she was just Robert's type. "No," Sawyer said, not even looking at Robert.

"Hey, it's no problem. I like to watch you try to use that old-fashioned Southern charm."

"I don't need any help." Sawyer looked at his lieutenant and got the nod of approval he needed.

"Fine," Robert said. "Go ahead and drag your sorry ass over there again. I'll just stay here. In the air-conditioning."

Lieutenant Fischer shook his head. "No, you don't. You're going to the hotel to interview the maid again. She doesn't speak much English."

"Doesn't anybody else speak Spanish?" Robert moaned.

"Not like you do. I've got officers who grew up in Mexico that don't speak it as well."

Robert grinned broadly. "It's hell to be brilliant." He ducked out the door right before the telephone book hit it.

A HALF HOUR LATER, Sawyer parked his car in front of the brick two-story. He walked past a couple brown-eyed, brown-skinned children, carefully stepping around the pictures they'd created on the sidewalk with colored chalk.

Sawyer nodded at the two old men sitting on the steps. When he'd left OCM the day before, he'd taken the time to speak to them personally, hoping they'd seen the shooter. From his vehicle, just minutes before the arrival of what he still believed was Mirandez's band of dirty men, he'd seen them in the same spot, chatting.

They'd seen the shooter. It didn't help much. He'd worn a face mask.

He took the steps of OCM two at a time. He just needed to get inside, talk to Liz Mayfield and get the hell out of there. Before he did something stupid like touch her. He'd thought of her skin for most of the night. Her soft, silky skin. With legs that went on forever.

Sawyer glanced down at the street-level window. Plywood covered the opening, keeping both the sun and unwanted visitors out. He didn't stop to wonder how unwelcome he might be. He walked through the deserted hallway and down the steps. He knocked once on the closed door and then again when no one answered. He tried the knob, but it wouldn't turn.

"She left early."

Sawyer whirled around. He'd been so focused on the task that he hadn't heard the woman come up behind him.

"Sorry." She laughed at him. "Didn't mean to scare you."

Looking at her could scare almost anybody. She had bright red hair, blue eyeliner, black lips, and she wore a little bit of a skirt and shirt, showing more skin than material. She couldn't have been much older than eighteen. If she had been his daughter, he'd have locked her in the house until she found some clothes and washed the god-awful makeup off.

His son would have been just about her age. "What's your name?" he asked.

"Nicole." She held up the palm of her hand and wriggled her fingers. "Don't you recognize me?"

She was the part-time receptionist who had gotten her prints taken. An evidence tech had taken care of it for him. He'd been busy filling out case reports—one for the shooting, a separate one for Liz Mayfield's threat. "Sorry. Thanks for doing that, by the way."

"I'd do almost anything for Liz. Like I said, though, she's not here. She left early. Maybe to get ready for the dance."

Sawyer tried to concentrate. "A dance?"

"OCM is having a dance. A fund-raiser. Jamison says we're going to have to shut the doors if donations don't pick up."

Sawyer had finally had the opportunity to talk on the telephone with Jamison Curtiss, the executive director of OCM, late the evening before. The man had flitted between outrage at both the shooting and the note Liz Mayfield had received, to worry about the bad press for OCM, to despair about the neighborhood all in a matter of minutes.

Sawyer had told himself, several times while he was shaving this morning, that it had been that conversation that had spurred dreams of Liz Mayfield. Otherwise, there'd have been no reason to take his work home, to take it literally to bed with him.

Dreaming about a woman was something Robert would do.

"Dinner is two hundred bucks a plate," the girl continued. "Can you believe that? Like, I'd cook 'em dinner for half that."

"Where?"

"Like, at my house."

Sawyer shook his head. "No, where's the dinner?"

"At the Rotayne Hotel. Pretty fancy, huh?"

"As fancy as they get." *As long as they keep the dead bodies hidden in the alley.* "What time does it start?"

"Dinner's at seven. My grandmother wanted me to go. Thought I might meet a nice young man there." She wrinkled her nose.

"Not interested?" he asked.

She shook her head. "Last one I met got me knocked up. Guess Grandma kind of forgot about that. I don't know what I would have done if Liz hadn't helped me find a family for my baby. Now she's living in the suburbs. Like, with a mom and dad and two cats." The girl's eyes filled with tears.

"Uh…" He was so far out of his league here.

"Anyway," she said, sniffing loudly. She tossed her hair back. "She's the best. Some lawyer guy helps her. He talks fast, drinks too much and wears ugly ties. Easy to spot."

"What's his name?" Sawyer asked.

"Howard Fraypish. Liz went to the dance with him."

Sawyer pulled his notebook out of his suit coat pocket and made a note of the name. Yesterday, after they'd gotten Liz Mayfield's prints, he'd asked her whether she was seeing anybody. It was a legitimate question, he'd told himself at the time.

She hadn't even blinked. Said that she hadn't dated anyone for over a year.

Going to a dance with somebody sounded like a date.

"I think she just feels sorry for him," the girl added.

So, she and lawyer guy weren't close. Maybe there was someone else. He had a right to ask. Maybe the connection wasn't Mary or Mirandez. Maybe the shooter's target had been the pretty counselor. It wouldn't be the first time a spurned love interest had crossed the line. "She seeing anybody else?"

"Not that I'm aware of."

He was glad that Liz hadn't lied to him. But it still surprised him. A woman who looked like Liz Mayfield shouldn't have trouble getting a date. She had the kind of face and body that made a man stupid.

He'd made that mistake once in his life. He wouldn't make it again.

HE TRIED TO REMEMBER THAT, two hours later, when he watched her glide around the room. She had on a long, dark blue dress. It flowed from her narrow waist, falling just shy of her ankles. It puffed out when she turned.

She'd pulled her hair up, leaving just a few strands down. Sawyer rubbed his fingers together, imagining the feel of the silky texture. The dress had a high collar and sleeves ending just below the elbow. She barely showed any skin at all, and she was the sexiest woman there.

Classy. It was the only word he could think of.

Determined to get it over with, Sawyer strode across the dance floor, ignoring the startled whispers or shocked glances in his wake. He felt as out of place as he knew he looked with his faded blue jeans and his beat-up leather jacket. He'd shed his suit earlier that evening before suddenly deciding that he needed to see Liz Mayfield tonight. She'd had her twenty-four hours. It wasn't his fault that she was a party girl and wanted to dance.

He met her eyes over the shoulder of her date. Her full lips parted ever so slightly, and her face lost its color. He shrugged in return and tapped the man between them on the shoulder.

The guy, early forties and balding, turned his head slightly, frowned at Sawyer and kept dancing.

Sawyer tapped again. "I need a few minutes with Ms. Mayfield."

They stopped. When the guy made no move to let go of her, Sawyer held out his hand. She stared at it for several seconds then stepped away from her date. Suddenly she was in his arms, and they were dancing.

He wanted to say something. But his stupid mind wouldn't work. He couldn't think, couldn't talk, couldn't reason.

She smelled good—like the jasmine flowers that had grown outside his mother's kitchen window.

He wanted to pull her close and taste her. The realization hit him hard, as if someone had punched him. He wanted his tongue in her mouth, her breasts in his hands and her thighs wrapped around him. He wanted her naked under him.

Sawyer jerked back, stumbling a bit. He dropped his hands to his sides. The two of them stood still in the middle of the dance floor like two statues.

Why didn't she say something? Hell, why didn't she blink? She just kept her pretty green eyes focused on his face. Sawyer kept his breaths shallow, unwilling to let any more temptation into his lungs. "Any more letters?" he asked. He kept his voice low, not wanting others to hear.

She shook her head. "Our mail doesn't usually arrive until after lunch. I left before it got there."

"So, no news is good news?"

"For tonight."

He understood avoidance. At one point in his life, he'd perfected it. He felt silly standing in the middle of the floor. He stepped closer to Liz Mayfield, and she slipped back into his arms as if it was the most natural thing in the world.

Which didn't make sense at all because it had to have been ten years since he'd danced with a woman. It felt good. She felt good.

He really needed to remember that he wasn't here to dance. "What did your little friend have to say?" he asked.

Her body jerked, and he realized he'd been more stern than necessary. "I'm sorry," he said.

"That's fine," she said. "It's just that I...I didn't see Mary today."

"She didn't show, did she?"

Liz shook her head and jumped in with both feet. "I had to cancel most of my appointments. I didn't feel well." That much at least was true. She'd been sick after hearing Mary's voice mail. *I'm not coming today. I'll see you tomorrow at the regular time.*

Liz had tried to call her a dozen times before giving up. Dreading that Detective Montgomery would find her before she had the chance to locate Mary, she'd left the office. She'd worried that a frustrated Detective Montgomery might take matters in his own hands and track Mary down.

Liz had never expected he'd show up at the fund-raiser. But she should have known better. Detective Montgomery didn't seem like the kind of guy who gave up easily. In fact, he seemed downright tenacious. Like a dog after a bone.

She tried to hold that against him. But couldn't. While it made for an uncomfortable evening, she couldn't help appreciating the fact that he'd held her to her twenty-four hours. He took his work seriously. She could relate to that.

"Are you okay now?" he asked, sounding concerned.

She nodded, not willing to verbalize any more half-truths. From across the room, she caught Carmen's eye. She was standing behind the punch table, pouring cups for thirsty dancers. Liz could read the concern on her pretty face. She'd had that same look since Liz had told her about the letter.

Liz shook her head slightly, reassuring her. Carmen was little, but she could be a spitfire. If she thought Liz needed help, she'd come running.

"Who's that?" Detective Montgomery asked.

"Carmen Jimenez. She's a counselor, too. I think I mentioned her yesterday."

"I remember. Did you tell her about your letter?"

"Yes."

"She hasn't gotten anything similar?"

Liz shook her head.

"I've got some bad news," Detective Montgomery said. "We found another dead body this morning. Right outside of this very hotel. He'd been shot. Up until a few weeks ago, he'd been a cook for Mirandez."

"Mirandez has a cook?"

He leaned his mouth closer to her ear, and she felt the shiver run down the length of her spine. "Not like Oprah has a cook. A cook is the guy who boils down the cocaine into crack."

"Oh. My."

"People keep dying," he said. "It's my job to make it stop. If Mary knows something, it's her job to help me."

She'd been wrong. He wasn't like a dog after a bone. He wanted fresh meat. She pulled away from him, forcing the dancing to stop. She couldn't think when he had his arms around her, let alone when his mouth was that close. "If you had enough to arrest her," she protested, "you'd have done it yesterday. You don't have anything but a wild guess."

He had more than that. The tip had come from one of their own. It had taken Fluentes two years to work his way inside. Sawyer didn't intend to sacrifice him now.

Push the counselor. He could hear Lieutenant Fischer's words almost as clearly as if the man stood behind him. "She was there. And you need to convince her to tell us what she saw. She needs to tell us everything. Then we'll protect her."

"You'll protect her?"

"Yeah." For some reason Liz's disbelieving tone set Sawyer's teeth on edge. "That's what we do. We're cops."

"She's eight months pregnant."

"I'm aware of that. We would arrange for both her and her baby to have the medical care that they need."

"And then what?" she asked, her tone demanding.

Sawyer threw up his hands. "I don't know. I guess the baby grows up, and in twenty years, Mary's a grandmother." Sawyer rubbed the bridge of his nose. His head pounded, and the damn drums weren't helping. "Look, can we go outside?" he mumbled.

She seemed to hesitate. Sawyer let out a breath when she nodded and took off, weaving in and out of the dancers, not stopping until she reached the exit. They walked outside the hotel, and he led her far enough away that the doorman couldn't hear the conversation.

She spoke before he had the chance to question her. "I'll talk to her. She's supposed to come to OCM at eight tomorrow morning. It's her regular appointment."

"And you'll convince her to talk to us?"

"I'll talk—"

"Liz, Liz. Back here. What are you doing outside?"

Sawyer turned back toward the hotel door. Her date stood next to the doorman, wildly waving his arm. The man started walking toward them, his long legs eating up the distance.

"He doesn't know about my letter," Liz said, her voice almost a whisper. "I'd like to keep it that way."

When the man reached Liz's side, he wrapped a skinny arm around her and tugged her toward his body. For some crazy reason, Sawyer wanted to break the man's arm. In two, maybe three, places. Then maybe a kneecap next.

"You had me worried when I couldn't find you," he said.

She stepped out of the man's grasp. "Detective Montgomery is the detective assigned to the shooting at OCM." She turned back to Sawyer. "Detective Montgomery, Howard Fraypish," she said, finishing the introduction.

The guy stuck his arm out, and Sawyer returned the shake. "I'm OCM's attorney," Fraypish said.

The man's hot-pink bow tie matched his cummerbund.

"I better get going," Sawyer said. "Thanks for the information, Ms. Mayfield."

"I certainly hope you arrest the men responsible for the attack at OCM," Fraypish said. "Where were the city's finest when this happened? At the local doughnut shop?"

Was that the best the guy could do? "I don't like doughnuts," Sawyer said.

"Are you sure you're a cop?"

Liz Mayfield frowned at her date. The idiot held up both hands in mock surrender. "Just a little joke. I thought we could use some humor."

Sawyer thought a quick left followed by a sharp right would be kind of funny.

"I should have called you, Detective. Then you wouldn't have had to make a trip here," she apologized.

"Forget it." His only regret was the blue dress. He knew how good she looked in it. He wondered how long before he stopped thinking about how good she'd look without it.

LIZ WOKE UP at four in the morning. Her body needed rest, but her mind refused to cooperate. She'd left the hotel shortly after midnight. She'd been in her apartment and in bed less than ten minutes later. She'd dreamed about Mary. Sweet Mary and her baby. Sweet Mary and the faceless Dantel Mirandez. Jenny had been there, too. With her crooked smile, her flyaway blond hair blowing around her as she threw a handful of pennies into the fountain at Grant Park. Just the way she'd been the last day Liz had seen her alive. Then out of nowhere, there'd been more letters, more threats. So many that when she'd fallen down and they'd piled on top of her, they'd covered her. And she hadn't been able to breathe.

Waking up had been a relief.

She showered, put on white capri pants and a blue shirt

and caught the five-o'clock bus. Thirty minutes later, it dropped her off a block from OCM. The morning air was heavy with humidity. It had the makings of another ninety-degree day.

She entered the security code, unlocked the front door, entered and then reset the code. She didn't bother to go downstairs to her office, heading instead to the small kitchen at the rear of the first floor. She started a pot of coffee, pouring a cup before the pot was even half-full. She took a sip, burned her tongue and swallowed anyway. She needed caffeine.

While she waited for her bagel to toast, she thought about Detective Montgomery. When he'd walked away, in the wake of Howard's insults, she'd wanted to run after him, to apologize, to make him understand that she'd do what she could to help him.

As long as it didn't put Mary in any danger.

But she hadn't. When Howard had hustled her back inside the hotel, she'd gone without protest. Jamison had made it abundantly clear. Attendees had coughed up two hundred bucks a plate. If they wanted to dance, you danced. If they needed a drink, you fetched it. If they wanted conversation, you talked.

Liz had danced, fetched, talked and smiled through it all. Even after her toes had been stepped on for the eighteenth time. No politician could have done better. She'd done it on autopilot. It hadn't helped when Carmen had come up, fanning herself, and said, "Who was that?"

"Detective Montgomery," Liz had explained.

"I suspect I don't have to state the obvious," Carmen had said, "but the man is hot."

Liz had almost laughed. Carmen hadn't even heard the man talk. Or felt the man's chest muscles when he'd held her close—not too close but close enough. She hadn't smelled his clean, fresh scent.

Detective Montgomery wasn't just hot; he was *smoking* hot.

Her bagel popped just as she heard the front door open. She relaxed when she didn't hear the alarm. Who else, she wondered, was crazy enough to come to work at five-thirty in the morning?

When she heard Jamison's office door open, she almost dropped her bagel. He probably hadn't gotten home much before two.

She spread cream cheese evenly on both sides and started a second pot of coffee. Jamison was perhaps the only person on earth who loved coffee more than she did. She had her cup and her bagel balanced in one hand and had just slung her purse over her shoulder when she heard the front door close again.

She eased the kitchen door open and glanced down the narrow hallway. Empty. All the office doors remained closed. "Hello?"

No answer. She walked down the hallway, knocked on Jamison's door and then tried the handle. It didn't turn.

She walked down the steps to the lower level. Her office door and all the others were shut. "Good morning?" she sang out, a bit louder this time.

The only sound she heard was her own breathing.

Liz ran up the stairs, swearing softly when the hot coffee splashed out of the cup and burned her hand. She checked the front door. Locked. Alarm set.

She relaxed. It had to have been Jamison. What would have possessed him to come in so early and leave so quickly? She hoped nothing was wrong. She walked back downstairs and unlocked her office. It was darker than usual because no light spilled through the boarded-up window.

She had to admit that the wood made her feel better.

Maybe she'd ask Jamison to leave it that way for a while. At least until she got her nerves under control.

Rationally, she didn't put much stock in the letter. It wasn't out of the realm of possibility that one of her clients or their partners had decided to jerk her chain a little. It didn't make her feel any better, however, to think that the shooter had been aiming for Mary.

She intended to somehow make the girl open up to her, to tell her if there was any connection between her and Dantel Mirandez. But in the meantime, she needed to get busy. She sat down behind her desk and opened the top file. Mary was not the only client who was close to delivery. Just two days before, Melissa Stroud had been in Liz's office. They'd reviewed the information on Mike and Mindy Partridge, and Melissa had agreed to let the couple adopt her soon-to-be-born child. Liz needed to get the necessary information to Howard so that he could get the paperwork done.

At twenty minutes to eight, she heard the front door open again. Heavy footsteps pounded down the stairs, and within seconds, her boss stuck his head through the open doorway.

"Hey, Liz. Nice window."

She shook her head. "Morning, Jamison. How are you?"

"Exhausted. It ended up being a late night. We didn't leave the hotel until they pushed us out the door. Then Reneé and I and a couple others went out for breakfast. I didn't want to say no to any potential donors. I've got a heck of a headache, though. It was probably that last vodka tonic."

"Jamison, you know better." Liz smiled at her boss. "Had you been to bed yet when you stopped by here this morning?"

"This morning? What are you talking about?"

"You stopped in about six. I had coffee made, but you left before I could catch you."

"Liz, how many glasses of wine did you have last night?"

Liz dismissed his concern with a wave of her hand. "Two. That's my limit."

"Well, you may want to cut back to one. Reneé had set the alarm for seven, and we slept through that. I barely had time for a two-minute shower just to get here by now."

Liz shook her head, trying to make sense out of what Jamison said. "I heard the door. The alarm didn't go off. I'm sure I heard your office door open. But when I came out, there was nobody around."

"It must have been a car door."

"No, it wasn't," Liz protested.

"Then it was Cynthia or Carmen or one of the other staff. Although I can't imagine why anybody would have gotten up early after last night. What were you doing here?"

"Mary Thorton is coming at eight. I wanted to get some stuff done first." No need to tell Jamison that she'd been running from her dreams. He already thought she was losing her mind.

"Have you talked to her since the shooting? Poor kid. She must be pretty shook up."

"I'm sure she was. Detective Montgomery thinks she knows more than she's letting on."

"Is that why he came to the dance last night?"

Liz was surprised. Jamison rarely noticed anything that didn't directly concern him. But then again, Detective Montgomery had a way about him that commanded attention.

"Yes."

"At least he wasn't in uniform. That wouldn't have been good for donations. How do you think the party went?" Jamison asked, sitting down on one of Liz's chairs.

"People seemed to have a good time," Liz hedged. When his eyes lit up, her guilt vanished. He could be a bit self-centered and pushy, but Liz knew he'd do almost anything for OCM. She would, too.

Even spend an evening with Howard Fraypish, who had
been Jamison's college roommate. After college, Jamison
had taken a job in social services and married Reneé. Howard had gone to law school, graduated at the top of his class,
married his corporate job and produced billable hours. Lots
of them, evidently. The man had a huge apartment with a
view of Lake Michigan, and he'd opened his own law office
at least five years ago.

The two men had stayed connected over the years, and
when Jamison had been hired as the executive director of
OCM, he'd hired Howard's firm to handle the adoptions.

"Want a warm-up?" Jamison asked, nodding at Liz's
empty cup.

"Sure."

They walked upstairs to the kitchen. Liz had poured her
cup and handed the glass pot to Jamison when his cell phone
rang. Liz started to walk away, stopping suddenly when she
heard the glass pot hit the tile floor.

She whirled around. Jamison stood still, his phone in one
hand and his other empty. Shards of glass and spilled coffee surrounded him.

"Jamison?" She started back toward her boss.

"There's a bomb in my office." He spoke without emotion. "It's set to go off in fifteen minutes."

Chapter Three

Detective Sawyer Montgomery arrived just minutes after the bomb squad had disarmed, dismantled and disconnected— she wasn't sure of the technical term—the bomb that had been left in the middle of Jamison's desk. It had taken them eleven minutes to arrive. The longest eleven minutes of Liz's life.

Beat cops had been on the scene within minutes of the 911 call that Liz had made from Jamison's phone after she'd pulled him, his phone and herself from the building. They'd blocked off streets and rousted people from their apartments. OCM's neighbors, many still in their pajamas, had poured from the nearby buildings. Mothers with small children in their arms, old people barely able to maneuver the steps, all were hustled behind a hastily tacked-up stretch of yellow police tape.

Liz had wondered if Detective Montgomery would come. She hated to admit it, but she'd considered calling him. In those first frantic moments before help had arrived, she'd desperately hoped for someone capable. And Detective Montgomery absolutely screamed capable. She doubted the man ever encountered anything he couldn't handle.

But now that he'd arrived, Liz wanted to run. She couldn't decide if she wanted to run to him to seek shelter in his embrace or run far from him to protect herself from his intensity, his questions, his knowing looks.

Liz watched him get out of the car and scan the crowd. He said something to the man who rode with him. Liz knew the exact moment he spotted her. It didn't matter that three hundred yards separated them. Liz felt the shiver run up her arm just as if he'd touched her.

"What the hell happened?" he asked when he reached her.

Liz swallowed, trying very hard not to cry. How ridiculous would that be? No one had been hurt. No one injured. And she hadn't even thought about crying until Detective Montgomery had approached.

"Bomb threat," she said. "Actually, more than a threat, I guess. The bomb squad removed it just a few minutes ago."

"Where was it?"

"In the middle of my boss's desk. In a brown sack." The tears that she'd dreaded sprang to her eyes.

"Hey." Detective Montgomery reached out and touched her arm. "Are you okay?"

He sounded so concerned. That almost made the dam break. "I'm fine, really. Everyone's just been great."

Detective Montgomery frowned at her, but he didn't let go. The most delicious heat spread up her arm.

"Come over here." He guided her toward the curb.

"Okay." Whatever he wanted. As long as she didn't have to think. Because then she'd think about it, the bomb and the look on Jamison's face. She'd remember the pure panic she'd felt as they'd run from the building.

He pulled his hand away, and Liz felt the immediate loss of heat all the way to her stomach, which was odd since his hand had been nowhere near her stomach. He unbuttoned his suit coat, took it off and folded it. He placed it on the cement curb. "Why don't you sit down?" he suggested, pointing at his coat.

"I can sit on cement," she protested.

"Not and keep those…short pants clean," he said. His face turned red. "I know there's a word for them, but I can't think of it right now."

He was smokin' hot when he was serious and damn cute when he was embarrassed. It was a heck of a combination. "They're called capri pants."

He smiled. "It might have come to me."

Oh, boy. She sat down. She knew she needed to before she swooned. "I'm sure it would have, Detective Montgomery."

"Sawyer," Detective Montgomery said. "Just Sawyer is fine."

Liz nodded. The man was just being polite. After all, in a span of less than forty-eight hours, their paths had crossed three times. They weren't strangers any longer. She was sitting on his coat. "Liz is fine, too," she mumbled.

"Liz," he repeated.

She liked the way the *z* rolled off his tongue. She liked the way all the consonants and the vowels, too, for that matter, rolled off his tongue. It was a molten chocolate center bubbling out of a freshly baked cake. Smooth. Enticing.

Maybe he could read her the dictionary for the next week.

"I need to ask you some questions," he said.

She wasn't going to get a week. "Sure." Why the heck not? Together they sat on the faded gray cement, hips close, thighs almost touching. Liz wanted to lean her head against his broad shoulder but knew that would startle the hell out of him.

She settled for closing her eyes. It seemed like a lifetime ago that she'd crawled out of bed and caught the five-o'clock bus.

"Sawyer?"

Liz opened her eyes. The man who had been with Sawyer when he'd arrived now stood in front of the two of them.

He was an inch taller and probably ten pounds heavier than Sawyer. He had the bluest eyes she'd ever seen.

Was the sky raining gorgeous men?

"What did you find out?" Sawyer spoke to the man.

"Bomb, all right. Big enough that it would have done some damage. Quick to shut down. Looks like they wanted to make it easy for us."

Sawyer didn't say anything.

"Who are you?" Liz asked.

The man's face lit up with a broad smile showing perfect teeth. "I'm Detective Robert Hanson. My partner has no manners. Otherwise, he'd have introduced us."

"I'm Liz Mayfield."

"I guessed that. It's a pleasure to meet you. I—"

"What else?" Sawyer interrupted his partner.

Detective Hanson shrugged. "We'll get the lab reports back this afternoon. Don't expect much. Guys thought it looked like a professional job."

"Professional?" Sawyer shook his head. "Half the kids in high school know how to build a bomb."

"True." Detective Hanson stared at Sawyer. "Did you get her statement?"

"Not yet," Sawyer said, pulling a notebook and pen from his pocket.

Detective Hanson frowned at both of them. Then he turned toward Liz. "Who got in first this morning?"

"I did," she said. "I got here about five-thirty."

Sawyer looked up from his notebook. "Short night?"

Liz shrugged, not feeling the need to explain.

"Door locked when you got here, Ms. Mayfield?" Detective Hanson asked.

"Yes. After I came in, I locked it again and reset the alarm."

"You sure?"

"I'm usually the first person in. I know the routine."

"Did you see anything unusual once you got inside?"

"No. I went to the kitchen and started a pot of coffee."

"Then what?"

"I heard the front door, and then I thought I heard Jamison's door open. It appears I was right."

"You didn't see anybody?" Detective Hanson continued.

"No. When I left the kitchen, I looked around."

"Then what—"

"You looked around?" Sawyer interrupted his partner.

"Yes."

"You should have called the police."

She frowned at him. His tone had an edge to it. "I can't call the police every time I hear a door."

"You got a threat mailed to your office, and then shots were fired through your window," Sawyer said. "Maybe you should have given that some thought before you decided to investigate."

"Maybe we should keep going." Detective Hanson spoke to Sawyer. "You're taking notes, right?"

Sawyer didn't respond.

"After I *looked around*—" she emphasized the words "—I went down to my office and started working. After Jamison arrived, we came upstairs for coffee."

"What time was that?"

"Almost eight. Jamison's cell phone rang and then...we called 911. That's about it."

"It sounds like you stayed pretty calm. That takes a lot of guts." Detective Hanson smiled at her again.

She smiled back this time. "Thank you."

Sawyer grabbed Robert's arm. "Come on. Let's go. I want to talk to the boss."

Liz stood—so quickly that her head started to spin. She

picked up Sawyer's suit coat, shook it and thrust it out to him. "Don't forget this," she said.

He reached for it, and their fingers brushed. The fine hairs on her arm reacted with a mind of their own. What the heck was going on? She'd never ever had this kind of physical re-action to a man. Especially not one who acted as if he might think she was an idiot.

Sawyer jerked his own arm back. "I'll…uh…talk to you later," he said. Great. She had him tripping over his own tongue.

Sawyer got twenty feet before Robert managed to catch him. "Hang on," he said. "What the hell is wrong with you?"

Sawyer shook his head. "Just forget it."

"You act like an idiot and think I'm going to forget it?"

"Maybe you've forgotten this. We're here to investigate a crime. We've got a lot of people to talk to. I didn't think it made sense to spend any more time with Liz."

"Liz," Robert repeated.

"Yeah, Liz." Sawyer did his best to sound nonchalant. "She told me I could call her Liz."

"Since when do you hang all over witnesses?"

"I wasn't hanging all over her. She seemed upset. I of-fered her some comfort. Perhaps you've heard of it. It's called compassion." Sawyer started to walk away.

Robert kept pace. "That wasn't compassion I saw. That was a mating call. What's going on here, partner?"

Sawyer didn't know. Didn't have a clue why he started to unravel every time he got within three feet of Liz. "Liz Mayfield is a material witness to a crime. We had questioned her. I figured we needed to move on."

"That's it?"

"What else could it be?"

Robert looked him in the eye and nodded. "Your timing

sucks. I could have had little Lizzy's phone number in another two minutes."

"Lizzy," Sawyer repeated.

"She's my type."

Sawyer clamped down on the impulse to punch his partner, his best friend for the past two years. "She is *nothing* like your type."

Robert cocked his head. "Really?"

"Yeah. Really."

"I'll be damned." Robert laughed, his face transformed by his smile. "You like her."

"You don't know what you're talking about." Sawyer walked away from his partner.

Robert ran to catch up with him. "You're interested in a witness. Mr. Professional, Mr. I-always-use-my-Southern-manners. This has got to be killing you."

"Liz Mayfield is going to help me get Mirandez. That's my only interest," Sawyer said.

Robert slapped him on the back. "You just keep telling yourself that, Sawyer. Let's go talk to the boss."

When Sawyer and Robert reached Liz's boss, the man held up a finger, motioning them to wait while he finished his telephone call. From the one side of the conversation that Sawyer could hear, it sounded as if the guy was making arrangements to refer his clients on to other sources. After several minutes, the man ended the call and put his smartphone in his pocket.

"Detective Montgomery." The man greeted Sawyer, giving him a lopsided smile. "I have to admit I was hoping there wouldn't be any reason for us to talk again."

Sawyer felt sorry for him. He looked as if he'd just lost his best friend. "This is my partner, Detective Robert Hanson."

"Nice to meet you, Detective Hanson. I'm Jamison Curtiss, the executive director of OCM."

Sawyer watched Robert shake the man's hand, knowing Robert was rapidly cataloging almost everything there was to know about Jamison.

"I understand you got the call this morning, warning you of the bomb," Sawyer said.

"Yes. I'd just gotten to work. It was probably about ten minutes before eight."

"What happened then?"

"Liz and I left the building."

"Then what?" Sawyer prompted the man, reaching into his pocket for his notebook.

"Then I got a second call."

"What?" Sawyer stopped taking notes.

"The second call came in just after they'd found the bomb. Same guy who called the first time. Congratulated me on following directions. Then he told me that unless I closed the doors of OCM, there would be another bomb. I wouldn't know when or where, but there would be one."

"Liz Mayfield didn't say anything about a second call." Sawyer couldn't believe that she'd withheld information like that.

"She doesn't know. I'm not looking forward to telling her."

"Anybody else hear this call?" Not that Sawyer didn't believe the guy. The man looked shaken.

"No. It lasted about ten seconds. Then the guy hung up."

"What are you going to do?" Sawyer asked, keeping one eye on Jamison and casting a quick glance back at Liz. His heart skipped a beat when he didn't see her right away. Then he spied her. She had her back toward him. It took him all of three seconds to realize he was staring at her butt and another five to tear his glance away.

Robert laughed at him. He was quiet about it—just loud

enough to make sure Sawyer heard him. Jamison Curtiss looked confused. Sawyer nodded at the man to continue.

"In the past forty-eight hours," Jamison said, "one of my employees received an anonymous threat. On top of that, my business has been shot at and almost blown up. Whoever is trying to get my attention has it. Unless you can tell me that you know who's responsible, I don't think I have a lot of options."

"We don't know—" Robert spoke up "—but we will. Who has a key to OCM?"

"All the counselors. And our receptionist. Everyone has a slightly different schedule."

"And everybody knows the code to turn off the alarm?" Robert asked.

"Of course."

"Keys to the office doors all the same?"

"Yes."

"Same as to the front door?"

"Yes."

Sawyer and Robert exchanged a look. One key and a code. Child's play for somebody like Mirandez.

"You already gave us a list of employees with their home addresses. I'd like their personnel files, too," Robert said.

Jamison wrinkled his nose. "Is that really necessary?" he asked.

"Yes." Sawyer answered in a manner that made sure Jamison knew it wasn't an option.

"Fine. I'll have them to you by this afternoon."

"Anybody else have a key? A cleaning service, perhaps?"

"We all know how to run a vacuum. We can't afford to pay someone to clean."

"Anybody really new on your staff?"

"No, we've all been working together for years. Liz and Carmen came at about the same time."

"Carmen?" Robert asked.

"Lucky for her, her brother wasn't feeling well this morning. She came to work late." Jamison pointed to the group of counselors gathered across the street. "Carmen Jimenez is the dark-haired woman standing next to Liz."

"My God, she's beautiful," Robert said, then looked surprised that the comment had slipped out. "Sorry," he added.

Jamison shrugged. "That's the reaction most men have. Many of our clients are Spanish-speaking. She's a big asset."

Sawyer studied the two women who stood close together, deep in conversation. Carmen stood half a head shorter, her black hair and darker skin a stark contrast to Liz's blond hair and fair complexion. "Liz and Carmen close?"

"Best friends. We're all like family." Frustration crossed Jamison's face. "I've got to talk to them," he muttered. "They deserve to know what's going on."

Sawyer watched him walk across the street, joining Liz, Carmen and one other woman, who looked about ten years older. He assumed it was Cynthia, the counselor who just worked mornings. He couldn't hear what Jamison told them, but by the looks on their faces, they were shocked, scared and, he thought somewhat ironically, Liz and Carmen looked downright mad.

It took another ten minutes before the group broke up. Jamison walked back to Sawyer and Robert. "Well, they know. I told them that I've already started making arrangements for our current clients to be referred to other agencies. We have a responsibility to these young girls."

Sawyer understood responsibility. After all, he'd made it his responsibility to bring in Mirandez. "I'm going to go talk to Liz," Sawyer said to Robert.

Robert gave Liz and Carmen another look. "I'll go with you," he said.

When Sawyer reached Liz, he realized that Mary Thorton sat on the bench directly behind her. The young girl looked up when Sawyer and Robert approached. She didn't smile, frown or show any emotion at all. She just stared at the two of them.

Sawyer couldn't help staring back. The girl had on a green shirt and a too-tight orange knit jumper over it. With her big stomach, she looked like a pumpkin. Then the dress moved in ripples.

Sawyer remembered the first time he'd felt his baby move. It had rocked his world. He'd first put his hand on his girlfriend's stomach, then his cheek. It had taken another hour for the baby to roll over again, but the wait had been worth it.

Sawyer stuck his hand out toward Carmen Jimenez. "Ms. Jimenez," he said. "I'm Detective Montgomery."

"Good morning," she said.

"This is my partner, Detective Hanson."

Robert reached out his own hand. "It's a pleasure, Ms. Jimenez." Robert smiled at the woman. It was the same smile Sawyer had seen work very well for Robert in the past.

Carmen Jimenez didn't have the reaction that most women had. She nodded politely and shook Robert's hand so briefly that Sawyer wasn't sure that flesh actually touched.

Sawyer turned his attention to Mary, keeping his eyes trained on her face. He didn't want to make the mistake of looking at her baby again. "Mary." He spoke quietly. "Where were you at six o'clock this morning?"

"Sleeping."

"Alone?"

Mary gave him a big smile. "I don't like to sleep alone."

"So, I guess whoever you were sleeping with could verify that you were in bed this morning?"

"I don't know. Maybe."

"Come on, Mary. Surely he or she would know if you'd slipped out of bed."

"Trust me on this, Cop. It wouldn't be a she."

"Didn't think so," Sawyer said. "What's his name?"

"I can't tell you."

The girl's eyes had widened, and Sawyer thought her lower lip trembled just a bit. Liz must have seen it, too, because she sat down next to Mary and wrapped her arm around the girl's shoulders.

Sawyer deliberately softened his voice. He needed Mary. Hated to admit it but he did. "Mary, we can help you. But we need to know what's going on. You need to tell us."

"I don't know anything. You'd need to talk to him."

"Mirandez?"

Mary shook her head and frowned at Sawyer.

"No."

"Who, Mary? Come on, it's important."

She hesitated then seemed to decide. "Well, okay. His name is Pooh."

"Pooh?"

"Yeah. Pooh Bear. He's been sleeping with me since I was six."

He heard a laugh. Sawyer whirled around, and Robert suddenly coughed into his hand. Carmen, her dark eyes round with surprise, had her fingers pressed up against her lips. Sawyer looked at Liz. She stared at her shoes.

Damn. He could taste the bitter metal of the hook. The girl had baited her pole, cast it into the water and reeled him in. It was all he could do not to flop around on the sidewalk.

"Funny," he said. "Hope you're still laughing when you're sitting behind bars, waiting for a trial."

Liz stood up and jerked her head toward the right. "May I speak to you in private, Detective?"

Sawyer nodded and walked across the street. When he stopped suddenly, Liz almost bumped into him. She was close enough that he could smell her scent. It was a warm, sticky day already, but she smelled fresh and cool, like a walk through the garden on a spring night.

"Don't threaten her," Liz warned. "If you're going to charge her with something, do it. Otherwise, leave her alone. This can't be good for her or the baby."

Sawyer took a breath and sucked her into his lungs. As crazy as it seemed, it calmed him. "She's a little fool."

"She's a challenge," Liz admitted.

Sawyer laughed despite himself. "Paper-training a new puppy is a challenge."

Liz smiled at him, and he thought the world tilted just a bit.

"I'll talk to her," Liz said.

"How? Isn't she being referred on?"

Liz glanced over her shoulder, as if making sure no one was close by. "I'm going to keep seeing her. She needs me."

"Your boss is closing shop."

"I know. Carmen and I already discussed it. We'll see clients at my apartment."

Calm disappeared. "Are you nuts?"

She lifted her chin in the air.

He pointed a finger at her. "You received a threat. Which may or may not have anything to do with the shooting. Which may or may not have anything to do with today's bomb. Which may or may not have anything to do with Mirandez or Mary or the man in the moon. What the hell are you thinking?"

"I have to take the chance."

She'd spoken so quietly that Sawyer had to lean forward to hear her. "Why?" The woman had a damn death wish.

"I just have to," she said.

Was it desperation or determination that he heard in her tone? All he knew for sure was that nothing he could say was going to change her mind. "When? When are you starting this?" he asked.

"Mary's coming to see me tomorrow."

Great. That gave him twenty-four hours to figure out how to save them both.

Chapter Four

Liz's small apartment seemed smaller than usual after she set up shop at the kitchen table and Carmen took the desk in the extra bedroom. Girls came and went, and while the surroundings were different, the conversations were much the same as if they had occurred in a basement on the South Side.

It was late afternoon when Carmen made her way to the kitchen. "I thought Detective Montgomery might have a stroke yesterday." She took a swig from her water bottle. "He looked like he wanted to wring your neck."

Liz laughed and reached for her coffee cup. She took one sip and dumped the rest down the drain. No coffee was better than cold coffee. "He thinks we're idiots."

"He might be right." She hesitated. "What time was Mary's appointment?" she asked softly.

Liz looked at the clock. "Three hours ago."

"Did you call her?"

"Four times."

Carmen didn't say anything. Finally, she sighed. "There's something very wrong here."

"I know. I just don't know what it is." She ran a hand through her hair. "Are you done for the day?"

"I am. I could stay with you."

"Don't you dare. Your brother is still sick. Go home. Pick up some chicken-noodle soup for him on the way."

"You're sure?"

Liz nodded.

"Okay. I'll call you tomorrow."

Liz watched her friend leave. She waited fifteen minutes before trying Mary's cell phone again. It rang and rang, not even going to voice mail. She tried her three more times in the evening before finally giving up and going to bed.

She woke up the next day, tried Mary, didn't get an answer and finally admitted to herself that she needed help. Carmen was right. Something was very wrong.

Liz called Sawyer. He answered on the second ring.

"This is Liz Mayfield. Mary had an appointment yesterday, but she didn't show or call. I'm worried about her."

She wasn't sure, but she thought she heard him sigh.

"Can't the police do anything?" she asked. "She's just a kid."

"I'll put the word out to my contacts. If anybody sees her, they'll call."

"What about a missing-person report? Should I do one of those?"

"You can." Sawyer didn't think it would hurt but he doubted it would help much. Every day there were lots of teenagers reported missing. Most showed up a few days later safe and sound, sure that they'd taught their parents a thing or two. The true runaways usually called home a couple weeks later, once their money had run out. The smart ones anyway. The dumb ones slipped into a life of prostitution that killed them. Even those who were still technically breathing, working the streets each day, were as good as dead.

Fluentes had made contact late the night before. He had heard that Mirandez had slipped out of town but didn't have specifics. Sawyer thought it likely that Mary had gone with him. For all he knew, the two of them were hiding out in some fancy hotel somewhere, living off room service, enjoying all the benefits that drug money could buy.

"Do you think we should check the hospitals?" Liz asked.

"Probably a good idea. Hell, maybe she had her baby."

"I doubt it. Mary's scared to death of labor. I think she'd call me."

If she could. But maybe Mirandez had put the screws to that. "Are you this tight with all your clients?" Sawyer asked.

"No. But Mary really doesn't have anybody else."

"She has Mirandez," Sawyer said.

"He must have opted out. Maybe he's afraid of blood?"

"Only of seeing his own," Sawyer said. "What about her family? Anybody around here that she'd stay with?"

"Her mother died several years ago. I've met her father. He kicked her out when he found out about the pregnancy. I tried to reason with him, but it was no use. Something along the lines of she's made her bed, now let her lie in it."

His parents had been furious when he'd come home and confessed that he'd gotten his girlfriend pregnant. His mom had cried. His dad had left the house for four hours. But then he'd come home, quietly conferred with his wife, then the two of them sat Sawyer down so that they could discuss what he intended to do about the situation.

He'd wanted to marry Terrie. He found out it didn't much matter what he wanted. Terrie's parents refused to even consider the idea. He'd been the poor kid from the wrong side of the tracks. They'd wanted more for their daughter.

Sawyer had been standing at his son's freshly dug grave when Terrie's father had confessed that not allowing his daughter to marry Sawyer had been a mistake. Sawyer hadn't even responded. Sawyer knew the man thought he could have pulled Terrie back from the drugs that crushed both her body and mind.

Sawyer knew better. He hadn't been able to help Terrie. A marriage license wouldn't have helped him wrestle her away from the cruel grip of addiction. He'd believed Terrie when she'd promised to quit the drugs. In doing so, he'd failed her. That haunted him. He'd failed his helpless son. That had rocked his soul, causing it to crack and bleed.

"She have any friends?" Sawyer asked.

"She talked about a couple girlfriends. But I never met them."

"Okay. Then I guess we wait. See if something comes up."

"There is one place we might check," Liz said. "Mary mentioned a children's bookstore that she liked. Said she spent a lot of time there, looking through books."

"Got a name?"

"I've got an address. I wrote it down. I had planned on finding it and picking out a baby gift." She opened her purse, pulled out the slip of paper and read it to him.

He whistled softly. "Are you sure that's right?"

"Yes. Mary raved about this store. She said Marvis, the owner, was really cool. It's not an area I'm familiar with."

"I'd hope not," Sawyer mocked. "I don't think there're a lot of bookstores in that neighborhood. There are, however, a lot of really great crack houses. I'll go check it out and let you know."

"You're kidding, right?"

He didn't answer.

"Look, Sawyer. You need Mary. I'm the best link you have to her. But if you cut me out—if you even think about leaving me behind—that's the last information I'll share with you."

Sawyer counted to ten. "To interfere with a police investigation is a crime. To willfully withhold evidence is a crime."

"You'd have to prove it first."

Sawyer almost laughed. He'd used his best I'm-a-hard-ass-cop voice. The one that made pimps and pushers shake. But she didn't even sound concerned. "What about your clients?"

"I'll call Carmen. We both had a light day today, so she should be able to cover my clients. She can meet them at a coffee shop near OCM."

"Fine. Be ready in twenty minutes."

Sawyer hung up the phone. He ran his fingers across the stack of manila folders that had been delivered late last night, hot out of the filing cabinets of OCM. Personnel files. Liz Mayfield's file.

He sifted through the pile. When he found hers, he flipped it open. Copies of tax forms. Single with zero exemptions. Direct-deposit form. Emergency-contact form. Harold and Patrice Mayfield, her parents. They had a suburban area code.

He set those papers aside. Next was her résumé. With plenty of detail.

He scanned the two-page document. The label Ph.D. jumped out at him. Liz had a doctorate degree in psychology from Yale University. Up until a few years ago, she'd worked for Mathers and Froit. The name meant nothing to him. He read on. She'd been a partner, responsible for billing out over a half million a year. That was clear enough. She'd been in the big time.

But she'd left that all behind for OCM. Why? With a sigh, Sawyer closed the file. He stood up and snatched his keys off the desk. He almost wished he'd never looked. Even as a kid, he'd been intrigued by puzzles.

He opened his car door just as Robert pulled his own vehicle into the lot. He waited while his friend parked.

"I've got a lead on Mary Thorton," he said when Robert approached.

"Need me to go with?"

"No. It's probably nothing. The personnel files are on my

desk. Spend your time on them. Maybe the connection to OCM isn't Mary. Maybe it's something else."

WHEN SAWYER AND LIZ pulled up to the address, Sawyer started to laugh. A dry chuckle.

Liz looked at the slip of paper and then checked the numbers hanging crooked on the side of the old brick building. There was no mistake. Mary's bookstore was the Pleasure Palace. Brown shipping paper covered the front windows. "What do you think?" she asked.

"I think it's not a Barnes & Noble," he said, smiling at her.

"Let's get this over with," she said, opening her car door.

Sawyer caught up with her fast. "Stay behind me," he instructed. "It's too early for the drug dealers or the prostitutes to be doing business, but there's no telling what else lurks around here."

Liz slowed her pace and let him take the lead. He pushed the door open with his foot. "Also, no telling where people's hands have been that turned that handle," he said almost under his breath.

There were magazines everywhere. Women, their bodies slick with oil, in every pose imaginable. Men with women, women with women, women with dogs. Where the magazines ended, the ropes, chains and harnesses took up.

"I don't believe this." Sawyer let out a soft whistle and pointed.

There, surrounded by DVDs, handcuffs, and plastic and rubber appliances in all shapes and sizes, was a table piled high with kids' books. They were used but in good shape.

Sawyer picked one off the pile. It was the familiar Dr. Seuss book. "I hate green eggs and ham," he said, "Sawyer, I am."

"You think this is funny, don't you?" Liz hissed.

"It's hilarious. It's worth the price of admission."

"There was no admission."

"Trust me on this. There's always a price. We just don't know what it is yet."

"Hello." A voice sang out from the corner.

"But we're just about to find out," Sawyer whispered.

A woman, almost as tall as Sawyer and pleasantly plump, wearing a flowing purple pantsuit floated toward them. She had big hair and bright red lipstick. "Welcome to the Pleasure Palace. I'm Marvis. May I help you find something? A nice DVD perhaps? Or we have some brand-new battery-operated—"

"We're trying to find a book for our friend," Sawyer interrupted. He nodded at the table.

"A children's book?"

"Yeah."

"Well, you've come to the right place. Everything is half-off the cover price. All of these belonged to my grandchildren. They are in good shape. The books, that is." Marvis laughed at her own joke, her double chin bouncing. "Not that my sweet babies aren't fit as a fiddle, too. They can run circles around me."

It would be a fair amount of exercise just getting around Grandma Marvis. Liz caught Sawyer's eye and knew he was thinking the same thing.

"There are over two hundred books here. Every one of my eight grandkids could read before they were five."

"Our friend comes here all the time. She's about five-three, fair skin, freckles, blondish-red hair and pregnant." Sawyer pretended to browse through the pile, all the while keeping an eye on the door.

"Let me think." The woman tapped her polished pink fingernail against her lips.

Sawyer walked over to the counter. He picked the top

DVD off the rack. He looked at the price and pulled a fifty out of his pocket.

"Oh, now I remember. Mary, right?" The woman's doubled chin tucked under when she smiled.

"That's the one."

"Wonderful girl. Loves her books. Always takes one of the classics." She waved her hand toward the end of the table. "Last time she was here, she got *Little Women*. Said she hoped that if she had a daughter she'd be as pretty as Winona Ryder."

"When was she in last?" Sawyer asked.

"It had to have been at least a week ago. I was telling Herbert, he's my man friend, just yesterday that I bet she had her baby. What did she have? She was carrying it so low, I couldn't help but think it was a boy."

"No baby yet. In fact," Sawyer said as he pulled a book off the children's table and threw another twenty at the woman, "if she happens to stop by, would you tell her to call Liz?"

"I'll do that. You all have a nice day. Are you sure I can't interest you in something? We've got a whole new line of condoms. Cartoon characters."

"No thanks." Sawyer literally pulled Liz out of the store and back to the car. He unlocked her side, threw the merchandise in the backseat and got in on the driver's side. He started to drive away without another word.

"I wonder if they come in an assorted box," Liz said.

Sawyer almost ran the car into a light pole.

Not that he needed to worry about causing an unexpected pregnancy. A quick trip to his physician ten years ago had taken care of that. But there were other good reasons to wear protection. With a woman like Liz Mayfield in his bed, he'd probably be hard-pressed to remember that. He'd want her, all of her, without anything to separate the two of them. He'd want—

"Hey, are you all right?" she asked. "You look a little pale."

Sawyer whipped his eyes back to the road. In another minute, she'd start to analyze him. If she found out what he was thinking, she'd probably jump out of the car. "I'm fine," he said.

"So, now where?" she asked.

"I'm taking you home."

"We can't just give up."

"I'm not giving up. But until a clue turns up, we wait. Maybe Mary will get smart and call you."

"You're determined to think the worst of her, aren't you?"

"She's up close and personal with a drug dealer. It's hard to think of her as Mother Teresa."

"Why don't you try thinking of her as a mixed-up, scared, lonely kid?"

"I can't do that." He risked a quick glance at her.

Liz folded her arms across her chest and stared straight ahead. When she spoke, he had to strain to hear her.

"You need to try harder," she said.

He tried. Every damn day he tried. Tried to rid the streets of scum. Tried to arrest just one more of the human garbage that preyed on young bodies and souls. She had no idea how hard he tried. Just like she had no idea that he wanted her more than he'd wanted a woman in years. Maybe ever. And that, quite frankly, scared the hell out of him.

Yeah, he needed to try harder. He needed to keep his distance, needed to remember that getting Mirandez was the goal. Not getting into Liz Mayfield's pants or letting her get into his head.

LIZ WASHED HER DISHES, cleaned her bathroom, sorted some old photographs and even managed to force down a peanut-butter sandwich. She went through all the motions of a regular life. But what she really did was wait for Mary's call.

When the phone finally rang at seven o'clock, she jumped off her couch, ran to the kitchen and managed to stub her toe on the way.

She tried to keep the disappointment out of her voice when Jamison greeted her. "Liz, I talked to Carmen late this afternoon," he said. "I understand that Mary was a no-call, no-show yesterday."

Jamison would understand her worry. She knew she could confide in him. But she couldn't bring herself to utter the words. To somehow give credence to the fact that Mary might be in trouble. That Mary might be, at this very moment, crying out for help, but there would be no one around to hear. If she said it, it could be true.

"You know how these kids are. I'm sure I'll hear from her soon."

"I hope you're right," he said. "I don't know how much help this is, but I did get a lead on Mary that you can pass on to Detective Montgomery."

"What?"

"I reviewed some case files today, and I saw a note that one of my girls had heard about OCM from Mary Thorton. They met at a club."

"What's the name of it?"

"Jumpin' Jack Flash. I guess they have a dance contest every Tuesday night. The women don't pay a cover, and all the drinks are two bucks. It's somewhere on the South Side, on Deyston Street."

Liz knew just where it was. She and Sawyer had passed it this morning on their way to the bookstore. And today was Tuesday.

"He might want to check it out. From what I understood

from my client, it's a real hangout for the young crowd. I had thought about trying to put a few brochures there."

His business, her life.

"Thanks for the tip, Jamison."

"You'll tell Detective Montgomery?"

"I will. Thanks, Jamison." Liz hung up and dialed Sawyer. After four rings, his voice mail came on. "Hi, Sawyer," she said. "I've got a tip on Mary. It's a dance club on Deyston. Call me, okay?"

She waited an hour. She'd tried his line again. When voice mail picked up again, she pressed zero. A woman answered. Detective Montgomery was not in. Was it an emergency? Did she want to page him?

She almost said yes but realized he could be in the middle of trouble. The man had a dangerous job. He didn't need to be interrupted.

She'd just go there by herself, look around and ask a few questions. She'd only stay a short while. Then she could report back to Sawyer. It would probably be better if he wasn't there anyway. He'd do his tough-guy cop routine and scare away any of the girls who might know Mary.

Liz had learned a lot about teenage girls in the past three years. When they got scared, they clammed up. She didn't want the girls circling the proverbial wagons and making it impossible to find Mary.

Liz ran back to her closet and started sorting through her clothes. Business suits or jeans. Old life, new life. She didn't have much in the middle. But tonight, she needed a young, nonestablishment look. It took her twenty minutes to find something that might work. She pulled the short, tight black skirt on, hoping like heck that she wouldn't have to sneeze. The zipper would surely break. Then she put on a black bra and topped if off with a sheer white shirt that had come with one of her swimsuits. She left her legs bare and stuck her feet into high-heeled, open-toed black sandals.

She teased and sprayed her hair, put on three times the amount of makeup she normally wore and walked her body through a mist of perfume. For the finishing touch, she applied two temporary tattoos, one on her breast, just peeking over the edge of her bra, and the other on the inside of her thigh, low enough that it would show when she crossed her legs. She'd remembered them at the last minute. They'd come in a box of cereal. One was a snake and the other a flag. Not exactly what she'd have chosen but better than nothing. Every girl she met had some kind of tattoo or body piercing.

When she got finished and looked in the mirror, she wasn't too dissatisfied with the effort. She didn't look eighteen, but she thought she could pass for her mid-twenties. At least they might not guess she was thirty-two—so far into adulthood, from their perspective, that she couldn't possibly even remember what it was like to be young.

She grabbed a small black purse, stuck her cell phone in it as well as two hundred bucks. She remembered Sawyer's advice from earlier in the day. Everything had a price. She needed to be prepared to pay for information.

She waved down a cab and ignored the guy's look when she told him the address. Thirty minutes later, when he pulled up to the curb, she sat still for a minute, for the first time wondering if she had made a big mistake.

Music poured out of the small, old building. Ten or fifteen teens gathered around the door, lounging against the cement walls. Everybody had a cigarette and a can of beer. More boys than girls. And the few girls who were there were clearly taken. One straddled a boy who sat on a wooden chair. He had his hand up her shirt. Another girl, plastered from lips to toes to her boy, his hands possessively curled around her butt, almost blocked the doorway.

"You getting out, lady?" The cab driver raised one eyebrow at her. "I don't like sitting still in this neighborhood."

Liz swallowed. This morning, the neighborhood had looked gray. Gray buildings, gray sidewalk. The sky had even seemed a little gray, as if it were a reflection of the street below. But tonight, the street seemed black and purple and red. Violent and passionate, the colors of sex and sin. Firecrackers popped, music blasted, the air almost sizzled.

"Yes, I'm getting out." Liz threw a twenty at the driver and stepped from the car.

Chapter Five

"Oh, baby, I do like blondes." The voice came from her far left. Liz couldn't see him until he stepped away from the corner of the building. He looked older than the other teens, probably in his early twenties. He cocked a finger at her. "Come here. Let's see if they really do have more fun."

A couple of the other teens pushed each other around, laughing, but nobody else said anything. Liz ignored them all and walked into the club.

If it had been loud outside, it was mind-blowing inside. It made her head hurt. She managed to make her way through the crowd and got up to the bar. She stood next to a group of girls, most of them looking about Mary's age. Where the hell were the police? These kids couldn't be old enough to drink. Liz wanted them all busted but just not until she got the information that she wanted.

"I was talking to you outside, baby."

Liz felt heat crawl up her neck. She turned around. It was Creepy Guy from outside. She knew immediately that ignoring him wasn't going to work.

"I heard you." She smiled at him. "But I got to find my friend before I can have my own fun."

He stared at her breasts. Liz resisted the urge to slap him and tell him to get cleaned up and get a job. "I'll help you, baby. Who you looking for? I know everybody here."

She debated for all of three seconds. "Annie Smith. She likes to dance here."

"Don't know her." The man grabbed her arm and pulled her close. He smelled like cigarettes and cheap rum. "Let's you and me dance."

He stood five inches taller, probably eighty pounds heavier and had wrists twice as big as hers. Liz felt the fear spread from her toes to her head. It didn't matter that he was ten years younger. Age and experience didn't give her an advantage. Brute strength would win every time.

She took her free hand and stroked him under the chin with the back of her fingers. "I'd like that," she said. When he took his free hand and cupped her butt, she forced the smile to stay on her face. "You stay here," she said. "I'm gonna be right over there with those girls. You'll be able to see me." She opened her purse and pulled out a twenty. "Buy me a drink, sugar. Buy yourself one, too."

Then she pulled away from him and edged over to the group of girls that were still gathered just feet away. Several of them turned and stared at her when she joined the group. Then they started talking again as if she wasn't there.

Lord, it was just like high school.

She couldn't wait for them to warm up to her. She had only minutes before the creep at the bar got tired of waiting. She moved around the group, stopping when she stood next to a girl she guessed to be about five months pregnant.

"What do you want?" The girl took another drag off her cigarette.

Liz wanted to rip it away. Didn't she know what that was doing to her baby's lungs?

"I'm looking for Mary Thorton."

The girl looked over both shoulders then started to move away. "Stop, please," Liz pleaded, keeping her voice low.

"My name is Liz, and I think she's in trouble. I want to help her."

"Liz who?"

"Liz Mayfield. I work at Options for Caring Mothers on Logan Street."

Liz saw the flicker of recognition in the young girl's eyes. "You'll get in trouble asking about Mary," the girl advised, her voice low. "She ain't around anyway. She and Dantel went to Wisconsin. She said they were going fishing. Up by Wisconsin Dells."

"Are you sure?" Liz asked, aware that the man from the bar, a drink in each hand, walked toward her.

"That's what she told me. I don't think she wanted to go, but I don't think her boyfriend likes the word *no*."

Liz wanted to hug the young woman. Instead, she winked at her, took a step backward and loudly said, "Hey, if you don't know Annie Smith, you don't need to be such a bitch about it. I just asked a freakin' question."

She turned toward the door, but the guy with the drinks intercepted her before she got five feet. *Damn.* "Oh, thanks," she said and reached for the drink that she had absolutely no intention of sipping. She might be thirty-two and well past the bar scene, but she knew all about date-rape drugs.

Creepy Guy looked her up and down. Then he put his nearly empty glass and her full glass down on the nearest table, grabbed her hand and yanked her out into the sea of bodies. "Let's dance, baby. You can drink later."

The smell of sweat and cheap liquor almost overwhelmed Liz. When the man pulled her close and she could feel his erection, her mind almost stopped working. He had his hands on her butt and his mouth close to her ear.

She thought she might throw up.

Suddenly, the crowd parted and girls started screaming. Twenty feet away, two men were fighting. One had picked up a chair, and the other had a knife. Liz watched as yet another man, holding a beer bottle like a club, stepped into the mix.

Creepy Guy let go of her.

"I gotta pee," Liz said and ran for the bathroom.

There was no damn window in the bathroom. She moved into one of the stalls and grabbed her phone out of her purse. She dialed Sawyer's number. It rang and rang.

"Hey, don't take all day. The rest of us got to pee, too." An angry fist pounded on the door.

"Just a minute," Liz said. Sawyer's voice mail kicked on. Liz flushed the toilet so that she could talk. "Sawyer, I need help. I'm at 1882 Deyston." She disconnected that call and had just started to dial 911 when the door to the stall was kicked open.

"Everybody out," a female cop yelled at her. "Put your hands in the air and walk to the door."

Liz wanted to put her arms around the woman and hug her. But the gun pointed at her told her that wouldn't be appreciated.

Liz walked out into the club area. Some of the grayness from the daytime had eased back in. The lights had been turned on, and the music had been turned off. There were at least ten cops, with more pouring through the open door. Within minutes, the cops paired off, breaking the group into smaller groups. Everybody had to empty their pockets, their purses. A female officer patted Liz down, looking for weapons. She didn't care.

Liz didn't even care when she had to sit on the dirty floor, her hands on top of her head. Anything was better than dancing with that man, his erection pressed up against her, his hands grabbing at her butt. Thank God he hadn't tried to kiss her. Even now, the thought of it made her gag.

She sat quietly. The girl next to her cried; the boy on the other side screamed obscenities at the cops who stood around the perimeter of the room. Liz scanned the area for the pregnant girl who'd given her the info, but she was nowhere to be seen. Somehow, she'd managed to slip out.

Liz tried to remember every cop show she'd ever watched. When did people get fingerprinted? When was the mug shot taken? Would she get to make a phone call before or after all that?

Who the heck would she call? Sawyer hadn't been at his desk. She couldn't ask Carmen to come down to the police station at eleven o'clock on a Tuesday night. The only person she could call was Jamison. He'd have a cow, but then he'd come.

A minute later, when Sawyer, with his partner Robert on his heels, came through the doors, she realized that Jamison wasn't the only one likely to have a cow.

Sawyer literally skidded to a stop. He didn't say a word. He couldn't.

"Damn," Robert said.

"Hi," Liz said.

"What the hell are you doing here?" Sawyer demanded. God, he'd been scared. When he'd gotten her messages, he'd driven like a crazy person to the bar, calling Robert on the way. They'd gotten there almost at the same time. When he'd seen more than a dozen squads outside, all kinds of crazy thoughts had entered his head.

Now that he was sure she wasn't hurt, he wanted to wring her little neck. "You came here, looking like *that?*" he said.

She put her chin in the air. "I had to fit in. I couldn't wear my jeans."

"Did you have to dress like a damned hooker?"

He regretted it the minute he said it. But he was scared. He hadn't been there to protect her. What if she'd gotten hurt? Raped? Killed?

"I didn't think a three-piece suit would fit in," she said.

"You didn't think. Period."

If anything, she put her nose a bit higher in the air. "I called you. I tried to reach you."

"You left a stupid message. Page me. That's why I leave the number."

"I didn't want to bother you," she said.

"Bother me?" This woman drove him crazy. "All you've been is a bother since the day I met you."

"Look, Sawyer," Robert interjected. "There's no harm done. She's fine. We're all fine. Don't be an idiot about this."

Sawyer rubbed a hand across his face. He could see the pain in Liz's pretty green eyes. It was hurt he'd caused.

He took a deep breath. When he spoke, he raised his voice just enough that Liz could hear but that the rest of the people in the room would have to make up their own story. "I'm sorry, Liz. I'm more sorry than you can imagine. I was worried and…and I'm not handling this well." His voice cracked at the end.

"I want to go home," Liz said. "Will you take me?"

He felt the weight of the world lift off his shoulders. "Yeah, I'd be glad to." He looked at Robert and nodded his head at the officer who seemed to be in charge. "Can you…"

"No problem. I'll give our boys the CliffsNotes version so that they understand why she's making a quick exit. Get going."

Sawyer nodded, wrapped an arm around her and walked her out of the bar.

He wished he had a coat, something that he could throw over her, cover up some skin. What in the hell had she been thinking?

Once inside his car, Sawyer kept his hands firmly wrapped around the steering wheel, afraid that he might just reach out and shake her. Of course, once he touched her, he'd be toast. It would all be over for him. He'd end up kissing and touch-

ing her and maybe more if she didn't have the good sense
to stop him.

It would be wrong. She deserved better than what he had
to offer. Which was nothing. Liz Mayfield was young, pretty
and someday would make some man a fine wife. They'd have
pretty babies, and God willing, she and her husband would
see them grow up, go to their first baseball game, drive a
car, go to college, have a life.

He'd thought he'd had it. Then he'd lost it. His baby's
precious body had grown cold in his arms. The nurses, the
professionals who were used to saying the words *baby* and
death in the same sentence, let him be. They walked around
his rocking chair, careful to keep their voices down, their
eyes never quite meeting his.

Much wiser now, he knew what he had. He had his work,
his career. He made important arrests that got scum off the
streets. He made a difference every day. That was more than
some people had in a lifetime. It had to be enough for him.

He'd been half out of his mind with worry when he'd gotten the two voice mails from her. He'd listened to the first
and realized that she intended to go to Deyston Street and
then the second; when he'd heard the panic in her voice and
knew she was scared and possibly hurt, his heart had almost stopped.

It had been a huge relief when he saw her. And then he'd
turned stupid. The worry eating at his soul had burst from his
mouth, and he'd hurt her. He regretted that. But she needed
to understand how big of a mistake she'd made. For her own
sake. She didn't understand how violent, how cruel, how hu-
miliating the street—and those who called the street their
home—could be.

He would take her back to her apartment, and they would
talk. He wouldn't yell, and he wouldn't accuse. It would be
a civil conversation, one adult to another. He'd make her

understand that she needed to let the police look for Mary. That she needed to stop seeing OCM's clients at her apartment. Then he'd leave.

Sawyer found a spot near the front of Liz's apartment building. "I'd like to come in," he said. He was proud that he sounded so calm, so reasonable. See, he could do this.

"I'm not sure that's a good idea."

"We should talk. I'd be more comfortable talking in your apartment." Wow. *He* should be the shrink.

He waited until she nodded before he quickly got out of the car. Yep, everything would be fine. They'd have a nice quiet conversation, and he could leave, knowing that she'd be safe.

He walked around the car and opened Liz's door. Oh, hell. From this angle, her legs went on forever. She had them crossed, one sexy, small foot, with painted red toenails, dangling over the other. Tanned legs, absolutely silky smooth. Round knees, firm thighs and a…a snake. No way! It couldn't be! He squatted down next to the open door, and with his index finger, he tapped against the tattoo.

"What the hell is this? Are you nuts?"

"Sawyer, it's just…"

"It's not just a tattoo," he yelled. "You have the most beautiful, incredibly sexy legs." He pulled his hand back and rubbed his temple, as if he suddenly had a very bad headache. "How could you even think about getting a tattoo? And a snake. Were you drunk on your butt or what?"

"Stop yelling. My neighbors will call the cops. I'm not dealing with that again tonight."

She unbuttoned the top three buttons on her shirt. "It's a rub-on. See? Just like this one."

He did not intend to look. There was really no need. But he couldn't stop himself. And when she stuck two slim fingers in her mouth, wet them with her tongue and then rubbed her breast, blending the stars and stripes of the American flag, his knees almost gave out.

Chapter Six

"You need to stop doing that," he warned.

"But…" She looked up at him, confusion clear in her green eyes. "I just wanted you to see—"

"I see. I don't need to see another thing. Let's go." He turned away, not looking as she maneuvered those long legs out of the car.

"They came out of a cereal box," she said.

He'd never be able to eat his Cheerios again. "Fine. Let's not talk about tattoos anymore, okay?" He motioned for her keys, and she handed them to him. He unlocked the apartment door. He held up his palm, stopping her. He went inside, took a quick look around the apartment, and when he came back, he pulled her inside and shut the door.

"You and I are going to talk. But first, go take a shower. I'll make coffee."

"I don't really drink coffee at night. I'd prefer some tea. Something herbal. It's in the cupboard."

Herbal. He needed strong, get-a-grip caffeine and she wanted herbal. "Fine. Whatever. Just get that stuff off your face and get rid of those tattoos."

He made the stupid tea and tried not to think about how she'd look in the shower, the water sliding over her slim, firm body. The woman truly had an incredible shape. He'd appreciated it before, but now that he'd seen a bit more of it, he might have moved into the worship stage.

He had already finished one cup of tea when she came back to the kitchen. Her long hair, looking a bit darker when wet, was pulled back in a loose braid. She had on a T-shirt, a pair of jogging shorts and white socks. No makeup. Not a speck. She looked about sixteen. He felt better. He wouldn't be tempted to stick his hands up her shirt if she didn't look legal.

"Here's your tea."

"Thanks."

She sat on the stool next to the kitchen counter and took dainty little sips. Neither of them said a word for a few minutes. When she did speak, she surprised him.

"I did a stupid thing tonight," she said.

Yeah, that was exactly what he'd intended to tell her.

"Something bad could have happened, and it would have been my own fault."

Right. That about summed it up. Why didn't it give him more pleasure to hear her say it? To have her admit that she was out of her league?

"I didn't want to miss meeting Mary's friends. I didn't stop to think about all the other people who would be there."

He hated—absolutely hated—seeing her this beaten. "Just forget it," he said. "It's over."

And then she started to cry. She might sip daintily, but she cried loud and rough. Her nose got red, big tears slid down her cheeks, her shoulders shook and she made choking sounds. Knowing it was stupid, knowing he'd probably regret it, he walked around the counter and wrapped his arms around her.

"Now, now." He tried to comfort her. "You had a tough night. Everything will be better in the morning."

"I hate being a girl. I hate being smaller, shorter, weaker. I hate being afraid."

The muscles in his stomach tightened.

"Did somebody threaten you?" He pulled back just enough so that he could look her in the eye.

"No. It's nothing. I'm just tired."

She was lying. "Did somebody touch you tonight?" He felt a burn. It started in the pit of his stomach, then exploded into his arms and legs, making him shake. He was going to kill the bastard.

She shrugged her shoulders, trying to dismiss him. He stopped her. "I told you once. Don't lie to me. Don't ever lie to me."

She gave one last sniff and lifted her chin in the air. "When I got out of the cab, there were a bunch of teenagers outside of the building. One of them said something. He looked a bit older than the rest, maybe twenty or so. I just ignored him. But when I got inside, I couldn't shake him."

"What did he do?" He didn't want to know. He didn't want to hear it.

"He wanted to dance."

"Okay."

"I tried to get out of it. He was too strong. I couldn't get away without making a scene. I'd gotten the information I needed. All I wanted to do was get out of there without a bunch of people wondering who I was and why I was there. I think he might have been high on something. He seemed just on the edge of being out of control."

She'd gotten information about Mary. He didn't care. "What did he do to you?"

"He pulled me close and I could feel…him." She blushed but recovered quickly. "I could feel him poking into me and I got scared. I was in a strange place, I didn't know a soul and he outweighed me by at least eighty pounds." She blinked her eyes, where tears still clung to her thick lashes. "Then there was a fight. I guess that's why the cops came. Anyway, I told him I had to pee and I ran to the bathroom. When the cops came, I almost hugged them."

He pulled her close, held her next to his heart and bent his mouth very close to her ear. "I'm sorry that happened to you. I'm sorry he touched you. I'm sorry he scared you. But you need to forget it. You're never going to see him again."

She moved even closer, and her curves suddenly filled his hands. Her heat warmed him. She kissed the side of his neck.

Let it be enough, he prayed. *Let it be enough.* But he knew it wouldn't. He wanted her mouth, he wanted her hands, he wanted her legs spread apart. He wanted to make love with her for about a day. That might be enough.

"I'm very grateful," she said, making him feel like a lecherous old man. She looked sixteen, and she'd just given him a shy, sweet little kiss and a gracious thank-you. And all he could do was think about pushing her backward, getting her legs hooked over his arms and coming inside of her until one of them passed out.

Then she wrapped her arms around his back and hugged him. He could feel the whole length of her body. It pressed up against him, tempting him. She smelled so good. Sweet and fresh. He bent his head over her wet hair, breathing in the scent of her shampoo. He moved his hands across her back, fingering the bottom of her T-shirt. God help him, he needed to touch her.

He put one hand under her shirt, lightly rubbing her bare back. He moved his fingers over her warm skin, loving the silky feel of her. He moved his hand a bit higher, finding only skin. The woman hadn't put a bra on. Was she crazy? Didn't she have a clue what that did to him, to feel her warm skin, to know that he was just inches away from holding her breast in his hand?

And when she lifted her face and her lips were just inches from his, he went down for the count. He kissed her. Long and slow. And when he slid his tongue into her mouth and she suckled lightly on it, he got instantly hard.

Never taking his mouth away from hers, he moved his hand across her ribs and cupped one breast, loving the feel of the heavy weight, loving the softness, the warmth. He brushed his fingers across her nipple, groaning when she arched her back and pressed her breast more fully into his open hand. He shifted, pressing his hardness against her softness.

She jerked her head back, her eyes wide open.

Her soft, liquid warmth had turned into a hard, solid block of ice.

He was an idiot. A senseless, selfish idiot. She'd already had one man tonight poking into her, causing her to be scared. And now he was doing the same thing. With grim resolution, he pulled away from her, putting a good foot between their bodies.

"I'm sorry," he said. "I can't believe I did that. I…I should be shot."

She laughed. A bit shaky perhaps but it gave him a little hope. "I think that's extreme," she said.

"I'm not so sure. I'm attracted to you," he said. "But you don't have to worry. It would be unprofessional for me to pursue a relationship with you."

She stared at him.

"I'm a cop," he said, reminding both of them. "I'm investigating a murder. I can't do anything to compromise that investigation."

He could tell that she was starting to get it.

"Never mind," Sawyer said, thinking he'd rather be just about anywhere else than explaining to her why he couldn't

even think about sleeping with her. "I think I'd better go."
He grabbed his keys off the counter.

Liz's braid had flipped over one shoulder, and she played
with the wet ends. "Don't you even want to know what I
learned about Mary?" she asked, her voice subdued.

Yes. No. Hell, he'd been so far gone that he'd forgotten
all about Mary. He moved behind the counter, needing the
physical barrier. "What?"

She took a sip of tea. "Mary and Dantel Mirandez are
fishing in Wisconsin."

He laughed, glad that he still could. "Sure they are."

Her cheeks turned pink. "I talked to one of Mary's friends
tonight. At first, she wouldn't tell me anything. But then I
think she decided that I might be able to help Mary."

"Did she say Mary needed help?"

"No, but she acted nervous, like she didn't want to be
caught talking about Mirandez or Mary."

"Smart girl. Liz, I can't see Mirandez with a fishing pole.
Not unless he'd diced somebody up and was using them for
bait."

"You said Mirandez was smart. If he wanted to disappear, doesn't it make sense that he'd go somewhere you'd
never think to look?"

"Yeah, but fishing? And anyway, even if I believed it,
there has to be at least a thousand lakes in Wisconsin. We'd
never find him."

"It's someplace near Wisconsin Dells."

Near Wisconsin Dells. Or The Dells, as all the vacationers
called it. One of the detectives he worked with had just taken
his family there. He'd called it Little Disney. There were
lots of water parks, miniature golf courses and restaurants.
Home of the Tommy Bartlett ski show and the boats shaped
like ducks that cruised up and down the Wisconsin River.

He couldn't for the life of him see Mirandez at a place

like that. "It just sounds too bizarre," he said, absolutely hating to see the look of disappointment on her face. "Even if he's there, we wouldn't have a clue where to start looking."

"Yes, we do. He's at a cabin. We just have to check out the cabins in the area."

"It's Wisconsin. The state is full of cabins and campgrounds. Even if we know it's around The Dells, it's a big area to search."

She didn't look convinced. "I have to try," she said.

He got a bad feeling in the bottom of his stomach. "You're not trying anything. Wasn't tonight enough of a lesson?"

She swallowed hard, and he felt bad about throwing it in her face. But if that was what it took to keep her safe at home, he didn't feel that bad.

"Yes, tonight sucked. I got hit on by a kid and spent a half hour sitting on a dirty floor. But it's nothing in the grand scheme of things. I have to find Mary."

"The police will find Mirandez. And Mary will be there. We've got a huge amount of manpower out on the street. It's only a matter of time."

"Not if he's fishing."

"Gang leaders do not fish." Sawyer pounded his fist against the kitchen counter.

"You can't be sure of that." Liz started to pace around her apartment. "I don't know what's going on here. I've thought about it for days, and nothing seems to make sense. Well, maybe one thing. That first day we met, after the shooting, you said that it seemed like Mirandez wanted Mary's attention. That he wasn't actually trying to hurt her."

"Right. She's his girlfriend. Maybe he's partial to sleeping in the same bed every night."

"No. It's more than that. I think Mirandez thinks it's his baby."

"You told me it belonged to a student at Loyola."

"Yes. But I think Mary told Mirandez something different."

"Why?"

"Because she's young and alone and probably desperately wanted someone to want both her and the baby."

"Then the Loyola kid was just convenient."

"Perhaps. But he didn't deny that he'd slept with Mary."

"Who knows how many men she slept with?" He hated to be quite so blunt, but Liz needed to stop looking at Mary with rose-colored glasses. She surprised him when she didn't look offended.

"You're right. We don't know. And maybe Mirandez doesn't, either. You said that Mary had been his girlfriend for the past six months. She's eight months pregnant."

Sawyer sat down on one of the counter stools, tapping two fingers against his lips, deep in thought. "So, she's two months along before she ever sleeps with Mirandez. But he doesn't know it."

"Maybe she didn't even know it. But she probably figured it out fast enough. By that time, Mirandez was taking care of her, giving her money, making her feel important."

"So, she doesn't want to walk away from a good thing." Sawyer didn't bother to try to hide his disgust.

"Or she was afraid to try to walk away. Especially once she saw the murder. Maybe that's why Mirandez tried to frighten her. To let her know that he wasn't going to let her walk away."

"Because he loves her?" Sawyer shook his head. "It's possible, I suppose."

"Maybe he wants the baby?" Liz raised an eyebrow.

Sawyer shook his head. "He's a killer. Why would a gang leader, a professional drug dealer, want a baby? And what's so special about this baby? Who knows how many kids he already has running around the city?"

"I don't know. But if I'm right and he does want the baby, then Mary's life isn't worth the price of bubblegum once she gives birth."

Sawyer didn't say anything for a few minutes. "Or maybe she and Mirandez are playing house somewhere, and she doesn't want to be found. She might not be in any danger at all."

"I can't take that chance. Mirandez might be holding her against her will. She's the one person who can send him to jail. Once she has that baby, she's a loose end that he can tie up."

"She should be safe enough for a couple weeks. Didn't you say that the baby wasn't due until September?"

"Babies are known to come early."

"We'll alert every hospital in the state. In Wisconsin, too. Hell, in the whole damn country. If someone comes in matching Mary's description, we'll have her."

"But what if he won't let her go to the hospital?"

"He's a drug dealer, not a doctor." Even Mirandez wouldn't be stupid enough to try to deliver a baby.

"Blood probably doesn't bother him."

Yeah, but delivering a baby? Sawyer had watched the obligatory films in the academy. But in all his years on the police force, he'd never had to deliver a baby. Even before that, when his son had been born, his girlfriend hadn't called until it was all over. He'd raced to the hospital to see his four-hour-old son. He'd barely left the hospital for the next thirteen days. He'd slept and eaten only when he'd been on the verge of falling down. He'd stayed there until they'd taken the body of his son from his arms, leaving him forever alone.

"I gave her a chance to come forward. If she was scared of Mirandez, why didn't she say something?" Sawyer asked.

"I don't know. Maybe she thought that Mirandez would

kill her, too. Maybe she thought Mirandez would rest easy once he found out that she didn't intend to turn him in."

"I don't think he's the type to forget. They don't teach you to turn the other cheek in the hood."

"I don't think she has lots of experience with men like Mirandez."

"No one does. They all die first."

Liz shrugged. "That's why I'm going after her."

No way. Evil surrounded Mirandez. He wouldn't risk letting that evil leak out and touch Liz. "That's not possible. It's a police matter."

"But you said the police are searching in Chicago. They aren't going to find Mirandez or Mary."

"We know Mirandez has dropped out of sight. But we don't have any reason to believe that Mirandez is in Wisconsin. I told you that we have people on the inside. There's been no talk about fishing. He would have told somebody in his organization. And our guys would know."

"I think the girl at Jumpin' Jack Flash told me the truth."

"What was her name?"

Liz blushed. "I didn't ask. I didn't want to scare her. She had dark hair, about shoulder length, with olive-colored skin. Late teens. I'd estimate she was five or six months pregnant."

"Of course."

Liz raised an eyebrow when she heard the bitterness in his voice. "Are you automatically discounting everything she said because she's young and pregnant?"

Young pregnant women lied. His girlfriend had lied to him. Mary had lied. Why wouldn't this one lie? "No. But I don't accept it as gospel."

Liz shook her head, clearly disgusted with him. "I'm going to Wisconsin. She needs me."

"You don't even know where to begin," he protested.

"I'll get a map. I've got some recent photos of Mary. I'll

show them around, and somebody will have seen her. Someone will know where I can find her."

If it was that easy, they wouldn't have a stack of missing-person reports. "It's too dangerous. I can't let you do it." When she opened her mouth to protest, he held up a hand. "I'll ask Lieutenant Fischer to send a few guys north. We'll expand the search. We'll notify both local and state authorities in Wisconsin." It was the best he could do. Probably better than the half-baked lead deserved.

"Thank you. But I'm still going. I have to."

She wasn't going to let him keep her safe. "Mary doesn't deserve this kind of loyalty. She lied to you. She told you that she didn't even know Mirandez. You know that she's been living with him for the past six months. Don't you even care that she looked you in the eye and lied to you?"

"Mary's in a fragile state right now. I'm not sure she's able to make good decisions."

"*You're* not making good decisions," he accused. When she shrugged in return, he knew continued arguing would get them nowhere.

"You should probably go," she said. "I want to get an early start."

"I hope to hell she's worth it," he said as he pulled the door shut behind him.

Chapter Seven

Sawyer called Lieutenant Fischer from his car, knowing he had a responsibility to give the man any information that might lead to Mirandez's capture. The older man listened, asked a couple questions and agreed it was a long shot. That said, he'd assign a few resources to Wisconsin. They couldn't afford to ignore any lead, no matter how preposterous.

"There's one other thing, Lieutenant," Sawyer said. Now that he'd had a minute to think about Liz going to Wisconsin, he realized that there was one good thing about it. If whoever had sent the threat was serious about it, it got her out of harm's way here.

"Yes."

"Liz Mayfield intends to search, as well. Would you… Could you get the word out? I don't want her getting caught in any cross fire."

Lieutenant Fischer didn't answer right away. When he did, he surprised Sawyer. "We should use Liz Mayfield."

The department didn't use civilians. They weren't trained. They could botch up almost any action, putting officers at risk. "I don't understand, sir."

"You think that Mary Thorton willingly went with Mirandez?"

"I think there's a high probability of that," Sawyer answered. "She's been living with him for months. She didn't turn on him when she had the chance."

"If that's true, she's going to run if she thinks the cops are closing in. Or she's going to tell Mirandez and they'll both run, or there's going to be a bloody battle between Mirandez and us. But if Liz gets close, she may be able to talk to the girl. You said yourself that there seemed to be a really strong bond between the two of them. That if anyone could get to Mary, it would be her."

Sawyer regretted ever having said those words. "Sir, you *cannot* send her after Mirandez. He's a monster. He wouldn't think twice about killing her."

"That's why I'm sending you with her. It's your job to keep her safe. If she gets hurt, I'm going to have the mayor and her boss and God knows who else wanting my head. Stick to her like glue."

There was no damn way. "No."

"Why not?"

He couldn't tell his lieutenant about what had happened in Liz's kitchen, that he'd almost exploded from wanting her. "She's not going to like having me as her shadow."

"Too bad. She doesn't have a choice. Some things just can't be negotiated."

He was a doomed man. "Will you let Robert know where I am?"

"Sure. By the way, I talked to him just a little while ago. He told me that the two of you had sprung Liz from Jumpin' Jack Flash."

Good call on Robert's part. Better to tell the boss rather than let him hear it through the grapevine. "Seemed like the right thing to do," Sawyer said.

"It's fine," his boss said.

Sawyer understood. Lieutenant Fischer wasn't going to worry about the small stuff when he was close to snagging Mirandez.

LIZ FROZE WHEN SHE HEARD the knocking on her front door. In the mirror, she could see the reflection of the digital alarm clock. Eight minutes after four. No one knocked on her door at that time of the morning.

Mary. She spit out the toothpaste, took a gulp of water and grabbed a towel. She wiped her mouth on the way to the door. "Just a minute," she yelled. She wanted to yank the door open but took the extra second to check the peephole. She looked, pulled back, blinked a couple times and looked again.

Sawyer. She twisted the bolt lock to the right, pulled the chain back and opened the door.

"What happened?" she said.

"Can I come in?"

She opened the door wider. "It's Mary, isn't it? Oh, God, is she all right?"

"Liz, calm down. I don't know anything more than I knew last night when I left here."

"Oh." She felt the relief flow through her body. No news wasn't necessarily good news, but it wasn't bad news, either. Swiftly on the heels of the relief came annoyance. "What are you doing here?"

She thought he looked a bit unsure. But that must be her imagination. *Capable* Detective Montgomery didn't do unsure.

"You said you were leaving early." Sawyer gave her a slight smile. "I know you sometimes get up at the crack of dawn. I didn't want to miss you."

"It's four o'clock," she said.

He shrugged his broad shoulders. "I didn't wake you."

No, he hadn't. She'd already showered, dried her hair and packed her bag. In another ten minutes, she'd have been gone.

"Why are you here?" she asked again.

"I'm going with you. To look for Mary."

She backed up a few steps and shook her head. Her tired mind must be playing tricks on her.

"Do you have any coffee made?" Sawyer asked.

"No." She didn't intend to offer him coffee. First of all, the man had kissed her like crazy and then stopped. It was the stopping she was mad about. Then he had compounded his errors by dismissing the notion that she might have gotten a viable lead on Mary. Now he acted as if he had every right to come to her house at four in the morning for conversation and coffee.

He crinkled his nose and pretended to sniff the air. "Funny. That smells like coffee."

She'd been done in by hazelnut beans. "I've got a timer. It must have turned on."

"Great. I could use a cup."

He could pour his own. She intended to go finish packing, and then they would go their separate ways.

"Fine. Cups are on the counter. I've got things to do."

He nodded and pointed at the corner of her mouth. "You've got just a speck of toothpaste there."

Oh, the nerve of this guy. "I was saving it for later," Liz said, her voice dripping with sweetness.

Sawyer laughed. "Good one. You're funny in the morning."

He'd think funny when she left him standing on the curb.

Ten minutes later, Liz walked into the kitchen. Sawyer stood at the counter, drinking out of her favorite cup and eating a piece of toast. "I made you some," he said. "I didn't know if you liked jelly."

"Sawyer." Liz smiled, purposefully patronizing. She felt

calmer now that she'd had a few moments to herself. "This is bizarre. You can't come to my house at four in the morning and have breakfast."

"I packed enough to last a week. I suggest you do the same."

A week? He expected her to spend a week with him?

Liz grabbed for the piece of toast he held out to her. She needed food. She surely had low blood sugar. He couldn't have said *a week*. It would all be better once she'd eaten.

"I did an internet search last night," Sawyer continued, as if he had every right. "I've identified the most likely places."

Likely places? "Sawyer, stop. You're giving me a headache. First of all, when did you have time to do an internet search? You left here just hours ago. Did you sleep at all? And more important, why are you doing this? Last night you didn't seem to think that my information had much value."

"Any lead is better than no lead."

"Well, you can't go with me." She couldn't spend a week with him. Heck, she couldn't spend an hour with him without itching to touch him. Mr. Can't-compromise-the-investigation had no idea that given another two minutes last night, she'd have been all over him. The man had no idea just how much at risk he'd been. The desire had been swift, hot, almost painful.

Throughout the very short night, she'd relived the scene over and over again. By morning, she'd been almost willing to admit that he'd probably done the right thing. There was no need for the little spark between the two of them to grow into a really big flame. With air, a little encouragement and fresh sheets, it could be spontaneous combustion. They'd both be burned, hurt worse than they could imagine.

Which was ridiculous. Absolutely not necessary. They both wanted Mary. He wanted to use the girl. She wanted to save her. Same goal, different objectives. No common values or mission statement. There was no need to share strategy. Certainly no need to share a car.

"I want to go by myself," she stated.

"No."

Who had died and put him in charge? "You can't stop me."

"I can," he said, suddenly sounding very serious, more like he had the night before. "I'm the lead detective on the case. If you don't cooperate with me, I'll have you arrested for interfering with a police investigation."

"You wouldn't do that," she accused. He just stood there, not blinking, not moving.

"I'll do what I have to do."

"You…you…" she sputtered, unable to find the word that captured her anger. "You cop." It was the best she could do at four in the morning.

He shrugged. "I want Mirandez. Mary's my ticket. She testifies against Mirandez and we get to throw away the key. I haven't made any bones about what I'm trying to do. You think they're in Wisconsin. That's as good a guess as any right now. Are you ready to go?"

She wasn't going anywhere with him. "I'm packed. I'm leaving. Solo. Alone. You can follow me if you want, but we aren't going together."

"That's a waste of gas if we're both going the same way."

He didn't *really* care about wasting gas. "You're afraid that I'm going to warn Mary. You don't trust me."

He looked a little offended. "I trust you. About as much as you trust me."

She didn't trust him one bit. He'd steal her heart and never give it back. She'd be the Tin Man looking for the Wizard.

"I want Mirandez to pay for his crimes," Liz said. "If you're right and Mary can testify against him, I'll do everything I can to persuade her to do so."

"You still refuse to accept that she might be part of this."

"She's not."

"Fine. I'll be the first to say I'm wrong. But if I'm right, I'm going to arrest both of them. Maybe it would be in Mary's best interests if you were with me when I find them."

Mary wouldn't talk to Sawyer. Liz knew that. He was everything she despised. She'd clam up, or worse yet, she'd spout off and probably irritate the hell out of him. She didn't think Sawyer would arrest her out of spite. He wasn't that type of cop or man. No, Sawyer wasn't the wild card. But Mary was. She needed to be there when the two of them met up again.

"All right," she said. "We'll go together. But you'd better not slow me down."

"Don't worry. We'll be there in three hours. Then we start working the river."

"Working the river?"

"Yes. In that area, most of the major campgrounds and resort areas are close to the Wisconsin River. We'll pick a point and then work both sides of the river, north and south. The girl at Jumpin' Jack Flash said he was fishing. He's got to be staying in the area. Could be a tent, a cabin or a damn resort. We'll check them all. If we're going to do this, we do it right."

That seemed like a whole lot of *we*. "Fine." Did she just say *fine*? What was she thinking? "Let's go."

"We can take your car or I'd be happy to drive."

"Oh, no," she said. "Let's take my car."

"Then follow me over to the police station. I'll drop my wheels there."

How had this happened? She was drawn to Sawyer like some cheap magnet to a refrigerator. He could see the attraction, yet he had some crazy ethical, moral or puritani-

cal code—she wasn't sure which—that prevented him from
acting on it.

So, however much she tried to avoid it, she'd be squirming in her seat for days, and he'd be determined to withstand
it. To prevail.

It made her furious. With herself and with him. "I'll get
my bag," she said. "While you're waiting, find a thermos. I
think there's one in those cupboards. I'm gonna want coffee."

SAWYER PULLED INTO a truck stop shortly after seven. They'd
beaten the rush-hour traffic, scooting out of the Chicago-
land area before lots of commuters hit the road. It had been a
straight shot north up I-94, and now they were headed west,
just twenty minutes shy of Madison.

Liz hadn't said a word to him since they'd left his car
at the station and he'd climbed into hers. Not even when
he'd ask her if he could drive. She'd just looked at him and
dropped the keys to her Toyota into his open hand. He'd
pushed the seat back and tried to get comfortable. She'd sat
on her side of the car, drank coffee, fiddled with the radio
stations and generally ignored him.

He didn't care. A little dislike between him and Liz could
go a long way. He hoped it went far enough that it kept him
from wanting her, from taking her into his arms, from pulling her under his body.

He didn't think he'd be satisfied with less. He knew he
didn't have a right to ask for more. He needed to keep his
hands on the wheel and let her be pissed off at him. It was
safer and ultimately easier and better for the both of them.

"I'm hungry," he said.

"Fine." She barely spared him a look before she turned
her face to the window.

"We need gas, too."

"Fine," she repeated. She reached down between her feet, opened her purse and pulled out a twenty.

"I'll buy gas," Sawyer told her. "This is police business."

"Your boss knows you're going?"

"Of course. He thinks it's probably a wild-goose chase. But since Mirandez has had us chasing our tails for over a year, he's pulling out all the stops."

"When we find Mary, I'd appreciate it if you'd let me talk to her first. She'll be scared."

She had no idea she was playing into Lieutenant Fischer's hands. That was exactly what the man had hoped for. The lieutenant wanted Liz to draw Mary in, to get her to testify against Mirandez. Lord, he hated using Liz like this. "I'll do my best." Sawyer heard the stiffness in his voice. He ignored the quick look Liz shot in his direction and pulled the keys out of the ignition. "Let's go."

Sawyer took the lead, but no one even glanced up when they walked through the door. Not until Liz walked past the two men who were sitting in the middle booth drinking coffee. Sawyer heard the soft whistle first, then "Wouldn't mind having those wrapped around my waist."

Sawyer stopped in his tracks. He balled up his fist and turned.

Chapter Eight

"Sawyer, please," she said. "Let it go."

It was the look in her eyes that stopped him. She didn't want a scene. Sawyer gave the men a look, and they had the good sense to take an interest in their eggs. He turned, walked another ten feet and slid into the empty booth at the end of the row. He faced the door. "They're stupid," he said.

"Agreed," she answered.

"You should wear pants," he lectured her. "No," he said, shaking his head. "That's not fair."

She waved a hand. "Nor practical. It's going to be a hundred degrees today." She picked up the plastic-covered listing of the day's specials.

"I imagine women get tired of men acting like idiots."

She sighed. Loudly. "Yes. Especially when they have dirty hair, food on their faces and bellies that hang over their pants."

It didn't take much for him to remember how he'd ogled those same legs last night. Yeah, his face and hair had been clean and his stomach still fairly flat, but that didn't make him much better than those creeps.

"How much farther?" she asked.

"We're twenty minutes east of Madison. Then it's another hour or so north to Wisconsin Dells. Our first stop is Clover Corners."

She shook her head, apparently not recognizing the name. "Why there?"

"Like I said earlier, we look everywhere. But there are a few places that seem more logical than others, so we start there."

"I'm not sure I understand the logic."

"I know Mirandez. He's a low-profile kind of guy. That's what has kept him alive so long."

"I thought you said he was twenty-six."

"You meet very few middle-aged gang leaders."

"I suppose. What kind of fishing would a low-profile type of guy do?"

"He'd look for a place where he could stay, eat and buy his bait without ever having to venture out. Especially because he probably can't go anywhere without dragging Mary with him. People notice pregnant women."

Liz nodded in agreement. "Last week when I went shopping with her, four people stopped to pat her stomach. Four complete strangers."

He didn't want to talk about Mary's pregnancy.

"It's like her stomach has become community property," Liz continued. "I told her she should get a sign for around her neck."

Despite himself, he wanted to know. "What would it say?"

"Something along the lines of Beware of Teeth. Then they wouldn't be able to sue her when she bit their hand."

There'd been a couple times that Mary had looked as if she wanted to bite him. Maybe a quick couple of nips out of his rear.

"But the really sick part is that I—"

"Two coffees here?" A waitress on her way past their booth stopped suddenly. She dropped a couple menus down on the corner of the table.

"Just water, please," Liz replied.

"Coffee would be fine," Sawyer said. Liz hadn't shared in the car. She'd been too busy being mad at him.

The waitress walked away. "What's the really sick part?" Sawyer asked.

Liz leaned forward. "Sometimes, I just can't help myself. I just have to touch their stomachs. I always thought that a pregnant woman's stomach would be soft, like a baby is soft. But it's this hard volleyball. It's so cool."

It had been cool. Cool and magical. His girlfriend had been thin. She hadn't actually showed for the better part of four months. And then one day, her flat little stomach had just popped out. And suddenly the baby had been real. He'd had no trouble at all suddenly visualizing what his son or daughter would look like, how he or she would run around the backyard at his parents' house, how he or she would hold his hand on the first day of school.

Even though he was just a kid himself, becoming a dad hadn't scared him.

He'd been too damn stupid to be scared.

He hadn't even considered that his child would be born weak, suffering, too small to take on the world.

He'd learned the hard way. Babies weren't tough at all.

The waitress came back with their drinks. "What can I get you this morning?"

"A bagel and cream cheese, please," Liz said.

"That's it?" Sawyer frowned at her.

She nodded.

Well, hell. He couldn't force her to eat. "Ham, eggs, hash-brown potatoes, and a side of biscuits and gravy," Sawyer said. The waitress wrote it down and left.

"Work up an appetite driving?" Liz asked.

Yeah, but not for food. But he wasn't going there. He'd managed to pull back last night. It had cost him. He'd spent most of the night mentally kicking his own butt. It hadn't helped that he knew he'd done the right thing. No, he'd been wound too tight, been too close to the edge. He'd wanted her badly.

But he couldn't sleep with Liz. Not with the possibility that he was going to have to arrest Mary. He knew that once he slept with Liz, once he let her into his soul, he'd be hard-pressed to be objective about Mary. And he couldn't afford to let up on the pursuit of Mirandez now. Not when they were so close.

"You may be sorry," he said. "We're not stopping again until lunch."

"It'll be okay. If I get hungry, I'll gnaw off a couple fingers."

"Mine or yours?" The minute he said it, he was sorry. He didn't need to be thinking about her mouth on any part of his body. "Just remember," he said, working hard to keep his voice from cracking, "the per diem reimbursement rate is $50 a person per day. They actually expect us to eat."

"Last of the big spenders, huh?"

"Big spender? The city? No. They barely buy us office supplies."

She put her elbows on the table and rested her chin on her hands. "Did you always want to be a cop, Sawyer? Was that your dream?"

His dream had been to raise his child. "No."

"How did you end up wearing a badge?"

It had seemed like the only thing to do. "I didn't go on to college right out of high school. I worked for a while." He'd worked like a dog when he'd found out Terrie was pregnant. He'd been determined to provide for her and his child. It was afterward, when he faced the truth that Terrie had continued to use drugs during the pregnancy, that he thought he'd worked too much. He'd been so focused on providing for his child that he'd neglected to protect him.

"But then…things happened, and I decided I wasn't going to get anywhere without an education. I started at the junior college and then went on for a bachelor's degree. I've been a cop for fifteen years. I don't know how to do much else."

"You haven't been in Chicago for fifteen years."

"How do you know?"

She looked over both shoulders and leaned forward in the booth. "Like Mary said," she whispered, "you talk funny."

"I do not. You people in the north talk funny."

"I wouldn't say that too loudly. A body can go missing in the woods for a long time before somebody stumbles upon it."

"Duly noted."

"Why Chicago?"

"Why not?" He took a drink of coffee. That was probably all he needed to say, but suddenly he wanted to tell her more. "My father died two years ago. My mom had passed the year before. With both of them gone, there was no reason to stay in Baton Rouge."

"Aha. Baton Rouge. I had guessed New Orleans."

"I spent some time there."

She settled back in her booth. "Drinking Hurricanes at Pat O'Brien's? Eating beignets at Café du Monde? Brunch at the Court of Two Sisters?"

He'd been working undercover, mostly setting up drug buys with the underbelly of society. "Sounds like you know the place."

"I did an internship there when I was working on my doctorate. I loved everything about it. The food especially. After I left, I dreamed of gumbo."

"I can do a crawfish boil better than most."

She sighed. "Don't tease me. You don't really know how to cook, do you?"

His mother had believed that cooking was everybody's

work. In the South, family meant food. Hell, maybe when this was all over, he'd have Liz over for dinner.

Maybe they'd eat in bed. He'd feed her shrimp creole and drizzle the sauce across her naked body.

Lord help him. He reached for his water and knocked his silverware on the floor.

She scooted out of the booth and reached over to the next table to grab him a fresh set. He saw the smooth, tanned skin of her back when her shirt pulled up.

He did a quick look to make sure the two goons in the middle booth weren't copping a look.

Nope. It was just him.

"No other family there?" she asked.

"What?" He shook his head, trying to clear it.

She slid the silverware toward him. "Do you have other family in Baton Rouge?"

He'd brought Jake with him. That had taken some doing, but there'd been no other option. "No." She was getting too close. He needed to change the subject.

"How about you?" he asked. "Did you always want to be a social worker at OCM?"

"No, I worked in private practice for several years. Sort of chasing the American dream. You know, a fancy house, a new car, trips to Europe, three-hundred-dollar suits."

He knew that much. He wanted to know why she'd left it all behind. "Doesn't sound all that bad."

"It's not bad. Just not enough."

He let her words hang. When she didn't continue, he jumped in, not wanting the conversation to die. "Just decided you'd had enough of living in the lap of luxury?"

She smiled, a sad sort of half smile. "You got it. Decided I couldn't take any more caviar and champagne."

He thought about pushing. Over the course of his career, he'd persuaded street-smart drug dealers, high-priced hookers and numbers-running bookies to talk. Some had been easier than others. But he rarely failed.

But he didn't want to pry or coerce Liz into offering up information. Maybe it was as simple as she made it sound. Maybe she just got tired of the fast lane. If so, no doubt it would lure her back, sooner or later. She'd get tired of slugging her way through the day at OCM, the hours filled with fights with belligerent teens.

If she didn't want to talk, okay with him. He didn't care what had driven her to OCM.

Right. He wanted to know. Wanted to know everything about her. Might have asked, too, if the waitress hadn't picked that moment to slam down their breakfasts in front of them. He picked up his fork, dug into his eggs, grateful for the diversion.

They didn't speak again until they were both finished eating. "I've got a picture of Mirandez in the car," Sawyer said. "It's a good shot, shows his face really well. When we get to each place, you can go into the office and show Mary's picture as well as Mirandez's."

"And if they haven't seen them?"

"We move on. But leave a card. Put my cell-phone number on the back." He reached out, tore off a corner of the paper place mat and wrote down the number. "Oh, by the way—" he tried for nonchalant "—when I was doing my internet searches, I got us a place to stay."

Liz was glad she had finished breakfast. Otherwise, she might have choked on her bagel. He made it sound so married-like. As if they were on vacation and he'd taken care of the reservations: *Hey, honey. We're going to the Days Inn.*

Problem was, they weren't married and this was no vacation.

"Where?" she managed to ask.

"Lake Weston. It's on the west side of The Dells. It's centrally located to the search. There weren't a lot of vacancies. I guess this is prime vacation season. Everybody's here with their kids, a last fling before school starts."

Please, Liz, let me come before school starts. Jenny had called her at work. It had been a crazy summer for Liz. One of the other partners had been gone from work for months. He'd had a heart attack, and Liz had worried that the rest of the staff would have one, too, if they kept up the pace. Everyone was working six days a week, twelve hours a day. But still, when Jenny had called, she'd agreed to let her come. Jenny, at sixteen, loved the city. Its diversity, its energy, its passion for music and art.

Liz had managed to squeeze out time to shop, to go out to eat and even for a concert at Grant Park. Four days after she'd arrived, Liz had kissed Jenny goodbye and sent her home on the train. Three months later, Jenny had been dead.

"What are you thinking about?" Sawyer asked. "You look like you're a million miles away."

Liz debated whether she should tell him. Even after three years, it was difficult to talk about Jenny and the hole that her death had made.

"My little sister used to visit me in the summers. She told me it was better than a weekend at Six Flags."

Sawyer laughed. "Not bad. You edged out an amusement park. How old was she?"

"Sixteen." She'd always be sixteen in Liz's mind.

"Wow. A lot younger than you. Second marriage for one of your parents?"

"No. Just a bonus baby. I was thirteen when she was born."

"She in college now?" Sawyer asked.

"No." Liz gripped the edge of the Formica-topped table. "She's… Jenny's dead."

She could see his chest rise and fall with a deep breath. "I'm sorry," he said. "What happened?"

"She killed herself. In the bathroom of my parents' house. She bled to death in the bathtub."

He didn't know what to say. "Did she leave a note?"

"No. I'm not sure if that makes it more or less horrible."

"Do you have any idea why?"

"She was eight weeks pregnant. According to her best friend, the father of the baby had taken back his ring just two days before."

Sawyer shook his head. "I'm sorry."

He was sorry, and she hadn't even told him the worst part. The part that had almost destroyed her until she'd found OCM.

"I guess I understand why it's so important for you to help Mary."

He had no idea. "Let's just say I don't want another girl to fall through the cracks." It was the same thing she'd told Jamison. There wasn't really a better way to sum it up.

"Right." Sawyer folded up his paper napkin. "You know," he said, his voice hesitant, "Mary might be hiding in one of those cracks. She and Mirandez. She had the chance to point the finger at him. But she wouldn't."

"I don't know why," Liz said. "Maybe she's afraid of him?"

"If she's smart, she is. If she's lying about him being the father, maybe she's trying to get him to marry her? Maybe he's a meal ticket?"

It was possible. She might see it as a better alternative than working her whole life. "When we find them, I'll ask her."

Sawyer slid out of the booth. "I hope like hell you get the chance."

Chapter Nine

At each place, it was the same. Liz showed Mary's picture first, then Mirandez's. Then she'd tell the story. She'd been working in Europe for the past year and had missed her sister's wedding. Having just returned, she hoped to surprise the bride and groom.

Everyone had looked at the pictures, shaken their heads, taken her card and agreed to call her if the couple checked in. Sawyer had concocted the story, hoping that people's inherent love of a good surprise would keep any clerk from telling Mary and Mirandez that someone had asked about them. And if someone did have loose lips, perhaps Mirandez wouldn't be too nervous if he thought only Liz had followed Mary.

They'd stopped at ten places before noon. "How's that bagel holding up?" Sawyer asked.

"We can stop if you're hungry," she said.

"You don't eat lunch?"

She waved a hand. "Sure I do."

"Uh-huh. What did you have for lunch yesterday?"

Liz chewed on her lip. "Chips and a can of pop."

"The day before?"

"Oh, for goodness' sake. I had…chips and a pop."

He leaned across the seat and inspected her. "You don't *look* like you've got scurvy," he said.

She let out a huff of air. "I take a multivitamin every day. Oh, damn." She smacked herself on the forehead. "I think I forgot my vitamins."

Sawyer shook his head. Ten minutes later, he turned the car into a gas station. Half the building was a convenience store. "I'll get us some lunch." He opened his door. "So, what kind of chips do you like?"

She smiled. "You're not going to try to reform me?"

"I'm smarter than that. Do you want to come in?"

"No. I need to call Jamison. I left a message on his machine early this morning. That was before I knew we would be traveling together."

"What's he going to think about that?"

"He'll be thrilled. He'll think I'm safer."

"You like Jamison, don't you?"

"He's a great boss. He trusts all of us. He knows we work hard, and he's really loyal in return. He treats us more like good friends than employees."

"He and Fraypish are friends, right?"

"For over twenty years. Jamison really respects Howard's legal judgment." Liz pulled out her cell phone and started dialing. "And he works at the right price, too."

Sawyer slammed the door shut. He didn't really care about what Jamison thought about Fraypish. He wanted to know what Liz thought about the man.

Why? He pushed open the door of the convenience store. Why did it matter? He and Liz had shared a couple kisses. Okay, a couple of really hot kisses that had made his knees weak, but still, it meant nothing. They would hopefully find Mary safe. She'd turn on Mirandez, and months from now, if he and Liz happened to run into each other at the grocery store, they'd nod politely and go their separate ways.

He grabbed an extralarge bag of potato chips. What did he care if she got fat and had bad skin?

He walked over to the counter and picked out two ham-and-cheese sandwiches. He stuck two cans of pop in the crook of his arm. A young woman at the cash register stopped filing her nails so that she could ring him up.

"Will that be all?" he asked.

"You don't happen to stock multivitamins?"

She shook her head.

"Got any fresh fruit?"

She pointed to the back of the store. "Bananas. Fifty cents apiece."

"I'll take six." When he got to the car, Liz was just snapping shut her cell phone. He dropped the bag into her lap. She reached inside and pulled out the chips.

"A big bag," she said, looking pleased. She pulled out the soda. "Thank you very much," she said. She handed him the bag, but he didn't take it.

"There's something else for you," he said.

She peered inside the plastic bag. A smile, so genuine that it reached her pretty green eyes, lit up her face. "You bought me bananas."

You'd have thought it was expensive perfume or something that sparkled. He opened his own soda and took a big drink. Liz Mayfield made a man thirsty. "I can probably find us a picnic table somewhere," he said.

She shook her head and ripped open her bag of chips. "Let's just keep going."

They stopped at another eleven places before Sawyer finally pulled into the parking lot of Lake Weston. It was after seven, hadn't had dinner and Liz looked exhausted. She had dutifully gotten out at each stop, given her spiel and returned to the car, looking more and more discouraged.

"Look, here's our place. I think we should call it a night," Sawyer said. "Neither of us got much sleep last night. Let's get checked in, I'll find us some food, and you can crash."

"No."

It was the first word she'd said in two hours.

"What?"

"No. We have to keep going. Let's just grab a sandwich. We can probably hit three or four more places tonight."

"Liz, be reasonable. It'll be dark in another hour. We'll get a fresh start in the morning."

Liz picked the map up and spread it across her lap. "Look, there're two places just ten miles or so up the road. We're wasting time."

He was going to have to strap her down. But he didn't think he had the energy.

He shook his head. "We have to get checked in. They close the office at eight. We need to get a key to our cabin."

"Cabin?" she repeated.

"I got a *two*-bedroom cabin. It was all they had. I hope you don't mind sharing a bath."

"Oh. No, of course not. It sounds great. I mean, it sounds like it will suit our needs. Enough space, you know."

She was blushing. He didn't get it. Had she really thought he'd only book one room? Maybe in his wildest dreams. "You're going to have to register. It's in your name. If Mirandez happened to track you back here, I didn't want there to be any record of me. Only problem is, you'll have to put it on your credit card. The department will reimburse you."

"That's fine." She opened her car door. "I'll get us registered. And then we're going to the next two on the map. Their offices might close around eight, too. We'll need to hurry."

The woman was a workhorse. "Fine. We'll go to those two. But then we're done. And I'm picking the restaurant. Get prepared because there may not be chips on the menu."

IT WAS ALMOST NINE O'CLOCK when Sawyer ordered steaks for both of them. He'd found a supper club alongside the high-

way. The parking lot had been full, and he'd taken that as
an endorsement.

The lighting was a little too dim, the music a little too
loud. But the chairs were soft, and the cold beer he held in
his hand tasted really good.

He thought Liz might fall asleep in her chair. Her eyes
were half-closed. She looked pale, tired and defenseless. And
it made him want to slay dragons for her.

If—or when, he corrected himself, trying to think a bit
more positively—he found Mary, he would kick her butt
for making this woman worry. For making the two of them
traipse across the country in a hot car that didn't have a
working air conditioner.

He wished he'd learned that little piece of information
earlier. Like before he'd left his own car at the station and
decided to take a road trip in the Toastermobile. He'd turned
the knob just after breakfast this morning, when the temperature had already hit the low nineties, and hot air had
blown in his face. He'd looked at Liz, and she'd shrugged
her shoulders and looked the happiest she had all morning.

Looking back, it had been an omen of how the day would
go. One big bust.

But through it all, Liz had moved forward without com-
plaint. He'd driven, and she'd read the map, directing him
from place to place. Her instructions had been clear and suc-
cinct. At each stop, she'd gotten out and flashed her pictures.
She hadn't whined or complained. Hell, she could probably
slay her own dragons. She was tough enough.

"We'll go north tomorrow," he said. He picked up a roll,
buttered it and held it out to her. She shook her head no. He
kept his hand extended and raised one eyebrow.

"I'm too tired to fight," she said, and she grabbed it out
of his hand.

He waited until she took a dainty little bite before continuing, "Thank you. You don't eat enough."

"I ate a banana."

"So you did. Maybe that will be enough to keep you from falling down."

"If it's not, just prop me up and drive to the next place."

He laughed until he realized she was half-serious. "You're not going to give up, are you?"

"No. I can't. I won't."

"What happens if we don't find Mary?"

"We will. If we look hard enough, we will."

God, he hoped he didn't have to disappoint her. "Probably no need to start so early tomorrow. Maybe you could catch up on your rest."

"I'm not tired."

No, of course not. "Yeah, well, I am."

She blinked twice. "No, you're not." She shook her head at him. "You think by saying that you're tired that I'll implicitly understand that it's okay if I'm tired."

Why did she have to be a psychologist? Why couldn't she have been an accountant or an engineer?

"Did it work?" he asked.

"No. I'm fine. Don't worry about me."

"Okay. But could you at least drink your water? Just being in the car today was enough to dehydrate a person."

"Where did you get your medical degree?"

He didn't take offense. She'd smiled at him. The first one of those he'd seen in a couple of hours.

"Off the street of hard knocks. It's a fast-track program. You do your internship at a homeless shelter and your residency in the emergency room at Melliertz Hospital. They don't have metal screeners there for nothing."

"I'll bet you've seen a lot of violence, huh?"

She leaned her head back against the chair. The flickering

light from the cheesy candle on the table danced across the long lines of her graceful neck. She was a beautiful woman.

"I'll bet you've *heard* about a lot of violence," he replied. "I wonder what's worse. Seeing it or hearing about it."

A cloud of sadness drifted across her face. "I think seeing it," she said. "When you hear about it, you can't imagine how horrific it really is. Your mind just won't let you go there."

He had a bad feeling about this. He figured there was only one way to ask the question. "You're the one who found your sister?"

"Yes."

"What happened?" He braced himself, having investigated a few of those types of calls over the years. It was gruesome, ugly work.

"I tried her on the telephone but didn't get an answer. After a couple of hours, I drove out to my parents' house. They were gone for the weekend. She'd been dead for several hours when I found her."

He knew exactly what it had looked and smelled like. He hoped like hell that they didn't run into something similar with Mary. That Mirandez hadn't spirited the girl away just so he could kill her and dump her body up in the boondocks. "I'm sorry," he said, thinking it sounded a bit inadequate.

"I am, too," she said, her voice trembling just a little. "But thank you. It's still hard for me to talk about it. For some reason, you made it easier."

It wasn't a dragon but close. A sense of satisfaction, a sense of peace, filled him.

The waiter arrived at their table, his arms laden with heavy serving platters. He set two sizzling steaks down in front of them with sides of baked potato and fresh green beans.

Sawyer picked up his fork. "Bon appétit," he said. In return, she smiled and picked up her own utensils.

Twenty minutes later, the dishes had all been cleared away. Sawyer sipped a cup of steaming-hot coffee and watched Liz. She'd done better with dinner than she had with breakfast or lunch. She'd managed to eat at least half the steak and most of the potato. "Let's get out of here," he said when he saw her head jerk back. She was literally falling asleep sitting up. Within a couple of minutes, he'd settled the bill and walked her out of the restaurant. He kept his hand firmly planted underneath her elbow. It felt so right that he refused to think about all the reasons it was wrong.

A ten-minute drive got them back to the cabin. "Let me check it out," Sawyer ordered. He opened the compartment between the two seats and pulled out the gun that she'd seen him shove inside earlier. When he got out, he quickly walked to the cabin door, the barrel of the gun pointed upward. He twisted the doorknob, evidently found it locked, because she watched as he unlocked the heavy door with the real key the office had given them. Then in one fluid motion, he swung his body inside. Within seconds he was back, motioning for her to get out of the car. "Looks okay," he said. He waited for her to get inside, then pulled the door shut behind them, turned the lock and looked with some disgust at the flimsy chain before hooking it.

"What were you expecting?" she asked.

"I didn't know. A good cop just expects something."

Sawyer Montgomery was a very good cop. She stood somewhat awkwardly by the door. The cabin wasn't big but comfortable enough. The small sitting area had two chairs, a lamp table and a stone fireplace. A sign posted on the fireplace warned against actually using it. To the right, pushed up against the wall, was a double bed. To the left, two doors. She walked across the scarred but clean wooden floor and peeked into the first one.

Okay. Small but neat. The bath had a white tile floor and

pale blue walls. Above the shower stall was a small, high window with a faded yellow shade.

She moved on to the second door. Reaching inside the door, she found the light switch. A single bed with a dark green bedspread and small dresser almost filled the space. The switch controlled the floor lamp next to the bed. Its dim light barely reached the corners of the room.

"It's kind of a two-bedroom," Sawyer said, standing directly behind her.

"It's fine," Liz said. "Which bed do you want?" she asked.

Sawyer edged past her and in four steps walked across the small room. He lifted the inexpensive white plastic blinds and inspected the windows. They were double-paned and locked from the inside.

"I'll take the one in the other room."

The room with the door that had the no-real-protection lock. Yes, Sawyer Montgomery was a good cop. Even though she was more than a hundred miles from home, physically exhausted and in a cabin with a man she'd only known for a couple days, she felt safe.

"If you hear anything, and I mean anything," he continued, "you come get me. I'm a light sleeper."

Thinking about him sleeping just twenty feet away from her did funny things to her insides. "I'm sure it'll be fine," she said.

"Just don't hesitate," he said. "Why don't you use the bathroom first? I've got to make a couple calls and check messages." He pulled one of the chairs closer to the lamp table. Liz grabbed her bag by the door and took it into the bathroom with her.

Sawyer waited until he heard the shower running before dialing Robert's cell phone. When it rang four times, Sawyer got worried that Robert had some hot date. He breathed a sigh of relief when it was answered on the seventh ring.

"Why, it's Fisherman Sawyer," Robert said.

There were times when caller ID was inconvenient. "I figured the lieutenant would fill you in."

"Oh, yeah. Where are you?"

"Halfway between Madison and Hell."

Now it was Robert's turn to laugh. "I've been there. Lots of potholes and greasy-spoon restaurants. Is our little piranha biting?"

"No. I didn't really expect him to. I think I'm on a wild-goose chase."

"How's Liz?"

Wonderful. Gorgeous. Strong. "Fine. A little tired. It's been a long day."

"You planning on letting her get any sleep tonight?"

Sawyer could hear the tease in his partner's voice. It didn't matter. *Liz* and *bed* in the same sentence wasn't funny. "None of your business," he said.

"She's gotten to you, hasn't she?" Robert asked, his voice more serious than usual.

"She's…interesting."

"Six-legged spiders are interesting."

"Them, too. Look, I better go."

"Well, before you do, you might want to know this. Fluentes thinks Mirandez has a sister somewhere in Wisconsin."

"What? I don't think that's possible." Sawyer ran his hands through his hair. "I've never seen any mention of siblings. Not anywhere."

"Well, rumor has it he's got a much older sister. Hardly anybody has ever seen her, but she evidently came home for their old man's funeral a few years ago."

A sister? Was it possible that Mirandez had sought refuge with his family?

"Fluentes have a name?" Sawyer asked. "Was the sister married?"

"I told you everything I know."

"Okay. Thanks." Sawyer hung up just as Liz came out of the bathroom. She had on clean shorts and a T-shirt. She gave him a quick wave and slipped into the bedroom, closing the door behind her.

Liz closed the door and flipped the light switch off. In two steps, she reached the bed. She pulled the bedspread and thin blanket back all the way, leaving them at the end of the bed. She slipped under the cool sheet and hoped for sleep.

She rubbed her elbow. In the shower, she'd almost scrubbed it raw, in some silly hope that she could erase the feel of Sawyer's hand as he'd cupped her elbow and guided her across the parking lot. She could still feel his heat, his strength, his goodness.

It had been a long time since a man had taken care of her. The last serious relationship she'd had, she'd taken care of the man. Not in the physical sense certainly but in almost every other way.

She'd been a twenty-five-year-old virgin when she'd met Ted. Theodore Rainey. They'd dated for two years before he'd asked her to marry him. She'd accepted both his engagement ring and the invitation to sleep in his bed. A year later, after three wedding dates had come and gone, canceled due to Ted's work schedule, it had seemed as if they'd never manage to get married.

She knew she should have looked beyond his feeble excuses and tried to understand the real reason he avoided marriage. She supposed that was why psychologists never treated themselves. They had no objectivity. Had one of her patients described the relationship that Liz had with Ted, Liz would have advised her to get out of it.

In the end, they'd parted almost amicably. By that time, the sex was infrequent, generally hurried and rarely fulfilling. It had been a relief not to have to pretend anymore.

Liz pulled the sheet up another couple of inches, snuggling into the cool bed. As she drifted off to sleep, she thought about the lucky woman who shared Sawyer's bed, knowing in her heart that that woman wouldn't spend much time pretending.

Chapter Ten

Liz woke up when she heard the shower turn on. The walls of the cabin were perhaps not paper-thin but pretty darn close. She heard a thud and a soft curse. Sounded as if Sawyer was having a little trouble with the narrow stall.

She slipped out of bed, walked over to the window and peeked through the slats of the blinds. Looked like a pretty day. Bright sunshine with just a few puffy clouds. Maybe it would be a few degrees cooler than the day before. It had been a real scorcher. She'd known her air-conditioning didn't work, but in some juvenile way, it had been her way of one-upping Sawyer. He'd been so high-handed about coming with her that she figured she owed him one.

But then later, when he remained in the hot car while she at least got a few breaks going into the mostly air-conditioned offices, and he didn't complain even once, she began to feel bad. When he'd bought her bananas, she'd felt very stupid and very petty. She intended to start this day off better. She'd seen the sign in the office area last night that promoted the free continental breakfast for guests. She could go grab a couple cups of coffee, maybe some chocolate doughnuts if she got really lucky and be back before Sawyer got out of the shower.

She slipped her feet into sandals and grabbed her purse off the old dresser. When she opened the front door, she sucked in a deep breath, cherishing the still-cool early-morning air. It was probably not much past seven. When she got to the office, she had to wait a few minutes while a young family, a man, woman and three small children, worked their way past the rolls and bagels, assorted juices and blessed coffee.

No chocolate doughnuts but there was a close second—pecan rolls. She put two on a plate and then grabbed a bagel and cream cheese for good measure. Sawyer ate a lot. She poured two cups of coffee and balanced them in one hand, grateful for the summer she'd spent waiting tables. When she got to the door, the young man who'd gotten his family settled around the one lone table got up and opened it for her.

Liz strolled across the parking lot, loving the smell of the hot coffee. Unable to resist, she stopped, took a small sip from one of the cups, burned her tongue just a bit and swallowed with gusto. Little topped that first taste of coffee in the morning.

When she got outside the cabin door, she carefully set both coffees and the plate of pastries down on the sidewalk. She used her key to open the door. Then she bent down, picked up her cache and pushed the door open the rest of the way with her foot. She went inside and turned to shut the door. And then she almost dropped her precious brew.

Sawyer, wearing nothing but a pair of unsnapped jeans, had a gun pointed at her chest.

"What the hell do you think you're doing?" he asked.

What was *she* doing? "Are you going to shoot me?"

"Don't ever do that again," he instructed, ignoring her question.

"Do what?" She threw his words back at him. Darn, he had some nerve. He'd scared ten years off her, and he acted as if *he'd* been wronged. Before she dropped them, she put the coffees and the pastry plate on the table.

He closed the gap between them, never taking his dark

brown eyes off her face. He carefully placed his gun next to the plate. "Well, for starters," he said, his words clipped short, his accent more pronounced, "don't ever leave without telling me where you're going."

He acted as if she'd been gone for three days. "Sawyer, you're being ridiculous. I walked across the parking lot."

He grabbed both of her arms. "Listen to me. You don't open a door, you don't answer a phone, you don't—"

She tried to pull away, but his hold was firm. "I'm not your prisoner. You're not responsible for me."

He was close enough that she could see the muscle in his jaw jerk. "I am. Make no mistake about that. You do what I tell you to do when I tell you to do it. This is police business, and I'm in charge."

"I thought you might appreciate coffee. If I'd known that I might get shot for it, I wouldn't have bothered."

He stood close enough that she could smell him. The clean, edgy scent of an angry man. His bare chest loomed close enough that all she had to do was reach out and she would be touching his naked skin. She let her eyes drift down across his chest, following the line of hair as it tapered down into the open V of his unbuttoned jeans.

Oh, my.

She flicked her eyes up. His breath was shallow, drawn through just slightly open lips. His eyes seemed even darker.

And then he closed the distance between them and pulled her body up next to his, fitting her curves into his strength. He pushed his hips against hers, confirming what her eyes had discovered.

He was hard.

"This is crazy," she said. "We can't—"

"Just shut up," he murmured, and then he bent his head and kissed her. As wild as his eyes had been, she expected the kiss to be hard, brutal. But it wasn't. His lips were warm and soft, and he tasted like mint. She opened her mouth, and he angled his head, bringing them closer until she no longer knew where he stopped and she began. He rocked against her, and she thought she might split apart because the pleasure was so intense.

She moved her hands across his broad back, then lower, dipping her fingertips just inside the waistband of his jeans. She lightly scraped her nails across his bare, hot skin, and when he groaned, she felt the power of being a woman. It soared through her, heating her.

He moved his own hands, pushing them up inside her loose shirt. When all he encountered was bare skin, his big body literally shuddered. She pushed her hands deeper into his jeans, under the cotton material of his briefs, cupping each bare cheek. He pulled his mouth away from hers. "You're driving me crazy."

That made her braver, made her feel even more powerful. She found his lips again and kissed him hard. And she arched against his body, greedy with her need to touch him everywhere. "I want you to—"

The shrill ring of a cell phone cut her off. Sawyer pulled away from her and reached across the table to check his phone.

"It's mine," Liz managed. "It's in my purse."

She grabbed the still-ringing phone. Remembering his orders that she couldn't answer the phone without his permission, she looked at him. The phone rang two more times before he nodded. Liz hurriedly pushed a button. "Hello," she said.

"Liz, you were supposed to call me yesterday."

Howard Fraypish. She'd forgotten all about him. "I'm sorry, Howard. I had a few things to take care of."

She covered the mouthpiece with her hand and whispered to Sawyer, "I'll be just a minute. It's Howard."

Sawyer raised an eyebrow.

"We're working on a placement."

"Sure. Whatever." He walked across the room. She watched him pull a T-shirt out of his bag. He pulled it on in one smooth motion.

"...and I need to make sure that Melissa hasn't changed her mind. The Partridges don't want to be disappointed."

She'd totally missed the first part when she'd been ogling Sawyer's bare chest. "No, Howard. I spoke with her just a couple days ago. She's definitely giving the baby up for adoption. I don't think she's going to change her mind. She should deliver by the end of next week. And then two weeks after that, she leaves for college."

"Call me the minute she delivers."

"I will, but don't worry. She knows you're handling the legal work. I told you that I'd told her to call you directly if she can't reach me."

"Oh, yeah."

He sounded so distracted. "Is something wrong, Howard?"

"What could be wrong? I'm just busy. Really busy. I've got to go. Goodbye, Liz."

Liz snapped her phone shut. Sawyer stood next to the table, drinking one of the cups of coffee.

"You want the bagel?" he asked.

So, he wanted to pretend that the past ten minutes hadn't happened. That they hadn't argued, that they hadn't practically swallowed each other up. No, she wouldn't let him do it. Even if it meant that she had to admit that she'd come close to begging him to take her to bed.

"What's going on here, Sawyer?"

He stared at her for a long minute. "When I got out of the shower and I couldn't find you, I got worried. It was less than a week ago that somebody made a threat to your life.

Now, I know you think that it was just some kid but maybe not. Even if it was, we're on this crazy chase after Mirandez. I know you don't understand how dangerous he is. But if you're right that he and Mary are here and he finds out that you're looking for him, there's no telling what he might do. The man has no conscience. He kills people like the rest of us kill bugs."

Well, okay. "I'm sorry. I should have said something before I went for coffee."

He shrugged his shoulders. "Just forget it."

Forget that he'd kissed her? Was it that easy for him? "We got a little carried away here," she reminded him.

He nodded. "You're right. I'm attracted to you, Liz. But to act upon it would be absolutely wrong on my part. Whether you like it or not, I am responsible for this operation. And that includes you."

"I'm a big girl, Sawyer. I take responsibility for my own actions."

"And I take responsibility for mine."

He didn't sound too happy about it. "Sawyer, I don't understand why we can't—"

"Because I can't lose focus. My job is to find Mirandez. And to arrest him, with solid enough evidence that the guys in suits have no trouble getting a conviction."

"I'm trying to help you."

"I appreciate that. But what happens when Mary is part of that evidence? What happens if I have to arrest her, too? I can't let you and how you feel about Mary keep me from doing my job."

"I wouldn't ask you to do that," she said, not understanding why he couldn't see that. She'd never put him in that position.

"You wouldn't have to," he said, his voice soft.

IF POSSIBLE, LIZ THOUGHT the temperature had shot even higher than the day before. By ten o'clock, after just a couple hours in the car, they both looked a little wilted. They'd already been to four smaller campgrounds. One hadn't even had an office, so they'd had to be content with just driving through the camping area, looking at the various campsites. At the other three, the response had been virtually the same.

"Nope. They don't look familiar. But then again, we get a lot of people passing through. It would be pretty hard to remember everybody. Sure, you can check back. We're here from sunup to sundown most days."

Good old-fashioned Wisconsin charm. Liz wondered why she felt compelled to wring the next person's neck. Between the heat outside, the worry about Mary and the sexual tension radiating off Sawyer, she thought murder looked like a fairly good alternative.

He hadn't touched her again. Hadn't really said more than ten words to her. But each time she got out of the car and walked into one of the campground offices or when she walked back, she knew, just knew, that he watched her every step of the way. And while it seemed a little crazy, she thought she saw a hunger in his eyes. But then she'd get in the car and he'd be all business, all silent business, and she decided she had a case of wishful thinking and wicked thoughts.

She wanted Sawyer. She wanted to kiss him. After all, the man had the kind of lips that you could kiss for about three straight weeks without coming up for air. And then she wanted him naked.

She'd only ever slept with one man. But now all she could think about was getting it on with a man she'd known for less than a week.

It made her feel disloyal to Mary. Mary had to be the priority. And Liz knew what happened when priorities got mixed up. She couldn't bear for that to happen again. Mary deserved more. Liz respected Sawyer's ability to stay on task. She felt slimy that her focus had slipped momentarily. It had been jarred by the incredible warmth of his body pressed up against hers.

But thankfully, Sawyer had pulled back in time. He'd done the right thing. So, she needed to stop being mad at him.

"How much farther north?" she asked.

Sawyer risked a quick look at her. He'd told himself he might get through the day if he just didn't have to look at her. Didn't have to see her pretty green eyes with the dark eyelashes that had literally fluttered down across her cheeks when he'd kissed her. Or her pink lips, the bottom one fuller than the top, that literally trembled when he'd brushed his hands across her breast.

She'd gathered her long hair up, twisted it in that way that only women knew how to do and clipped it on top of her head. In deference to the heat, she had on a white sleeveless one-piece cotton dress, the kind of shapeless thing that seemed so popular these days.

Not that the dress did him much good. He could still remember what every one of her curves felt like. Hell, the woman even had curvy feet. She had white sandals on that showed off her red-painted toes and the delicate arch of her small foot.

He put his eyes back on the road. Safer by a long shot. "I thought we'd go about thirty miles. Then we'll need to cross over and come down the other side. If we don't get it all done today, we'll have to come back tomorrow."

"Then what?"

"Tomorrow we'll go west toward Route 39. That's one of the main roads. Lots of tourists head up this way. There're a couple large lodges and camping areas."

"This is kind of like looking for a needle in a haystack, isn't it? I guess I didn't fully appreciate how difficult it might be."

"You want to turn back? You could be in your apartment by midafternoon."

"No. Absolutely not. I'm not giving up."

He hadn't expected any different. Liz seemed almost driven to help Mary.

"You must care a great deal about Mary," he said.

"I know it may be hard to understand. She's not all that easy to be around. She's at the stage of her life where she's very inner focused. Her needs, her wants, her pleasures take priority."

"Sounds like most teenagers."

"True." Liz smiled and he felt better. Lord, she was sunshine, all wrapped up into a nice portable package.

"Thankfully, most people grow out of it," she said. "Some never do. Some can't ever love another more than they love themselves."

It was the opening he'd waited for. He just didn't know if he had the courage to ask the question. "Sounds like you're speaking from experience?"

"Years of study."

Right. *Be bold or go home.* That was what the bumper sticker said that Robert had tacked up on his computer a couple years ago. "How's Howard feel about your leaving town with me?"

"Howard?" She looked genuinely puzzled. "How would he know?"

"He doesn't know you're with me? I thought that's why he called."

"He called about an adoption that he's working on."

"I figured that was just a pretense. I thought Jamison probably called him, and Fraypish decided it might be in his best interests to remind you not to forget him. I'm surprised he didn't demand that you come home. I know if you were dating me, you wouldn't be spending the night in a cabin with another man."

"Dating you?"

Now she looked a little green. Clearly the idea didn't have a lot of appeal. "Never mind," Sawyer mumbled. He sucked at bold.

"I'm not dating Howard."

"You two looked pretty friendly at the dance."

"We were dancing. It's hard to look like strangers when you're doing that. Howard wanted to take a date. I didn't have one. So, when he asked, I said yes. We met there. He didn't even pick me up."

"Hard to believe that you wouldn't have a date." *Lame. Lame. He was so lame.*

She chuckled. "There are worse things."

"Agreed. Still, seems like you'd have them lined up outside your door." He kept his eyes on the road, too scared to look at her and say the words.

She didn't say anything for a minute. He wondered if he'd offended her. He risked a quick look over.

"I almost got married a few years back," she said so matter-of-factly that he almost missed it. A hundred pounds, like barbells falling from a rack, seemed to land square on his lungs, making it hard to breathe.

"Married?" He managed to spit the word out.

"Someone that I used to work with," she said. "He's a nice enough guy. We just didn't want the same things."

He could imagine what the guy wanted from her. What every man, including him, would want. "What did you want?"

"Marriage. I suppose children."

She should have that. "Sounds reasonable," he managed

to say. Not for him, but then again, they weren't talking about him.

"Have you ever been married, Sawyer?"

"No."

"Come close?"

"Once."

"What happened?"

He wanted to tell her. Wanted to tell her about the whole stupid mess. But then she'd know he was a failure. That he hadn't been able to protect his son. That he hadn't been smart enough or brave enough. And then he'd see the pity in her eyes, the same pity he'd seen in the nurses' eyes, the doctors' eyes, the hospital chaplain's eyes. He couldn't stand that.

"We were both young," he said. "It probably wouldn't have worked out."

"Do you ever see her? Run into her at class reunions?"

"She's dead."

"Oh. I'm sorry."

"Yeah. Me, too." He meant that. He'd hated her. Hated her for what she'd done to his son. But even so, when he'd heard that she'd died of a drug overdose, just a couple years later, he'd mourned her loss. Another tragedy caused by drugs. And by the people like Mirandez who bankrolled the drugs into the country and then built a distribution system, mostly of kids, that rivaled those found at blue-chip companies.

"You must have loved her very much," Liz said.

He knew what she was thinking. She thought he was still in love with his dead girlfriend. He really wished it was as simple as that. "Sure," he said, choosing to let her continue down that path.

"Don't you think she'd have wanted you to go on?"

No. She hadn't really cared if he'd lived or died. All she'd cared about was where she was going to get her next hit of heroin. "It doesn't matter. I know what's best for me."

"I guess we'd all like to think we do," she said.

"If we don't, who does?"

"Sometimes it's difficult for us to see ourselves as clearly as others can see us."

She was probably right. But he didn't want her looking too closely at him. Otherwise, she'd see that he had a hole, a big, dark hole, all the way down to his soul. "Is that Liz or Liz the psychologist talking?"

She looked a little offended. His goading tone had done what he'd intended. "I'm not sure I can separate Liz from Liz the psychologist. It's who I am."

For the hundredth time, he was glad he'd managed to put on the brakes at the cabin. She deserved better. Better than some guy who was so afraid of losing what he loved that he wouldn't love at all. He didn't need a damn psychologist to explain it to him. "Well, I'm hot and hungry. Let's keep going."

Chapter Eleven

The next morning, Liz woke up with the birds. They were singing outside her window, welcoming the new day with their high-pitched tune of joy. She turned over, reached out her hand and with one finger separated the blinds. The bright sun made her squint her eyes.

Darn it. She'd overslept. They should have been on the road two hours ago. Why hadn't Sawyer woken her up? Was it possible that he'd overslept, too? Swinging her legs over the edge of the bed, she grabbed a pair of shorts from her suitcase and slipped into them, stuck her feet into her sandals and left the room.

Sawyer's bed was empty. The bathroom door stood half-open, telling her that he'd left the cabin. She made a quick trip to the small room and felt immeasurably better after having brushed her teeth and washed her face. She walked out of the cabin, saw her car and wondered where Sawyer might be.

Maybe he'd gone to the office for coffee today. Oh, she wished she had a gun. She'd love to just shock the heck out of him. He'd open the door, and maybe she'd shoot at his feet just to give him a taste of his own medicine. And then she'd kiss the heck out of him again.

As delightful as that sounded, with nothing more threatening than a nail file, Liz tossed that option. Still, the coffee sounded good. She walked across the parking lot to the office and helped herself to a large black coffee. She passed on the sweets. A few more days of pecan rolls and she'd be one big roll.

On her way back, she discovered Sawyer almost hidden behind the cabin. He was doing push-ups. She didn't know how many he'd done before she started watching, but she saw him do thirty. Then he flipped over onto his back and started in on the sit-ups.

Her throat went dry. The man had on a pair of loose cotton shorts but no shirt. Sweat clung to his skin, and the sun glinted off his broad chest. With each sit-up, the muscles in his stomach rippled. A hundred sit-ups later, he collapsed on his back, his legs spread.

She felt a bit like a voyeur.

When Sawyer sprang up from the ground in one fluid motion, she realized she must have sighed.

"Liz?"

"Good morning," she said. "I'm sorry. I didn't mean to disturb you." *Or stop you.*

"No problem. I needed to stretch out a bit."

"We have spent a lot of time in a car lately."

"Yeah."

Okay. If he could pretend that she hadn't been staring at him, she could, too. "I'm sorry I slept so late."

"You must have needed it."

"Right. Do you want to shower first or should I?"

"You go ahead. I'm going to run for a little while. Just around the parking lot. The cabin won't be out of my sight."

She wondered if she stood on her tiptoes if she could catch a glimpse out the bathroom window. Sawyer was being vigilant in protecting her. She was just being greedy. "Well, I'll see you in a few minutes, then."

He nodded.

By the time she'd showered and dressed and Sawyer had done the same, she felt almost calm. Not at all like a woman who had almost thrown herself on a sweaty, half-naked man in a hotel parking lot.

They drove into town and grabbed a quick breakfast at one of the local eateries. Back in the car, Liz spread the map across her lap. She looked at it then folded it.

"What's wrong?"

"Nothing. I figure you know where you're going."

"I do. South. Then we'll work our way back up on the other side."

It sounded an awful lot like yesterday and the day before. A day of stops and starts and disappointments. Liz resisted the urge to pound her head against the window.

As if Sawyer had read her mind, he asked, "You up for this? We can always go back to the city."

Giving up wasn't an option. Being late had grave consequences. These were the lessons she'd learned. "No, let's go. The sooner we get started, the sooner we find them."

To his credit, Sawyer didn't even respond. He just started driving.

By the middle of the afternoon, Liz felt horrible. She'd worn her most lightweight shirt and shorts, but still the material clung to her skin. It had to be ninety-five degrees in the shade. They'd already stopped at seven campgrounds, two parks and four small motels that crowded the river.

"Next stop is Twin Oaks Lodge," Liz said, holding the map a couple inches off her legs. If she let it rest, it would probably stick to her.

"Yeah, that sounds right. I actually tried to get a cabin there, but they were full. Said they book up by the beginning of April for the whole summer."

"Not a bad position to be in," Liz said.

"It's not all gravy. They have long, cold winters up here," Sawyer reminded her.

"So? We have long, cold winters in Chicago."

With that, he turned the wheel, pulling the car into the large parking lot of Twin Oaks Lodge.

As usual, he pulled off to the side, out of view of the office windows. His cell phone buzzed just as Liz opened her door. He scanned the text message.

"Is it work? Is it Mary?" Liz asked.

"It's work, and I don't know if it's Mary."

"If it's Mary…"

"Then I'll tell you what I can. I just have to respect the privacy and the security of the person who's calling me. Even having you listen in on one side of the conversation could jeopardize that. I won't do that to this person."

"This person? I can't even know if it's a man or a woman?"

"No. Better for you and better for the person."

She nodded, apparently realizing he wasn't going to budge. There was a lot he probably should apologize for, but this wasn't one of the things.

"Fine. I'm going to go into this office, ask my questions and pretend to look at the brochures. If I—" she paused for effect "—would happen to get us both a cold drink, will you promise not to shoot me when I come back?"

It took him a minute to realize that she was kidding, that she was in some way trying to smooth things out between the two of them. He shrugged. "It depends. Make sure it's a diet."

"It's always the details that get a person into trouble, isn't it?" Liz opened the car door and walked across the parking lot. He watched her until she got inside.

He dialed Rafael Fluentes. The man had infiltrated the organization deeper than any other undercover cop had been able to. His calls rarely meant good news.

"It's me," Sawyer said when Fluentes answered.

"I hear you're working the river. How's the fishing?"

"Nobody is biting."

"Sucks everywhere. There's talk of a rumble," Fluentes said.

Damn. It was an unusual night when there wasn't an intergang slaying. Turf battles waged fierce and frequent. Fluentes wouldn't have called about that. This must be a big-time, bring-out-your-big-guns war call. "When?" Sawyer asked.

"Soon."

Sawyer regretted being two hundred miles away. Robert would keep him informed, but it wasn't the same as being there. "Hope the fish bite better there."

"Yeah, me, too. I don't care if the small ones slip through our nets, but I'd like to hook a few of the big ones. By the way, I've got a little info on the sister fish. Mirandez is the only child of Maria and Ramon Mirandez. However, Maria had a child ten years before she married Ramon. We're not even sure Ramon knew about the kid. In any event, Mirandez has a much older half sister out there somewhere."

Maybe that made some sense. She'd come to Mirandez's father's funeral. If Ramon Mirandez hadn't known about the child, Maria Mirandez would have finally been free to have both her children with her to comfort her in her time of need.

"What's her name?"

"Angel."

"Angel what?"

"I don't have a last name. Maria's maiden name was Jones."

"Jones?" Sawyer frowned at the phone.

"Yeah. Mirandez's grandfather was as white as you and me."

"Bet that's not well-known in the hood."

"Remind him of it when you arrest him."

"Angel Jones," Sawyer repeated. "Or Angel whatever. She's probably married by now. Where's she live?"

"Not sure. Maria Mirandez moved to one of those independent living centers a couple years ago. A real nice expensive one."

Sawyer couldn't help but interrupt. "Guess what's paying for that?"

"I know. If we didn't have the drug money, the economy would be in real danger. Anyway, we got one of her old neighbors to talk. She remembers Maria visiting a daughter who lived up north."

"Up north?" Sawyer repeated, even more discouraged than before. "That's it? That's all you got?"

"Maria evidently never drove at night. She could get from her daughter's place to home all in daylight. So, I'm guessing it's not Alaska."

"You're funny."

"Hey, I said it wasn't much. But at least we know there's a sister."

"Yeah, I know. I'm sorry. I'm just getting discouraged."

"Patience is the fisherman's friend. Try to remember that," Fluentes said before he hung up.

Sawyer wouldn't brag about catching Mirandez. But he would get some real pleasure out of seeing him stuffed and mounted on a plaque and hung on somebody's wall. Not his. He didn't want to look at the son of a bitch every day.

He'd been off the phone for three minutes before Liz came out of the office. She was carrying two big cups. She got in and handed him one. He opened the straw, poked it into the hole and took a big drink. "I like a woman who can follow directions."

"Just tell me what to do and I can do it."

She hadn't meant it to be provocative. He could tell that by the sudden blush on her face. But the double meaning hadn't been lost on either one of them. He rubbed his jaw, and his whole damn face felt hot. What a bunch of idiots they were.

"News about Mary?" she asked.

He shook his head. "Mirandez has a sister. A half sister on his mom's side."

"Where?"

"Nobody knows. They'll keep digging. I've got a name. Angel. Might be Angel Jones. Every place we go from now on, we ask for her, too. Maybe we'll get real lucky."

TWO STOPS LATER, luck struck. Liz flashed the picture, told her story and waited for the standard answer. When the young man behind the desk gave her a crooked smile and said that she'd be able to find Mr. and Mrs. Giovanni at cabin number seven, she almost wept.

"My sister's pregnant," Liz reminded the clerk, wanting so desperately to believe but knowing she couldn't be too optimistic.

"I know. I was surprised when her husband told me that the baby wasn't due for another couple of months. They wanted to rent a boat yesterday, and I was nervous as heck. Thought she'd probably pop that kid out when she hit the first wave. But they docked it back in last night, safe and sound. Although I don't think your brother-in-law knows much about fishing. Your sister had to show him how to bait a hook."

"Yes, she's a talent. Well, I can't wait to see them. My car is in the parking lot. If I just keep driving on this road, will it take me past cabin seven?"

"Sure thing. And if they aren't there, look for them out at the dock. That's where they seem to spend most of their day. She reads books, and he throws his line in the water and spends most of the day on his cell phone. That's not how I'd spend my vacation. But since your brother-in-law tips twice as good as anybody else, I ain't gonna judge."

Easy to tip when it was with dirty money.

"Well, I'm going to try to surprise them. You won't call them or anything, will you?"

"Couldn't if I wanted to. Cabins don't have phones."

"Well, okay, then. I guess I'll see you later."

"Sure. Just make sure your brother-in-law knows how helpful I was."

Liz managed a smile. She walked quickly back to the car, opened the door and slammed it shut before she turned to Sawyer. "They're here. Cabin seven. Mr. and Mrs. Giovanni."

Sawyer's eyes lit up, and his hands clenched the steering wheel. "Giovanni," he repeated.

"Dark hair. Dark eyes. Guess he figured people in Wisconsin wouldn't know the difference between Hispanic and Italian."

"Suppose. It's not like he could have picked Anderson or MacDougal."

"Now what?" They hadn't really ever talked about what would happen if they actually found them.

"We call for backup. Damn, I wish Robert were here."

"What do I do?"

"Stay here. Once I make the call, I'm going in for a closer look. I want to get the layout of the cabin."

"The clerk said they might be down at the lake. There's a path that runs behind all the cabins."

"Okay. Thanks."

"I don't want Mary getting hurt. You need to let me get her out of there."

"You're not going anywhere near Mirandez. He'll kill you. Without hesitation, without second thoughts."

"But—"

"But nothing," he said. "Don't fight me on this, Liz. I've

been straight with you all along. This is a police operation. You have to stay here. You have to stay safe."

She didn't intend to give up that easily. "You'd have never found her if it wasn't for me. Why can't I just go look around with you?"

"No. Mirandez is a crazy man. Look, Liz, I'll do my best to make sure Mary doesn't get hurt. You've got to trust me."

She would trust him with her life. If Capable Sawyer couldn't handle the trouble, the trouble had a destiny. But she couldn't walk away from Mary now. Not when she was this close.

"It's not a matter of my trusting you. Mary doesn't trust you. She doesn't like you. She's not going to listen to you. She'll do something stupid."

He seemed to consider that. "You'll do exactly what I tell you to do?"

"Yes."

"You won't call out to her or say anything until I give you the sign?"

"No."

Sawyer shook his head as if he couldn't believe what he was about to do. "All right. But don't make me regret this." He picked up his cell phone and dialed the number he'd evidently memorized. He gave the party on the other end a terse description of their location and the suspected location of Mirandez and Mary. He listened for a minute, responded with a terse yes and hung up.

"Who was that?"

"Miles Foltran. He's the sheriff of Juneau County. I made contact with him before we left Chicago so that he knew we were in the area. He'll have backup here in ten minutes."

"Now what?" Liz asked.

"I never should have listened to Fischer," Sawyer muttered.

"What?"

"Never mind. Just be quiet. I need to think."

Liz wasn't even offended. The man had more on his mind than being polite to her.

"Now we go take a look," he said, starting the car. He threw it into Drive and slowly eased out of his parking spot.

"Shouldn't we wait for backup?"

"We are. We're going to keep a nice safe distance away."

Sawyer drove down the narrow blacktop road, keeping his speed around twenty. They saw the first cabin and then ten or twelve more look-alikes. Sawyer continued past cabin seven, all the way until a stand of evergreens took over where the road stopped. He turned his car around, angling it so that he could get a view of the shorefront that ran behind the cabins.

"I don't believe this." Sawyer reached between the seats and pulled out his gun.

"What?" Liz craned her neck to see.

"Look between those two cabins, about a hundred yards out. That's Mirandez."

A short, thin man, wearing a baggy white T-shirt and blue jean shorts that fell below his knees, paced up and down the dock. He had a beer in one hand and a phone in the other.

"Keep talking," Sawyer muttered. "Keep talking, you bastard."

But almost as if that had been the kiss of death, Mirandez lowered his arm, snapped the cell phone closed, walked over to the lawn chair at the edge of the water, held out his hand and helped Mary pull herself out of the chair.

"Mary," Liz murmured, more scared now than ever that she'd actually seen Mary. "You've got to make sure she doesn't get hurt," Liz said. "Promise me."

"Damn," Sawyer said, totally focused on Mirandez. "They're leaving."

Liz stared at the young couple. Sure enough, Mary and

Mirandez were walking toward the black SUV that was parked almost on the sand. Mirandez evidently hadn't wanted his vehicle far from him.

Before she could even think about what to do, Sawyer threw the Toyota into Drive and pulled up to the end of the driveway. "Get out now. My side."

He opened the door, stepped out, grabbed her arm and literally pulled her from the car. He gave her a quick, hard kiss. "Run like hell for the trees."

"What are you doing?"

"What I ain't gonna do is let the bastard get away. He can't get around me. He's going to have to go through me. Now get the hell out of here."

LIZ HEARD MIRANDEZ'S SUV engine kick to life, and she knew she had mere seconds. "Mary," she managed to choke out.

Sawyer spared her a quick glance. "I'll do the best I can."

She ran for all she was worth, reaching the trees just when she heard the horn. Mirandez leaned on it, obviously irritated that someone had the audacity to block his way. Liz could see him looking around, and she prayed that he wouldn't see either her in the trees or Sawyer, who had somehow managed to get behind a big oak tree about twenty yards to the left of the car.

When she heard the scrunch of car on car, she knew that Mirandez had gotten tired of waiting. With the bumper of his SUV, he pushed the rear of her car aside. In another fifteen seconds, he'd have enough space to squeeze out.

And almost as if in slow motion, Sawyer stepped out from the tree, fired twice, hitting the front wheel of the SUV. Mirandez reached his arm out of the open window, a deadly-looking gun extended from his hand, and fired at Sawyer, who had slipped once again behind the tree.

Liz wanted to scream but knew she couldn't distract Sawyer. The bullets bounced off the tree, the only protection Sawyer had against the horrible gun. Liz, almost without thought or intent, grabbed some rocks from the ground, and with all her strength, she flung them across the road, straight toward the cabin. One hit the door, another the roof and the rest scattered across the ground.

It was enough to momentarily distract Mirandez, and Sawyer didn't miss his opportunity. With Mirandez's attention on the cabin, Sawyer swung his big frame out from behind the tree.

The bullet caught Mirandez's forearm, and his gun fell to the ground.

Sawyer ran to the SUV, kicked the gun a hundred feet, all the while keeping his own gun leveled at Mirandez's head. "Police," Sawyer announced. "Turn off the engine."

Mirandez looked up, maybe to judge his chances, and Liz held her breath. Then, with a slight shake of his head, as if he couldn't believe what was happening, he turned off his vehicle.

"Mary, get out of the car," Sawyer instructed, his voice steady.

For just the briefest of seconds, Mary didn't move. Then she almost tumbled out in her haste.

Liz met her halfway. She reached for her and held her as close as the pregnancy allowed. She thanked God. They'd found her in time. This time she hadn't been too late.

Mirandez screamed and yelled obscenities at Sawyer. But when Sawyer took a step toward Mary, Mirandez changed tunes.

"Get the hell away from my baby," the drug dealer yelled. "You don't have any right. I'll kill you. I swear to the Holy Mother that you're a dead man."

His baby. Liz pulled away from Mary, wiping a gentle hand across the girl's teary face. What the heck was going on?

"Oh, Liz," Mary cried, "I was so scared. I didn't think I'd ever see you again. I—"

Just then, four squad cars rounded the corner. Six officers piled out, guns drawn.

"I'm a police officer," Sawyer called out. "The man in the SUV is Dantel Mirandez. He's wanted on suspicion of murder."

The tall one in the front of the pack held his hand up in the air, motioning those behind him to stop. "Detective, your voice sounds about right. But given that I've only talked to you on the phone, put your gun down now and show us some ID."

Sawyer nodded. "That's fine. Come a little bit closer. If he moves, shoot him. He dropped his gun. It's to my right, twenty-five feet out."

Sawyer laid his own gun on the ground and watched while the officers secured Mirandez's gun. He unclipped the badge on his shirt pocket that he'd hastily attached right before he'd pushed Liz from the car and run for cover himself. He tossed it at the man who'd spoken.

The man glanced at it for a moment, and then a big grin spread across his face. "Welcome to Wisconsin, Detective Montgomery. Looks like you've had quite a day."

Sawyer thought he might have the same silly-ass grin on his own face. "Watch him," he warned again before he picked up his gun and put it back in the car. Then he strode over to Liz and Mary.

"You both all right?" he asked.

"We're fine," Liz answered.

Sawyer took a long look at Mary. She looked tired and pale, and she was holding on to Liz so tightly that he was surprised Liz could still breathe. "What's the story here, Mary?"

"He's a monster," Mary answered, her voice brimming with tears.

"Did he hurt you?" Sawyer asked. "The baby?" Suddenly he knew killing Mirandez wouldn't be enough. He'd have to torture him first.

Mary shook her head and took a couple of loud sniffs. "Dantel has a sister who lives around here. She's a nurse. They were going to cut me up. And then take my baby."

"What?" Liz asked.

"But they had to wait. His sister said I had to be at least thirty-six weeks so that the baby would be big enough."

"But aren't you almost thirty-eight weeks, honey?" Liz brushed her hand gently over Mary's hair.

"Yeah. But he didn't know that. He was gonna keep me up here until his sister thought I was ready."

"It's not his baby, is it?" Sawyer asked. Liz had been right. Suddenly it was all starting to make some sense. "But he thought it was."

"Dantel treated me like a queen, bought me anything I wanted, took me anywhere I wanted to go. I couldn't tell him I was already six weeks pregnant before we ever slept together."

More lies. When would the damn lies stop? Sawyer pushed the disgust back. "He wants the baby?"

"His mother is dying. She wants a grandchild before she dies. His sister can't have any kids."

Sawyer wanted to make some sick joke about Mirandez being a mama's boy. But he couldn't. Dying mothers weren't funny. "How'd you find out what he had planned?"

"I didn't know at first. When we left Chicago, he said that he just wanted to get away and relax for a few days. I didn't want to go but you…you can't turn Dantel down. He doesn't like it."

Sawyer bet not. "Then what?"

"I thought we were going fishing. But he didn't have a

clue what he was doing. I started getting scared. There isn't even a phone in the room."

"What happened?"

"We went to his sister's house. At first she was really nice, talking to me about the baby and everything. But then I had to pee so I went upstairs to the bathroom. When I came down, I heard her telling Dantel that it would be a couple weeks before she could take the baby. That she didn't want to take a chance on the lungs."

The devil seed had taken root and sprouted in the Mirandez family. "Then what?" Sawyer asked.

"I pretended that I didn't hear them. I ate dinner with that horrible woman and pretended that nothing was wrong. I thought I might have a chance to get away. Dantel had been on the phone all the time. Another gang issued a challenge. There's going to be a big fight soon."

"Where?" Sawyer asked. "Did you hear him say where and when?"

"Yes. Maplewood Park. On Sunday night."

"Good girl," Sawyer said. "That information is going to be very helpful."

"Dantel hated that he wasn't in Chicago to control things. He went crazy on the phone one night, talking to somebody. I thought it might be my chance. But he saw me. I told him I stepped outside for some air, but I knew he didn't believe me. Since then, he's been watching me like a hawk." Her lower lip trembled, and a fresh set of tears slid down her face.

The girl had a lot of guts. "You did good," Sawyer told her. "You saved yourself and your baby. You should be proud."

When Liz threw him a grateful glance, Sawyer felt his heart, his stone-cold heart, heat up just a bit.

He was about to do something stupid like thank her when Sheriff Foltran interrupted him. "We've read him his rights, Detective. He needs medical attention. We'll see that he gets that at the local emergency room, and then we'll get him booked. My friend Bob owns this place, and I don't think he'll appreciate us hanging around until all his other guests show up."

Sawyer nodded at the man. "Right. Put him in one of your cars. I'll ride with you." He turned back to Liz and Mary. "I'm going to have to deal with this. He crossed state lines, so it's a bit more complicated to get him back into our jurisdiction. And then I need to arrange secure transport back to Chicago."

"How long will that take?" Liz asked.

"Probably a day or so. You two can go back now. Take the car. I think it will still run."

"It's over?" Mary asked.

"This part is over. I still need your testimony."

Mary nodded. "I want the bastard to pay. He was going to let that woman cut my baby out."

"You'll testify about the murder you saw?"

Mary didn't say anything for a full minute. She just stared at the ground. Then she looked at Liz. "Dantel said he'd kill me," she said, her voice very soft. "He said he'd kill you, too. He sent you that letter just to scare you. And he shot up your office just so we'd both know he was serious and that he could get to us anytime he wanted. He had the bomb put there, too. I don't know how but he did it. I'm so sorry."

"It's okay," Liz assured her. "He'll be in jail."

God willing, Sawyer thought. God and a smart jury. His gang would still be on the prowl. Sawyer wondered if Liz had any idea the risk Mary was taking. He should tell her.

"He beat that man and killed him," Mary said. "He was laughing while he did it. The guy was screaming and crying, and there was blood everywhere."

Hell, maybe he ought to do everybody a favor and manage to drop Mirandez in the Wisconsin River. With a fifty-pound sack of cement around his neck.

But he wouldn't. Even given the number of times he'd seen the system fail the community it served, Sawyer still believed in it. Believed that if he did his job right, the next guy would do the same, and so on. It was what separated them from the animals, both the four-legged and the two-legged like Mirandez.

Right now what he wanted most in the world was to take Liz into his arms. But he knew that couldn't happen. Even with Mirandez in custody, it wouldn't be fair to Liz to pursue a relationship. He didn't intend to offer marriage. He couldn't offer children. He needed to make a clean break of it now.

"I'm going to be pretty busy for a few days. He'll need to be processed."

Liz nodded.

"I need your written statement," Sawyer said to Mary.

"Now?"

"That would be best." He pulled the ever-present note-book out of his shirt pocket.

"Don't I have to sign a form or something?"

"You write it, date it and sign it. I've accepted statements written on crumpled-up paper towels. It doesn't matter what it looks like. What matters is what it says."

Mary assessed him for a long moment. "You know, you're not so bad for a cop."

Didn't rank up there with Liz looking at him as if he walked on water but it still made him feel real fine. "You're not so bad yourself. What are you two going to do when you get back to town?"

Mary was back to her shrugging.

Liz saw it, too. "Mary, I want you to stay with me. For at least a couple of days."

He didn't miss the pure relief that crossed Mary's face.

It reminded him of how much of a kid she really was. That didn't stop him from wishing that Liz hadn't made the offer. Mary attracted trouble. He didn't want Liz getting caught in the cross fire. He wouldn't be there to protect her.

"Your car should drive fine even though Mirandez did dent it up a little. I'm going to call Robert and ask him to meet you at your apartment. Just to make sure it's still secure."

"What?" Liz looked at him as if he'd lost his mind.

"I think we have a good chance that the judge will deny Mirandez bail. He's clearly a flight risk. We'll keep the lid on the fact that Mary's going to put him in the hot seat. Given that he still thinks Mary's pregnant with his baby, she's probably safe for now. You, too. But I don't want to take any chances. I'd feel better if Robert meets you there."

"Oh."

He knew immediately that if it were just her, she'd argue until she turned blue. But she wouldn't take a risk with Mary.

"You remember him, right?"

She nodded. "It's just a bit embarrassing."

"What?"

"The last time I saw Robert, I wasn't exactly dressed for success."

Sawyer remembered exactly how she'd been dressed. Or mostly undressed. He'd bet his last dime Robert did, too. "He won't even mention it." Sawyer would make damn sure of that.

Chapter Twelve

Liz was an hour from home when her cell phone rang. She answered it, keeping one hand on the wheel. "Hello."

"Everything okay?"

She'd left Sawyer more than two hours ago. Capable Sawyer clearly didn't like having things out of his immediate control and he probably figured he was due an update. "We're fine. No trouble."

"Good," he said.

The relief in his voice made her insides do funny little jumps. *Slow down, girl. He's a cop. With a misguided sense of responsibility.*

"I called Jamison and told him everything," Liz said. "Now that Dantel Mirandez is in police custody, he wants to reopen OCM, especially since we know Mirandez sent that letter to me. Do you have any concerns about that?"

Sawyer didn't answer right away. When he did, he didn't sound too happy. "I guess not," he said. "There's always some risk. But I don't think we can expect the man to keep his business closed forever."

"He'll be glad to hear that."

"I suppose you're planning on going back right away?"

"Of course. Why wouldn't I?"

He sighed. "By the way, I talked to Robert. Pull into the alley behind your building. He'll meet you there."

"Okay."

"If you don't see him right away, don't get out of the car. Just keep driving until you get to the closest police station. And call me."

"I'm sure everything will be fine."

"I know. It just doesn't hurt to have a plan B."

She imagined Capable Sawyer always had a plan B. "Mary has slept most of the way."

"That's good. By the way, I read her statement again. She did a good job. Lots of detail that will be helpful. Just remember, when she wakes up, remind her not to tell anyone that Mirandez isn't the father. That's the best protection she has right now."

"What happens when she delivers within a couple weeks and it's obvious the baby is full-term? What happens if Dantel tries to claim that he's the father?"

He didn't answer right away. When he did, he surprised her. "If Mary's telling the truth, a simple blood test will rule out Mirandez's claim. Of course, then her life won't be worth the paper that the test is printed on. When Mirandez finds out that she's going to testify against him, she's going to be in real trouble."

"What is she going to do?"

"She's going to have to get out of town, Liz."

"Are you crazy?"

"No. Don't say anything to her yet. I don't want her freaking out."

Liz gave Mary a quick glance. The girl snored, her head at a strange angle against the headrest.

"Well, I'm freaking out. She hasn't signed adoption paperwork yet. What if she decides to keep her baby? She can't just go off on her own with a newborn. She's going to need help."

"That can be arranged."

Liz realized with a sinking heart that he'd had time to

think it through. He'd known from the moment Mary confessed that this was how it had to end. Liz stepped on the gas a bit harder, wishing it was his head. "You should have told her. Before she confessed that she'd been there. You should have told her that her life would never be the same again."

"We need her. She's the one who can put Mirandez away. I never pretended anything—"

"But leaving town?" Liz interrupted. "That's huge. It means...it means I'll never see her again."

There, she'd said it. She didn't want to lose Mary.

For a minute, she thought he'd hung up. There was absolutely no noise on the other end of the phone. When he did speak, he sounded a bit strange. "Liz, I'm sorry. I probably should have said something. I couldn't. I just couldn't give Mary a reason to not do the right thing. A man died that night. Mirandez killed him, and he needs to pay for that. I know this is tough. But Mary would have drifted out of your life sooner or later. This way you'll know she's safe."

She absolutely hated that he made sense.

She wanted to hang on to her anger, to somehow let it soothe the pain of loss. But really the person to be angry at was Dantel Mirandez. It wasn't Sawyer's fault. "So, this is real-life witness-protection stuff?"

"Yeah. It doesn't just happen on the television shows."

"She's not going to take this well."

"Don't tell her yet. I just wanted you to have a chance to hear it first. When I get back to town, we'll tell her together."

She let up on the gas, and her stomach started doing those funny little jumps again. "Thank you, Sawyer." It sounded awfully inadequate, but she couldn't yet verbalize her feelings. They were too fresh, too unexpected, too much.

"It'll be okay, Liz. I promise. Just trust me on this one."

"I've always trusted you, Sawyer." *Even before I loved you.*

She jerked the wheel when the right-side tires swerved off the highway.

She felt hot and cold and sort of dizzy. "Traffic's picking up," she said. "I've got to go."

"Okay. Be careful. Please."

Careful? It was a little late for that. She'd fallen in love with Sawyer Montgomery.

Forty-five minutes later, she pulled into the alley and found her regular parking space. She'd barely turned the car off when someone tapped on her window. Even though she'd been expecting Detective Hanson, she still jumped several feet.

He smiled at her, but when a blue car pulled into the alley and headed toward them, his smile and easy demeanor vanished. "Get as close to the other door as you can. Lie down on the seat," he ordered.

Liz did as she was told, grateful that Mary still slept, slumped down in the seat. She saw that Detective Hanson had left the car door open and moved behind it. He had his gun out.

Liz held her breath and waited for the shots. All she heard was the engine of a car badly in need of a tune-up. It sounded as if it never even slowed down as it went past.

"It's okay." Detective Montgomery stood up. "Two old ladies. Both with blue hair."

Liz laughed. "Not part of Mirandez's gang?"

"I doubt it." He looked at Mary. "She sleep all the way here?"

"Yes. I don't think she's had much sleep the past couple of days."

"Let's get her inside. Street is pretty quiet. I've been here for about fifteen minutes and haven't seen anything unusual. I don't expect any trouble."

"Okay. Mary." Liz leaned over to tap the girl on her shoulder. "Wake up, sweetie. We're home."

Mary's eyes fluttered open. She looked at Liz first, then at Detective Hanson. "Who are you?" she asked.

"Detective Robert Hanson."

"Oh, yeah. I remember you. You were with Detective Montgomery. I guess you're the babysitter?"

Detective Hanson didn't look particularly offended. "I'll bet you can't wait for my microwave popcorn."

Mary snorted.

He ignored it. "Let's go," he said. "Stay close. Do what I tell you to do when I tell you to do it."

Liz knew the past several days had taken their toll on Mary when she didn't argue with Robert.

They got inside without incident. Robert checked each of the rooms. Mary stood in the kitchen, waiting for him to finish. When he did, she gave Liz a hug and went off to sleep in the spare bedroom. Liz gave her an extra blanket and shut the door behind her. Then she sank down onto her couch, loving the feel of the leather fabric. It was good to be home.

"Can I ask you something, Ms. Mayfield?" Detective Hanson asked. He stood near the kitchen counter. "How is Sawyer?"

"Stubborn. Bossy. Opinionated." She held up three fingers and ticked off the list.

Robert rubbed his hands together. "I knew it. I knew it from the first day I saw the two of you together. Like a match and dry kindling."

"Oh, but we're not…" She stopped, unwilling to share the private details of her relationship.

Robert laughed. A quiet chuckle. "Well, I hope you are soon. Otherwise, he's going to be a real pain in the ass to work with."

WHEN THE PHONE RANG late that night, Liz practically vaulted off the couch. The apartment had gotten very quiet after Robert had left and Mary had gone to bed. "Hello?"

"Ms. Mayfield?"

She didn't recognize the voice. "Yes."

"This is Geri Heffers from Melliertz Hospital. Melissa Stroud asked me to call you. She had a baby girl tonight."

Melissa. She wasn't due for another week. "Is everything okay?"

"Everything's fine. I understand you're Melissa's counselor and that you've been helping her arrange for an adoption. She's going to be released the day after tomorrow."

Liz knew what that meant. Melissa needed to sign the paperwork before she left the hospital. According to state law, she'd have seventy-two hours to change her mind. The baby would either stay in the hospital or be released to temporary care in a foster home until that time period elapsed. Only then could she go to the adoptive parents.

"I'll be there tomorrow. I'll come late afternoon." Liz promised the nurse and hung up. She dialed Howard's number from memory.

When he answered, she didn't waste words. "Howard, it's Liz. Melissa Stroud had her baby today at Melliertz. It's a girl. Healthy. She wants to sign papers tomorrow. Can you meet me there around four in the afternoon?"

"Excellent. The Thompsons really wanted a girl."

"The Thompsons? I thought Mike and Mindy Partridge were the adopting parents."

"No, they wanted to wait another couple months. Mike's traveling a lot these days."

"Have I met the Thompsons?"

"No. But they're great. I've done a full background check. You couldn't ask for better. I've talked to Jamison about them."

She didn't like it when she hadn't met the adopting parents. This had happened before. But when she'd mentioned something to Jamison, he'd told her not to worry about it and that he trusted Howard's judgment. "I'd like to see the background report," she said.

"Oh, sure," Howard said. "I'll bring it with me to the hospital."

Liz hung up the phone and went to check on Mary. She'd been right. It looked as though Mary would sleep through the night. The pregnancy, the worry, it had worn out the young girl.

Liz wished for just a bit of Mary's sleepiness. She turned on the television. Ten minutes and bits and pieces of three sitcoms later, she turned it off. She picked up a new magazine that had been waiting for her in the mailbox. Flipping page by page, she got halfway through it before she admitted defeat.

She couldn't stop thinking about Sawyer. What was he doing? Was he still interrogating Mirandez? Had he had dinner? Had he returned to the cabin? Had he gone to bed?

That was where her thoughts got her into trouble. She wondered if he slept in underwear. She didn't have to imagine whether he wore basic white. That little puzzle had been solved when he'd greeted her at the door with a gun and a pair of unsnapped jeans.

She'd been so darn busy looking at his zipper and the equipment underneath that she'd barely given the gun more than a passing thought. She hadn't worried that Sawyer would shoot her. Capable Sawyer didn't make mistakes like that.

Robert thought they were like a match and dry kindling. What he didn't know was that with a few choice words about responsibility and professionalism, Sawyer had effectively doused the flames, looking every bit like a man afraid of fire.

It made her wonder exactly what or who had burned Sawyer in the past. She'd wanted to ask Robert but knew it would be useless. Sawyer was his friend. He would guard his secrets.

Why hadn't Sawyer called? He'd said he *might* call, not that he *would* call. Why would he call? When she picked up a paper and pen, no longer content to silently argue with herself, and actually started to make a list of whys and why nots, she knew she'd gone around the bend.

Nothing would ever be the way it was before she'd met Sawyer. Heck, she'd never even be able to enjoy a big bowl of gumbo again. If she saw flowering vines climbing up a wrought-iron railing, she'd probably burst into tears. She'd never be able to go south of the Mason–Dixon line again.

Liz got up and walked over to the shelf where she kept her favorite CDs she'd purchased years ago. She pulled out two, walked into her kitchen, opened the cabinet door under her sink and dumped them into the trash.

She was done with New Orleans jazz.

She returned to the couch and reached an arm toward the light switch. She might not sleep, but at least she could brood in the dark.

LIZ ALMOST SLEPT through her appointment with Howard. She had gotten up once, around nine, and fixed breakfast for Mary. She steered Mary toward the television and then went back to bed. When she woke up the second time, she had a headache, a stuffy nose and a sore throat. As irrational as it was, she blamed Sawyer.

She showered and got dressed as fast as her ailing body allowed. She walked out to the kitchen and poured half a glass of orange juice. Her throat was so sore she knew she'd be lucky to get it down. "You doing okay, Mary?"

"I didn't know you had cable," Mary said, holding the remote control.

"Enjoy. I've got to go meet OCM's attorney. I'll be back by dinner. There are snacks in the cupboard. Help yourself."

Mary waved and flipped channels. Liz left the apartment. Halfway to the hospital, her stomach rumbled with hunger, but unless she could find somewhere that pureed eggs and bacon, she was out of luck.

Howard waited for her outside the front doors of the hospital. When he bent to kiss her cheek, she pulled back. "Don't get too close. I have a sore throat. I'm probably contagious."

When he jumped back a full foot, she couldn't help but compare him to Sawyer. Somehow she just knew that little short of the plague would keep Sawyer Montgomery from kissing his girl.

Oh, God, how she wanted to be that girl.

"You look horrible," Howard said.

"Thank you. I worked all night on this look."

He frowned at her. "If you didn't go gallivanting around the countryside, you'd probably stay a lot healthier."

Gallivanting? She'd saved an unborn baby from a crazy woman's knife. She couldn't have a lot of regrets. "Did you bring the background report?" she asked.

Howard put a hand over his mouth. "Oh, no. I completely forgot. Trust me, it's fine. They're great people."

"I'm not comfortable with this," Liz said.

"Come on. We're both here. You don't feel well. You surely don't want to stick around while I run all the way across town to get them from my office. You won't want to come back later. You'll probably be sleeping. So, let's just get this over with."

Unfortunately, everything he'd said was true. "Okay. But fax them to me tomorrow. Please don't forget. I need the information for my files."

After a quick stop at the hospital gift shop to pick up a box of candy, they checked in at the nurses' desk on the Maternity floor. They got the room number and walked down the long hallway. When they got there, they saw Melissa sitting up in her bed, watching a game show.

"Hi, Melissa," Liz spoke softly from the doorway, not wanting to scare the young woman. "How are you?"

"Hi, Liz. I'm okay, I guess."

Liz smiled at her client. Melissa Stroud had graduated from high school just three months earlier. She'd been the valedictorian of her class. Her gown had been big enough that the visitors, all the parents and aunts and uncles and grandparents proudly coming to see their offspring, probably hadn't realized that she was six months pregnant.

They'd have all been shocked that a smart girl like that could have gotten herself in trouble.

The father of the baby had been the salutatorian. First and second in their class.

Two smart kids having dumb sex.

"I've brought Howard Fraypish with me. You've talked to him on the phone."

"Okay."

Liz wasn't worried that the girl didn't show more emotion. Generally, that was how most of the girls got through the adoption process. They simply shut off their feelings.

"How's the baby?" Liz asked.

"Good. The nurses said she was real pretty."

Liz thought she caught just the hint of pride in the girl's voice. "You haven't seen her?"

"No. They said I could. Even after I told them I was giving her away. But I couldn't. I just couldn't." And suddenly, a tear slipped out of Melissa's eye, running down the smooth surface of her eighteen-year-old face.

She brushed it away with the back of her hand. "It's stupid to cry. I'm giving her away. That's what I want. That's what I planned on."

Liz felt her own tears threaten to fall. She blinked her eyes furiously. No matter how right the decision was, it was always painful. "You're a very brave girl, Melissa."

The girl shook her head. "I'm never going to sleep with another boy again as long as I live."

Liz smiled and patted the young girl's arm. "Someday you will meet a fine man. He'll make your heart race and your palms sweat." Just like Sawyer did to her. "The two of you will get married, and you'll have beautiful, brilliant children. Your heart will heal. Trust me."

Melissa sniffed. "It's hard to think about things like that. I hope she understands why I had to do this. I hope she realizes that it wasn't because I didn't love her."

"She'll understand," Liz assured the young girl, whose circumstances had forced her to become mature fast. "After all, she has a very smart mother. She'll understand all kinds of things."

Melissa smiled. "Well, let's get it over with."

Howard pulled up a chair. He opened his briefcase and pulled out a stack of papers. In a matter of minutes, Melissa had officially given away her child.

"Do you want me to stay?" Liz asked.

"I think I'd rather be alone. But thank you. I don't think I could have gotten through this without you."

Liz knew from previous experience that Melissa wasn't through it yet. She'd spend many hours sorting through the myriad of feelings, traveling down the dozens of paths her mind would wander around and through until she came to terms with her decision.

Liz hugged the girl. "I'll call you tomorrow."

Liz took the time to stop at the grocery store on the way home. She was anxious to get back to Mary, especially after seeing Melissa, and she was still feeling as if she'd gotten run over by a bus, but her cupboards were pretty bare. She needed to stock up if she intended to have a houseguest. She knew that Mary should have milk and fruit and vegetables.

Thinking about that reminded her of Sawyer buying her bananas, and she walked through most of the grocery store with tears in her eyes. Lord, she was an emotional mess.

She drove home and lugged her sacks inside. She set them on the floor next to the fridge.

"Mary," she called out. "I got Double Stuf Oreos."

No answer. The television was off. Liz listened for the shower. But nobody was running water in her apartment. In fact, she couldn't hear anything. Her apartment sounded empty. The truth hit her, almost making her stagger backward.

Mary was gone.

Chapter Thirteen

She ran from the kitchen to the spare bedroom. The bed was sort of made with the sheets and blankets pulled up, just not tucked in. A white sheet of notebook paper lay on the pillow.

It took every ounce of courage that Liz had to close the ten-foot gap. The message was short and sweet.

Liz, thanks for everything. You and that cop saved my life. By the way, he's not such a bad guy. I've talked to an old friend. She's going to let me share her place. I'll call you soon. Love, Mary.

Liz wanted to rip somebody's head off. Either that or sit down and cry for about a week. Or something in between those two extremes. She felt as if she was on a seesaw. She'd been high in the air, and the other person had just jumped off, causing her to hit the ground with a thud. Every bone in her body ached with the pain of betrayal, of abandonment.

She wanted to damn Mary to hell and back.

Why couldn't the girl have stayed put? What possessed her to leave? Why couldn't she just accept Liz's help?

Liz didn't have any answers. All she knew was that she wouldn't be able to rest until she was sure Mary and the baby were safe. She got herself off the floor, walked over to the phone and dialed Sawyer's cell phone. She'd given the number out so many times in Wisconsin that she knew it by heart.

He answered on the third ring. "Montgomery." His voice sounded so good, so solid.

"Sawyer?" she said. "It's Liz."

"What's wrong?" he asked immediately.

She laughed. She couldn't help it. So much for trying to hide anything from Capable Sawyer. "Mary's gone. She left a note."

There was a long silence on the other end of the phone. She realized that Sawyer wasn't surprised. It made her angry with herself that she hadn't seen it coming, as well.

"You're not surprised, are you?" she asked. "That's why you made her write down her statement. You knew she wouldn't be around to do it later."

Another pause, although this one was shorter than the last. "I didn't know," he said. "Not for sure. I had an idea she might run."

"I didn't see it." It broke her heart to admit it. How could she keep her girls safe if she didn't anticipate, if she didn't plan ahead?

"Liz," Sawyer said, "don't beat yourself up. She's a fickle kid."

A kid living in an adult world with adult dangers. "I've got to find her. I've got to know she's okay."

"No! That's crazy talk. You aren't going after her again. You know what happened the last time."

Sawyer's tone no longer held sympathy, but now a warning. A couple weeks ago she'd have taken offense. Now she could hear the caring behind his harsh tone.

"I'll be careful," she said. "I won't do anything foolish."

"You're not listening. You won't do anything. It's over. She's gone. Let her go."

"I can't do that." She knew he didn't understand. Knew that he couldn't. She needed to help him. "Sawyer, I told you that my sister, Jenny, died. What I didn't tell you was that I had the chance to save her."

"What?"

"Two days before she killed herself, Jenny left a message on my machine. 'Call me,' it said. I tried. No one answered. I wasn't worried. She'd left messages like that before. I got home from work the next night, and there was another message. 'Please call me,' it said." Her voice cracked, and she swallowed hard, knowing she needed to get through this.

"Liz, sweetheart, it's okay. You can tell me later."

"No. I need to tell you now. I didn't call. My friend and I had tickets to the opera. I'd left work late. She was already waiting outside my apartment when I got home."

She heard him sigh. It made her want to reach through the phone and hug him.

"I tried first thing the next morning. Couldn't get an answer. I remembered that my parents were out of town for the weekend. So, I drove to the house. You know the rest."

"I'm sorry," he said. "It's not your fault. There's no way you could have known."

"Perhaps not. But what I learned is that people reach out for help in different ways. I don't know if Mary's reaching out. Maybe she's not. Maybe she's pulling away and I'm just scared to let go. But I can't take the chance."

There was a long silence from his end. "Promise me," he said finally. "Promise me that you won't do anything until I get there. I'll leave in fifteen minutes. I won't stop for gas, for dinner, for anything. I'll be at your apartment in three hours."

No doubt about it—Sawyer Montgomery defined good. "I'll wait," she promised.

"Thank you," he said, and then he hung up.

THREE HOURS and twenty-seven minutes later, Sawyer pulled his borrowed car up in front of Liz's apartment building. He owed Sheriff Foltran a case of cold beer. That was the price the older man had quoted.

After Sawyer had hung up with Liz, he'd called him, given him a brief update and asked where he might rent a car. The sheriff had quickly set him straight, telling him that wasn't how it was done in the country. Within fifteen minutes, Sawyer had been on the road in a 2004 Buick, courtesy of the sheriff's wife.

He knocked on Liz's door. "Liz, it's Sawyer."

And when she opened it and walked into his arms, it felt right. He held her close, his chin resting on her head, content to let the heat of her body warm his soul.

"Thanks for coming," she said.

Three simple words. But the way she said it, it didn't seem simple at all. It seemed huge, bigger than life itself. It filled his heart, his whole being.

He bent his head to kiss her.

She jerked back. "I had a really sore throat this morning. It's better, but you still might catch it."

He shook his head. "I don't care." He reached for her again.

She slipped into his arms. "I knew you wouldn't care," she said. "I just knew it." She lifted her lips and kissed him.

He felt as if he'd come home. He wanted to consume her, to take sustenance from her strength, her goodness, her essence.

When he slipped his tongue inside and swallowed her answering groan, he knew, beyond the shadow of a doubt, that life would never be the same.

He kissed her for a very long time then wrapped his arms around her slim body and held her close.

"I missed you," he said.

"I know," she said, her words muffled, her lips pressed against his chest.

"Are you okay?" he asked. He put his fingers under her chin and lifted her face up for inspection. She had her long hair pulled back in a rubber band, and she didn't have a speck of makeup on. She looked pure and sweet and so beautiful.

"I'm fine," she said. "Now that you're here, I'm fine."

His chest filled with something that threatened to overtake him, to humble him, to bring him to his knees. "What happened, sweetheart?"

She grabbed a sheet of notebook paper off the lamp table and handed it to him. He turned it over and read it. "Damn kid," he said.

He noticed Liz didn't bother to defend her. But he doubted that her resolve to find Mary had lessened.

"Any thoughts on where she might be?" he asked.

"I want to go back to the bookstore. On the way here, before she went to sleep, Mary talked about getting more books for the baby. I don't know if that woman will tell me anything, but I have to try."

"Okay. I'll take a ride down there. I'll let you know what I find."

"I'm going with you."

"That's not necessary. You stay here. You don't feel well."

She shook her head. "I need to do something. I can't stay here."

He knew better than to try to argue. She had such strength, such sense of purpose, such commitment to a goal. He respected that. It was one of the things he loved about her.

Loved her. It hit him like a bullet against a Kevlar-lined vest. Bruising him, shaking him, shocking him. No longer sure his legs would continue to hold him, he sat down on the couch, hard.

"Sawyer, are you okay? What's wrong?"

Everything. Nothing. He shook his head, trying to make sense of it. He didn't want to love her. He didn't want to love anybody. If you didn't love, then it didn't hurt when you lost.

He needed air. "Let's get out of here," he said, standing up in one jerky movement.

She cocked her head, clearly not understanding his quick turnaround. Hell, he didn't understand it, either. He didn't understand much anymore.

"Sawyer, you're scaring me," she said.

He scared himself. "Liz, let's go. We're wasting time here."

"Are you sure?" she asked.

Oh, yeah, he was sure. Sure he loved her. Just not sure what to do about it.

He nodded. "Let's go. I'd like to get out of that neighborhood before it gets too late."

Sawyer called Robert from the car. "Hey, partner, where are you?" he asked.

"I'm working," Robert said. "Where the hell are you?"

"I'm working, too. Look, I need you to help me with a little surveillance at the corner of Shefton and Terrance."

"Are you in town? I didn't think you were coming back until tomorrow."

Sawyer looked at Liz. He'd used the hands-free speakerphone because of heavy rush-hour traffic. "My plans changed."

"What's at Shefton and Terrance?" Robert asked.

"There's a porn store on the corner of Terrance."

"That desperate, huh?" Robert laughed at his own joke.

"Funny. Mind your manners," Sawyer said. "I've got a lady in the car."

"Hi, Robert," Liz interjected.

"Hi, Liz," Robert said. "Sawyer, you did say *porn store?*"

Sawyer shook his head. "We'll be there in ten minutes.

Meet us at the corner of King and Sparton—that's two blocks north of the target. I'll fill you in then."

"Can you give me a hint?" Robert asked.

"Sure. We're looking for Mary Thorton," Sawyer said. "She's AWOL. The porn store is one of her old haunts. I don't think it's a trap, but I don't want to take a chance."

Ten minutes later, Robert walked into the porn store while Sawyer and Liz waited in the car, a block away. He returned ten minutes later carrying a brown paper sack. They watched him get into the car. Within thirty seconds, Sawyer's phone rang.

"Store's empty," Robert said, "with the exception of a greasy-haired old guy in overalls behind the counter."

"No woman, about sixty with gray hair?" Sawyer asked.

"Not that I saw."

Sawyer looked at Liz. "Maybe Grandma Porn only works the day shift?"

"At night, she bakes cookies for her grandchildren," Liz replied.

"Anything is possible," Sawyer said. "When it comes to Mary, I'm beginning to expect the unexpected."

"Let's talk to the guy in the store. Maybe he knows something."

"Okay. Hey, Robert, we're going in."

"Take money. The guy will probably block the door if you try to leave without buying something."

Liz pulled a twenty out of her purse and stuffed it into her shirt pocket. "Thanks, Robert," she said. "By the way, what did you buy?"

Robert laughed. "None of your business. All you need to know is that I'll be right outside the back door."

Sawyer pulled his car up in front of the store. When he and Liz entered, the man never even looked up from watching the small television behind the counter. Liz could just make out the familiar sounds of CNN.

They walked around the store for a few minutes. Finally, the man looked up. "Can I help you find something?" he asked.

"You must be Herbert," Sawyer said.

Liz wanted to smack herself on the head. She'd completely forgotten that the woman had mentioned her man friend Herbert. But Sawyer hadn't. Once again, he amazed her.

"That's me," the man replied.

"We're friends of Mary Thorton's. She talks about how nice you and Marvis have been to her."

"She's a great girl."

"The best," Sawyer agreed. "In fact, she called this afternoon and left a message on our machine. She said she was back in town after being gone a couple of days."

Liz wondered how he did it. The lies just rolled off his tongue.

"She was in Wisconsin," said Herbert.

"That's what she said. Nice time of year to go north," Sawyer added. "Anyway, she must have been having a blonde moment because she told us to call her later, but she didn't leave a number."

"Let me think." The man rubbed his whiskered chin. "I don't have her number. But Randy's place is just a few blocks from here."

Randy? Liz desperately wanted to ask, but Sawyer was on a roll.

"Good enough," Sawyer said. "We bought a stroller for the baby. We might as well deliver it."

Herbert picked up a notepad and scribbled an address on it. He held it in his hands. "You folks need anything as long as you're here?" he asked.

Liz pulled the twenty from her pocket. She walked over

to the stack of boxed condoms. She picked out the brightest, most garish design. She handed Herbert the twenty. "Thanks for asking. These should last a couple days," she said.

She heard Sawyer make a choking sound behind her.

"Keep the change," she said. "We'll tell Mary hello from you."

"You two come back anytime." Herbert handed her the slip of paper.

The phone rang seconds after they got back to the car. "Montgomery," Sawyer answered, leaving the phone on speaker. Liz noted he still sounded a bit hoarse.

"Everything okay?" Robert asked.

"Yeah. We got an address. Follow us."

"No problem. By the way, what's in *your* bag, Liz?"

"None of your damn business," Sawyer said and hung up.

"That wasn't very nice," Liz scolded him.

"When this is over," Sawyer said, his voice barely audible, "when we don't have the shadow of Mary or Mirandez or anything else standing between us, we're going to have a long talk."

The heat from Sawyer's body filled the small car. He wanted her. He might deny it, fight it and condemn himself for it. But he wanted her. "Take it from one who knows," she said, "talk isn't always the answer."

She heard the sharp intake of his breath and knew that he'd gotten her point.

She picked up the sack, opened it and peered inside. "I'm glad I bought a big box," she said, happy to let him chew on that for a while.

ONCE AGAIN, ROBERT COVERED the rear of the building, in the event Mary tried to make a run for it. Liz and Sawyer waited for him to get into position before knocking on the apartment door that matched the address Herbert had given them. When Sawyer gave her a nod, Liz rapped on the door.

"Just a minute," a female voice called from within.

Not Mary's voice. Liz looked at Sawyer and knew that he'd had the same thought. When the door opened, Liz knew why the voice sounded familiar. She looked different, of course, without a couple pounds of makeup on, but Liz recognized her. It was the girl from the bar. The one who had given her the original lead on Mary.

She didn't say anything, just simply stared first at Liz and then at Sawyer.

Liz looked past her. Mary sat on the couch.

"Liz?" Mary maneuvered her pregnant body off the cushions. "How did you find me?"

Sawyer stepped into the apartment. His eyes swept the room. "Anybody else here?" he asked.

"No," both girls answered at the same time.

"Mind if I look around?" Sawyer asked.

"You are such a cop." Mary shook her head at him in disgust. "Look around, peek in the closets, look under the beds. I really don't know what Liz sees in you."

Liz felt the hot heat of embarrassment flow through her. Had the two of them been that obvious?

Sawyer looked as if he couldn't care less that she'd put two and two together and come up with four. "Where's Randy?"

The girl who had opened the door held up her hand. "That's me. With an *i,* not a *y.*"

"That your real name?" Sawyer asked.

"Yeah. My dad wanted a boy. Hey, if he's lucky, he'll get a grandson." She rubbed her stomach and laughed at her own joke. "Of course, he'll never know. I haven't talked to him in two years."

"Her dad's a bigger jerk than mine," Mary interjected.

Liz dismissed the comment. Now wasn't the time to try to deal with it. "Are you all right, Mary?" Liz asked.

"I'm fine. I left you a note," she said.

"You did," Liz acknowledged. "I appreciate that. I was still worried. You hadn't said anything about leaving."

"I didn't have anywhere to go. Then I called Randi, and she said I could stay here."

Liz looked around the room. Not much furniture but clean. The biggest mess was on the couch, where Mary had been sitting. When she'd gotten up, the big bag of chips on her lap had spilled. An open carton of milk, propped against the cushions, tilted dangerously.

"I know what I'm doing, Liz. Getting mixed up with Dantel was stupid. I'm not going to make a mistake like that again. But I can't live with you. I need to take care of myself. I need to prove that I can do it."

Liz didn't answer; she couldn't. She walked over to the couch and moved the milk carton from its precarious position to the lamp table, all while trying to sort out her chaotic thoughts. Chips and milk. A contradiction. Just like Mary. Sweet, yet bitter. Young, yet mature beyond her years. Considerate, yet selfish. Independent, yet so dependent.

Liz knew she needed to take a step back. Hated it, but knew it all the same. Otherwise, she ran the risk that she'd alienate Mary and cause her to cut off ties completely. She looked across the room. Sawyer stood absolutely still, watching her. She wanted to run to him and beg him to help her, to tell her what to do. But she knew she had to make the decision. She had to live with the consequences, good or bad.

"OCM is reopening next week. Will you come see me?" she asked.

Mary nodded. "Sure."

Liz swallowed hard, pushing the tears back. She pointed to the chips. "Eat some vegetables, okay?"

"No problem. Randi fixes broccoli every day. She said that we're going to have smart babies because they're getting lots of folic acid."

"You're both going to have beautiful and smart babies," Liz said. She gave Mary a hug first, then Randi. "Take care," she said. "Call me if you need anything."

She walked out of the apartment, hoping she'd make it to the car before she made a complete fool out of herself. Sawyer didn't say a word, somehow knowing that she needed a few moments of silence to sort out her thoughts.

He picked up the phone and held it to his ear, choosing not to use the speaker. He dialed. "Mary's fine," Sawyer said. "Thanks for your help, Robert."

Sawyer paused, listening. "Yeah, she is," he said. Another pause. "I'm not sure. I'll see you tomorrow." Then he hung the phone up.

"What did Robert have to say?" Liz asked.

Sawyer looked very serious. "He said you were a hell of a woman, and he wondered what I was going to do about it."

"Oh." She knew what *she* wanted him to do about it.

"I'm proud of you," he said.

She hadn't done it for Sawyer. But it felt darn good to hear him say those words. She leaned over toward him and kissed him on the cheek. "Thank you. That means a lot to me."

Sawyer put the car in Drive and pulled away from the curb. Neither of them said a word until they were just blocks from Liz's apartment. "You're awfully quiet," Sawyer said. "Are you sure you're okay?"

"I'm fine," Liz lied, knowing that she wasn't a bit fine. She was needy and wanting, but it had nothing to do with Mary and everything to do with Sawyer. Did she have the guts to tell him? If not now, when? When it would be too late? She'd just have to take the chance.

"I want you to make love to me. Tonight. Now."

Sawyer gripped the steering wheel so tightly that his fingers were white. He didn't say a word.

"Don't tell me it would be a mistake," she said. "Don't tell me that it would be inappropriate. It's all I've been thinking about for days."

"Stop," he said. "We'll be at your apartment in five minutes. Don't say another word until we get there."

It took them eight minutes. During that time, Liz didn't spend time regretting acting on the impulse to tell him. She contemplated all the ways she might make love to him. By the time the car stopped, she was practically squirming in her seat.

Sawyer put the car into Park and with deliberate movements turned off the engine and pulled the keys from the ignition. When he turned toward her, her heart plummeted. Liz knew what he'd done in the eight minutes. He'd figured out a way to tell her no. She could see the answer on his face.

"A man would be half-crazy not to want to take you to—"

"Don't give me your speech," she interrupted, refusing to let him walk away. There was more than one way to get her point across. She leaned over the seat and kissed him on the lips. She ran her tongue across his bottom lip.

She heard the quick intake of breath, and she felt the absolute stillness of his body.

"You want me," she stated.

He didn't deny it. She felt her confidence soar.

"Liz," he said, looking miserable, "I'm sorry. It would be a mistake. I can't give you what you want."

"I think you can," she said, looking pointedly at his zipper, which did little to hide his state of readiness.

He blushed. In her lifetime, she'd never expected to see Sawyer Montgomery blush.

"I can't pretend not to want you," he said. "I can't pretend that I don't go to bed hard at night for wanting you."

He spoke softly, but his words had an icy edge to them. She felt the answering heat pummel through her body, landing right between her legs. "There's no need to pretend," she said.

"You want commitment. You want marriage. I'm not offering that. I can't."

The words seemed torn from his soul. She didn't want him to suffer. She wanted them to celebrate life.

"You didn't bring a ring?" she asked, her voice full of accusation.

"No. Listen, I'm not..."

"Sawyer, I'm kidding. It was a joke."

He held her at arm's length. "I don't understand," he said.

"That's what I wanted from Ted. That's not what I want from you."

He looked a bit shocked, then fury crossed his strong features. He chuckled a dry, humorless noise. "Now, that's sweet," he said. "I'm good enough to sleep with but—"

"Sawyer," she said, "I'm sorry. I said that poorly."

He didn't respond.

She needed him to understand. "You're only the second person that I've ever told about Jenny. I told Jamison when I applied for the job at OCM. I thought he deserved to know what had driven me to his little counseling center. I told you because I wanted to share with you the joy of Jenny's life and the despair of her death. I wanted you to understand that both of those experiences make me who I am today."

"I'm glad you told me," he said.

"I want you to hear the rest. Jenny was a bright spot. For sixteen sweet years, she lit up my life. Since her death, I've been mourning that the time wasn't longer. I should have been celebrating the light."

She put her head against his chest. "People pass in and out of your life. They leave you changed, forever different.

You helped me understand and accept that Mary, too, will pass in and out of my life. I can't control that."

"Damn kid." He said it without malice.

"She's very brave."

"She is," he admitted. "Damn brave kid."

She lifted her head from his chest and looked him squarely in the eyes. Now wasn't the time to duck her head, to hide her feelings. "You're going to pass in and out of my life. You've been honest about that from the beginning. I'm not asking for forever. I'm asking for now."

He looked very serious. "I don't deserve you," he said.

She saw the hunger, the pure need, and knew it matched her own. It gave her courage.

"Take me inside," she urged. "Make love to me."

"I cannot resist you," he said. And then without another word, he opened the door and the two of them tumbled out of the car. He walked so quickly to the building that she almost had to run to keep up. When they got to her door, he took the key. Once inside, he shut the door, flipped the bolt lock and kissed her. Long and hard until both of them struggled for breath.

He moved her so that her back was against the wall. He pressed up against her, his chest against hers, his hips grinding into hers. So strong, so big, so much. She pushed her hands up inside his shirt, running her fingers across his bare stomach. His skin burned, and she could feel the muscles underneath. She traced his ribs and, with the tips of her thumb and index fingers, gently pinched each flat nipple.

He groaned and arched his back.

It made her feel powerful, as if she could tempt him beyond thought. It made her feel in control. But when he pulled away suddenly and grasped the hem of her shirt, she knew how quickly control shifted. "I want to see you," he said. "All of you." He yanked her white T-shirt over her head and ran his fingers across the edging of her bra, then lower, just lightly grazing her nipples. And when they responded to his touch, he bent his head and sucked her, right through the sheer material.

"I've been dreaming of this," he whispered against her skin. "Of what you'd look like in lace. You're more beautiful than I could have ever imagined."

His words, his barely there voice, floated around her, assuring her. But then his mouth was back, first on one nipple, then the other, and she couldn't think at all. His mouth moved across her body, lavishing wet kisses on her warm skin. He nipped at her collarbone, sharp licks of his tongue against her neck, before returning his lips to her mouth to kiss her thoroughly.

He reached behind her, releasing the clasp on her bra. She shrugged out of it, never taking her mouth off his. And when he slipped his warm hands into her shorts and cupped her bottom, pulling her against him, she ground her hips into his.

He pulled her shorts and panties down in one quick jerk. They pooled around her feet. Only then did he tear his mouth away. He stepped back a foot and looked at her. He didn't say a word for a moment, just looked at her. Then he took his hand and ever so lightly, with just the very tips of his fingers, brushed her cheek, tucking a strand of hair behind her ear. He let his hand drift downward, across her breast, then down, lingering just moments on her stomach, stopping just at the apex of her thighs. "You're perfect," he said, his voice soft.

He made her feel beautiful. She moved her feet apart, spreading her legs, inviting him to touch her. But he lifted his hand, moving it to the back of her head, working his fingers into her hair, and gently pulled her mouth to his. He kissed her gently, barely touching her at first, stroking her lips with his tongue, nipping at her bottom lip. He angled his lips, thrust his tongue into her mouth and kissed her.

When her knees started to buckle, he swept her up into his arms. With sure and confident steps, he carried her to the bedroom. He lay her down on the bed and gently pulled both her arms above her head. Moving across her body, he nudged her thigh aside. She spread her legs and he kneeled between them.

"Oh, my God," he whispered, running his fingers across her naked body. She shivered, and he gave her a smug smile. Then he bent down, kissing first one breast then the other.

"I need you." She arched her back, pressing her nipple into his mouth. She would beg soon.

He sucked her, sending shivers from her breast all the way to her very core. When he pulled back, he moved his strong hands under each thigh, pulling her legs wide. He moved his mouth down her stomach, coming finally to the place where she needed him most. She forgot about being embarrassed, forgot about wanting to please him, forgot about being lady-like, and she simply enjoyed. She took and took from him, the pressure building inside of her until it burst out of control, the waves of pleasure slamming through her.

He held her. He stretched out next to her and pulled her close, his arms wrapped around her. With every ounce of strength she had left, she threw one bare leg over his.

Oh, my God. She'd come apart, and he still had every stitch of his clothes on. Sensing her distress, he held her just a bit tighter. "Relax, sweetheart. It'll be my turn soon."

"But that's not fair," she protested, her voice weak.

"You don't have any idea, do you, what it does to a man to have a woman do that for him? To know that he's brought her pleasure?"

She realized he sounded just a bit smug.

She let him enjoy it for just a moment, then she reached

up and slipped a hand underneath his T-shirt. When her fingers crossed his nipples, she rubbed the tiny nubs. Breath hissed out from between his lips. He had his eyes closed. She trailed her finger down his stomach, following the line of hair. She ran her fingers across his jeans, tracing the ridge of his erection. He arched his hips off the bed. "Oh, sweetheart. You make me feel like a sixteen-year-old again."

His confession gave her courage. She moved quickly, straddling his hips with her legs. She rubbed against him, and he reached up, stilling her. But she wouldn't be stopped. She pulled his T-shirt up. Then she moved down so that her knees touched his. She unsnapped his jeans and pulled his zipper down slowly. He literally groaned.

"I'm a dead man," he said. She laughed. Then with a sure hand on each side of his hips, she pulled his jeans and briefs down.

She made love to him. Her fingers, her lips, skimmed his body, teasing, caressing. When she wrapped her hand around him, his whole body jerked, coming inches off the bed.

"I want to be inside of you," he said.

"I want that, too," she answered.

With one swift movement, he gently flipped her onto her back. He positioned himself above her and gently pushed himself into her. He held himself back, allowing her body to stretch, to adjust to him.

"Oh," she said.

He kissed her face, soft, gentle brushes of his lips. "It's okay. Just a little bit more."

She forced herself to relax and to take him.

"Perfect," he said, his voice a mere whisper.

And then he started to move. Within minutes, she shattered once again. Barely before she could catch her breath, he pounded into her, faster and faster, until his whole body tensed, and with one last powerful thrust, he exploded inside her.

For long minutes, there was no sound at all in the room. Then, with a sigh, he lifted his weight off her. He kissed her—a long, gentle kiss. Then he carefully pulled away from her, then fell onto his back in a clumsy movement. He threw one bent arm over his forehead. "That almost killed me," he said.

It was hard to keep the smile off her face. Now who was feeling smug? she thought.

"I liked it," she said. "Can we do it again?"

He opened one eye and stared at her. "You liked it? You *liked* it?" he repeated. "People *like* apple pie and long walks on the beach."

"I like cherry pie and long walks in the woods. A lot. But trust me on this—I don't like either one of those things as much as I liked this."

"*This* almost gave me a heart attack."

"I know CPR," she said. She boldly wrapped her hand around him, winking at him when he immediately responded.

"Oh, baby." He flipped her onto her back and proceeded to make her own heart race not once but several times over.

Chapter Fourteen

Sawyer woke up happy and warm. Liz slept on her side, her naked body wedged up against him, her bare back against his chest. He had an arm wrapped around her, and her breast filled his hand.

He moved just a bit. She stretched in response. He let go of her breast, pulled his arm back and gathered her long hair in his hand and moved it out of the way. Then he gently kissed the back of her neck. "Good morning," he said.

"I'll give you a dollar if you make coffee," she said.

He laughed. "I'll give you five dollars if you make breakfast."

She rolled over and laid on her other side, facing him. "I'll give you my last twenty if you'll make love to me again." She winked at him.

"Your last twenty? What happens then?"

"I'm hoping you'll take pity on the poor. I could be your own personal charity."

He rolled onto his back and pulled her on top of him. "I've been known to be a very generous man in the past. Giving of my own personal assets."

"Donate away, baby," she said.

And he did.

And later—much later—when they finally stumbled into

the kitchen, it was closer to lunch than breakfast. "Be careful," she said.

He thought the warning probably saved him a broken leg. He'd surely have tripped over the piles of soup cans, cereal boxes, pots and pans, glasses, silverware and cleaning products scattered on the kitchen floor.

"I like to clean when I'm nervous," she said. "I had some time to kill yesterday between when Mary left and you arrived."

"Anything left *in* the cupboards?"

She shook her head. "Nope. I'm nothing if not thorough."

"Next time you get really nervous, come to my house. My cupboards haven't been cleaned since I moved in."

"Yuck. Sounds gross."

She started coffee and he started lunch. For the first time in seventeen years, he started to think about a future.

"I'm going to go take a shower," she said.

"Okay." Good. He needed time alone, time to sort out his thoughts.

He loved her. He loved her playfulness, her sense of humor, her dedication to her clients, her willingness to help others. He loved her body.

She had wanted commitment and marriage from another man. She didn't expect it from him. He was, in her words, just passing through. He flipped the grilled cheese with more force than necessary, sending it flying out of the pan. It landed on the counter. He picked it up, dusted it off and returned it to the skillet.

Just maybe, *he* wanted a little commitment.

He opened a can of tomato soup. By the time it was hot, Liz had not only returned to the kitchen but he also had a plan.

"If you don't have anything else to do today," he said

carefully, "I thought we might go to Navy Pier. You like Ferris wheels?"

"I love Ferris wheels. But I can't. I have to get my office organized at OCM. I'd brought a lot of my files here. I'll need them back at work when we reopen."

Okay. She wasn't saying no just to say no. She had a commitment to work. He knew how important her work was to her. That was one of the things that made this perfect.

"You really like your job, don't you?" he asked.

"I love my job. Just like you love yours."

Yeah, Sawyer thought as he poured himself a second cup of coffee. Liz didn't need all those things that he couldn't give. She didn't seem concerned about her biological clock like most of the women he'd met over the years. She'd mentioned wanting children, but that was before. Now she had her career. A job she loved. One that she was passionate about.

He wouldn't get in the way. He'd make sure she understood that he didn't intend to disrupt her work. That he valued her dedication. He'd also make sure she realized they weren't ships passing in the night. He'd convince her that she could have both a career and a relationship with a man.

She'd wanted marriage at one time. He'd give her time to adjust to the idea again, and then once she saw that it could work between the two of them, he'd pop the question.

But for now, he'd give her space. He got up from the table, intending to put the dishes in the dishwasher.

"We didn't use my condoms," she said.

She spoke so matter-of-factly, as if she might be discussing the weather or what to have for dinner. He felt the world tilt, causing all the good and beautiful things that had happened last night to slide together, combining into a dark and ugly mess. He held on to his dirty plate tightly, afraid that he might drop it.

He should tell her now. He should have told her before. But now, if she had questions or concerns, it was the right thing to do.

No. He hadn't had a chance to win her over, to convince her of his love.

"I just want you to know that I think the chances are pretty good that we're safe. But if I'm wrong and I am pregnant, I won't expect anything from you. I can handle it myself."

Tell her, you fool. Tell her. "You'll let me know?" he asked.

"Of course. I'd never hide something like that."

Coward. "No problem. I'm sure it will be fine. I'll call you later today."

"HE'S NOT GOING to call," Liz moaned, her head resting in her cupped hand. It was late afternoon, and she'd worked like a dog all day, trying to reestablish connections with all her clients.

"It's been five hours," she said, looking at the clock.

Jamison walked past her office. He poked his head in, looking around. "Who are you talking to?"

"Myself."

"Fascinating. By the way, Sawyer called."

"What?"

"You must have been on your phone. It rolled over to my line. I told him you'd call him back."

"Oh." She'd been waiting all day, and now that he'd finally called, she didn't know what she was going to say to him.

"Snap out of it, girl," Jamison said. "Just remember. Play a little hard to get. It'll make you more interesting."

"Really?"

"I read it in one of Renée's magazines."

She was about ready to try anything. She picked up the phone and dialed.

"Montgomery."

"Hi, Sawyer. It's Liz."

"Hi. Thanks for calling. Is this a bad time?"

"No, it's fine. Jamison and I were…we were just discussing a case."

"Everything okay with Mary?"

"Yes. Thanks for asking."

There was an awkward moment of silence. Could that be the only reason Sawyer had called? She felt the loss, the sense of disappointment spread through her body.

"I was wondering if you'd have time for a late dinner tonight. I know you're busy and all."

Play a little hard to get. Jamison's advice rang in her ears. Hell. It would be hard to pull that off when she threw herself at him later. "I'd love to."

"Great. I'll pick you up at seven."

Come naked. "I'll be ready." Liz hung up the phone.

When Mary walked by unexpectedly ten minutes later, Liz still stared at her blank computer screen, unable to get much past the fact that in just a few short hours, she'd have another opportunity to seduce the very serious Sawyer Montgomery.

"Hi, sweetie," she said when the young girl dropped into the chair in front of her desk. "How are you?"

"I'm starting to waddle."

"It always looked good on Donald and Daisy."

"I saw the doc this morning. He thinks the baby is already over seven pounds."

No wonder she beamed. "Good. Your due date is coming up fast."

"I know. I've been a real pain about this adoption thing.

I know you've been worried that time is going to run out. I've made up my mind."

"That's wonderful, Mary. I know it's been difficult. What do you want to do?"

"I'm giving her up for adoption."

"Her?"

"They did an ultrasound. The doc is ninety-nine percent sure the baby is a girl."

"And you're sure? About the adoption?" In her heart, she believed the decision was best for Mary and for the baby. Mary probably knew that, as well. Knowing it and acting upon it were two different things.

"Yes. I'm too young to raise a baby. I need to go back to school and get an education. I don't want to work in some stupid job my whole life. I'm going to go to college. Maybe that's selfish, but that's what I want."

"It's not selfish, Mary. You're young. You have hopes and dreams. College is one way to make those things a reality."

"You know what made me decide adoption was the right thing?"

"What?"

"I was thinking about all those things, and then I realized that I wanted my baby to have all the same things. But I'd never be able to give her that. That's what made me decide."

Mary wiped a tear off her face. Liz hoped she could be strong for both of them. "I'll contact our attorney. We'll get the paperwork done immediately."

"No."

"But, Mary, you just said—"

"You didn't let me finish. I'm giving her up for adoption under one condition. I want you to adopt her."

Liz felt the floor tip. "Mary. Sweetheart. I…I'm flattered. Really. But I can't possibly adopt your child."

"Why not? You already have your education and you

have a great job. You're home at night and on the weekends. You live in a safe apartment. You can give her everything she'll need."

She could. But that wasn't the point. "Mary," she said, not sure where to begin. "Any number of people have the means to provide for a child. That does not mean that they would be good parents."

"I know that. You couldn't grow up in my house and not realize that. But with you, it would be different. You would be such a great mom."

A mom. A single mother. A statistic. A concern.

But those were the black-and-white facts and figures. Liz knew better. While it wasn't a perfect solution, single mothers were quite capable of raising great, well-adjusted kids. But could she do it?

She hadn't thought about babies for herself. At least not since it had become abundantly clear that Ted never intended to marry her. While they'd been engaged, she often thought about the children she hoped to have. They'd talked about it. But when she'd finally stopped waiting for him, she'd stopped thinking about children, never considering pursuing motherhood on her own.

Why not? Why the heck not? Mary was right. She had a good job. Even if OCM wasn't around forever, she had the background and the credentials to land another job quickly. She had a nice savings account courtesy of her previous work. She was healthy and strong. She was—

"But the most important thing," Mary said, interrupting her thoughts, "is that you'll love her. And she'll love you."

Now Liz and Mary were both crying.

"Oh, Mary. Are you sure?"

"I'm sure. More sure about this than anything. Please say you'll do it."

It wasn't really much of a decision. How could she say no?

She loved Mary. By default, she loved the baby that Mary carried. She had a connection to this baby that would carry her through the difficult months to come. She could do this. She wanted to do this.

What would Sawyer think? Did it matter? She knew it did. They'd never even discussed children. There'd been no need to. She hoped he'd be happy for her, that he'd understand what a gift Mary had given her.

"I'd be honored, Mary. I will love her and care for her. When she grows up, I'll tell her about her biological mother and what a wonderful young woman she was."

Mary wrapped her arms around Liz. "Thank you. Now I know everything will be okay."

LIZ HAD A THREE-PAGE LIST by the time her hand cramped up, and she was forced to lay down her pen. So much to do and so little time. She had to get the spare bedroom decorated. She needed a crib, a car seat. Clothes. She needed to tell Jamison. He'd be worried about the appearance of things. After all, someone on the outside looking in would say it was unethical for a counselor to adopt the child of one of her clients. But that was the legal mumbo jumbo. On paper, it might look weird. In her heart, Liz knew it made perfect sense. She also knew that once Jamison got past his shock, he'd do everything he could to help her.

She didn't want to wait another minute to do it. She walked up the stairs to his office. He sat at his desk, calmly reviewing the budget numbers, not having any idea that she was about to upset his world. She almost felt sorry for him.

"I just talked to Mary Thorton. She's agreed to put her baby up for adoption."

"That's probably a good decision on her part."

"Yes. Here's the kicker, Jamison. She wants me to adopt the baby."

He pushed his chair back from the desk. "You told her no, I assume."

She shook her head, almost laughing when all color left his face. She felt so good about the decision that his doubts couldn't dispel her joy. "No. I said I would."

She gave Jamison a moment to recover before continuing, "I know it's highly irregular. I know others might question the decision. But you know me, Jamison. You know I wouldn't agree to this if it weren't the right thing for me and for the client. I can do this. I can adopt this baby and make a difference in the baby's life."

"But, Liz, you're a single woman. You know we always try to place the babies with two-parent families."

"I know. But we've made exceptions in the past. This is at the client's request. We always give special consideration to that."

He stared at her. Then he stood up, walked around his office twice, then sat down again. He didn't say a word. "You're sure?"

"Absolutely. I'm scared. I'm not going to try to lie about that. It's such a huge commitment. What if I'm no good at this?"

"You've been good at everything you've ever done."

Liz walked around the edge of the desk and placed her hand on Jamison's shoulder. "You know what drove me to OCM."

"Is that why you're doing this? Is this more of the same? More of having to make up for not being there?"

Liz didn't take offense. Jamison had always known her better than most. "No. Jenny's gone. I will forever miss her. I'm not doing this for her or because of her. I'm doing it for me. I pray that I'll be the kind of mother this sweet child deserves."

Jamison put his head in his hands. "We're going to need an ironclad release from Mary."

"She'll sign it," Liz said.

"I don't want her coming back in five years claiming that you coerced her into the decision. You don't want that."

She understood the legal issues. "You're right. That's why I'm here. I want you to handle the paperwork from here. I know you won't miss anything."

He looked up and let out a big sigh. "Okay. Let's call Howard. He's going to have to work his magic."

But Howard didn't answer. Jamison left a message on his machine. Liz got up from her chair, walked around the desk and kissed Jamison. "Thank you," she said. "Thank you for supporting me."

"What's your friend the cop going to say about this?"

She couldn't wait to tell Sawyer. Mary had barely been out the door, and Liz had been reaching for the telephone. She'd dialed the first five numbers before common sense prevailed. She couldn't just call him, chat about the weather for a couple of minutes and drop the bomb. *Hey, Sawyer. Great news. I'm adopting a baby.*

He might be worried that a baby would change their relationship. After all, she wouldn't be able to drop everything to go out to dinner. But babies did sleep. Maybe they could still work in sex and breakfast.

"I'm not sure what he'll say," she said. "I'll see him tonight."

Chapter Fifteen

Sawyer rang her doorbell at seven minutes before seven. She looked out the peephole. He had on a blue sport coat, tan slacks and a white shirt. He looked good enough to eat.

She opened the door. "I've missed you," she said.

"Really?"

"Oh, yeah." She reached out, caught his striped tie in her hand and hauled him into the apartment. She released the tie, cradling his face with both hands. Then she kissed him. Hard.

She squirmed, pressed and arched, her hands racing across his back. She yanked at his coat. He helped, never taking his lips off hers. She pulled his shirt out of his pants, then grabbed for his belt buckle. Unzipping him, she boldly stuck her hand down his pants, wrapping her hand around him.

He bit her lip and pushed her against the wall. "Damn," he said.

"I want you inside me."

He grabbed her bottom, whipping his head up when he found nothing but skin under her dress. He stepped back and shucked his pants. Then he picked her up, braced her back against the wall, wrapped her legs around his waist, and in less than a minute, when she started to climax, he followed her over the edge.

Sawyer, his chest heaving, having come so hard he thought

he might pass out, gently unwrapped Liz's legs from his waist. He held her steady when she swayed. He rested his forehead against the wall, not certain if he'd ever be able to move.

The mantel clock chimed. Seven delicate rings.

Liz looked up and kissed his chin. "Thanks for coming early," she said.

He chuckled, knowing he didn't have the strength to laugh. He lifted his head and stepped back. His sport coat lay near the door. His pants and underwear a mere foot away. He'd taken her with his shirt and tie still on.

"You okay?" he asked.

"Wonderful."

"You look happy," he said.

"I am. I had a great day. How was yours?"

"Okay. I've got news about Mirandez," he said. He tucked his shirt in and zipped his pants. "Let's sit on the couch."

"Tell me," she said.

"We got Mirandez back to Chicago today. He's taken up residence at Cook County Jail. There's a hearing tomorrow. The judge will deny bail. That's a given."

"That's great."

"Yeah. There's something else. We had to turn over Mary's statement to his attorney. We put it off as long as we could."

"What should I tell Mary?"

"Tell her that we've arranged for her to go to a safe place. There's a hospital nearby. We've also arranged for help for a few weeks after the baby's born."

Mary wouldn't need help. "That won't be necessary."

"Are you sure? It's not a problem."

"Mary's giving the baby up for adoption. She wants to go to school. If there's no college nearby, you're going to have to pick a new place."

He looked a little shocked. "Yeah, actually, there's a great school about twenty minutes away. When did she decide all this?"

"Just today." This wasn't how she'd planned to tell him. He'd surprised her. It shouldn't matter. Maybe it just made everything easier. "Oh, Sawyer. The most wonderful thing has happened. Mary asked me to adopt her baby."

If he'd looked shocked before, now he looked absolutely stunned. She could see the color drain out of his face.

"What did you say?"

"Yes. I said yes. I'm adopting the baby. We think it's a girl."

"Are you crazy?" He stood up and paced around the room. "Have you lost your mind?"

She'd expected surprise. The anger hadn't even been on her radar screen. "Sawyer, what's wrong? You're acting weird."

"How could you do this? You have your career. You love your job. You told me so."

"I do love my job. But this gift, this totally unexpected, wonderful gift, has been given to me. I want the baby. I want to love her and watch her grow. I want to make a difference in her life. I want her to make a difference in mine."

"No."

He said the word as if it had two syllables, as if it had been torn from his soul.

"Sawyer, for God's sake, tell me what's wrong."

"I love you," he said. Where his voice had been loud before, it was now quiet. She could barely hear him. "I've loved you for weeks."

It should have made her dance with joy. But the anguish in his voice stopped her happiness cold.

"I wanted to give you time to get used to the idea. I didn't want to push. I wanted you to get used to me."

"Sawyer, I didn't know. I—"

"Now," he said, interrupting her, "everything has changed. I can't be with you."

Her chest hurt. She clenched her hands together.

"I don't understand," she said.

"I had a son," he said. "He died. In my arms. His tiny heart just couldn't do it."

A son. Why hadn't he ever told her?

"His mother?" she asked.

"Terrie was a young drug addict. I didn't know it when I got her pregnant. It was painfully clear by the time she'd had the baby. My son paid for her sins. He paid for my sins."

"Your sins?"

"I didn't protect him. I failed."

It started to make sense, in some horrible kind of way. "That's the girl who died? Your baby's mother died?"

"The drugs killed her, too. Just took a few years."

Oh, the pain he'd suffered. Liz wanted to reach out to him, to hold him, but she knew she had to hear it all.

"We never got married. I only saw her once after our son died. But I still didn't want her to die. It was just one more damn useless death."

His relentless passion for tracking Mirandez suddenly made a lot more sense. "Sawyer, I'm so sorry that happened to you. It must have been horrible."

"You have no idea."

She let that one pass. She hadn't lost a child. But she had lost a sister. She knew the emptiness, the absolute gray that had filled her world for months. She wouldn't try to compare her loss to his. To do so would trivialize both. "It was a long time ago, Sawyer. You have to move on."

"I moved on. I made a decision that I'd never father another child. I had a vasectomy ten years ago."

Well! How could she have fallen in love with a man she didn't really even know?

That wasn't exactly true. She knew Sawyer Montgomery. She knew what she needed to know. He was a good man, a loving man, capable of sacrificing his own safety to help a young, pregnant teen. She didn't want to lose him. "Sawyer, you have to let go. Not of the person, but of the anger, the absolute rage that you've lost someone."

The look he gave her was filled with contempt. "I'm not some jerk paying a hundred bucks an hour so that I can lie on your couch and you can try to heal me."

"Sawyer, that's not what this is. This is Liz and Sawyer, having a conversation. Nothing more. Nothing less."

"I'm not angry," he said. "Who the hell would I be angry at? A dead woman?"

She knew better than that. Even as a kid, Capable Sawyer would have wanted to handle everything. But he hadn't been able to handle this. He still hadn't forgiven himself. He tried to find peace. With every scumbag of a drug dealer he put away, he tried to buy peace. Only, peace wasn't for sale. It had to be delivered. That only happened when a person gave up the hate, the absolute despair of being left behind.

"You're asking me to choose between this baby and you," she said. "That's not fair. I shouldn't have to choose."

He looked at her, and a tear slipped out of his very brown eyes. He didn't bother to wipe it away. "No, you shouldn't," he said. "I can't let another child into my life. I won't risk it."

Liz's heart, which had started to crumble away at the edges, suddenly broke right down the middle. The pain, as real as if the strong muscle really could just crack, sliced through her body.

With trembling legs, she walked over to the door and opened it. Not able to look at him again, she stared at the floor. "I'm sorry about your son. If I had known, I'd have done this differently."

"You're saying you wouldn't adopt the child?"

"No, I'm not saying that. But I wouldn't have just blurted it out. You should have told me. Everything now seems like such a lie."

He slammed his hand against the wall. "I never lied to you."

"You let me think you were in love with your dead girl-friend. I had no idea that there had even been a child. You lied by omission. For God's sake, Sawyer. You let me worry about an unplanned pregnancy."

He didn't respond. She didn't really expect him to. She suddenly felt very old, as if her bones might splinter. She forced herself to straighten up, to lift her head. "I don't want to see you again," she said. "Jamison can be your contact. Give him the details about the arrangements for Mary."

LIZ HAD BEEN IN BED for just a few minutes when the tele-phone rang. "Hello," she answered.

"Liz, it's Mary. My water just broke."

Liz sat up in bed, fear and excitement making her heart race. "Have you been in labor long? How far apart are your contractions?"

"Hey, you sound strange. What's wrong?"

Liz covered the phone and cleared her throat. She'd spent the better part of the past hour crying. Her eyes burned, she could barely swallow and her head felt as if she'd been kicked. "I've got a touch of a cold. Nothing to worry about. Now, what about the contractions?"

"I'm not having contractions. I don't think I'm even in labor."

"You're sure? No pain of any kind?"

"My back has ached all day," Mary said.

While Liz was no expert on childbirth, she had heard about back labor. She wanted Mary at a hospital. Now. "Honey, do you think you can take a cab to the hospital?"

"Yeah."

"Perfect. I'll meet you there. We should arrive about the same time. Just hang on. And breathe. Don't forget to breathe."

She'd arranged just that morning for her car to be picked up and the dents repaired. She grabbed the phone book out of the drawer, dialed the number for the cab company and waited impatiently while it rang three times. They said ten minutes and she was ready in eight. The ride to the hospital seemed to take forever. Yet, still, she beat Mary's cab by ten minutes. When it finally pulled up, she yanked open the back door. She helped Mary out and threw a twenty at the driver.

"How are you?" she asked, hoping she didn't sound as scared as she was.

"I don't want to have a baby," Mary said. "I'm not doing this."

Liz wrapped her arms around the girl, holding her close. "Don't worry. It'll be over in no time."

No time turned out to be twelve hours later. Twelve long, ugly hours filled with swearing, yelling, moaning, groaning and crying. But when Liz placed the beautiful baby girl in Mary's arms, the look on the girl's face told her that it had all been worth it.

"She's so pretty," Mary said, stroking the baby's head and face. "Isn't her mouth just perfect?"

Liz nodded. The baby was a healthy seven pounds and two ounces and just eighteen inches long. Almost plump. The doctor had delivered her and said, "Look at those cheeks." He hadn't been talking about her face.

"She's gorgeous," Liz said.

Mary stared at the baby. "I love her," she said, her voice filled with awe. "I just love her so much."

How could anyone not love something so perfect, so absolutely perfect in every way? Liz swallowed, almost afraid to ask the next question. She'd known she was taking a chance by letting Mary hold the baby. But Mary had been explicit. She wanted to see her child.

"Having second thoughts about giving her up for adoption?" Liz asked, wondering if she could slip back into the role of counselor after having embraced the role of mother.

"I'm not giving her up."

Liz nodded, afraid to speak.

"I'm giving her to you. That's different. I'm giving her to someone that I know will care for her and love her and give her all the things that I can't give her."

Liz didn't think her legs would continue to hold her. She sank down onto the edge of the bed. "Are you sure, Mary? Are you absolutely sure?"

"Yes. I've screwed up most of my life. I'm not screwing this up. She's my daughter. That will never change. But she's your daughter, too. She's going to call you Mom. And you're going to take her to her first day of kindergarten and make her Halloween costumes and make sure she has braces and gets into a good college. I know you'll do that. If you're half as good to her as you've been to me, she'll be a very happy girl."

Liz couldn't have stopped the tears if she'd tried. But she didn't. She let them fall, in celebration of mothers and daughters, in thanks of second chances, in hopes that Mary would someday have another daughter to love. In a different time, in a different place.

Mary held the baby out to Liz. "Here, take your daughter. She needs to start getting used to you. What are you going to name her?"

"I don't know. I hadn't thought about it."

"Would you call her Catherine? That was my mother's name."

Liz swallowed hard. "Catherine is a beautiful name. She fits it perfectly."

LIZ HELD CATHERINE for two hours before finally returning her to the nursery. She left the hospital, choosing to walk instead of catching a cab. She needed the fresh air. It had been a long stretch in a stuffy hospital.

She also needed to call Jamison. He had to get Mary's signature on the adoption agreement and get Catherine released to a temporary foster home for a couple of days. Liz hated that part. She wanted to bring her daughter home right away. But she knew the rules. She wasn't going to do anything that would jeopardize the legal standing of the adoption.

By the time Liz could pick up Catherine, she assumed Mary would be well on her way to her new home. Mary had accepted the news that she would be relocated under the witness-protection program with cautious optimism. Liz knew the young girl was scared but that she also welcomed the chance to have a new life.

At one point in the discussion, Mary had joked about calling Sawyer to thank him. Liz hadn't been able to even smile. The pain of losing Sawyer tasted too fresh, too bitter.

She would go on. She had Catherine. She had her work. Assuming Jamison would let her bring Catherine with her. That was just one more thing to talk to him about. She pulled her cell phone out of her purse. She'd called him shortly after she and Mary had arrived at the hospital last night. But then things had gotten a little hectic.

Jamison answered on the first ring. "Yes," he said.

"Jamison, it's Liz. It's over. She had a little girl. She's a beauty."

"Mom and baby okay?"

"Yes. Pretty tough delivery but Mary did great."

"Did she hold the baby?"

"Yes. And then she handed her to me and said that I better get to know my daughter."

For once, Jamison seemed speechless.

"Have you heard from Detective Montgomery?" Liz asked.

"Yes. He called late last night. I told him Mary was in labor. He said he would have some guards posted outside of Mary's room. Did you see them?"

She had. She'd appreciated them, but it had been just one more painful reminder of the man she'd loved and lost. He took care of things. He made things happen. He made it tough on the bad guys. "Yes, I did."

"I'm supposed to call him once I talk to you. They want to move Mary as soon as possible. He was going to have somebody talk to the doctor."

She knew it was for the best, but it still hurt to know that she would soon lose Mary from her life. "She can't be moved until she signs the adoption agreement. Or, at the very least, she needs to be moved somewhere we can get to her. You need to call and tell him that."

"Why can't you call him?"

She didn't bother to answer.

"What's going on here?" Jamison asked.

She didn't want to talk about it. Not yet. She'd managed not to think about Sawyer the entire time Mary had been in labor. She couldn't let her mind go there yet. She wasn't ready. "Jamison, I know I'm not making much sense. But you need to trust me."

"I don't understand."

"I'm not going to be seeing Sawyer again. I want something that he won't let himself have."

"It's still not all that clear," Jamison said.

"I don't understand it. Why should you?"

"You okay?"

Trust Jamison to get down to the nitty-gritty. "Yes. I'm fine. And next week, I'll be better. And in a year or two, I might even be good."

"Anything I can do?"

"Yes. Get that paperwork to Mary. I want to bring my daughter home."

Liz put her cell phone away. She walked another two blocks to the grocery store. There she filled her cart with bottles, formula, diapers and lotion. The next stop was a department store. She got some blankets, T-shirts and one-piece sleepers. She knew she'd need a hundred more things but she could always ask Carmen or Jamison to help her out.

Funny. When Mary had first asked her to adopt the baby, Liz had thought Sawyer would be around to help. Had looked forward to sharing the baby with him. That wouldn't happen. And she needed to stop hoping, stop praying that it might change. He was gone. She better start getting used to it.

When she got home, she dropped her purchases on the kitchen counter and went back to her bedroom, taking her clothes off on the way, leaving just her bra and panties on. She lay back on the bed, closed her eyes and assumed sleep would come. After all, she'd been up for thirty-some hours. But sleep, being a slippery fellow, danced just out of her grasp. She tossed and turned, her body too keyed up to get any real rest. After an hour, she got up.

She made herself a cup of tea and a grilled-cheese sand-wich. She checked her voice mail. No calls. Not able to be patient, she dialed Jamison's number.

"Yes," he said.

"Have you been to see Mary? Did she sign?"

"You should be sleeping, Liz."

"I know. Well?"

"It's the strangest thing. I can't get in touch with Howard. He's not answering his cell phone. I've left four messages on his pager, and his assistant doesn't know where he is."

Howard Fraypish was never unreachable. He carried a backup cell phone just in case his primary one went dead. "Are you sure you have the right number?" She rattled it off.

"I know the number. I've left messages. I can't do anything until I get the paperwork from him."

If Mary hadn't gone into labor a week early, Liz would have had all the loose ends tied up. Now she needed Howard. "I'll go over to his office."

"He's not there."

"Maybe his assistant can find the documents on his PC. She'll print them off for me. I've known her for years."

On her way out of the apartment, she stopped to check her mailbox in the odd event that Howard had mailed the information to her. She opened the slot and pulled out an assortment of bills, a magazine and…a plain white envelope with her name scratched across it.

She slid her thumb under the flap and pulled out the single sheet.

Stay away from Mary Thorton and her baby. Otherwise, they die. You don't want that on your conscience.

Liz slammed her mailbox shut. Damn it. It was supposed to be over. Mirandez was in jail. She waited for the fear to hit her, but all she could feel was bone-deep anger. Somebody had threatened Catherine. Her child.

She would not let them win.

She grabbed both the envelope and the sheet of paper by the edges and slid them into her purse. Once she'd seen Howard, she would take the letter to the police.

"I'M SORRY, LIZ. Howard didn't leave any paperwork for either you or Jamison."

She was not in the mood to be put off. "Can't you just get it off his computer?"

The woman looked a little shocked. "I don't know his password," she said. "Even if I did, I'm not sure that would be appropriate."

"Look, Helen. What's inappropriate is for Howard to have left his office without providing us with the necessary paperwork to complete this adoption. Now he won't return any calls. I want to know what's going on. This is so unlike him."

Now the woman looked really nervous. "I...I'm not sure what's going on," she confessed. "Howard has been acting so strange. Real nervous. Almost jumpy. Have you seen him lately?"

"Yes." She'd seen him at the hospital when Melissa Stroud had her baby. "He seemed a little scatterbrained but nothing unusual for Howard."

"Twice in the past week, I've caught him sleeping at his desk in the middle of the afternoon. When I arrive in the mornings, I can tell he's been working all night."

It didn't sound good, but then again, she had her own sleep issues. "Maybe he's just working too hard. Does he have new clients?"

The woman shook her head. "No, just the opposite. Business is off. If it wasn't for OCM and a couple other agencies that he works with, I'm not sure I'd have a desk to sit at. Last week I wanted to order a new fax machine and he told me to hold off—that cash was a little tight this month."

Liz did not have time to worry about Howard. She had plenty of her own worries. She stood up and slung the strap of her purse over her shoulder. "If you talk to him, tell him it's imperative that he call Jamison. We need the paperwork, and we need it now. If I don't have it within twelve hours,

I'm going to recommend to Jamison that OCM find a new attorney."

Liz left Howard's office and tried to grab a cab to take her to the police department. Two passed her by without even slowing down. In her hurry to leave the apartment, she'd forgotten her cell phone. She changed her path and headed back toward her apartment. Once there, she could call for a cab.

She was four blocks from home when three men jumped out of the bushes. All three wore dark coats and blue jeans, and each had a ski mask over his face.

Liz looked around for help, but the residential street was empty. "What do you want?" she asked, forcing words around her fear.

"Shut up," one man said. Then he put his hand on her shoulder and pushed her hard. Liz stumbled back and stuck both arms out, breaking her fall. Sharp rocks cut into the palms of her hand. She scrambled to her feet, unwilling to let them tower over her.

Another man grabbed for her purse, yanking it so hard that the shoulder strap broke. Liz didn't try to fight him for it. The first man stepped forward again. Liz braced herself for another push. She didn't expect the fist to her jaw, sending rockets of pain through her whole face.

She tasted blood.

"You stay away from Mary Thorton and her baby," the third man said. "If you don't, you'll be sorry. This is just a little sample. Just because Dantel's in jail doesn't mean he's not still in charge." Then he hit her in the stomach. She doubled over. When she managed to catch her breath and straighten up, they were gone.

It had all happened in less than a minute. She'd been attacked in broad daylight. She took stock of her injuries. She gently moved her jaw back and forth, very grateful when everything seemed to work. Blood oozed from several small cuts on the palms of her hands. She bent down to pick up her purse, and pain shot through her midsection. Damn. She probably had a broken rib or two. She sank to her knees and managed to grab the strap. Awkwardly, she got to her feet and half walked, half ran the rest of the way to her apartment.

Once inside, she got to the sink and spit out the blood in her mouth. She walked over to the telephone, careful not to look in the mirror on the way, and dialed 911.

Chapter Sixteen

Two officers and an ambulance responded. The police questioned her briefly. She gave them the best description she could of the men and told them what they'd said about Dantel Mirandez. She handed over the letter and envelope. Then the ambulance transported her to the hospital, the same one she'd left just hours earlier literally walking on air. Now she lay flat on her back, wheeled in, presented to the nurse on duty like a stuffed turkey on Thanksgiving Day.

The doctor put six stitches in the inside of her cheek, where her teeth had cut into the tender flesh. He also cleaned out the rocks in her hands and wrapped them up in white gauze. Then someone else took films of her ribs and substantiated that one was cracked. The doctor didn't even bother to wrap it, just told her to move carefully for a couple days.

She'd just snapped her jeans when Sawyer burst into the exam room. When he saw her, he stopped so suddenly that his body almost pitched forward over his feet.

He stared at her. First at her swollen jaw, then at her wrapped hands. When he finally spoke, his voice seemed rusty, as if he hadn't used it for a while.

"Are you okay?" The minute he said it, he knew it was an insane question. One look at her told him she wasn't okay.

"How did you know I was here?" she asked.

"The responding officers ran Mirandez's name through

the database. I came up as the arresting officer. So, they called me."

It sounded so simple. It didn't give any clue to the absolute terror he'd felt when they'd told him about her injuries. "He'll pay for this," Sawyer told her. "I promise you. He will pay for this."

She didn't say anything. Just stood there, holding her blouse together with one hand. He could see the pale blue silk of her bra against her soft skin. So beautiful. So fragile.

It was his fault this had happened. He never should have let Lieutenant Fischer talk him into taking her to Wisconsin in the first place. Mirandez wouldn't have any reason to be going after her now.

"I'm sorry," he said. "I'm sorry that bastard hurt you. I'm sorry I let him."

She looked at him as if he'd lost his mind.

He tried again. "I expected him to go after Mary. I never thought you'd be the target. That was stupid of me. Now you're paying the price."

She dismissed his concerns with a wave of her free hand. "How could you have known? He's been told the baby isn't his. Why would he care about warning me away from Mary or the baby? Did they tell you about the letter?"

"I swung by the station and took a look at it. He spelled your name right this time," Sawyer said, feeling the disgust well up in the back of his throat.

"I guess I didn't notice," she said.

"What exactly did the men say to you?" Sawyer asked. "Word for word, if you can remember."

"They told me to stay away from Mary and the baby. Then they said that just because Dantel was behind bars it didn't mean he wasn't still in charge."

Sawyer rubbed his forehead. He had a hell of a headache. It didn't make sense. None of it. Not that he questioned that

Mirandez had been able to communicate with his gang. That happened all the time. Prison bars didn't prove to be a very strong barrier. Sometimes it was a phone conversation in code. Other times, a dirty guard willing to carry messages back and forth for a price.

Perhaps the order had come down before Mirandez learned that the baby wasn't his. Whatever the reason, Sawyer would find out. "Is it okay for you to leave?" he asked.

She nodded. "Yes."

"I'll take you home."

"No." The word exploded from her. He hadn't expected less.

"Liz, be reasonable. You're hurt. You can't walk home. Just let me drive you." He wanted to make sure she got safely inside her apartment. It was the least he could do.

"No," she repeated. "I'm not ready to leave. I want to see Mary as long as I'm here."

"I'll wait," he said.

"That's not necessary," she said.

She looked as if she'd rather be anywhere but with him. He couldn't blame her. "We're moving Mary tomorrow," he said. "Guards will remain outside her door until then. We're placing a plainclothes cop in the nursery just in case he'd go for...the baby."

"Her name is Catherine."

Catherine. He didn't want to know that. Didn't want to know anything about the baby. But Liz deserved to know that her baby would be safe. "Your boss told me that the baby goes to a temporary foster home for a couple days. The detective can go with her just in case."

She chuckled, a dry, humorless laugh. "The foster parents should love that."

"It's not great, I agree. But it beats the alternative."

"What happens when I bring her home? Does the detective stay until she's in college?"

He could hear the sarcasm. "I don't think that will be necessary. But maybe for a couple of weeks. We're having the doctor certify that Mary was at or near a full-term pregnancy. We'll provide that to Mirandez's attorney. Just in case, we're asking permission from the court to run a DNA match. We need to get a blood draw from Mirandez. That will prove conclusively that he's not the father. But it will take several weeks before those results are available."

"Capable Sawyer."

"What?"

"Never mind. It was stupid. I'm just tired. I need to see Mary. You need to leave." She buttoned her shirt. He looked away, not wanting to watch her hands, not wanting to think about how his own hands had unbuttoned her shirt, how he had literally shook with wanting her.

Because perhaps, in a lifetime or two, he might forget.

He heard her groan. She had her sweater half-on with one sleeve hanging free. The arm that should have filled it was wrapped around her waist. She was even paler than before. "What's wrong?"

"Cracked rib."

He hadn't thought he could hate Mirandez any more than he already did. "Any other injuries that I can't see?" he asked. He knew she hadn't been raped. When the officers had contacted him, he'd asked that. Knowing that if she had, he'd have killed the men responsible. He would have laid down his badge and gone after them and ripped their hearts out.

She shook her head. "No. All in all, I think I got lucky."

Lucky. As absurd as it sounded, she was right. With no witnesses to stop them, it would have been easy for Mirandez's men to slit her throat or put a bullet through her temple. But they hadn't. They'd roughed her up and scared her, but they'd left her standing.

He took a step forward, then another, stopping just a foot away from her. Gently, he took her arm and pushed it through the sweater sleeve. With unsteady hands, he pulled both sides together, fastening the top button. Then the second one. The third.

Liz didn't breathe. Couldn't. Sawyer had his head bent, concentrating as he worked the buttons into the small holes, his strong fingers being so careful, so gentle. She thought her legs might not hold her. The man was helping her, dressing her like an adult would a child, and it was the most erotic thing that had ever happened to her.

When he finished with the last button, he lifted his head, meeting her eyes. He leaned forward, and ever so softly, he brushed his lips across her sore and swollen jaw. Then he reached for her bandaged hands, raised each one to his lips and gently kissed the tips of her fingers.

Then he gathered her small hands in his much larger ones, brought them to his chest and bent his head forward so that his forehead rested on hers. She could feel the beat of his heart pulsing through her body, sending crazy, wild, zigzag waves through her. His breath was hot, his skin cool, his body strong. She felt safe and protected. Yet weak and wanting for more.

"I love you," he said, his voice just a whisper in her ear. "I'm so sorry you got hurt."

She took in a deep breath, wanting to always remember the scent of Sawyer. She focused on his hands, which were still wrapped around hers. She wanted to remember the feel of his skin, the lines of his bones, the strength of his muscles. It wouldn't be enough. But it would be all she had.

"Sawyer, you need to go." She said it softly, all the malice gone. He was a good man. He'd suffered a great loss. She didn't want to drag out the goodbyes, making either one of them suffer more.

He nodded and pulled his hands away. He looked her straight in the eye. He slowly raised his right hand, reaching toward her face. She caught his fingers with her own and gently pushed his hand back to his side. Then she deliberately and carefully reached up and on her own, all on her own, tucked the wayward strand of hair behind her ear.

He gave her a sad half smile. Without another word, he left the room.

THE NEXT MORNING, Sawyer waited impatiently while they brought Mirandez up to see him. The door opened, and his slimy attorney came in first, carrying a briefcase almost bursting at the seams. Mirandez shuffled in next, his hands cuffed in front of him.

Sawyer hadn't wanted to come. He didn't want to even look at the murdering bastard. But he'd come up empty-handed in his search for the men who had terrorized Liz. Even the guys on the inside couldn't shake loose any information.

"This is highly irregular, Detective," the attorney said, setting his briefcase down on the table with a thud. "What is it that's so important that you had to talk to my client at the crack of dawn? It's barely seven o'clock."

He didn't care whose butt he'd had to drag out of bed. He'd been up all night. But still he had nothing. "Your client arranged to have Liz Mayfield beaten and threatened."

"That's impossible," the attorney said, disregarding Sawyer's statement.

Sawyer didn't bother to respond. He'd been studying Mirandez. For the briefest second, the man had looked surprised, then he'd completely closed down, pulling his usual sneer back in place.

"Are you charging him?"

"I want to ask him some questions."

"Under the circumstances, I will advise my client not to answer."

Mirandez sat up straighter in his chair. "Shut up, Bill. You talk too damn much."

The attorney's face turned red. Sawyer almost felt sorry for him until he remembered that the guy made his living defending killers. He deserved to be treated like dirt.

Mirandez rocked back in his chair. "Do you lie awake at night thinking these things, Cop?"

Mirandez was half-right. Since he'd let Liz slip out of his life, Sawyer had spent most of his nights staring at the ceiling, afraid to close his eyes, afraid to give in to the temptation to remember what it felt like to be wrapped in her arms. Last night, after walking away from her yet again, he'd worked himself to death, poring over reports, talking to informants, hoping he could forget the look in her eyes when she'd told him goodbye.

"You need to hire better help," Sawyer said. "Your guys ID'd you. They said you sent them. We've got both letters. You're not going to get away with this."

"You bore me." Mirandez put both hands on the table and twirled his thumbs. "What do you think I am? Stupid?"

"I think you're the scum of the earth."

Mirandez laughed. "Yes, well, I think you're pretty much an SOB yourself."

"Mr. Mirandez," the attorney began before a sharp look from his client had him shutting his mouth.

Mr. Mirandez? How freaking much was Mirandez paying the guy to get him to suck up that way? There wasn't enough money in the world. *Mr. Mirandez?* It made Sawyer sick. Nobody in his right mind would give Mirandez that kind of respect.

As suddenly as that, Sawyer figured it out. Mirandez. Not Mr. Mirandez, not Dantel Mirandez. He only went by Mirandez. Mary called him Dantel. Nobody else did. Nobody in his gang would. They probably didn't even know his first name.

"The baby isn't even mine. I don't care what happens to it."

Whoever had sent the men hadn't known that the baby wasn't Mirandez's. The men had warned Liz to stay away from Dantel's baby. Someone smart enough to throw the blame on Mirandez had hurt Liz. Why? Who? Would they try again?

Sawyer stood and grabbed his coat.

"Hey, what's your hurry?" Mirandez looked around the room. "While it's not Vegas, I thought we might play some cards. I'll stake you a couple hundred. I know you cops don't make much of a living."

"At least we make it honestly," Sawyer said and left before he followed through on his urge to slam Mirandez up against the wall.

He walked to his car, dialing Liz's number on his cell. The phone rang four times then the voice mail kicked on. He didn't want to leave a message. Wasn't sure what he even had to tell her. Just knew he needed to talk to her, needed to hear her voice. Needed to know that she was okay. He dialed OCM's main number next. Jamison answered on the second ring.

"Yes."

"Jamison, it's Sawyer Montgomery. I'm trying to get in touch with Liz. Is she there by any chance?"

"No. I haven't heard from her. She's supposed to be here at noon. We're meeting with Howard Fraypish. I talked to her early this morning. She had some errands to run and then she planned to stop by. I'll let her know to call you."

"Do that."

He redialed Liz's number. This time, when the voice mail kicked on, he left a brief message. "Liz, it's Sawyer. I don't think it was Mirandez's guys who attacked you. So, be careful, okay? Please call me. I know you probably don't want to talk to me. But just let me know you're okay. That's all you have to do. Just let me know."

He hung up before he started to beg. He couldn't shake the feeling that Liz was in danger. Not knowing what else to do, he drove. He went to Liz's apartment and pounded on the door. He dialed her number again and again. When her voice mail kicked on the last time, he said, "Liz, damn you, where are you? Call me."

He called Mary's room at the hospital. She hadn't seen her. He got the number of Randi's apartment and called there just in case. No luck. He called Robert and told him what was going on.

He was going to be too late. Something horrible had happened to Liz, and he was going to lose her. She'd never know how much he loved her. He hadn't been able to tell her. He'd chosen to let her believe that it wasn't enough.

Life is about choices. That was what she'd told him. Liz had chosen to live. She'd survived her sister's death, she'd learned to let go, to forgive herself for not being there. She'd chosen to make a difference in the lives of countless young women, allowing them to fully understand and appreciate that no matter how desperate the situation, they always had a choice.

They could lie or tell the truth. Give or take. Laugh or cry. Love or be empty forever.

Sawyer wiped the tears from his eyes as he drove down the familiar street. Without thinking, he went to the one place that gave him peace. He found his regular spot and parked the car. It had started to rain. It didn't matter. The cold, wet day couldn't touch him. He opened the gate of the small cemetery nestled between a church and a school. He took the path to the left. Then he knelt next to his son's grave and placed a hand on the shiny marker.

When he'd left Baton Rouge, his son had come with him. It had been the only choice.

The rain fell harder, hitting his head, his face, mixing with the tears that ran freely down his cheeks. He couldn't hear a thing besides the beating of his own heart.

Choices. He didn't want to give up his last chance to make the right one.

So, he bent his head, all the way to the ground, and he kissed the wet, cold earth that sheltered his child. He didn't kiss him goodbye. Never that. His son would always have a special place in his heart. But his heart needed to be bigger now. It needed to hold Liz and Catherine.

He'd been a coward. He knew now that he'd rather have one minute, one day, one week with Liz than a lifetime of being alone and afraid.

He knew he couldn't keep Liz or Catherine safe from all harm. He couldn't wrap them up in cotton and hide them from the danger that lurked in dark corners. They might get hurt. They might get sick. But he wanted to be there every step of the way, holding them, supporting them, making sure they knew they were loved more than life itself.

WHEN HE GOT BACK to the car, he tried Liz's apartment again. Still no answer. He checked his machine at work. No messages. Damn it.

He checked the time. Ten minutes after ten. Jamison had said they had a meeting with Fraypish at noon. Not knowing what else to do, Sawyer tried Jamison again.

"Yes," Jamison answered.

"It's Sawyer Montgomery. Any word from Liz?"

"No. I've tried a couple times. I swear this meeting is doomed. I can't reach Howard, either."

Fraypish. Liz had gone to see him and then been attacked. "Jamison, how well do you know Howard Fraypish?"

"We're like brothers. Why?"

"I don't know. It's just that there's something about him that nags at me."

"He's odd, but if you're thinking that he would harm Liz, that just wouldn't happen. When Liz got that first death threat from Dantel, Howard was just outraged."

Sawyer remembered Liz standing outside the hotel, whispering, *He doesn't know about the letter. Please don't tell him.*

"How did he know about the letter, Jamison?"

"I don't know. I might have mentioned it, I suppose."

A slow burn started in Sawyer's stomach. Mirandez's goons hadn't written the second letter. No, it had been somebody who knew about the first letter but hadn't actually seen it. Somebody who hadn't realized that Mayfield had been spelled wrong or that the grammar had been rough. Somebody who knew how to spell *conscience* and what it meant. Somebody who knew Mirandez as Dantel. That was what Mary called him. Sometimes Liz, too, especially after she'd been talking with Mary. Jamison had just referred to him as Dantel. That was likely the name he'd used when he'd been chatting with his buddy.

Sawyer turned a sharp left. "Jamison, what's Fraypish's address?"

The man hesitated, then rattled it off.

Sawyer hung up, called for backup and started praying. He couldn't lose her now. Not when he'd just found himself.

When he got there, he parked his car in front of the three-story brownstone. He took the steps two at a time. He had his fist just inches away from the door, ready to knock, when he heard a crash inside the house. He put his ear to the door and pulled his gun out of his holster. He could hear Liz and then another voice. An angry voice. A man's voice.

She was alive. He stepped away from the door, pulled out his cell phone and called for backup. He debated all of two seconds before he tried the handle. Locked. He heard a car pull up and realized that Jamison had also come.

He held up a finger warning the man to be quiet. "Do you have a key?"

"Yes. I feed his cats when he's not home." Jamison pulled out a ring and pointed at a gold key.

Sawyer inserted it quietly and opened the door just inches. He could hear their voices more clearly. Fraypish was yelling.

"You stupid woman. I am not going to let you ruin everything."

"Howard, you're never going to get away with it."

"I've been getting away with it for months. Your boss, Jamison, my good buddy, always was a trusting soul. And a fool."

"Why, Howard? At least tell me why you had to sell the babies."

"I'm not lucky at cards. At craps, either."

"How could you?"

Sawyer could hear the disgust in Liz's voice. Silently, he made his way down the hall.

"Easy. You'd be amazed at how desperate some people are to have a baby. Especially healthy, white infants like your little Catherine. They'll borrow from friends and family, mortgage their house. Whatever it takes. They'll drop a hundred thousand without blinking an eye."

"You make me sick," Liz said.

"You don't understand, Liz. I tried to convince you to stay away from that baby. When that didn't work, I hired a few guys to make my point. But still, you won't stop. I have to stop you."

"Howard, please, don't do this. We'll talk to Jamison. We'll get you help."

"It's too late. I borrowed money from the wrong people. If I don't make regular payments, they'll hurt me. Bad. They're due a check this week. I don't have any other babies in the pipeline. I need yours."

"You'll never get away with it. Jamison will figure it out."

"No, he won't. When you don't show up for the noon meeting, Jamison and I'll come looking for you. We'll find the body, I'll console Jamison, and your little Catherine will be on the market by dinnertime."

With that, Sawyer came around the corner. With one sharp downward thrust on Fraypish's arm, he knocked the gun out of his hand. Then he tackled the man, sending his fist into the guy's jaw. That was for the bruised jaw. He hit him again. That was for the cracked rib. He had his arm pulled back, ready to swing again, when two sets of hands pulled him off Fraypish.

"That's enough, Detective. We'll take it from here."

Sawyer shook his head to clear it. Two officers stood on each side of him. He took a step back. Liz sat on the bed, her arms wrapped around her middle. Tears ran down her face.

He pulled her into his arms.

"Thank you for getting here in time," she whispered. "I feel so stupid. I had no idea."

He held her. "Me, neither, honey. I focused on Mirandez, and I missed Fraypish."

"It's not your fault," she assured him.

Maybe not but he couldn't even think about what might have happened if he'd arrived five minutes later. He pulled back, just far enough that he could see her eyes. "I love you," he said, not willing to go another second without her knowing exactly how he felt. "I've been a stupid fool. I don't want to lose you. Tell me I haven't lost you. Tell me I'm not too late."

"What about your son?"

He brushed a tear off her cheek. "I loved him before he was born. Once I'd held him, he was the moon and stars and everything that was perfect. And when you love that much and you can't hold on to it, it hurts. It rips you apart. I didn't ever want to hurt like that again."

She kissed him, a whisper of lips against his cheek. "I never meant to hurt you."

"You were right. Life is about choices. When you love someone, there's a risk. You can choose to avoid risks, to never take the big leap off the cliff into the water, but then you never know the absolute joy of coming to the surface, the stunning glory of the bright sunshine in your eyes. I don't want to stand at the top alone."

"What are you saying?"

"Liz, I'm ready to jump. You have my heart. Take my hand. And together, with Catherine, we'll build a family. I'll take care of you, I promise. I love you. Please say you'll try."

She kissed him on the lips, and he allowed himself to hope. "You are the kindest, most loving and most...capable man I've ever met. I know you'll take care of me. I want a chance to take care of you." She reached out and took his hand. "And I want us to take care of our daughter together."

* * * * *

A sneaky peek at next month...

INTRIGUE...

BREATHTAKING ROMANTIC SUSPENSE

My wish list for next month's titles...

In stores from 19th July 2013:

☐ Sharpshooter – Cynthia Eden

& Falcon's Run – Aimée Thurlo

☐ The Accused – Jana DeLeon

& Smoky Ridge Curse – Paula Graves

☐ Taking Aim – Elle James

& Ruthless – HelenKay Dimon

Romantic Suspense

☐ Colton by Blood – Melissa Cutler

Available at WHSmith, Tesco, Asda, Eason, Amazon and Apple

Just can't wait?

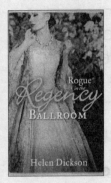

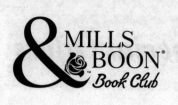

Join the Mills & Boon Book Club

Subscribe to **Intrigue** today for 3, 6 or 12 months and you could **save over £40!**

We'll also treat you to these fabulous extras:

- FREE L'Occitane gift set worth £10

- FREE home delivery

- Rewards scheme, exclusive offers...and much more!

Subscribe now and save over £40
www.millsandboon.co.uk/subscribeme

Mills & Boon® Online

Discover more romance at
www.millsandboon.co.uk

- **FREE** online reads
- **Books** up to one month before shops
- **Browse our books** before you buy

...and much more!

For exclusive competitions and instant updates:

Like us on **facebook.com/millsandboon**

Follow us on **twitter.com/millsandboon**

Join us on **community.millsandboon.co.uk**

| *Visit us Online* | Sign up for our FREE eNewsletter at **www.millsandboon.co.uk** |

What will you treat yourself to next?

 HISTORICAL

Ignite your imagination, step into the past...
6 new stories every month

INTRIGUE...

Breathtaking romantic suspense
Up to 8 new stories every month

 *Medical Romance*

Captivating medical drama – with heart
6 new stories every month

MODERN™

International affairs, seduction & passion guaranteed
9 new stories every month

n o c t u r n e™

Deliciously wicked paranormal romance
Up to 4 new stories every month

 RIVΛ™

Live life to the full – give in to temptation
3 new stories every month available exclusively via our Book Club

You can also buy Mills & Boon eBooks at
www.millsandboon.co.uk

Visit us Online

M&B/WORLD2